P9-EKY-374

BOOKS BY ICE-T

The Ice Opinion
*Ice: A Memoir of Gangster Life and Redemption—From South
Central to Hollywood* (with Douglas Century)
Kings of Vice (with Mal Radcliff)

*A Forge Book

ICE-T
AND MAL RADCLIFF

A TOM DOHERTY ASSOCIATES BOOK

NEW YORK

KINGS OF VICE

Copyright © 2011 by Ice Touring, Inc.

Management: Jorge Hinojosa

A Forge Book
Published by Tom Doherty Associates, LLC
175 Fifth Avenue
New York, NY 10010

www.tor-forge.com

Forge® is a registered trademark of Tom Doherty Associates, LLC.

Library of Congress Cataloging-in-Publication Data

Ice-T (Musician)
      Kings of vice / Ice-T and Mal Radcliff.—1st ed.
         p. cm.
      "A Tom Doherty Associates book."
      ISBN 978-0-7653-2513-6 (hardcover)
      ISBN 978-0-7653-3098-7 (trade paperback)
      1. Organized crime—New York (State)—New York—Fiction.   2. Street
life—New York (State)—New York—Fiction.   3. Revenge—Fiction.
4. Urban fiction.   I. Radcliff, Mal.   II. Title.
PS3609.C4K56 2011
813'.6—dc22

                                                                2011019774

First Edition: September 2011

Printed in the United States of America

0 9 8 7 6 5 4 3 2 1

Special thanks to everyone who's supported me for twenty-five years and counting. Love to all my fallen homeys, dead and locked away in prison. You are missed dearly. Eternal love to my inner circle of friends, family, and my wife, who really know what I go through and work to keep me focused and healthy. Peace to all the young street hustlers, players, and gangstas. To win the game you must devise an exit strategy. We all saw the last scene in Scarface.

—ICEBERG

1

Everything was the same, but different. Twenty years after Marcus Casey had first walked into Attica Correctional Facility, he walked out again, dressed in the same clothes he'd worn back in the day.

The tailored suit and custom shoes had once been the height of urban fashion. The waist of his pants still fit right, even a little loose now. The jacket and button-down shirt, with the collar open in the city heat, were a degree or two snug, given that his torso was more heavily muscled than when he'd last worn these clothes. He carried a small nylon sports bag that held the rest of his worldly possessions.

Eyes always scanning, he neared the end of the pedestrian tunnel that would let him out from Central Park onto 110th Street. At the tunnel mouth, a gaunt, stooped figure leaned against the wall, but roused himself as Casey approached. Casey casually switched the soft-sided equipment bag to his left hand. He liked to lead with his right.

"Say, man, gotta dollar I can hold?" He rattled coins in a small, foil-lined bowl he pushed toward Casey. The panhandler's dirty clothes billowed on his skeletal frame. It seemed the only thing anchoring him to the ground was the brand-new black and orange backpack hanging off one shoulder. His face was whiskered and creased, his eyes bleary, but his teeth were surprisingly even and showy white.

Even crackheads can afford new dentures nowadays, Casey thought. "Can't do anything for you today, homes. I'm a little light myself." He frowned, a memory shaking loose as he stared at the scrawny bum.

"You sure?" It was more pleading than threat.

Casey stared back at him, the corner of his mouth crooking up in a thin smile. "Tol' you that shit would bite you in the ass some-day, Ten Spot."

The other man reacted to hearing his street name as if he'd just been punched. "Huh? Who you?"

"Guess it has been that long, hasn't it?"

Ten Spot peered closer at Casey, the stoned cloud momentarily lifting from his gaze. "Fuck." He pointed a greasy, trembling finger. "That you, Crush? Thought you was dead."

Several teenagers skateboarded past on the street, the wheels clicking on the sidewalk making Casey tense for a moment. *Gotta watch that shit, jumping at every shadow, every noise out here. Just been gone a while, that's all.* He tuned back in to Ten Spot's slurred mumbling.

"You bust out?"

"Paroled. They cut me loose this morning."

"Da-yamn."

"Yeah."

Ten Spot frowned. "So, you gonna get back into it? You know?"

Casey said, "I got an idea or two." He started to walk away.

"You gonna need soljahs, Crush."

Casey stopped, but didn't say anything, only stared at the other man out of the corner of his eye.

Ten Spot cackled. "Aw, man, I'm'a get right. Now that you're out, I got a goal, dawg. You know, hope and shit."

"'Kay," he answered noncommittally as he walked off again.

"You'll see," Ten Spot called to Casey's back. "You'll see."

Casey walked north along Malcolm X Boulevard in the early afternoon. One thing certainly hadn't changed—it was still damn hot in July, whether in the can or on the streets. His nose filled with the many smells of the city in summer—the acrid bite of car exhaust, the reek of stagnant water, melting tar on the hot asphalt. But he smelled other things as well—the green trees in the breeze, the smell of dry grass browning under the merciless sun. The wafting scent of a woman's perfume as she strolled by. That one made Casey pause a moment as he drank in a smell he hadn't known since forever.

He had enough gate money, what he'd earned inside on his book when the prison authorities released him, to afford a bus or a subway MetroCard, but he walked instead. He needed to take it all in again—let the energy of the city and its denizens soak into him. He needed to feel how the streets had both changed and were still the same.

A friend on the outside had also offered to pick him up, but Casey had declined. He'd wanted to walk out of Attica. He wanted to stride away from that cage that had held him for the past two decades, feel the screws' eyes on him for the last time, and know with absolute certainty that he wasn't ever going back inside. Either he was gonna do what he had been planning for the last 7,300 days, or he'd be dead. There would be no arrest, no surrender this time.

There was another reason he wanted to leg it into the city proper—he wanted to see what had become of the place while he was away. The city that had been his at one time. Not so much in title or name, but when he'd been at the top, there'd been no doubt that Marcus "Crush" Casey had ruled the streets of New York City as the head of the Vicetown Kings.

Now he was back, and he wanted to immerse himself in the neighborhoods he hadn't seen in what seemed like forever—he wanted to see and hear and smell everything he had missed over the past twenty years. His friends could wait a bit. His enemies— their turn would come soon enough.

Casey stopped at a hot dog cart. He set his bag at his feet, standing over it protectively. Some habits never died, whether on the street or in the *cantone*.

A young woman in a watch cap and dreads was leaving with her hot dog. She was chewing and looking at the small screen of an instrument. He'd read about these new phones. They could take your picture or shoot a video the world could see in seconds. "Gimme one with heavy mustard and relish, the other with onions," Casey told the vendor. The smell of the hot, cooked meat intoxicated him.

"No problem," the black man said, a multicolored knit skullcap on his head. Without looking at his hands, he completed the order while glaring at a brightly painted catering truck parked across the street offering Thai fusion tacos and burritos. Several patrons stood in a line to order at its window. Casey figured the interloper would find his tires slashed soon, and probably not for the first time. Refreshing to see that New York City street vendors were still very territorial. Casey smiled as he paid for his food, appreciating a wolfish mentality.

Holding both hot dogs in one large hand and his bag in the other, he found an alcove step of an empty storefront and sat down to enjoy his meal. He could feel the inside of his mouth water and tighten in anticipation of his first bite. He chewed slowly, appreciating the individual flavors, the tang of the mustard, the bite of the onions, all over the rich, juicy meat. The damn hot dogs were magnificent. His enjoyment was interrupted by the memory of eating hot dogs with his son. That was a lifetime ago. Those days were over. Casey pushed the memory out of his head and thought about having two more, but that would make him sleepy, and he had far too much to do today before securing a place to lay his head and enjoying a short dog of real whiskey.

Casey wiped his mouth and chin with a napkin and got up to toss it in the trash before continuing on his way. A blue-and-white came down the street, but paid him little attention as it passed, the two cops inside chatting away. Although he felt a prickle of unease between his shoulder blades as his gaze met one of the officers', the patrol car turned the corner and sped off. Casey felt a mix of relief and sadness. Twenty years ago he could have bought those cops—or had them killed—with a few words in the right ears. Now they looked past him like he wasn't even there.

A voice echoed in his head, like the man who would have said the words was standing right behind him. *"O divine art of subtlety and secrecy! Through you we learn to be invisible, through you inaudible and hence we can hold the enemy's fate in our hands."*

Casey grinned. As usual, Mack D was right. He was effectively invisible—to the police, and more importantly, to those he would soon be moving against.

He began walking again, passing people and places, graffitied walls—including some with a familiar capital *V* and a crown over it—beauty shops, bodegas, outlets of fast-food hamburger and fried chicken spots next to boarded store fronts. Those who were out kept to themselves, eyes averted, in a hurry to get wherever they were going. Casey had read that crime in New York City had dropped by double digits over the past decade, but he couldn't have told that by looking around. Everyone seemed worried or nervous about something.

. . .

Eventually he arrived at his destination, a rehabbed five-story walk-up on a relatively quiet street not far from the City University. He stood in front of the neatly maintained building, taking it in, then went up the steps to the metal gate. He searched the directory and pressed the button labeled MANAGER.

"Who this?" a deep voice growled from the speaker.

"Who you think, fool?"

"Look here, whoever's out there messin' around betta step off. I ain't got time for no bullshit."

"You never did, Kenny, now open up, playa."

A pause, then the voice boomed forth again. "Marcus Aurelius. Ha ha! Get your ass in here, dawg."

The door buzzed, and Casey entered. "Come on up," Kenneth Saunders called from above as Casey ascended the staircase to the second-floor hallway.

Casey reached out and hugged the plus-sized handyman in his customary plaid shirt and work jeans. A ring of noisy keys dangled from a clip on his belt.

They broke, and Saunders took him in. "You look damn good. I knew you was big, but you sure put your yokes on in there, didn'cha?"

"Ad seg agreed with me," Casey said with a shrug.

"Sheeit, guess that's one way to put it," the big man said. "This way." He turned and led the way to his third-floor apartment. Along the way to the stairs, a door opened and a woman of at least eighty looked out, her eyes magnified behind old-fashioned, thick-framed glasses.

"I knew I heard your voice, Kenny. About my bookcase?"

"Miz T, I promise I'll fix it today. Before dark."

"Okay, now," she said warily as she peered at Casey through thick lenses.

He smiled. "He won't let anything happen to your first editions, Mrs. Tolivar."

The retired librarian leaned out, blinking hard at Casey. "Lord preserve us," she exclaimed, opening the door wider. "What a treat this is!" She spread her arms.

They hugged, Casey careful not to squeeze the old lady's spindly body too hard. Past her head, he saw into the small apartment. Two of the walls of her front room were covered with shelves rising from carpet to ceiling, each one packed with books. On the floor were four even piles of books and the broken shelf sat on top of them. To the left was a short hallway lined with glass-enclosed bookcases. On another wall was a large oblong plate painted with the knowing visages of John F. Kennedy, Martin Luther King, Jr., and Barack Obama.

"I was so sorry to hear about Antonio," the old lady whispered.

"Thank you," Casey said, refusing to show any emotion at the unexpected mention of his son. "And thank you so much for those books. They helped keep me sane."

"My pleasure, child. Let me fix you something to eat," the old lady said as they separated and looked at each other. "Just washed some fresh greens this afternoon."

"I'd dearly love some of your cooking, Mrs. Tolivar," Casey said.

"But we got men's bid'ness to conduct," Saunders added.

"Hmmm," she replied, giving the duo a dubious look. "Well, make it soon, okay?"

"Yes, ma'am," Casey said. The two men walked down the hall as the old lady closed her apartment door.

On the next level, Casey and Saunders entered the manager's apartment. In contrast to his workingman's image, Saunders's abode was decorated tastefully in modern furniture.

"What's your poison?" Saunders asked.

Casey hesitated. "Got any Glen Moray?"

"Bet." Saunders touched a button on the wall beside a recessed cabinet. The double doors swung open and simultaneously the main body of the wet bar rose from below into a serving position. He made the drinks, neat, and handed a squat, squared-off glass to

Casey, who remained standing, looking around at the understated elegance of the place.

"Good to have you back on deck," Saunders said.

"Here's to it." They clinked their glasses. Casey pursed his lips and blew a small stream of air as the whiskey warmed his insides. "Damn, that was long overdue."

With a broad grin, Saunders motioned toward the living room area. Selecting a plush chair angled toward the window, Casey sat, sinking into it as the soft, overstuffed cushions shaped themselves around his muscles. Saunders set his drink on a coffee table carved from a large piece of driftwood. "Be right back."

He walked into another room and, over the street traffic, Casey faintly heard electronic mechanisms whir. Saunders returned holding a thick file folder with a large rubber band around it under one arm, and two thinner ones under his other arm. He handed the big one to Casey. "This is what I got on that muthafuckah Rono since the funeral." His voice was hollow.

Casey looked at his friend as he hefted the file, then closed his eyes, taking a deep breath. The plain manila folder felt cool under his fingers, a stark contrast to the white-hot fire banked deep down inside him, a fire that threatened to flare up again at hearing the name of his enemy. Casey held his breath for a moment, then exhaled slowly, taking the edge off his anger with the stream of air whooshing out of his lungs. The time would come to let it rip loose soon enough.

"Probably could've gotten more, but I didn't want to risk greater exposure," Saunders said, plopping down on the couch. "Old Gerty taught us never to peep our hole card, right?"

"She sure did," Casey said quietly.

Saunders continued. "There's no electronic file, no memory sticks, computer discs floating around, nada. You're holding the one and only copy." He sampled more of his scotch.

Casey leaned forward and gingerly placed the file on the coffee table as if it were a bomb primed to explode. "Thanks, brother, I uh . . . ," he began, but the words wouldn't come.

The big man fixed him with a look and a shrug. "Come on, man, ain't no need for that."

Casey nodded, looking out onto the cityscape. "Inside, nothing ever changed—except the people there. Prison did its damnedest to change me too, and it did in some respects, but not like you might think. I'm back on the streets, and change is coming with me too, only it's gonna be delivered my way." He downed the rest of his drink in one gulp. The whiskey's burn as it slid down his throat was like a candle compared to the inferno inside him. "What about the others?"

Kenny set the files on his lap and leaned back in his chair. "Word on the street is you brokered some kinda 'understanding' while you was on the inside? You really gonna try to make peace among all the gangs in the city?"

Casey nodded. "Didn't want it to leak till I was out, but yeah, the major godfathers on the inside are all on board. It's all copacetic— they know I got my shit straight, even promised to look the other way if something were to happen to Rono in the next few days. All I hadda do was promise that the benjamins would keep flowing, and everyone would get their fair cut of everything."

"Tall muthafuckin' order, sounds like."

"Never said it was easy." Casey smiled. "Guess they musta responded to my winnin' personality." *That, and my promise that the drug pipelines would keep flowin'*, he thought with a grimace. That was something he'd have to take care of later—he had plenty on his plate in the here and now. "Anyway, got most on my side— except for the two I told you to start eyeing a few months ago."

Saunders handed the two smaller folders over. "Here's what I been able to pull together so far. Both these crews are small, but vicious and ambitious. The Lotus even tangled with the VKs a few weeks ago, and are still around to tell the tale. I don't need to tell you, but y'all better watch your step around both of 'em. Them Latino gangs don't mess around, and the Asians are worse."

"I'll keep that in mind." Casey tapped his fingers on the stack of folders in his lap, torn between diving in and just taking it easy for the rest of the night. Another thought occurred to him, and he let it flow. "Caught a vibe out there. The citizens seem pretty uptight as well—whassup with that? I thought the mayor and his crew were shapin' things up out here."

"Sheeeit, you read the papers, nigga, you know what's been goin' down. The fuckin' fat cats on Wall Street done fleeced ever'body, from big charities to your grandmamma, if you had one. Then the gov'ment stepped in, bailed 'em out, and pretty much let 'em go back to doin' the same thing they was doin' before. Meanwhile, millions lost their jobs, their savings, their homes. Crime ain't up— yet, but the ways things are goin', it will be soon, and po-po ain't helpin' neither."

Casey sipped his whiskey. "Yeah, I heard they trippin' a lot more than usual?"

"Yeah, well, the goddamn commissioner claims it's for 'future case involvement,' like they tryin' to say it's only a matter of time 'fore any of us who ain't white gonna commit a crime. They're compiling their own dossiers, I'm surprised you didn't get the red-eye on your way over."

Casey shot his cuffs and twitched out the lapels of his jacket. "You see these threads I'm wearin', nigga? Ain't no one gonna mess with a brother dressed as fly as me."

Saunders's dark expression broke at Casey's self-mockery, and the two men laughed again.

Several moments passed until Saunders broke the silence. "What kinda broad you want tonight? Big titties, small waist, or an ass you can throw a saddle on and ride like a jockey? Or how 'bout one of each? Being my age, I got a shitload of Cialis 'round here some damn where."

He chuckled deep in his chest, and so did Casey, who held up his glass. "This'll do me for now, big stump."

Saunders gave him the Spock raised-eyebrow look.

"Don't trip, nigga. I ain't gotten fond of new fish booty." They both laughed again. *When was the last time I had a real laugh?* Casey poured and they drank again.

They had some more whiskey with a delivery of Chinese take-out with plenty of fried shrimp and hot mustard. They ate and talked of nothing special for a while, Casey enjoying every minute of it.

"Goddamn," he said, finishing off a breaded prawn sopping with hot sauce and sighing with pleasure. "Swooping Yee's still burns like a mother."

"You ain't never lied, I will be up all night." Saunders settled into the couch. Old-school R&B played on the sound system. He waved at the doorway on the far side of the room. "The spare room's all ready. You can bunk here long as you like."

Casey nodded his thanks, then got serious. "I'll stay tonight at least. But one, Rono don't know you exist, and we wanna keep it that way. And two, I gotta report to my PO tomorrow and I don't want him to get all bloodhound up in here either."

"Can't see why," Saunders said as he picked up a TV remote control and punched in a sequence of numbers. There was an audible click as the handyman rose and went over to the marble-topped kitchen island seen through an archway. Casey watched as Saunders swiveled the top up and over on hydraulic hinges. He grasped a handle in the middle of the opening and up sprang a display board on oiled hinges, festooned on each side with various handguns, compact submachine guns, flash-bang and smoke grenades, serrated knives, and other assorted weaponry. "As you can see, I been doing more than just remodeling over the years."

Now Casey's eyebrows arched in surprise. "Apparently—you fixin' to start some kind of war without me?"

Saunders shrugged his broad shoulders. "Man's got to protect his castle, ya know?"

"Protect it, or hold off a few SWAT teams—looks like you could do either without breaking a sweat." Casey leaned inside the archway, arms folded while Saunders pointed out several items.

"Got the SIG P229 in .357, good stopping power," he said, like a country salesman offering his wares. "That Beretta Bobcat .22 caliber is small, easy to conceal, and very efficient." He looked over at a bemused Casey.

"There'll be time enough for that later," the freshly minted ex-con said. "I need to get situated and do some recon first, dig?"

"As Sly Stone used to say, Solid, my brother." They knocked fists.

Later, Marcus Casey lay on his back in a more comfortable bed than he'd known in the past two decades, hands behind his head, sleep a stranger for once. A copy of Sun Tzu's *Art of War* lay on the nightstand. He turned on the Tensor light next to it, got up, and found a pad of paper and a pen. He began making a list of names, crossing some off and adding others. Some were those he'd known before going down and others he'd met in prison. A few on the list he put question marks beside. He regarded the names, conjuring up images of some as he remembered them.

He tore the paper from the pad, folded it in half, then lay back down on the bed, the sounds of the city his lullaby. For a moment, he compared the noises outside—passing cars, the occasional bit of conversation from passersby, the rattle of window-unit air conditioners—to what he'd heard for the past twenty years as he'd tried to get to sleep. Crying, furtive whispers, the squeak of too-thin mattresses as cons gave it up to each other, grunts of pain and the thick, meaty sounds of fists on flesh.

Shaking his head, Casey turned over and tried to banish those memories. It was impossible to rid himself of so much this fast, so he settled for pushing them back into a corner of his mind and concentrating on the present. A room that didn't smell of sweat, toilet hootch, and dead hopes; clean, crisp sheets; and a door he could leave through any time he wanted. Casey glanced at the door, then got up and turned the knob, opening it wide to the rooms outside. First time in a long time. He nodded, satisfied, and went back to bed. Finally, sleep overcame him.

2

The next morning, Casey went out to the Vidalgo Auto Restoration facility in the Iron Triangle in Queens. A dense industrial area in Willets Point, the Triangle was populated with various scrap yards, garages, and auto body shops. Male and female teens hawked for the shops as cars in need of body or engine work slowly rolled along, their drivers looking for the best deal.

"Right here, Miss Lady!" a young Latino man with spiky hair and a Spider-Man T-shirt yelled at a middle-aged woman piloting a dented Mercedes. "We can fix it like showroom new."

"Hey, now we got the best discount, you can't go wrong," a pretty young black woman in a too-tight halter top announced. "We got the best. I guarantee."

Casey walked past a mechanic bent over the engine of a family van, a heavyset woman worrying her bottom lip as she watched him work. He entered the Vidalgo establishment, brushing past several customers haggling with personnel and others busy in the mechanics' bay. The whole place smelled like grease, gas, and industrial solvent. Past a faded Ford Taurus on a lift, three men talked inside a second-story glass-and-wood office that looked out over the shop floor. One was an older white man with a silver head of tangled hair. Gino Vidalgo. He took a dead, chewed stub of a cigar out of his mouth and shook it at the other two men, underscoring whatever point he was making. Noticing Casey, he nodded briefly at him and resumed his animated conversation.

Casey reached the rear at the open end of the shop. This led into a junkyard of crushed car hulks, stacked and stripped of various parts. He stopped for a moment, getting his bearings, then went over to a row midway down on his left. Searching around, he found the wreck of a Volvo station wagon toward the bottom of a particular stack.

"We missed you, Crush."

He straightened and turned to two men standing at the head of the row he'd just come down. The speaker, a smaller man wearing a loose, multicolored shirt, was in front. The second thug was large, at least six-four, with prison-chiseled arms sticking out of the openings in the leather vest over his bare chest.

Slipping, Casey admonished himself. He'd tried to stay on point, but hadn't picked up Gulliver Rono's welcoming committee. Given Rono knew a few of the enterprises Casey still had a piece of throughout the five boroughs, he'd most likely had those staked out since he knew Casey'd been released yesterday. It was what Casey would have done in Rono's shoes. *Hafta be more cautious,* he reminded himself.

"That makes me all warm and tingly, fellas," Casey replied, facing the two as they came down the row. He glanced around as they approached. Due to the narrow aisle, they had to advance one behind the other.

The smaller man grinned, showing two gold-fronted teeth. "Now we just wanna make sure you understand to keep your head down and go about your own business. And understand that your business ain't VK business anymore."

"Uh-huh." Plucking a triangle of broken side mirror from a pan-caked Nissan Maxima, Casey slashed up and across with it. He caught the talker on the side of his face, the man rearing back in pain as he clapped a hand to his slashed cheek.

"Muthafuckah!" he bellowed.

Casey pistoned his big foot into the thug's chest, sending him stumbling back into his partner. Rather than run and give his at-tackers a chance to come at him from two sides, Casey came straight at them.

The smaller one was going for a gun under his colorful shirt when Casey hit him with the heel of his hand under his chin, putting all his weight behind it. The dazed man's teeth cracked together, and he reeled against the stack of cars.

The larger man, whose face hadn't changed its impassive ex-pression, lunged forward and grabbed Casey's upper arms. He pulled the ex-con to him, curling one of his ham-sized hands into a fist and raising it to do some real damage. Casey managed to duck the blow, but got tangled with the talker, who was now back in play. The trio fell against the cars, grappling with one another as the larger man let Casey go so he wouldn't get pulled off bal-ance. Falling against a stack of flattened cars, Casey scraped his lower back against a jagged piece of metal, tearing his jean jacket.

"That's your ass, chump," the talker promised, his cheek and neck covered in blood as he clamped his hands around Casey's throat. Oddly, Casey couldn't see any stains on the bright shirt. They spun about, Casey shoving the talker between him and the larger man. Grimacing, Casey jabbed his knee hard into the smaller man's groin, bending him over.

"Shit," he wheezed.

Casey snatched the man's gun from its belt holster and pointed the matte-black Colt .45 at the larger man, who remained stone-faced.

"Tell Rono you delivered your message." Without taking his

eyes from the man-mountain, Casey clubbed the talker hard over the head with the gun butt, sending him crashing to the ground.

The larger man remained motionless, unsure of what to do. Casey shot him in his right thigh, the report echoing off the walls of crushed metal. The silent man grunted as he momentarily buckled against the stack, his face showing surprise and pain. "Fuck," he seethed.

"Go on now, Chatty Cathy," Casey repeated, the gun steady on the wounded man.

The two men hobbled off, beaten and humiliated. Casey shook his head, knowing Rono would enact his own punishment for their failure.

Casey went back to the rear of the Volvo and got the rusted lift gate open after bracing a foot against the body and tugging hard several times. Tossing out some junk from the cargo area, he crawled inside. He unlatched the backseat and propped it forward, exposing a sealed compartment. Opening it required a key Saunders had given him last night. From inside, Casey extracted a sizeable rectangle wrapped in thick sheaves of acid-free paper. Inside were several thousand dollars in twenties and fifties.

"There's my benjamins." He put the brick in his empty equipment bag.

Making sure no one else was looking to brace him, Casey left the facility, walking briskly to get to the subway stop near Shea Stadium. He didn't want to be late for his first meeting with his parole officer.

"They called you Crush because you crushed the competition by any means necessary," Ike Lomax stated as he patted down his charge, who leaned on the man's metal desk, palms down.

"Or maybe 'cause I like orange soda."

Lomax finished his search and asked, "What happened to your

jacket, Mr. Casey?" Casey hadn't had time to change before his appointment and had entered the parole officer's office with the torn garment over his arm. But he'd hung the jacket up when the PO requested him to submit to a pee test and body search.

"Must have caught it on something. I hadn't noticed." *A sharp-eyed po-po,* he thought. *Gonna have to stay on my toes 'round him.*

Lomax was as impassive as the big man in the junkyard, but there was a practiced cynicism to his demeanor. "You can sit down, Mr. Casey."

He sat in one of those molded plastic chairs prevalent in bureaucratic agencies from motor vehicle to welfare. "Nice bling." Lomax indicated the gold medallion on Casey's neck. "St. Jude. Patron saint of lost causes. Is that what you think you are, Mr. Casey?"

"You tell me."

Lomax eased his tall, rangy frame into a creaking, wheeled office chair on the other side of the desk. He was a black man in his late fifties, with thinning hair cut bristle-short on his scalp. He wore glasses and was in shirtsleeves and a fashionable tie, which Casey noted was of quality silk. There was an orderly stack of files on his desk that also contained a push-button phone from the '70s, with duct tape around the handset. Most of the accoutrements of the small office were decades old, except on one wall, where there was a map of the five boroughs and parts of New Jersey. Overlaid on it was a clear pane of plastic divided into a grid that looked vaguely like a circuit board with numerous red glowing pinpoints. From time to time some of the pinpoints changed position on the grid.

"What are your job prospects?"

"I've got a few leads from the program." Casey had taken one of those job readiness programs, run by a religious charity, prior to coming up for parole. He'd been lucky, and his paperwork had already been in the pipeline before the mayor had gone on TV to sift the political discourse, ultimately slowing down the rate of paroled releases. New York City, like the rest of the country, was in a huge budget crisis, with its city services already overburdened before the shortfall. But the prison system was a powerful lobby, and prison labor filled several monetary gaps.

"Restaurants still need dishwashers and fry cooks." Lomax frowned. "Though it's hard to imagine you being satisfied doing that. I mean, what with all them fine bitches you used to have and all the whips and bling-bling." A shadow of a smile came and went across his face as he chuckled.

Now Casey was the one who remained impassive. "Thought I might work with kids, give them the benefit of my hard-learned lessons."

Ignoring that, Lomax asked, "What about lodging?"

Casey hunched a shoulder. "Got enough for the Y till I find something." He was aware he'd have to give this man an address where he could be found soon, as the PO could make unannounced visits any time he wished.

Lomax idly tapped his fingers on Casey's unopened file. "Thinking Brooklyn?" He glanced at his map. "Manhattan's still expensive, even now."

Where's he going with this? Casey shifted in his chair, eyeing the PO calmly, even though all his senses were suddenly on low alert.

Lomax studied him some more. "I might have a place or two you could check out."

"Halfway house?" He damn sure wasn't going to stay in one of those. Not with what he had planned.

This time Lomax let his smile out. It wasn't pleasant. "I'll make some calls. Let you know. Got a cell yet?"

"No."

"Okay, well, get one, today."

He was tempted to say something sarcastic, but squelched it. "Yes, sir."

A beep sounded on the map, making Lomax glance over with a frown. "Okay, once you get settled, report in. Any other change in your status, you immediately let me know that too." He indicated his relic telephone. "We have a central message system and you have my extension. I don't want to hear nothing 'bout you 'lost my card.'"

"Absolutely." Casey started to rise.

"Of course, you know no fraternizing with known associates and so forth."

"Understood." Casey took his jacket off the old-fashioned coatrack. At least he wasn't going to fraternize with any of them today.

As he left, he saw Lomax pull an electronic device the size of a large calculator from his desk's middle drawer, turn it on, and consult its monitor screen.

Lomax studied the monitoring device as he listened to Casey's footsteps fade down the hallway. "Shit, these morons gonna be the death of me yet." He made a mental note to check up on the possible offender that afternoon, see if he needed to be sent back inside.

When he was sure Casey was out of earshot, he pulled out his cell and dialed a number from memory. "Fulson, it's Lomax."

"This about your ten thirty appointment?"

"Yeah, he just left. Arrived right on time, like a good little parolee."

"How you readin' him?"

"Oh, I have no doubt he's scheming to get back into the high life as soon as possible."

"And you still wanna let him do that?"

"If the chatter on the street's true, then having Marcus Casey walkin' around outside will do more for us than sending him back inside."

"Tigers don't change their stripes, you know."

"This one won't have to. Hang back and observe for a while,

let's let this play out. If he does what I think he's gonna do, he'll do our job for us. If not, we'll have plenty of options to send him back to Attica."

Fulson chuckled. "No one ever said you didn't have balls as big as boulders, Lomax. You realize if this goes south, they'll hang your ass out to dry. You best be sure of who's playin' who here."

"Shit, no guts no glory. Sometimes unconventional opponents need unconventional tactics. I'll know soon enough if Casey is the guy, and you best believe I'll be watching him like a hawk."

Lomax hung up and put his phone away, still staring at the flashing light on his grid. *Now, if there was only some way I could take care of this problem as easily. . . .*

Riding down in the elevator, Casey considered Lomax's surveillance board. He'd heard in the joint that probation was using GPS and other forms of electronic tracking to keep tabs on parolees. That buzz on the map must have meant one of them had gone astray, some chump on a tight leash. Casey couldn't be on a leash, tight or otherwise. He'd just do what he had to do, but keep the volume on two.

Outside the brick-and-concrete building, he walked east, then took a left at a tight alleyway between buildings. In the middle of plastic trash bags and loose garbage in a Dumpster, he collected his bundle of cash. There had been no other place to stash it between the auto place in Queens and the parole office, and he damn sure couldn't explain that kind of money to Lomax. There was something about that dude he couldn't nail down. He was a hard-ass, for sure. But he didn't act like the bulls in stir or other POs he'd observed over the years. There was definitely more going on in his head than marking the months to retirement.

Still, Casey had to admit, it had been a much better reception than what he'd gotten on his first day inside way back when.

3

Marcus Casey walked into Attica Correctional Facility in his best suit. Every swinging dick in here, from the hacks to rival gangs, knew he was coming today. Plenty of them were jonesing at the thought of moving up in the ranks by icing him. The Aryan Brotherhood, jealous over his command of the New York City streets and their hatred of "niggers," had spread the word through the prison wire that he wasn't gonna last twenty-four hours inside.

After processing, he was dressed in standard prison attire—blue jeans, blue cotton long-sleeved shirt, white socks, and tennis shoes with no metal eyelets, since those could be used for cutting. The two hacks escorting him to his cell suddenly turned him down a small, isolated corridor. Two other guards joined them.

"Oh, so this is how it goes—" His words were cut off by a heavy blow to his kidney, followed by a nightstick to the back of his knee that dropped him to the ground.

"Heard all about you, Casey," one of them said as he jammed the tip of a cattle prod hard into Casey's shoulder. The voltage made his muscles contract, and he cried out involuntarily, the shock convulsing his body. The guard removed the prod, leaving Casey on his hands and knees, gasping and winded.

"You may have been a hot-shit gangster out there, boy. But in here"—he jabbed the arcing metal contacts into Casey's back, driving him to the floor—"you ain't even shit. You got that?"

Unmoving, Casey lay on the damp concrete floor. He wasn't surprised at the reception. He just hadn't figured they'd strike so fast. He was angry too—the bribes he'd sent hadn't eased his way inside at all. Could be these ofays were taking the money and doing him anyway, or Rono had paid them, or they just wanted to show him who was boss.

On his hands and knees, he pretended to be weaker than he was. The head guard with the glove holding the cattle prod didn't disappoint. He walked around in front of Casey, tapping the device against his other hand. "You ain't gonna come into our nice little prison and start stirring up trouble, now, are you? I don't hear you, burr head. I said, now are you?"

"Fuck you!" Casey lunged upward, butting him in the stomach while manhandling him backward, doing his best to keep the stun baton trapped between his body and the guard. The other three reached for them but he had his target pressed against the wall. With hands all over him, Casey reared up, battering the top of his head into the man's jaw. Bone cracked under the impact.

The guard made a thick, injured wail and fell to the ground, Casey on top of him. He tried to hit him again, but the three other guards pulled him off, clubbing him to the ground in a rain of nightsticks.

The head guard, holding his jaw, lisped, "You just earned yourself ninety days in the hold, motherfucker."

Gonna be a long goddamn sentence, Casey thought just before the blackness took him.

. . .

He awoke in the infirmary, with a cast on his arm, one on his leg, and a concussion. The warden visited him, trying to find out who was responsible. Casey didn't say a word. He was hospitalized for a week, then moved to protective custody, meaning twenty-three-hour-a-day lockdown. The other hour was for exercise in what the prisoners called the dog kennel, a narrow fenced-in outdoor corridor.

Casey figured he could do solitary with no sweat, since his busted limbs needed time to heal anyway. But it was far from a cake walk. He soon ran into an enemy he couldn't defeat; the endless isolation. It was his constant companion, the lack of any human contact, and this wore on him. He tried everything to make the time go by; exercising until he was exhausted, sleeping for up to eighteen hours at a stretch, rapping endless tunes to himself until the words lost all meaning, walking the neighborhoods in his mind's eye, seeing every street, every building. But his favorite pastime was planning exactly how he was going to kill Gulliver Rono when he got out.

He replayed the events of that day over and over again, seeing Rono's Joker-like grin as he stuck the knife between Casey's ribs when the feds busted in. He held on to that memory, firing his rage, but with no outlet it overflowed into the cramped cell resulting in the destruction of his clothes, his mattress, anything and everything. Finally the ninja turtles came in to get him, the helmeted and body-armored guards who bum-rushed him with their plastic shields and dragged him out of the cell thrashing and roaring. He was sedated and put under observation in the psych ward.

Casey knew he had to play his time inside differently, or he was gonna end up either dead, crazy, or an institutionalized lifer. No way in hell was he going down like that. He knew cats on the street who got released only to break the law to get locked up again. Poor bastards couldn't handle life without a set routine.

When his seventy-two-hour observation period was over, Casey had said the right things to the prison doc, nodded at the right times, and ended up right back in solitary. He tried to maintain, but soon felt himself slipping toward breakdown again. The thought of losing his mind scared him even more than losing anything he had lost as the dethroned leader of the VKs. He held on, but came out a changed man—he'd seen hell, and would do anything not to go back.

Walking along the city streets got Casey revisiting the past again. He thought of Vasili Machinko, who'd been the VKs' banker when he was running the outfit. Machinko had washed the gang's dirty money into clean funds, investing in legitimate businesses such as real estate, an electrical supply wholesaler, and even a piece of a beachfront resort in St. Lucia. He'd formed limited and overseas companies as fronts to handle the infusion of cash as passthroughs.

The morning Casey was arrested, Machinko, an older man, was getting a steam at an Old World Ukrainian bathhouse in Coney Island. As the feds were happily handcuffing Casey, Rono's emissary was at the bathhouse using a cattle prod with its voltage amped up to extract all the financial secrets of Casey's empire from an indignant Machinko. Once Rono's henchman was given the all-clear that Casey's assets were transferred and under Rono's own laundryman's control, he went about his dirty work with the passion of a Nazi. One day Casey wanted to return the favor to Rono and his banker.

He took the subway to Midtown and the locker where he'd stashed the research file Kenny Saunders had prepared. He was right to have left the walk-up early that morning, before Rono's hounds had picked up his scent. Bad enough he hadn't spotted them at Vidalgo's, but leading them to Kenny would have been a fuck-up of epic proportions. Retrieving his file, he walked over to the Roosevelt Hotel on Madison at Forty-fifth.

"Does Izzy Latour still work here?" he asked the pretty female clerk behind the check-in counter.

"I'm sorry, sir." She smiled politely. "I don't know who that is."

"Never mind. I'd like a room."

She looked at her monitor. "I'm afraid we're all booked up. We have a couple of conventions in town."

Casey was about to protest when someone spoke over his shoulder. "I imagine we can find something for you, Crush."

Casey turned and it took him a moment to place the handsome Afro-Latina standing there in the DKNY tailored suit. "Damn, Carla, you don't age, do you, girl?"

"You're full of it, but I'll choose to believe you." She kissed him on the cheek and they hugged, patting each other's backs. She said to the younger woman, "I'll take care of getting Mr. Casey situated, Lisa."

"Very good, Ms. Aquila."

"Come on, let me buy you lunch."

"Mind if I store this first?" he asked. He'd put the file in the equipment bag and padlocked it too.

"No problem." She called a bellman over and he took the bag into her office.

"There's a nice little place a few blocks from here." She put her arm through his as they walked.

"So Izzy got you this job?" he asked.

"In a roundabout way, yeah. When did you touch down?"

He brought her up to date on his activities, including the dust-up in Queens. Contrary to her polished appearance, Carla Aquila was from the hood, just like Casey. She was one of the few people that knew him inside and out.

Now she smiled ruefully. "I get the feeling you're gonna ignore Rono's message."

Casey didn't answer, and as they crossed the street among a knot of people coming each way, he chuckled. "Everybody's either yakking on their cell phone or listening to, what do they call 'em?"

"IPods," she replied. "Welcome to the twenty-first century, old school."

Casey laughed. "Indeed."

They arrived at the modest eatery and got a table toward the rear. Carla ordered a salad and Casey a steak sandwich. He could have eaten two, but restrained himself.

Casey drank some water and asked, "You keep in touch with that ex of yours?"

She folded her arms. "What you want with Champa?"

"Can't a brotha look up an old pardner?"

"Don't you mean a running buddy who just happens to know how to blow shit up?"

He gave her an innocent look.

"Nigga, please," she said, sotto. "Last I heard, he'd hooked up with some other bumper-headed vets and was pulling down scores out west."

"L.A.?"

"No, the real cowboy and Indian west. Wyoming, Oklahoma, places like that."

"Can you get word to him on the DL?"

"I don't think I want to be a party to you and Champa's fun and games."

"As I seem to recall, you used to like that lifestyle once upon a time."

She screwed up her face. "That was then."

He reached over and put his hand on hers. "Uh-huh."

She frowned at him, but didn't move her hand. "I'll see what I can do."

As their food arrived they got caught up on various subjects, including Carla's daughter, who was in her second year at Brown.

"That's great, Carla. I know Sara'll do well." Casey willed himself not to get carried away and wolf down the food sitting before him in huge bites. The goddamn thing was the most intoxicating piece of meat he'd smelled in more than twenty years. It damn near gave him a hard-on. It was only with an effort that he didn't curl his free arm protectively around the plate as he ate. *Slow and steady, Casey, slow and steady.* He calmed down and took a bite, chewing thoroughly, savoring every bit as long as possible.

Carla paused, a speared cherry tomato on her fork that she pointed at him. "That's because I'm gonna keep her away from men like you and her father."

Casey laughed. "That's probably wise."

She ate her tomato, regarding him as she chewed and swallowed. "Because you're right, Marcus, I do have a thing for men who don't do the nine-to-five—unfortunately they usually end up doing five to ten." She let her gaze stay on his face. "Why else would I have written your conniving ass?"

"I was glad for those letters, they meant a lot," he admitted. "Look, Carla, I'm not looking to cause you drama, so say the word and I'll bounce, but I have something I gotta do and that's not gonna change. So let me know what's up, and regardless we always gonna be cool."

Carla looked at his face for a moment and Casey knew what she should say, but knew she wouldn't say it. "Okay, Crush, I'll talk to Champa."

They smiled thinly at each other and continued their lunch.

Afterward, in the suite Carla secured for him in the hotel, she playfully shoved him on the bed and began undressing. "Hope you're not sleepy after that heavy lunch."

Casey lay propped on his elbow and swallowed. "You know it's been more than a minute."

"We knew what we were doing then . . . and now." She started unbuttoning her blouse, revealing a light blue lacy bra supporting her full breasts. He was intoxicated, particularly with the color of the garment offset against her coppery skin.

"I meant," he said hoarsely, "me. I hate to admit this, but I'm as wound up as a fat boy trapped in a pie shop." But that didn't stop a creeping voice and an all-too-familiar image in his head. Much as he tried his former mentor's words wouldn't go away.

"A true player controls his impulses until the time is right." The voice sounded like it was coming from right beside him, but Casey knew that was bullshit.

Shut up, Mack D. Casey reached up for those lacy cups, but that calm, insistent voice in his head wouldn't let up.

"'Manhood is a struggle,' Benjamin Disraeli said. You know you got business to attend to before reaping the rewards." His former mentor's voice just wouldn't fade. Casey had to respond to his mentor's reproachful visage, and held up his hands in surrender.

"What's wrong?" Carla asked breathlessly.

"It's not you, baby." Casey sat up. "It's us."

She sighed. "Me and Champa have been through for a long time, Crush. More than a decade now. You know that."

"Yeah, I know. But me and him go way back too, and muthafuckahs have been known to be territorial."

Carla's full lips crooked in a wry smile. "Maybe I'll just drug you and have my way with you anyway."

He smiled, and asked, "Is that right?"

Carla laughed deep in her throat, then sat on the edge of the bed. Casey watched her as she buttoned her blouse. *Goddamn, she could get my ass distracted and shot.*

Carla turned serious. "I know it won't just be Champa you'll be reaching out to." She glanced at his profile. "Hasn't there been enough blood and death, Marcus?"

"What?! You want I should just ignore what happened? Just let the busta who took everything away from me walk the same streets I do?"

She got close to him. "Of course not. But Rono can't keep going forever. In fact—" But she didn't finish.

"What is it?" he asked.

"I'm sure I'm not telling you something you don't already know. Or will find out soon enough."

Impatiently, he said, "Come on, woman, what you talkin' about?"

"Word is Rono has diversified." She momentarily stiffened, then relaxed. "Not too long . . . after Antonio was killed."

Casey raised his head, all interest in her fine body vanishing at the mention of his son. "Yeah, and?"

"Sex trafficking with young girls." She glared up at him. "That's what that *pendejo*'s involved in now. I'm pretty sure it's not bullshit. There's been a couple of . . . representatives who've come around lately suggesting how I might make more on the side if I would enlist their services.

"Thing is," she continued, "seems it's some kind of Asian hookup he has, not Russian mob like I first thought."

Casey pretended this didn't affect him. "Rono always was an ambitious bastard."

"And that's one thing that hasn't changed." Carla looked at Casey for a moment and gave him a warm smile, which he returned. "This has been a trip, Crush. I'll let you know when I hear from Champa."

4

Casey spent most of the afternoon studying the file on the new VKs. Rono had expanded the gang's business into shady new areas. Although Casey had been no stranger to diversifying when he ran the show, he'd always stayed away from foul shit like sex trafficking, something Rono obviously had no problem with. From the string of underground chop shops, high-end B&E rings, computer scams, to a marijuana pipeline of the tastiest Pacific Northwest weed distributed up and down the East Coast, Casey had built up the Vicetown Kings from mere dope slangers to a highly efficient, disciplined operation involved in both underground and straight concerns.

He'd learned the lessons of others before him, like Cornell "The Ghost" Jones, Casper Holstein, and Frank Matthews, the Black Caesar, who skipped out on his bail in 1973, never to be seen again. Certainly no choirboy, Casey could chill a treacherous mother-lover as soon as blink, and go on eating his catfish and eggs. But he had rules. When he ran the VKs, crack was off-limits to the crew—that shit destroyed your concentration, your ambition, and your drive. It was a lethal virus that, once introduced, couldn't be contained. He'd always enforced strict internal policies on the limits of drug use and backed them up with hard-nosed sanctions— sometimes permanent when necessary to get the point across. He had to. He wasn't just running a gang, but creating a legacy the only way he knew how.

But Rono had stolen what Casey and others now dead had built into something special. Carla's assertions were backed up by what he read in the file, confirming the rumors he'd heard while he was locked down. Casey surmised the sex trafficking angle was a desperate move on Rono's part to keep growing profits. The Vicetown Kings were still a force to be reckoned with, but their reach had diminished under their current leader. When Casey had been double-crossed, Rono had ruthlessly assassinated several of his boss's inner circle. It was cold-blooded, but made sense from a tactical standpoint, as the new alpha dog had to eliminate those loyal to Casey. But that also meant Rono had to bring in those he could bend to his will, small thinkers with little or no experience. A number of his captains were as untrustworthy as he was. They'd broken off to form their own factions, and were now rivals. They could be persuaded, one way or another. Several were ready to roll with Casey's plan right now. The others would fall into line once he'd reestablished himself, or pay the price.

The white-collar avenues Casey had invested in for long-term stability were still on the books. But several of those pursuits, from real estate in the Hamptons to square but steady concerns like fast-food chains and a printing business, had been squandered by Rono. He and his zombies had sucked out the profits to maintain their bling-bling lifestyles, but had neither reinvested in the businesses nor paid attention to the market. That would all change once he was back in control.

Putting the VK file aside, he turned to the other files on the two gangs that stood in his way of ruling the streets again—the Blood Devils and the Black Lotus. The Blood Devils were a fast-moving, hard-hitting Latino gang that had appeared in New York about five years ago, part of the illegal immigration invasion flooding up from Mexico. They ran their own businesses—protection rackets, coke, grand theft auto, and guns—while holding their turf like pit bulls. They aligned themselves with no one.

The Black Lotus was a close-knit triad out of Hong Kong that had come east from Seattle, apparently in search of greener pastures. Like most of the Chinese gangs, they'd set up in Chinatown and immediately ascended to the top of the gang hierarchy, absorbing or eliminating their opponents. Casey was impressed at how methodical they were. Now they controlled the heroin distribution throughout the neighborhood, and also ran high-end prostitution, numbers, and a thriving designer knock-off business.

The leaders of both gangs had flatly refused Casey's offer to join the syndicate he was building. Therefore, they had to be removed. The only question was how to do it without the streets erupting in a bloodbath that could be laid at his feet. That didn't even take into consideration Rono and his lieutenants, all of whom had to be disposed of before Casey could move in. Three dangerous snakes that had to be grabbed by the tail and killed before they could bite him.

Casey leaned back, lacing his hands behind his head. Mack D's calm voice echoed in his head again, reciting one of his favorite maxims by the fourth century BC Chinese general Sun Tzu:

The military is a Tao of deception—
Thus when able, manifest inability
When active, manifest inactivity
When near, manifest as far.

When far, manifest as near.
Thus when he seeks advantage, lure him.
When he is in chaos, take him.
When he is substantial, prepare against him.
When he is strong, avoid him.
When he is wrathful, harass him.
Attack where he is unprepared.
Emerge where he does not expect it.

"Easier said than done, homes," Casey muttered. Rono was expecting Casey to move against him sooner or later, of that he was certain. And right now, he had no army, just himself. "Gonna take a whole shitload of deception to bring these muthafuckahs down. Just gotta figure out how to do it."

Remembering Mack's pearls of wisdom made Casey think back to when the older man had first gotten ahold of him at Attica. . . .

Aching all over from his latest beating. Casey was flung into the familiar solitary room, the hacks' laughter echoing in his ears.

"We got a pool ridin' on your black ass, boy. I got three-to-one sayin' you ain't gonna live through Christmas." The guard who had hauled him into the cell laughed as he slammed the door shut. "I'd sure hate for you to disappoint me."

Reaching for the hard bed, Casey pulled himself to his feet and spat blood and mucus into the stainless-steel sink bolted to the wall. Gingerly he probed his tender face, which had taken a hella beating from the three Latinos who had jumped him in the shower, hoping to put him down once and for all.

Casey, however, had been more than a match for them. He'd wrapped a bar of soap in a towel and improvised a crude blackjack, keeping it constantly in motion as he whaled on the trio. They'd gotten in some good licks, but one was now missing two teeth, another had gotten a concussion when Casey had rammed his head into the shower room wall, and the third had his ribs stove in when Casey had hammered him with his free hand before the hacks had broken it up.

And now here he was, all fucked up and back in solitary again for three months, just for defending himself. Casey washed his face, probing a loose tooth with his tongue, hoping it would stay put long enough so he could get out and have the prison dentist look at it. But that was ninety days away, and Casey wasn't sure if he could make it through the next twenty-four hours.

He turned from the sink and was about to lie down when he saw a neatly folded scrap of paper and a pencil on the pillow.

Casey looked at the door, and the closed judas hole. He knew the rules—nothing was allowed into the hole with an inmate except the clothes on his back. Any infraction automatically doubled a con's stay.

Casey didn't know if this was a setup or not, but the chance of contact with someone, anyone else, was worth the risk. The message was simple, yet caused a lot of head-scratching.

> *You believe you are a prisoner here. I say you are as free as you wish to be. The choice is yours.*

What the fuck? About to flush the cornball words down the toilet, Casey stopped. This was too goofy to be a trap. Okay, why not respond just for a laugh? At first he was going to be threatening, but instead wrote a brief, serious reply on the back of the paper. When he had his next exercise period, he dropped the note on the floor outside, aware that any communication between solitary inmates was also strictly forbidden.

When he returned, another slip was waiting on his bed. Next to Casey's scrawled reply—*I'm listening*—were four words.

That's the first step.

That was how Marcus Casey first communicated with Johnny Meachum, aka Mack D. He wouldn't actually meet him until much later, but their correspondence that first year in prison made a hell of a difference. It got him through.

Shaking his head, Casey returned to the here and now. Standing up from the desk where he'd been going over the file and making notes, he stretched and rubbed his face, realizing it was past ten at night, and he hadn't eaten since lunch. He could ring for room service, but wanted some fresh air. He put on his suit jacket over his T-shirt and jeans and walked down to the street. Passing his reflection in a plate-glass window, he made a note to see his tailor in the next few days to update his look. He knew Mal Yurik still had his shop of sartorial finery in Chelsea, because, like with everything else, he'd checked on it before he got out.

Of course, he'd be careful and not wear anything too fancy to one of his check-ins with Lomax. It was bad enough that the man could drop in announced. That reminded Casey that he still had to find a place to stay. An innocent-enough crib so as not to arouse the PO's suspicions, but also a place he could operate from if necessary. Solving both those problems wouldn't be easy.

Casey had two slices at a corner pizzeria, admonishing himself to watch what he ate. Too much rich food and lazing around would dull his instincts, not to mention soften his belly. Checking his watch, he decided to visit a particular nightspot, hoping that what he'd heard in the joint was still accurate concerning the locale and its owner.

Casey hailed a cab, leaning down to the passenger window once it stopped. He asked the driver if he knew the club he was looking for, and the cabbie shook his head. Casey waved him on and kept walking. He repeated this twice more, and on the fourth try he got into a cab with a lit mini-billboard advertising a cop show on the roof.

"So you wish to take my chariot to the Honsu Club, bruddah?"

"Yeah, it's supposed to be somewhere in Brooklyn, that right?"

"On Flatbush." He slid the car into the light traffic and engaged the meter.

"You been to it?" He looked at the cabbie's license. It read KAM WAIAKANA.

"Yeah, once or twice. Drinks okay and them *wahines,* whew, baby."

Casey grinned in the dark backseat, the city's lit signs sweeping by the car's windows. "What else you know about that place and who hangs there?"

Waiakana gave it a beat, then, "What else you want to know?"

Casey laid a fifty across the seat back. "I got the twin to lay on you plus the fare for whatever you can tell me."

The driver took the bill and began talking as the car headed toward the Brooklyn Bridge. Casey leaned back in the seat and listened. It was good to learn everything you could about unfamiliar territory.

In his penthouse high above Manhattan, Gulliver Rono bent over a line of finely chopped white powder. The small mirror rested on a beautiful, naked, black woman's rounded ass as she posed on her hands and knees in front of him. Rono massaged her splendid booty while he put a white ivory straw to his nose.

"Hold still, ho." He reached between her legs while deftly snorting the line in one smooth pass, trying to make her twitch. If she did, she'd earn a smack from him for messing up his hit, but the woman was a pro, and remained still, although a small moan escaped her lips as he roughly fondled her.

The cocaine hit his nasal passages, and he did two more lines in quick succession, feeling the high elevate his senses. "C'mere." He pulled the woman to him, reclining back into the soft cushions of the black leather couch as she straddled him, her experienced hands fondling his crotch as she kissed him hungrily. With one hand, she unbuttoned his raw silk shirt, revealing a body that had once been rock-hard, but had grown soft and thick over years of high living, rich food, and too much partying. The woman didn't pause, her high, tight, fake tits bounced in Rono's face as she moved lower to maintain his arousal.

"Yeah, bitch, you know what I like—gonna boss me up good—" A knock at the door snapped his head toward the interruption. "What the fuck ya want?"

"Boss, we gotta situation out here."

"God-muthafuckin'-damnit!" Swiping the whore off his lap with a sweep of his arm, he rose and stomped to the door, adjusting his pants as he cracked it open. "Muthafuckah, I'm 'bout to get busy up in here, what the fuck you trippin' 'bout now?"

"Big Sally and Low Rise just got back from Vidalgo's. They ran into Crush."

Rono's half-erection deflated the moment he heard his former boss and mentor's name. "Muthafuck." He opened the door just wide enough to slip out, calling back over his shoulder to the woman, "Stay the fuck there, I'ma be right back."

He stalked out into the living room, which was decorated in modern, glass-and-metal furniture that was showing its age after years of hard parties and indifferent care. The room smelled of old weed and stale takeout, the marble countertops in the adjoining kitchen a mess of dirty dishes and cardboard takeout boxes.

"All right, what the fuck's so important y'all gotta interrupt—" He stopped when he saw the two men standing next to Derek Webb, one of his chief enforcers.

Low Rise stood there like a whipped dog, a huge white bandage covering his cheek and a decided lean to his stance, like someone had stomped on his nuts, and even walking too fast hurt now. The expression on his face alternated between fear and pain.

Beside him, Big Sally was leaning on a heavy, black wooden cane, and Rono noticed the bulge of what was probably a thick bandage underneath his right pants leg. Expressionless as ever, only the slight twitching of his upper lip betrayed the pain he felt.

Rono quickly masked his surprise with disdain. "Oh, ain't this a bitch. What the fuck happened to you two?"

Low Rise cleared his throat. "Casey. We found him at Vidalgo's, went to give him that message you wanted delivered. He, uh—he got the drop on us."

Gulliver Rono rubbed a hand over his hairless head and the jagged scar on his scalp that he'd had since childhood. He'd never bothered with plastic surgery to remove or hide the defect, keeping it visible to show how tough he was. "What?! He got the drop on both you bitches? How does that work? This old muthafuckah just got sprung after doing a hard twenty, and you pair of pussies can't even handle his ass! Fuuuuuck!"

Rono paused, then in a low voice asked, "How'd he look?"

Low Rise frowned in confusion. "What?"

In a flash, Rono crossed the room and grabbed Low Rise by the cheek, making the smaller man wince in pain. He twisted his fingers into the banger's skin, feeling fresh stitches pop under his grip. "Casey, you dumb fuck! Who the fuck you think I'm asking 'bout? How'd he muthafuckin' look?" He saw dark red blood stain the bandage, but Low Rise didn't make a sound, even though his face had to be on fire. He knew the penalty for showing weakness in front of Rono.

"Hard enough to do this to us," Big Sally rumbled next to them. "That mutha had his shit goin' on. Like he never even went to the joint at all."

"Why was he at Vidalgo's?"

"Dunno. He was poking around in the junkyard, near some crushed cars."

Rono pondered this for a moment. "Prob'ly goin' after a stash of cash or some shit. Loose-lipped fucker was always braggin' about his hidey-holes all over the city, claimed he had loot stashed in every borough." He shrugged, affecting an aura of nonchalance. "No big thing. Even old toothless dogs gotta eat, right?"

He laughed, and the other three laughed with him, but Rono heard the forced undertone in it. Even worse, he heard the forced tone in his own voice, and he hated it. After twenty years, the mention of Marcus Casey's name still got him unglued. But he'd be goddamned if he'd let any of his soldiers see his fear.

Releasing Low Rise, he red-eyed him and Big Sally. "You two get the fuck out of here—go get cleaned up or something, just get the fuck out of my sight. Webb, call a muthafuckin' council in an hour—I want to get some shit straight with our boys." He turned to go back into the bedroom. "I'ma finish my business in here, and then I'll decide how to handle Casey."

He walked back into the bedroom, his earlier drug-fueled lust replaced by an urgent need to control, to dominate, to hurt someone. When the black whore saw the look in his eyes, she shuddered, but slunk toward him when he motioned her to his side.

Sixty minutes later, Rono faced his assembled captains. He was cleaned up and dressed to the nines, his tailored suit concealing his soft paunch. Idly, he examined his manicured fingernails, wiping a bit of skin and blood from under one with his silk handkerchief. Everyone in the room waited until he spoke.

"We all gonna remain cool about Crush for now, got it?" he said.

"How cool?" Derek Webb asked. "You still gonna remind him who runs shit, right? I know Big Sally'd want that. I'm damn sure Low Rise'd want it too, what with his face gettin' fucked up and all."

"Nigga, *I* say what Big Sally and Low Rise fuckin' want. If they'd done what they were supposed to, I'd still be in bed with my bitch instead of talking with you niggas," Rono declared, pacing the room. "We make any kinda move on Casey, who the fuck you think the cops gonna come after first, huh? We got the biggest damn deal with the Colombians in years locked up, and I don't need any drama flaring right now. Keep Crush in your crosshairs, but the trigger don't get pulled till I say so, got it?"

"Ain't nothing to flare up," Webb observed, "if we chill his shit first night he's back in the city. If homeboy's stupid enough to try and come back to the 'hood, that is." Nods and assenting laughter went around.

"Maybe your memory's coming up short, Dee, but more than once in all those years in the joint, Crush managed to keep breathin', despite the green light I okayed on his ass. He's got friends and allies inside and outside, and I need all our shit to be smooth for the time being."

Rono bore his gaze into their faces. "Nothin'—not a muthafuckin' thing—happens to him without my okay. Am . . . I . . . understood?"

Heads bobbed up and down, along with grunts of agreement.

5

There was a long line to enter Club Honsu. The cabdriver had told him the name of the bouncer/doorman, Clete, and that he got hungry 'round this time of night. Clete was easily six-six and a cock diesel. Casey handed a warm, paper-wrapped pastrami sandwich to two pretty women in the middle of the line. When they got closer, they giggled, handed Clete the paper bag, and told him the gentleman with them had bought it for him. After happily inspecting the contents with a deep sniff, he let them and Casey in over a chorus of groans from those skipped over. Casey took care of the cover for the three of them.

"Bye-bye, handsome," one of the ladies said as they went off to dance.

Club Honsu was a converted space that had once been a department store during its long and varied history. The main floor had twin bars, one along each length, with a slightly raised dance floor at the end. The DJ was on the open-air second level over-

looking the packed first floor. Casey assumed the requisite VIP
areas were up there as well.

He sauntered to the bar, edging around two busty, drunk women
whooping and rubbing their breasts together. Eyeing this display
as it broke up, he said sideways to the bartender, "Is Shin around?"

The inked, pierced man gave him a blank reaction. "Don't know
him, cousin."

"Give me a beer, okay? Whatever's the darkest you have on tap."

"That'll be eight even," the bartender said, setting a pint of
Samuel Adams Black Lager before him.

Casey produced a ten and walked around, attuning himself to
the vibe of the crowd, the chatter, and the driving music. Eventually, his glass empty, he leaned against a pillar. Briefly, as if transported in a time warp, he was carried back more than two decades.
He and Danielle were slow dancing while others frenetically moved
around them. His lieutenants had cleared out the entire second floor,
and were holding court, but he was content to steal these few moments alone with Dani.

"I'm quite fond of you, you know," she whispered in his ear,
kissing his neck.

"Dani . . . I . . . I'm so glad you're in my life."

She stopped and looked at him. "Then let's make a life together."

Although all his attention had been on her, his street instincts
had prickled, and Casey had glanced up to see Rono watching
them from the second level, a small smile on his lips. He raised his
rocks glass to Casey before melting back into the party. *If only I'd
recognized that smile for what it was . . .*

The memory and Dani's face faded as someone tapped Casey
on the shoulder. He looked at the woman standing next to him.
She was Asian, gorgeous, and dressed in a black suit coat, tailored
black slacks, white shirt, and black tie.

"Come with me, Mr. Casey."

She pivoted on her heels, military precise, and he followed her through the club to a rear door. *If this is an ambush, at least she's fine bait*, Casey mused as he admired her phat ass swishing back and forth. She opened the door, and they stepped into a wide back area where a red and tan fully restored Jaguar Mark V 1950 Drophead idled.

"Goddamn," Casey exclaimed. "Do you even know what inconspicuous means?" He laughed as a man exited the backseat of the classic car. Shinzo Becker, half Chinese and half black, stood lean and muscular in trendy casual wear.

The kung fu enthusiast walked up and put his hands on Casey's shoulders, shaking them. "You don't let a brotha know you landed? I'da thrown a party for you, man."

"Right on, brotha," Casey responded, "but I'm trying to keep my convict ass on the down low for the time being."

"Fuck that crooked dick muthafuckah Rono," Becker spat. "I don't need an excuse to quell his shit and bring peace to at least a couple of boroughs. Come on man, let's roll. Got a few errands to run." Becker got back in the car, Casey entering after him. The chauffeur got behind the wheel and effortlessly engaged the clutch.

"Here you go." Becker handed Casey a cheroot and inserted one in the corner of his own mouth, lighting the thin cigars for both of them. The two sat back, smoking and relaxed. The car went over the uneven roadway as if it were on a highway of smooth sheet metal. After a few minutes, Becker turned to him. "You need a crib?"

"You done got psychic on me, man." Becker had been the one to advise Casey to invest in real estate back in the old days.

Casey's host showed gapped front teeth. "One place for the squares and another for, extracurricular endeavors, shall we say?"

"We shall." Casey smiled.

"I'll see what I can procure. You got out at the right time, considering how shitty the market is now."

"Maybe some kind of, I don't know, office, too, for lack of a better term. Someplace to lay low and hide the firepower."

"Clear on that."

Casey drew and exhaled another lungful before he asked, "You at peace with Rono now?"

"Come on, nigga, you know that boy's always testing my limits. Remember when I caught him dry snitchin' back in the day when he was a youngsta and knocked out his tooth." Casey laughed. "Anyway he thinks he's King Shit now, but not everyone's buying it."

Casey cocked his head. "You think about putting him in check . . . again? Breaking off some of what he has? How deep is his respect?"

Becker snorted. "That's a negative number. But the question really is a matter of pragmatism." The gangster interlaced his manicured fingers. "Complicated, understand? Not that I wouldn't be willing to take a run at him if the cosmos, you know, aligned. That boy is treacherous, but then again, I'm not telling *you* anything new."

Casey hadn't asked Becker if his driver was cool. She wouldn't be behind the wheel if she didn't back his play. Casey was sure she was strapped like a car seat under that tailored jacket.

"I'm glad to see you, brotha, a lot of niggas go soft or crazy in the joint."

Casey lifted a shoulder slightly, blowing out a stream. "Yeah, well, hate kept me going the first eight."

"It's them other twelve that can kick your ass."

"You have to figure out what you need. Not what you want. What you want comes later."

"True dat."

"Life according to Mack D."

"Oh, wow, my man was up in there?"

"No lie."

"That cat was around when we was kids running things. I

remember that muthafuckah had a black mink interior in his Caddy. Fuckin' amazing!"

Casey nodded. "Yeah, he was no joke. Remember the Gault takedown?"

Becker cackled. "Man, that heist was legendary. Fuckin' inspired us, for damn sure."

"Twelve million in gold never recovered," Casey said admiringly. He reflected back on how Mack D kept him sane in a hellhole designed to drive everyone mad. Just like Casey, he'd been set up too. Mack D was down for life, not for his successful thefts but for killing a cop, an undercover who'd gone rogue and gotten greedy. But that hadn't mattered to the jury. He too had initially been fueled by the anticipation of revenge. In those years Mack D had raged against real and imagined enemies. This had sustained him for years, and nothing any counselor or con could say to him could get him to be anything but a mad dog. Until . . .

"Where you at, man, flashin' back to some prison riot?" Becker joked, pulling Casey out of his reveries. The car pulled to a stop. "Okay, we here. Let's go up, you gonna dig this shit."

Casey craned his neck. The car was before a modern high-rise apartment building. He stepped out with Becker, who turned to his pretty driver.

"You can amuse yourself for a while, huh, Li?"

"I'll see what I can find around here, daddy." The Jaguar rolled away as the two men stepped to the apartment building's glass door.

Inside were two security guards at a rotunda outfitted with monitors giving them regular views of exteriors and interiors. One of them got up to open the door.

"S'up, Shin?" The guard grinned.

"Just a bit of pimpin', baby," Becker responded. The guard burst out laughing and held the door open wider and let the visitors into the lobby.

"Nozinga's expecting you," the guard said. He led the way to a locked-off elevator bank. Inserting a hex-headed key in a corresponding opening in an electronic keypad, he freed up a car and brought it to the lobby.

"Thanks, playa," Becker said, tipping the guard a ten as he and Casey got on and rode up.

"Where the hell we going?"

Becker grinned at him cryptically. "To see the oracle."

"Some things never change."

"Shit, can't just keep layin' up with bitches and shinin' my nines all the time."

Casey laughed. "Whatever, man."

The door opened to a young, golden-colored woman draped in a silk print caftan. "Good evening, Mr. Becker."

"Hello, Ginger."

"Who's our guest?"

"Crush Casey."

"Indeed." She smiled at Casey. "Welcome."

The three walked along. Knowing Shinzo, Casey figured his friend had taken him to a voodoo priestess or a Indian Yogi. They took a left in the hallway and came before a set of double doors that weren't part of the building's original design. These were of dark wood, hand-carved with intricate filigrees and symbols Casey couldn't identify.

The woman opened one of the doors and let them into a somberly lit area containing a sunken conversation pit. The decor was a mixture of Middle Eastern with African touches. Sitting cross-legged on a couch in the sunken area was a dark-skinned woman of uncertain age, though Casey guessed she was at least fifty from her bearing. Another young woman, black-haired and dressed like Ginger, hovered respectfully near her.

"Shinzo, always a pleasure," the woman Casey presumed was Nozinga said. Becker stepped over and kissed her on the cheek. Folded money passed from him to her. "And Mr. Casey, pleased to meet you too. Your reputation would suggest a man of ruthless-ness, but who also operates by his own code of conduct." Her husky voice reminded Casey of the late Eartha Kitt.

Casey nodded and shot a discreet look at Shinzo.

"What will you have to drink?"

"Juice for me," Becker said.

Casey said, "I'll take a scotch. Neat."

The woman who'd been standing close went away. Casey and Becker sat on a couch facing Nozinga.

Becker said to his bewildered companion, "Nozinga is a kind of medium."

Casey managed not to laugh, but couldn't entirely contain his bemusement. "I see."

Nozinga didn't seem offended. Their drinks were brought to them.

"I consult with her from time to time," Becker said, entirely straight-faced. "Nozinga don't see what horse is gonna win at Aq-ueduct or what company is about to take off. Her abilities don't work like that."

"How do they work?" Casey addressed the supposed soothsayer after a sip of his drink. *If she's crooked, least she pours well.* The two young assistants sat nearby, observing.

"I get certain impressions," she answered, gesturing with both hands. "Currents, if you will, that emanate from you as an individ-ual, but also as someone who is part of the whole that is our shared cosmic personae. My task is to attune myself to your current to see where it's flowing. To peer into the fog of what could be several what-ifs that lie ahead."

"When I got the call telling me you were at the club, I knew you should see her," Becker added.

Casey glanced sidelong at Shinzo; he knew the man loved this Psychic Network shit. Shin was not alone; a lot of shot callers, Haitians and others in foreign cartels, subscribed to the powers of

Tarot readers and other mystics. And what the hell, he wasn't paying for the show.

He held his arms out. "Okay, I'm game."

Nozinga said, "Please relax, let whatever you wish to come forth . . . come forth."

A cell phone chimed the theme from *The Magnificent Seven*. Nozinga frowned briefly at Ginger, who produced the instrument from a pocket. She didn't silence the phone as Casey expected, but answered the call.

"Yes? . . . Uh-huh, sir," Ginger said into the phone, rising from where she sat and walking toward a curtained window.

Ginger came back to Nozinga and whispered in her ear. Casey caught the words "worried" and "press conference," but kept his face impassive.

"I'm sorry, I need to address this," Nozinga said, rising from the couch. "I'll be right back." The three women exited the room.

"It happens—Nozinga's in high demand," Becker said to Casey.

Casey laughed and said, "Yeah, I bet."

"Oh, okay, well, you can call bullshit on her afterwards but until then—"

"Hey, I'm cool, brother, I'm not trippin', I'm just curious to see her hustle—excuse me, 'gift.'"

Shinzo nodded and started to check his BlackBerry. Casey put himself in isolation state. He'd been alone a long time, so he was comfortable with remaining still, contained. It had been hard-learned, but in prison he'd seen how those twenty-three hours a day by yourself could steal your grip on reality. He'd certainly come close enough to the edge himself. But Mack D had shown him how to deal. Discipline of regularity, as those Zen books he'd read emphasized. Acting out or being openly defiant just to show how bad he was wasn't a strength, but a weakness. Still, you had to shiv a fool now and then.

. . .

Casey was getting nowhere fast. His days inside had fallen into a predictable pattern. He'd finish up his latest time in solitary, get out, and watch every sorry muthafuckah who wanted a piece of him take a number and get in line. He would end up defending himself, and wind up right back in protective custody again. He was always careful not to kill anyone, even though part of him sorely wanted to put every wannabe banger tits up. But he knew that would seal his fate, preventing him from ever leaving this hole except by a back-door parole, and he had too much shit he had to take care of on the outside.

He was already notorious as the man two other inmate groups had gotten into a fight over regarding which of them was going to kill him. The Aryan Brotherhood had won the argument, beating down a smaller set of Asians for the honor. They were still pissed as hell that he was breathing in the first place, and Casey always expected shit from them any place, any time.

When not embroiled in the bullshit gladiator games, Casey had weeded out the cats no longer loyal to him, and worked to expand his presence among those who were down. It had been slow going, but now he had a crew to watch his back, and he theirs. He was still communicating with his mysterious note writer, who only contacted him in solitary. Those notes kept his head straight, through the endless cycle of violence and isolation that was wearing him down a bit more every day. Even when he was out in circulation, he was constantly on his guard, trying to watch all directions at the same time, always trying to anticipate the next attack. To say he was jumpy would be an understatement—it had gotten to the point where his own homies were getting a bit nervous around him. Only later would he understand just how close to feral—to reacting instinctively, kill or be killed—he had become.

One afternoon in the mess hall, sitting with three of his crew at lunch, a glob of tobacco-laced spit landed on his plastic tray amid the erasers—chunks of processed, tasteless chicken. Casey looked up at a six-four, bald individual with a bushy red beard and eyebrows. Bare-chested, his arms were sleeved with numerous tattoos, variations on swastikas and ornate German calligraphy. This man was flanked by two smaller versions of Aryan manhood.

The big man pointed a thick finger at Casey. "Gonna take you apart with my bare hands, nigger."

Since his run-in with the guards, Casey had made it his first priority to get right. At the small of his back rested a shiv made from a triangular piece of plastic casing, the big end wrapped in electrical tape for a grip, tapering to a needle's point on the other end. His bribes had paid off, and the lethal weapon had been smuggled to him from the fabrication shop.

Casey leaned back and exhaled, signaling to his crew that he was about to go bo-bo keys on the man. Lightning-fast, he threw the tray of food in the cracker's face, then leaped on top of the metal table and drew his shank. He kicked the Aryan enforcer in the stomach before jumping on him, stabbing the shiv into his rib cage. He felt hands grab at his shirt and throat before they were ripped away. His crew was in the fight as well. Shouts rose from the mess hall, and above this he heard a steady grunting. As if standing outside of his body, Casey realized this sound was coming from him. He stabbed repeatedly, perforating the thug's side, blood spattering him and the concrete floor.

The enforcer slammed Casey into the side of the bolted-down table. Casey got an arm around the big bastard's throat while his other arm continued working the shank on his abdomen.

Getting his knees under him, the large man stood and pushed Casey against the wall and they fell heavily atop another table. Casey felt a rib crack, and couldn't maintain his grip. The bald man raised his scarred fists to pummel him and was swarmed by the hacks, batons swinging. Others in riot gear rushed through with their shields, pushing fighting inmates apart.

In moments the brawl was broken up. The room was cleared, and the prison put on lockdown. Casey was hauled off to solitary again, where he was left for more than a week before being taken to the infirmary for a doctor to examine him.

Once there, he was cuffed to a bed for an overnight observation stay in a long hallway. Oddly, he was the only one there. His only company was a trustee, an older black man with horn-rimmed glasses and close-cropped, heavily salted hair. He was neatly dressed, his blue shirt pressed and buttoned to the collar, his jeans spotless, and his bo-bos clean. He came by regularly, but didn't say anything until late that night, when no one else was around.

"The infamous Marcus 'Crush' Casey."

Casey regarded him, his side heavily taped. "Spread out, I'm not interested in makin' new friends." He clutched his side as a sharp pain shot through his body. He'd refused the offer of painkillers from the nurse . . . pain was clarity.

"Oh, is that right?" Neither his even expression nor his tone changed.

Casey squinted at the old man. "Nigga, do I know you?"

"You know of me, Mr. Casey, we've corresponded before."

Relaxing, Casey slumped against the pillow and realized he was staring at the infamous Johnny Meachum, aka . . . "Mack muthafuckin' D. What's with the house nigga routine?"

Mack D let the insult slide without a twitch. "Yeah, you right, I should be rollin' like you."

Casey frowned. "I'm just doin' what I have to do to survive in here, nigga. You should know that. There's a long list of muthafuckahs tryin' to build their rep off carvin' up my ass."

Mack D shook his head. "There are other ways of survival, my brotha. But perhaps another stay in solitary will help you figure that out." Without waiting for a reply, he pushed his cart along the hallway, leaving Casey staring after him.

Banishing the dark memory of those days in stir to the recesses of his mind, Casey remained stone-faced until Nozinga returned. He resurfaced. *Why did these fortune-tellers always go by one name, like they were Prince or Madonna?* Becker was playing some kind of video game on his smartphone, but put it away.

"Now, let's get back to where we left off." The woman sat down cross-legged on the couch again, fixing Casey with her penetrating gaze. "Please. Your full attention, if you would. Concentrate on the present, this very moment."

She closed her eyes, but didn't begin chanting or mumbling arcane words or anything else as far as Casey could tell. He glanced at Becker, who was transfixed, and resisted rolling his eyes. Even hardened street soljahs could be a sucker for some damn thing or another.

"We have to believe in that person or ideal which reaffirms our humanity," Mack D would remind Casey now and then. *"No matter how much we find ourselves trapped in the riddle of violence, as Kaunda informs us,"* he'd quoted Kenneth Kaunda, the nonviolent freedom fighter who was one of the leaders of the victorious struggle in ending colonial rule of his native Zambia.

Casey refocused. Nozinga had her eyes open and was speaking. She unfolded her legs and leaned forward. "You want revenge on Gulliver Rono. For what he took from you and what he caused to happen."

That didn't take any hoodoo power to figure out. She or one of her assistants could have street-Googled that information before they arrived. Casey sneered inwardly.

"But this is tempered by the insights you gained while incarcerated. Your steps are measured. You are sure of both yourself and the path you walk."

That could be said of a lot of dudes who'd been down a long time, Casey thought.

"I don't know, or rather, I can't see what your plan should be. The rightness or wrongness of it is not for me to judge."

Blah, blah, blah. At least Mack D and she agree on that one, he thought, sipping his scotch, and waited.

She halted, looking into the distance as if consulting with an unseen confidant before continuing. "The second and fifth names on your list should be approached now that you and Shinzo have reconnected. Mr. Munoz, who goes by Champa, and a Ms. Jupiter Jenkins, I believe."

Casey raised one eyebrow—now she had his attention. The list, still in his back pocket, hadn't been shown to another living soul. She might have guessed those names because of Becker, but how could she have known the order? "I've got an idea where one of them is, how about the other?"

"The one called Champa is in the desert—New Mexico, I'm fairly certain. . . . Taos, to be more specific. But he is coming this way." She paused, her eyes half closed. "As to Ms. Jenkins, she is much closer. There's machinery around her. Not far, across the Hudson." She suddenly deflated. "Sorry, that's all I have at the moment."

The two younger women, who had been out of the room, suddenly reappeared.

"Thanks, Nozinga," Becker said, rising.

"Yeah, that was something, all right," Casey agreed. He offered her his hand and she shook it. Ginger walked them to the door.

"How're your studies going?" Becker asked her.

She winked at him. "Can't beat the fieldwork."

"True dat." They said their good-byes and the two men walked back into the hallway.

Shin looked at Casey and said, "Ginger's a grad student in social anthropology. Working on a book about 'urban belief systems,' is the way she put it." He held up a hand, anticipating Casey's comment. "Don't concern yourself—she knows better than to use real names."

Riding down in the elevator, Casey asked, "So what was that business when we first got there?"

"What do you mean?" The elevator reached the ground floor and they stepped out into the lobby.

"Everything cool, my man?" It was the other guard who greeted them. The one who'd initially talked to Becker was off on his rounds.

"You know it," he said.

"Look," the guard began as Casey and Becker walked to the door. "How about that opening, Shin? You got anything?"

Becker said, "Teddy, I'm on it, okay? I'm not gonna forget you, brotha."

"Okay, okay, I know not to be a pest and shit. I'm just sayin' I can handle myself. I only need a chance to prove it."

"No doubt. I'll be in touch when the time is right." They bumped fists.

Outside, Casey and Becker drifted to the end of the block, waiting for Li to bring the car back.

"I meant the first time," Casey began, "the two honeys stayed in the room so we could hear part of the call. Then the second time when she came back, they didn't return until your girl Nozinga was done."

Becker offered another cheroot, which Casey accepted. "You think the call was to impress you? Making sure we overheard so you'd see how important she is?" He cupped his hands around the end of his friend's cigar as he lit it.

"It crossed my mind."

Becker shrugged. "Sometimes the girls stay and sometimes they don't. I've been there when only one was around, and she'd come and go." He waved a hand listlessly. "'Sides, I'm sure if they wanted to listen in on the sly, they could. All kinds of clients come to see

Nozinga." He regarded him sharply. "*All* kinds. From hustlers like you and me to law-and-order politicians."

"You know this for sure?"

He snorted. "Did Reagan's broad bring an astrologer into the White House to see him?" He took the thin cigar from his mouth, rolling it between his fingers, examining its irregularities. "What about what she told you?"

"I figured she might have got those names from you."

"And how would I know? That would make me a mind reader too. Shit, I'm good, homes, but I'm not *that* good."

Casey mulled this over as the Jaguar pulled up and they got in.

"Not to make you think this is some kind of conspiracy," Shinzo said, "but I do have a beat on where to find Ms. Jenkins."

"That right?"

Becker took a deep pull on his cheroot and exhaled. "Oh, yes, indeed."

6

A murder of cawing crows swept across the overcast morning sky. The subway cars below were bathed in gray tones. Sparks flitted from underneath one on a layup track as a welder repaired its undercarriage. In another car, Casey saw two workers busily refitting seats. Walking on, he went past a partially dissembled motorcar whose electric engines were being overhauled.

He arrived at a clearing in the middle of the cluster of cars, where several workers were on break. A beefy white man with longish hair stood over a thirtysomething black woman in overalls, who stared up at him fearlessly. Jupiter Jenkins had grown up to be video vixen fine, Casey noted.

"I still say it's bullshit," the man said.

The woman, who was sitting on the low ledge of a concrete wall, had her arms folded. She shook her head slowly. An open metal lunchbox was beside her.

The burly man stomped his heavy work boot. "It's bullshit and I'll put twenty on it."

The woman merely stared at him.

The loud man held up the twenty. "I say it's a trick, and you can't do it if I throw up the card."

The woman, still with her arms folded, twitched her shoulders.

One of the workers let out a loud "Haw, haw."

Another one said, "You're not making it worth her while, Tim."

Tim fumed. "Shut up, all of you." His jaw clenched as he glared at the woman. Finally he held up another twenty. "Forty says you can't do it."

The worker who'd guffawed said, "I got twenty that says she can, Timmy."

"I'll see some of that," another one said.

Tim's face turned red. "Fine. You cocksuckers want to bet against me? Fine. I'll cover it." He rapped the back of his hand against the woman's knee. "Come on."

Ms. Jupiter Jenkins sighed, closed her lunch box, picked it up, and got off the wall. There were some playing cards on a rickety table off to the side, with several folding chairs scattered around it. She walked over, set the box down, then turned to face the husky maintenance worker.

Tim took a playing card in his hand, his uneven teeth chewing on his bottom lip. The woman in overalls stood a few yards away from him, seemingly bored. Her arms were loose at her sides, her hands open. The man looked over at his coworkers, smirking and shifting his weight from foot to foot. The tip of his tongue crept out of his mouth and he flicked his hand, but didn't let go of the card. He chortled. The woman remained ready.

Seconds dragged by as Tim tried to catch the woman off guard. Finally with a huff he flung the card straight up into the air. The woman's left arm snapped out in a blur and the fluttering card suddenly fell back to earth, pierced by a slender, leaf-bladed throwing knife. *Ooooh*s and *ahh*s of amazement went around, followed by Tim's boys laughing their asses off at their friend's humiliation.

Jenkins retrieved her blade and walked over to the red-faced Tim, holding out her hand for the money.

He shook a finger at her. "I don't know how you did it, but it's a goddamn trick."

She crooked her fingers at him.

Tim stalked closer, snarling in her face. "I'm not paying you shit, girly. What you think about that?"

"Come on, Tim, don't be your usual asshole self," one of the workers said.

"Pay up, chump," another demanded, and laughed again.

"No!" Arms crossed, he said to the woman, "It was a trick, and you're full of shit! So what you gonna do about that, little miss?"

Casey watched, anticipating. This poor bastard had no idea he was messing with a deadly weapon.

Shaking her head Jenkins turned, walked to the card table, gathered up her lunch box, and started to walk away.

Tim gloated. "Typical bitch. Backs down when it really comes to it."

Without warning, she whirled around and flung her knife again with an efficiency of explosive motion. The spinning metal sheared off the hair hanging over Tim's left ear, nipping the top. The blade embedded itself in the side of a wooden tool shed with a loud *thunk*!

An open-mouthed Tim held a hand to his bleeding ear as the others gaped in silence. She walked over to the knife and plucked it from the wood, then stalked back to Tim. He silently handed over the money.

Somebody *haw, hawed* again.

Casey stepped forward. "Still playing with knives, Jupiter?"

She stared at him for a moment before approaching. "Crush," she finally declared. "Back among the living, huh?" She kept walking and he fell in step.

Like her, he got right to the point. "Good to see you, girl. So, you know why I'm here. The real question is, are you down?"

She grinned laconically. "I'm out of that life, playa. 'Sides, I can't get behind dealing in sex slaves, though I know plenty of women who do."

"You know I never did foul shit like that, I'm talking 'bout taking Rono out permanently and putting a stop to that shit." They entered the wheelhouse, a building with a large revolving circular center, with a section of track bifurcating the circle, used to turn subway cars around. Several individual subway cars were on tracks that entered the building through corresponding openings.

"Neither one of us are candidates for a peace prize." She crossed to a workbench covered in subway car parts. "But there's sin, and then there's evil, Crush." She looked up at him and smiled. "I heard about you now and then." Picking up a control relay, she used a screwdriver to loosen its housing. "No doubt you've got a reason to make him pay."

"Like you do," Casey said.

She pointed the screwdriver at him, her voice rising for the first time. "You're damn right I do. But since all that went down I've tucked my head and landed this square. I've got my kids back from child welfare and I intend to keep them, Crush. I haven't forgotten who their grandfather was or what happened to him. But it's their future I have to look out for now. Not running around playing avenger."

"All right, Jupe, I'm not here to argue with you. Just offering an opportunity."

"Yeah—for what? To get both our fool heads blown off?"

Casey shook his head. "To set our own terms. To be able to leave something more for those children of yours other than debt and grandma's brooch." He looked off for a beat, then back at her. "But it's not just about the money or the Kings, Jupiter. That's not what sustained me all those years inside."

She pulled the machinery apart. "Getting even."

"Getting things right. Letting Rono and everyone else doing his dirt know they can't get away with this shit any longer."

"You start this, there's no halfway."

"No, there isn't," he agreed. "Since we're just conversatin' and all, you seen Harwood around lately?"

"Last I heard, he was out on the West Coast."

"L.A.?"

"That's the word on the street."

"Keeping himself busy?"

She shrugged and continued to work on the relay. "I couldn't tell ya."

Time to go. "All right, girl, I gotta bounce."

"Good luck, Crush. No hard feelin's?"

"We cool. Stay up, Jupe."

Walking away, he remembered all the times Jupiter had his back, and hoped her "no" was just temporary. Turning the corner from the repair facility, he crossed a vacant lot of overgrown weeds and trash. On the side of an abandoned black TV he saw a capital *V* with a crown at its top spray-painted in silver. An omen or a challenge, Casey didn't know which.

From the subway yard in Hoboken he took the ferry over to Brooklyn. While he'd been gone, the transit authority had closed the slips, but reopened and refurbished the waterway terminal. That was when there was largess to be had from federal government coffers. Casey stood at the rail, taking in the salty air and the cityscape around him. Two seagulls pirouetted about each other in the sky then broke apart and dive-bombed for fish among the whitecaps.

Back on land, he started back to his hotel room, looking up and down the street as he walked. The more he was out and about, the more he felt exposed. It wasn't about Rono so much as it was about the growing impact of not being in a restrictive environment. Sure he had to report to Lomax, but that was more of an irritation, even given that the man had the power to violate him and throw him back inside. Loath to admit it, Casey hadn't escaped an institutionalized mentality yet. How many sorry sonsabitches had counted the days until they got released only to find themselves adrift, at a loss on how to hustle a roof over their heads or get a chump-ass job like mopping up some office building or washing dishes? Too many, that's for damn sure.

How much more comforting it was to fall into old habits, running with the kind of knuckleheads that got you put away in the first damn place. Deep in your subconscious you wanted to be caught, you wanted to be put back where you knew how to function, where the world made sense. He and Mack D had spent hours talking about the condition and how to combat it—to maintain your right mind. It wasn't enough to want Gulliver Rono broken and dead, though both had agreed that was certainly a laudable goal. But once that was accomplished, then what?

After the mess hall fight, Casey had endured another ninety days in solitary, and by the time it was done, he was ready to climb the walls. He continued his correspondence with Mack D, telling him that he wanted to take him up on his offer. But the older man had been strangely reluctant to get started, instead spouting various bits of philosophy, religious texts, and even verses of rap songs. This confounded and angered Casey, but he held back, trying to figure out what kind of game Mack D was playing.

At long last, his cell door opened, and Casey left to rejoin the mob again. The first thing he did was seek out Mack D, finding the man in the prison library, which was remarkably large. The older man had several books spread out around him on the table, and was reading one. He glanced up, regarding Casey over the top of his glasses.

"Mr. Casey."

Casey pulled out the chair on the other side of the table and sat. "Mack, I thought a lot about what you said in the infirmary, and I want—I want to know what you know."

Mack D closed the book in front of him and regarded Casey with his deep brown eyes. "Well then, the first thing you should know is that I know nothing."

"Say what?"

Mack D leaned back, resting his hands on his trim stomach. "Did you learn anything during your most recent time in the hole?"

"Yeah, I learned I never want to go back there again."

"Very good. Having a goal is the first step. Now, what can you do to make that goal a reality?"

"I gotta find a way to get everyone off my back. Can't kill 'em myself, 'cause that'll just put me in here forever."

"Exactly. Men in our line of work know violence has its place when properly directed and strategically used. But that doesn't mean that there is no place for anger in this world." Mack D pushed a thin, well-worn book across the table. "It's easy to go off your nut—anybody can do that—but to be angry with the right person to the right extent and at the right time, and in the right way— that is not easy, and not everyone can do that."

Casey nodded, committing those words to memory as he picked up the book. It was *Nicomachean Ethics*, by Aristotle. "This cat said what you just said first?"

Mack D nodded. "That, and a few other things." He stared at Casey. "Tell me you're a brother who knows how to read?"

"Shit, yeah, I only had to repeat kindergarten twice," he joked.

The other man chuckled. "Well, get ready for your graduate courses, Mr. Casey. Read that book—and I don't mean just flip through it and tell me you read it—*read* it. When you're finished— and it better not be in a week—come back to me, and we'll discuss it."

Casey flipped it open, first scanning, then slowing down and concentrating on the dense text. "Anything I should keep in mind while I'm looking this over?" he asked.

"Yes. Now that you've figured out you want to stay out of the hole, you need to figure out how you are going to do your time without going crazy, killing anyone, or becoming institutionalized. Once you have figured out how to do that, only then will you be free to plan what you will do once you're back outside. The trick for now is to compartmentalize all of the anger you have towards Gulliver Rono, and concentrate on the here and now."

Casey started to rise, then paused. "Why reach out to me?"

Mack D spread his hands. "Nobody does nothin' for nothin', Gerty used to say."

"That's right."

The older man leaned on the table. "I'm never getting out of here. I help you get your head right, you might see the outside one day. You might be in a certain position."

"To do you a favor?"

He tapped the book by Aristotle. "Let's concentrate on the here and now . . . for now."

That was the beginning of his long relationship with Mack D. Understanding the other man's philosophy had not come quickly or easily. Mack D had adopted the Socratic method of debate—he would pick holes in your argument until you had to admit that either you were wrong or that you had misunderstood the conversation in the first place. There were many times when Casey had stormed off after arguing a point until he was ready to chew nails and spit bullets.

But in time, he used what he and the older man talked about—philosophy, tactics, and more than a bit of the street—to not only survive, but even achieve a kind of strained equilibrium with those out for his head. Hell, he even held his own with Mack D once or twice.

And he created the blueprint for overthrowing Rono that he'd tattooed on the inside of his mind. He never let go of that plan, not even when his son was killed. Casey just had to be careful, not let the burning hate inside make him sloppy or reckless.

Casey trotted down into the subway, the echoes of voices and footsteps off the tiles embracing him. He searched the faces of his fellow passengers, wondering if the housekeeper there was contemplating ripping jewels off from her employer and going on the run or if the guy over there in the sharp suit was embezzling funds from his boss?

But these fine citizens would go on paying their taxes and worrying about the price of tomatoes, living out their mundane, boring lives until their mundane, boring deaths. Casey may have been sidetracked by prison, but he'd long ago made that step out of line, the determination that being the average Joe citizen was not going to be his thing. Not that he'd had much choice, given how he came up. Be a sucker or be dead, those were the only options for the children in his 'hood. He thought about his own father and how the old man had lectured him on not getting into trouble. He remembered the cops knocking on the door when he was eleven to tell his mother her husband had been shot and killed in a robbery.

From that day on, Casey was on his own. His mother had worked two jobs to keep a roof over their heads and food on the table, which meant her boy had plenty of time to run the streets. When his own seed was born, he was determined to make sure Antonio would have it better, that he wouldn't get sucked into the hard-core banger life, but that was not to be. Instead of being there for his boy, he kept running the streets and got jacked up by Rono. To make matters worse, he'd been stuck inside while his son had been out earning a tombstone. Casey shook his head. Ruminatin' on the past was a trap he had to avoid at all costs, he needed to look forward.

Grabbing one of his disposable cells, he called Carla. After pleasantries, he asked, "You got a number on that dude who came to you with the sex traffic offer?"

"Why?"

"Come on, Carla, you know what's up."

"Yeah, I guess I do. Let me see what info I can get on him."

"Just the digits, babe, I can handle the rest. I don't want you in the middle of this."

"Well, it's a bit late for that, ain't it, Crush?"

"Why you trippin'?"

"I guess I feel like I'm going down a bad road again."

"Come on, baby, it all be cool, just get daddy that number."

Carla let out a huge laugh. "Nigga, you crazy, don't lay that pimp shit on me, I'll get you those digits."

"Right on, in a minute."

Thereafter he found a working antique of a pay phone alongside a post office. Calling Lomax's number, he got the answering machine.

"Mr. Lomax, I'm making progress on a place and maybe a line on a job." Was that laying it on too thick? Did he sound too fuckin' eager, which Lomax would see through in a heartbeat? Casey didn't want to give the PO any excuse to sweat him. "Right now I'm staying with a friend, but I hope to be out of there by the next week or two." He gave him the address to Kenny Saunders's walk-up and hung up. Saunders had been prepped, and would provide the cover story, showing the parole officer the extra bedroom in his apartment that had been dressed up as if Casey were staying there. If Lomax were so inclined, he could look up the property records and would find a dummy company that owned the building. He doubted the PO would be able to figure out that it was Casey's company. The money salted away at the junkyard was his cut of the controlled rent all those years. The property taxes and utilities were paid on time and Kenny kept up on repairs—including his hidden improvements.

Then Casey called Kenny to ask him to see if he could get a line on Oscar "Slim" Harwood. Harwood was of the generation of crime bosses who'd come along in the wake of Frank Matthews and Leroy "Nicky" Barnes, who called himself Mr. Untouchable, and had his mug on the cover of *The New York Times Magazine*. He'd got his dick caught in the ringer once because he got bigheaded. Casey had a sit-down with Harwood early on in his career after returning to the States from Military service overseas. The older man had taught him about diversification and reinforced the edict of not hogging the lights and be all about staying in the cut. Too bad the old man hadn't followed his own advice.

Harwood had a stepson, Ricky, a knucklehead. But he and the boy were close. Despite warnings from his stepdad, Ricky got busted as part of a car chop outfit on the East Coast and did a nickel with Casey. Harwood had asked Casey to look out for the youngster, and Casey stepped in when some Aryan Brotherhood members were looking to shank the kid over a beef. He dealt with the attackers and brokered a truce, having made his own peace with the crackers years earlier. Slim Harwood wasn't one to forget such favors.

When Casey called, Ike Lomax was standing in a small, spare office in a high-rise on Thirty-second Street near Broadway, drinking tepid coffee from a Styrofoam cup while a technician adjusted his monitor. There were several more monitors side by side, some split-screen, on the three desks in this room. A ruddy-faced white man in a rumpled, button-down shirt with his sleeves rolled up and his tie loosened, turned to Lomax.

"We've got eyes and ears on this organic nursery in Long Island where Sinaloa buys his fertilizers and assorted other crap for that greenhouse. He recently placed an order, so we know he's coming back to town."

"Know when?" Lomax asked.

"Within the week is our guess," the man, McCormick, answered. "Wish I had it more precise, but the agency is happy that Captain Cifuentes likes his cocaine and hos, and likes to blab to impress." He was referring to a morsel of intel picked up on a bug in a high-end brothel on the outskirts of Mexico City. "So we know he's coming here too."

Lomax noted solemnly, "Up to much devilment."

"Speaking of which, what about your boy Casey?" McCormick asked. "How you gonna keep him contained as this plays out?"

Lomax looked up from his coffee cup. "Oh, I'm not trying to keep Crush Casey on any kind of leash—he'd only break it anyway."

McCormick chuckled mirthlessly as the tech signaled he'd fixed the monitor. "Okay, let's see what we can see."

Casey spent the rest of the day running down a few old street contacts, looking for more information on the VKs' sex trafficking ring. One contact was dead and another had vanished without a trace.

In the afternoon, he found himself out in Red Hook at the third-rate Furniture Land store of Hank Graves. Graves always had a beer gut and wore shirts too tight.

"What up, Hank?"

"Hey, hey, look who survived the joint."

"You're funny. I needs some info on Rono's sex trafficking shit."

Graves cocked his head, his squinty eyes getting tighter. "You lookin' to take running them girls over from your boy?"

Casey imagined Graves could see himself lording over a brothel of honeys, blowjobs available at the snap of his fingers. String him along, that's how he'd play it.

Casey spread his hands out. "I'm about getting my own thing going, Hank. Start fresh." Graves was slippery, and it wasn't much of a leap for him to make a call to Rono if things got hot. But he was also greedy, and if he felt Casey had the upper hand, he'd be loyal—to a point. "There's plenty of action to go around out there, so that don't mean going up against Rono. I'm just getting my legs back up under me and need to know where the land mines are. If I get something going, you know I'll break you off a piece, just like I did in the past."

"Yeah, that you did." Graves slurped soda.

"This Thai hookup of his, there's not a whole lot of them around here. Is it a gang from out of town, or maybe overseas?"

Graves shook his head. "My understanding is it's a family business of some sort, men and women both doing the work. They bring in the girls from Cambodia, Vietnam, all them slope countries. Got some Central Americans too."

"They got a big operation? They display the girls at a strip club or massage parlor they run, something like that?"

Graves cracked his knuckles. "They keep the broads holed up in an apartment and Rono spends a little change on grooming them so they look tighter than most."

"What about the Russians? I heard they got this market cornered."

"Don't know. Haven't heard nothin' about no dustups with them, but who knows? It seems like it's just a matter of time before someone has a beef with everyone."

Casey considered this as he stood up and finished his soda. "Thanks Hank."

Graves scratched the whiskers on his chin. "Kewel." They bumped fists and Casey left. He figured Graves was probably wondering if he should call Rono and score some points. But in the end, he knew Graves would recognize that Casey was not the guy to fuck with.

. . .

When Casey walked into his room, he spotted the phone's message light blinking as he looked at himself in the mirror. He pulled out his phone and made an appointment with Mal Yurik, the tailor. It was time to get his look tight. Before he split he checked the message. It was Kenny Saunders.

"That dude Lomax called to confirm you were staying here," his friend said.

"Yeah, how'd he sound?"

"Blasé, but I got the vibe he'd probably sound like that if he was cracking cuffs upside a fool's head."

"You think he'll drop by?"

"If he does, I just tell him you out looking for a gig or some shit."

"Maybe I better stay there tonight."

"Okay, cool. Also I heard from one of my boys that the last they heard of Slim Harwood was that he was running a rap label in L.A."

"He squared up?"

"Possible. I'll find out for sure, though."

"All right." Casey hung up, working out particulars in his head. The more he surveyed Rono's operation, the more he was hedging the confrontation they were sure to have sooner or later. That also meant he needed to be doing his recon and recruiting simultaneously. And that meant being able to get out of town if he was gonna get to some of the folks on his list. He was required to ask Lomax for permission, but what kind of excuse could he give him? A man could only have so many grandmothers dying.

7

"A woman named Grace Phan is the mastermind in all this," Carla told him over the phone later. "Fact is, except for the muscle, most of the players are women."

"What else you find out about Phan?"

"She kidnaps the girls, a lot of them underage, gets them hooked on dope and away from their families, and then makes them do tricks to survive. Business is booming with no sign of letting up. The girls are all scared shitless because every once in a while Phan makes an example out of one of them. The bitch is real foul."

That evening, Casey strolled past a refurbished brownstone on the Upper East Side, where Phan lived and operated her so-called business. Although Carla had obtained a phone number, he doubted he would learn much posing as a customer. Rono might have warned Phan about him, and damned if he was going to get his head blown off by some coked-up, terrified nineteen-year-old in her house of horrors. He snuck a quick glance through the glass doors as he passed by the entrance. There was a doorman on duty, and he had the requisite monitors at his desk.

Carla hadn't been able to find out if the girls were upstairs or if it was a call-in service with the money being taken care of electronically, and the girls meeting the john at some hotel. These types of operations were primarily focused on Asian clientele, so he paid closer attention to the Asian men who came and went. Carla had also told him one of the gang was supposed to be a Thai with blond locks. Casey took the fire escape up to the top of a building adjacent to Phan's place and surveyed everyone going in and out through night goggles.

Past eleven, an Asian man in a stylish, dark overcoat and open-collar shirt exited the building. In the green tinge of his binoculars, Casey wasn't sure his hair, done in an upward sweep, was blond, but it sure wasn't black. The man smoked at the curb until a black CTS Cadillac picked him up. Casey didn't have any wheels, but he memorized the plate number. Finishing his coffee, he climbed down and went for a walk up in Harlem.

"Long night, Mr. Casey?" Lomax said from his car, which was parked directly across the street from Kenny's apartment building. Lomax drove a late '80s Honda Acclaim. *One ugly-ass bucket*, Casey noted. He'd spotted the PO as he approached, wondering how long he'd been staking his supposed quarters out. He'd ditched the binoculars in some bushes a block away. No sense having to explain those if he got searched.

"Just getting some fresh air." He jerked a thumb over his shoulder. "Want to come up?"

Lomax gunned his car to life. "Maybe next time." He drove off, Casey frowning as he watched the car vanish into the night. *What's this dude angling for? And is he gonna trip me up before I conclude my business?*

. . .

Kenny Saunders had a contact at Motor Vehicles, and had them run the Caddy's plate. It was leased to an entity called Sunset International, which Carla had told him was a fashion accessories import company also run by Phan. Seems she was also in the knock-off market, and was importing human cargo along with her designer fakes. Looked like Shinzo had a little competition on the fake Louis Vuitton front.

The next morning, after chasing down several more leads, Casey ascended a narrow staircase in the Butler Houses projects in the Morrisania section of the Bronx. Using the stairs was out of habit; he never took the elevator in a housing project.

A door crashed open above him and a booming voice said, "Watch out, goddammit!"

There was a heavy thud, then hurried footfalls coming toward him. Casey was almost to the top of the stairs just as a thickset man in a doo-rag and a basketball jersey rushed at him. Behind him was the soldier Casey had come to see, Omar Atkins.

"Get the fuck off me, son!" Basketball Shorts yelled at Casey, shoving him in the chest. Casey pushed back hard, causing the guy to lurch off balance and stumble several steps backward.

"Crush—," Atkins yelled.

Casey tackled the other man, assuming he was running from Omar Atkins. What he didn't want to happen did, and the two of them went ass-over-end down the stairs to wind up entangled on the lower landing midway down.

"Bitch-ass muthafuckin' bitch!" the stranger swore, bringing 'round a pistol Casey hadn't noticed until it was right in his face. He deflected the piece with a reflexive swipe of his forearm as it went off, the bullet punching into the ceiling. *How'm I slipping like this?* he admonished himself.

"Wait, man!" Atkins yelled.

The angry man twisted his weapon toward Casey again, who reacted by uppercutting him, snapping Basketball Shorts's head back. The man wedged the gun between them, the muzzle flush with Casey's chest. But as he squeezed off another round, Casey grabbed his wrist and wrenched it upward, snatching the piece and leveling it at his head. The angry man fell back, glaring in shock. Casey's mind went into slow motion as he weighed the pros and cons of wasting this kid.

"Damn it, Clyde, check yoself! That's Crush Casey you fuckin' with," Atkins said.

The injured man tried to regroup, but his adrenaline was pumping way too hard. Casey looked him in the eye. "Could get a lot worse for you in the next few seconds, choice's yours." The man sat speechless on the landing with his legs out and his back against the wall.

"Whoa, hold up, Case. He won't talk. Be cool, brotha," Atkins said, partway down the stairs, his wide hand held up. "He's one of my soljahs, this's just a misunderstanding, that's all."

Casey glared at Atkins and lowered the gun, still keeping an eye on the man. "What the fuck, Omar?" Twenty years ago, he would have put the second fatal round in the man in a heartbeat. "I better not regret this."

"Come on," Atkins said, stepping past Casey. "Get the fuck outta here, Clyde, go get yoself cleaned up," he said to the young man.

Very aware they were in a public area, Casey glanced up and down the hallway. No doors had opened so far, but he knew curiosity would soon overtake apprehension. He didn't spot any housing police. "Let's bounce before any more surprises turn up." The two walked away from the building at a normal pace.

"What the fuck was that all about?" Casey asked, hooking a thumb behind him and dusting himself off.

Atkins scratched his close-shaven head. "Me and Clyde were making a house call on this cat that owed us some loot but was always busy when we tried to get paid."

"So who were you telling to watch out?"

Atkins showed blunt teeth. "Clyde got carried away and socked the dude and when he fell back he banged the door open. Then he saw you and panicked, I guess."

"That's one jumpy cat you rollin' with."

Atkins paused, brows bunched. "Yeah, well, good help is hard to find nowadays. How'd you find me, anyway?"

"Your boy Juicy told me you were on a collection run."

"Man, it's crazy to see you after so long." They walked past a newly refurbished playground where children played with abandon while their mothers chatted or texted on their cell phones.

Atkins rubbed the back of his neck. "So, what on your mind, Crush?"

"I want what's due me, Omar. I want the VKs back and Rono dead at my feet. You back me and I win, you're one of my captains."

Atkins looked at him, shook loose a cigarette, and held out the pack. Casey passed. Atkins lit his cigarette, took a drag, and said, "This is some major shit you talking. Rono's rollin' pretty deep these days, he's paranoid and well armed."

"I know this."

"Gonna be a lot of bodies 'fore we're done, son."

"Yep."

Atkins grinned thinly and smoked a bit more before he replied. "You figuring some kind of special ops thing, right? No way you going frontal on Rono. You don't have the weebles."

Casey said evenly, "Just like he did me, Omar. I'll have the right people in place at the right time when I make my move. I figure I take him and his number two guy Brixton out, and the rest will either scatter or fall in line."

Atkins nodded appreciatively.

"Can you get a tight squad together, ready to move when I give the word?"

"It's possible. I'm gonna need to lace them with some good faith bread."

"I figured that, just holla me what it is, and I'll set you up."

They bumped fists and parted company.

Later that evening, Casey returned to stake out Phan's building in a pickup truck he'd borrowed from old man Vidalgo. The truck was outfitted with a locked toolbox designed to sit crossways across the bed, right behind the cab. A common vehicle in New York City, though this one had a souped-up engine under its dented hood. He'd been out of practice driving, and had taken that afternoon to tool around the open fields in Willets Point and on residential streets to get the feel back. His lack of a valid driver's license could prove a bitch should the police stop him, but that was a chance he'd have to take.

Casey was hoping to see the well-dressed emissary of the madam or the driver of the Caddy, but had no luck.

The next night his patience paid off. He spotted the blond man behind the wheel of the CTS when he drove past. Casey fell in behind the Caddy and let a cab pull in front of him to act as a buffer. At one point, after the cab turned off, Casey thought he'd lost him until he saw the Caddy parked in an alley. Turning the corner, he parked the pickup at a hydrant and ran back in time to see the man in the overcoat exit from a metal door, along with a gorgeous Asian woman in a modest skirt and heavy waistcoat. They went past him, speaking in Korean or something as Casey pretended to talk on his cell.

The woman seemed neither affectionate nor rebellious as she got in the passenger side and they drove away. Casey went to the front of the building, noted the address, and quickly returned to the truck. He pulled out his cell and called Becker.

"Hey, man, can you run this address for me? It's 1632 St. Charles Street. Hit me back when you find out something."

"Hang on a sec. I can pull it up now. It's owned by Thomas Schultz in Scarsdale."

"That name mean anything to you?"

"Nah, let me see what else he owns. . . . Okay, he's got five other buildings in that area too."

"Okay, thanks, dawg, it may be nothing, we'll see."

Casey roared the truck to life and went back to Kenny's.

The next day, he returned via subway to get a look during the day. There was a sandwich shop around the corner of the building where he could sit and eat slowly and watch. He saw men and women come and go from the four-story apartment building. It didn't seem to have enough space to keep any number of sex slaves there, but maybe the woman he'd seen was someone else—one of the partners, perhaps. Carla had said most of the bunch were women. He considered waiting near the building's security door to slip in when someone came out again, but held off when he saw a security camera. He'd have to play this out another way.

Finally he had to quit the sandwich shop, but bought a *Post* at a newsstand and moved around at different angles to the building, pretending to read the tabloid. Casey was scanning the classifieds for the third time when the front door opened and the striking Asian woman stepped out. She was in jeans and a loose top, but there was no mistaking her. Casey had been down a long time, but he still appreciated a good chassis. In fact, he was pretty certain she was Filipina, and not just from the sway of those enticing phat hips.

He followed her into a Duane Reade drug store. She shopped for disposable razors, toothpaste and other sundries. Casey ambled along a few yards away, taking a few surreptitious shots of her on his disposable cell. She was young, within the age range of women who'd be trafficked, but would Phan give the girls this kind of latitude? *She must be playin' one hell of a skull game to keep her girls from runnin'*, he mused.

When the woman got a call on her cell, he realized she was definitely part of the crew. "No, F that dude," she said as Casey discreetly walked past her. "All those Jersey jerks are cheap." She giggled.

Casey stepped out to the street and spotted the Thai man from last night walking straight in his direction. *Fuck—ain't this a bitch.* He kept moving forward, hoping he wouldn't get made. The Thai was smoking and talking on his cell as he got closer, but no sooner had they passed each other than the man glanced back with a frown.

"Hey, I saw you last night," he blurted as the woman came out into the street with her purchases. "What the fuck, man?" The blond man advanced on Casey, who turned to face him, trying to bluff his way out.

"You trippin', better ease back, son."

"You a cop, that it? You motherfuckin' po-po?" The other man was up on Casey, yelling in his face, despite being a few inches shorter and much slimmer than his target. "You ain't no pig." He started reaching into his jacket.

Casey's prison instincts kicked in as he sized the shorter man up. "I said get to steppin', noodle." Onlookers were gathering. Everyone liked a street fight. Some things never changed in the city.

In a blink, the Thai flicked open a butterfly knife.

"Oh shit, Jai," the woman moaned, more annoyed than scared. Like she was going to miss her appointment at the nail salon again.

Jai the Thai came across with a side slash, but Casey crouched down and swept the man's feet out from under him. Whip-fast, he spun around and drove his elbow into the man's groin.

"Motherfucker!" the injured man yelled, grabbing his crotch.

Casey rose just as the woman tried to kick him. He caught her by the ankle and held her teetering off balance while he stomped on Jai's knife hand.

The Thai swore in a language Casey took to be his native tongue.

"Fuckin' asshole!" the woman declared.

Casey had her hopping on one foot and he let go. She stumbled backward, but didn't fall. He bent and picked up the butterfly knife. The woman was reaching into her small purse. Casey had a very distinct memory of witnessing a derringer's bullet do serious damage point-blank. He had no desire to find out what it could do to him.

He grabbed the Thai and pressed the blade against his Adam's apple. "Bitch, you better get your hand outta of that goddamn purse!"

Jai shrieked as the point pricked his skin. "Do what he fucking says!"

Casey hauled him to his feet, keeping his knife hand right at the man's throat, the other clamped around his upper arm. "Toss it," Casey ordered. She did so with a smirk.

"You don't know who you're fuckin' with, man," Jai said.

"Does this feel like I give a shit? Now shut the fuck up!" Casey had to end this quick lest the police rolled up and he'd be screwed for sure. Some shopkeeper must have called this in by now. The pigs were probably on their way already running silent.

Several of the people gathered were taking pictures on their cell phones. Just what he needed—souvenir shots of him holding this punk hostage going out on the Web. With Jai in tow, Casey backed up until he was in the middle of the street, cars screeching and honking at him. Here he was with a knife to a man's throat and drivers still barked at him to get the fuck out of the way as they passed. Fucking New Yorkers. A delivery truck rolled up and Casey shoved his prisoner toward it, causing the driver to stand on his brakes, the truck screeching to a halt.

"Jai!" the girl yelled, running toward him, snapping pictures on her cell phone.

The Thai stumbled and skidded on his knees, the top of his head smacking into the delivery van's front bumper with a nice *bonk. Muthafuckah ain't dead, but he'll have a helluva headache for a week*, Casey thought.

Using the high-paneled truck as cover, Casey took off in a straight line toward the residential streets of Greenwich Village. He jogged down a block and a half of storefronts, then cut down a quiet, tree-shaded street. Backing around a corner brought him to a row of trendy shops selling designer scarves, musical instruments, and the like.

Halfway down was an eatery, with its metal doors open from the sidewalk and leading down to its storage basement. An unlocked padlock hung in the loop of one. Casey went down the steps, closing the doors behind him. No sooner had he done so than he heard a car's tires squeal as it came around that corner, moving with enough urgency that he figured it was the pigs out looking for him.

Fortunately, there was no one else in the basement, just crates of produce and canned goods. But that meant the restaurant workers that were coming and going in here would be back soon. Casey had to take the chance and go back up. He waited a few beats, then pushed one of the doors open to a startled woman in a crisp white apron.

He stepped past her and saw the police car turn the far corner. Rather than run in the opposite direction, he walked briskly toward where the black-and-white had disappeared. That way, if they came back around the block, he'd be at the other end of the next block down.

Smiling malevolently, Casey felt exhilarated as he stalked away. Seconds away from being sent back for good, he felt as if live wires were sparking all over his body. It felt good to be back on the grind, using his wits to stay one step ahead of everybody. Then he remembered all the cell phone cameras.

"Muthafuck!"

8

The two-story clapboard house was off a narrow dirt lane; Casey estimated it must have been built sometime in the late nineteenth century. Behind it on the left was a dock with a tied-up rowboat on a small lake.

Casey had come upstate after placing a phone call on one of his burners, then trashing it. The man who'd returned that call walked around the far side of the house as Casey turned off the pickup's engine and got out. He was a tall, medium-built white man with sandy brown hair going gray at the sides, dressed in tan chinos and a patterned short-sleeved shirt. When Casey had last seen him more than twenty years ago, the name he'd been going by was Walker.

"Casey," he said, not offering a hand.

"Walker."

"Let's go on up to the porch." He led the way and as they approached, a woman appeared from behind the screen door. Casey bet she'd had a gun on him since he'd driven up. Walker was that kind of cautious.

"Bea, this is Casey," Walker said, easing his frame into a wicker chair and waving Casey to another.

"Pleasure." She offered her hand, which Casey shook. "Say hi to Champa if you see him."

"Sure will." If Casey had to guess, he'd put the dark-haired woman's age somewhere in the midfifties, same as Walker. She was toned and tanned, her exposed upper arms a testament to diligent gym work.

She went back into the house as Casey sat down. On a wicker garden table between them was a pitcher of lemonade and two glasses already filled. Casey seriously doubted this was Walker's touch.

The other man crossed one leg over the other, waiting on him.

No sense doing any kind of preamble or small talk. Business was the only topic Walker ever responded to. "I'm gonna take down Rono."

"Funny—you don't seem all twisted up with revenge," Walker observed.

"It's business," Casey answered.

"Taking down Rono has no interest to me," Walker said. "My work generally doesn't take me into his or what had been your orbit. Except that one time—and that's the only reason I returned your call." He uncrossed his legs and reached for a glass of lemonade, sipping silently.

"I know you'd never be part of a set crew, I'm just here to negotiate for your services."

"You have a specific set of tasks for me?"

"I do." It was humid on the covered porch, and Casey was thirsty. But he didn't want to reach for the glass. He couldn't help but see this as some kind of test. Walker wanted to see if the decades in prison had broken his discipline. "But I'm not going to sit here and bullshit you and say everything is already in place."

Walker nodded, enjoying more of his refreshment. He rolled the water-beaded glass across his forehead, the barest hint of a smile flitting across his lips. He looked out over the yard. "Things in your world are getting a little too complicated for my tastes lately."

"Looking to get out?"

Walker inhaled audibly, searching the horizon. "Not yet. Soon, but not yet."

Casey leaned forward, the balance having shifted in his favor. "This is a yes or no proposition."

"I know. I'm in."

Casey stood. "I'll be in touch."

"I look forward to it," Walker said.

In the pickup on his way back to the city, Casey reviewed their meet. Walker was a pro's pro, a thief for more than thirty years, security systems his primary specialty, but the man was handy with various types of guns too. He'd returned Casey's call because he was looking to make one final strike, a big enough haul to retire. And with his help, Casey was gonna make that happen.

Rono was overseeing the arrival of a diverted shipment of Blu-ray DVD players with a little extra cargo from Colombia packed in every box when his cell phone rapped out the refrain from "Low" by Flo-Rida. He flipped it open with one hand, motioning for the street crew to keep unloading.

"Whassup?"

The voice on the other end was so loud he had to pull the phone away from his ear. It was Jai, and he was pissed. "What the fuck, man! Your boy Casey was sniffin' around Phan's place. I saw him there last night, and this afternoon he was following Kelta and we got into it! I thought he wasn't a problem, Rono, so what the fuck?"

Rono had stepped away from the truck and spoke low and deadly into the phone. "I remember exactly what the fuck I said, jackass. Now watch your fuckin' mouth and tell me exactly what fuckin' happened."

Jai laid the entire confrontation out, trying to downplay how Casey had taken him down, but Rono wasn't buying it for a minute. He'd seen Casey beat the shit out of a hundred guys in the past. Jai was lucky he could still walk and talk. "So you tried to get flashy with that goddamn toy of yours, and he stomped you and took it away. Christ, Jai, you're lucky he didn't shove it up your ass."

"Whatever, Rono, I'm not the guy at the top of his list, that's why you the one trippin'!"

Rono spit out of the corner of his mouth. "Watch your fuckin' mouth, slant eyes! Now are you sure it was him?"

"Yeah, I'm motherfuckin' sure! Hold on, Kelta took his fucking picture."

Rono's phone dinged. He opened the file and looked at the picture of Casey standing behind Jai, trying unsuccessfully to hide his face. He looked a bit older—twenty years in stir would do that to you—but basically he was the same as when he'd gone in, maybe more solid from pumping iron on the inside.

Rono felt a chill come over him as he stared into Casey's eyes—it was like the man was fucking staring at him through the cell phone, like he knew Rono was looking at him, and was telling him *I'm coming for you, Rono. Ain't nowhere you can run or hide from me.*

"Well?" said Jai.

Rono hung up on Jai, hit speed dial and waited for the man on the other end to pick up. "Webb? . . . It's Rono . . . Casey's been sniffing around Phan's. . . . Yeah, in broad fuckin' daylight . . . I can't have him blowin' this deal . . . alert everyone to be on the lookout. . . . Yeah, there's a G from my hand for whoever sets the dogs on him first. Oh, and when all this blows over we're gonna have a little sit-down with Jai, that slope fuck's walking around like he's the King Shit lately, and it's 'bout time I show him how to use his fucking knife."

Rono snapped the phone closed and took a deep breath. No way was Casey gonna fuck up the biggest deal the VKs ever had, not when they were this close. Turning on his heel, he stalked back to the truck, snapping at the boys to offload that electronic shit even faster.

That night Casey took Carla out to hear a jazz quartet at a club over in Brooklyn. He hadn't been much of a fan prior to his incarceration, but Casey had come to appreciate various types of music behind the walls.

"Even classical, huh?" Carla touched his arm, grinning broadly. Her lips were an iridescent red against her bronze skin.

He matched her smile with his own. "Yeah, baby, two decades gave me a lot of time to expand my tastes."

"Is that right? Something to soothe the body and mind?" She put her face near his. They sat close together at a small table in the quiet club. The first set hadn't begun yet. Suddenly she leaned in and kissed him. Surprised, Casey didn't pull back right away, but did what came naturally, drinking in her subtle perfume.

After enjoying it for a few seconds, he subtly pulled back.

"What's the matter?"

"Ain't nothing wrong with you, girl. But your ex, that's another story."

"I told you, that's ancient history. Over and done with a long time ago."

"Yeah, but you ain't the only one got history with Champa here, and I'm not tryin' to put any salt in the game. My story's still unfolding. Fact is, I need him for some of these moves I'm 'bout to make. Someone I can trust hands down. He comes in, seein' we're getting all close—well, my life is complicated enough already."

Carla leaned back in her chair, her expression cool as ice. "Well, since you're so concerned about his emotional well-being, why don't you call him up right now and get this out of the way." She pulled her cell out of her purse and slid it across the table. "Here— use mine, that way you can be sure he'll pick up. He's waitin' on you."

Casey stared at her for a second, then swiped the cell off the tabletop and flipped it open. "Gimme a minute." He pushed his chair back, stood up, and headed outside, away from the club noise. Thumbing through her contacts, he reached "C." and hit OK. The cell rang in his ear, once, twice, three times.

"Carla, that you?" The voice on the other end was instantly familiar.

At that moment, Casey knew he'd fucked up—he should have used his own cell.

"Champa, hey, it's Crush, whassup, playa?"

Champa's voice turned ice-cold. "Oh, bit of this, bit of that. I heard you got sprung."

"That's right. So when you rollin' into town?"

"Don't know, I'll give you a holla when I'm on deck."

"Okay, cool—got some business to discuss."

"Seems like you're already in my business, nigga."

"Come on, man, you know I don't play that way."

Champa grunted. "You callin' me on her cell and all, what's a brotha to think?"

"Hey man, you puttin' too much on it. Ain't nothing going on here between her an' me, you know I don't play that—I got way too much other shit on my mind right now. I got some money moves I wanna bring you in on. Let's talk this over face-to-face."

"Yeah, well, you know I'm always looking to make some paper, Crush, but I ain't all that high on the revenge shit. No disrespect, I'm just not that guy, that's all."

"Is that the word on the street?"

"Come on, man, he's got it comin' and we've known each other too long to bullshit. But look, I got to bounce right now. I'm not sure when I'll be up on those streets, but I'll give you a holla when I'm local."

"Okay, in a minute, Champa."

Casey closed the phone. The first time he met Champa, they were in Juvy together. Champa always had a hair-trigger temper, even back then, but he'd also always had Casey's back. Hopefully, that hadn't changed. Casey walked back inside.

"We cool?" Carla asked as he sat down.

"I guess—we'll see." Their drinks arrived, and they clinked their glasses together.

"To no fear of the future," Carla toasted.

"To no fear," he echoed.

The lights dimmed and a man in a rumpled sport coat came out on the small stage to announce the band. The host, who was the club owner, was followed by the musicians, who came out to light applause. The pianist brought his mic on a swivel toward him as he sat down.

"Thank you, folks. Our first number is a rendition of 'I Didn't Know What Time it Was.'" He began tickling the keys and the others, a double bass player, guitarist, and drummer, fell into a smooth groove.

"You know," Carla drawled, "I really should stay away from men like you and him."

"Really? Now why's that?"

She put her hand on his, her fingers caressing the veined cords on the back of his hand. "What if I don't tell you? What would you do to make me talk?"

"I got to be crazy sittin' here with you." He laughed, removing his hand.

"Tease." She drank her wine.

"Look who's talking."

"I may have told Champa we'd banged."

He showed his teeth at her. "Bitch, have you lost your mind? Sheeit, no wonder he was actin' all salty on me. Why you plantin' ideas like that in his head? Don't you think I got enough to worry about without my homie comin' after me?"

She grinned at him. "Baby, come on, what do I gotta do?"

Shit. "Look, Carla, you're fine as hell, but I got to keep my head in this game. Don't be playin' me. Come on, let's go." They walked outside and hailed a cab to take them back to her place in Manhattan.

"Temptation is a motherfucker," Mack D had said far too many times. *"It distracts from the true mission."* Casey wished he could dismiss his mentor's teachings, if just for tonight. He'd always felt Carla was different than other broads, but since she was also Champa's ex, he knew he had to respect that. He turned and looked at her and her face twisted up.

"Oh fuck," she blurted, ducking as they drove past an elegant restaurant. She shot up and looked back.

Casey turned as well, looking in the same direction. "What, who's that?"

She'd reacted to a well-built, cappuccino-colored man exiting a sleek Mercedes McLaren roadster at the restaurant's valet station. He was dressed in a spotless, platinum-colored topcoat that matched the hue of both his hair and the car.

"Brix Bancroft," she hissed.

So there he was. Half Angolan, half German. Casey watched as Bancroft and a tall woman who carried herself like a model strolled arm-in-arm into the restaurant. "Rono's A-number one," he declared. "That one of his favorite spots?"

"Yeah, he owns it."

He made a mental note to follow up on Bancroft in the A.M. They pulled up at Carla's spot and she coaxed him upstairs for a drink.

He held the scotch in his hand, looking at her as she curled up on the couch. She was one bad bitch, and he'd been in the joint way too long.

"So Champa knows about us, huh?"

"What's there to know? We ain't done nothin'—*yet*."

"Cute," Casey said. He wondered how long he'd be able to resist Carla. And really, was it Champa or the memory of Dani holding him back? Carla wasn't no chick on the side, or a meaningless one-night booty bang.

She got up and traipsed toward the bathroom. "I know I'm repeating my damn self, but you're crazy to fall in with that squarehead Champa."

"You told me he'd been clean and sober for five years. Was that bullshit too?"

"No," she called from the bathroom. "Though it seems that's only made him more reckless. He still gets off on the thrill. He did when you knew him, and he does even more now."

He stretched and lay down on the wide couch, putting his hands behind his head. "And I don't?"

She didn't respond immediately and Casey let his eyes flutter closed, dozing. She returned and lay down next to him. "I don't want to have to be afraid for you."

"Then don't be."

"What you gonna do when you get the VKs back, shot caller?"

"We'll see."

"You always going to keep secrets from me?"

Casey kept his eyes closed and pretended he didn't hear her, mainly 'cause he didn't have an answer to her question.

Eventually she fell asleep, and Casey mostly dozed through the night, unsettled for various reasons, not the least of which was his growing feelings for the incredible woman lying beside him.

9

Casey stood in his pants and T-shirt, drinking coffee while staring out the cathedral window of Carla's loft at the busy construction site across the way. Raising the cup to his lips, he pointed the rim at the activity. "I know I been away for a while, but I've been watching these cats working, and seems to me those cranes are takin' beams down, not puttin' them up."

In a silk kimono, fresh from the shower, Carla joined him, snaking her arm around his waist. "That's right, they're taking the building down. It was gonna be high-end condos." She chortled. "When my folks first came here from Puerto Rico, they rented a roaches-so-big-you-could-saddle-'em coldwater flat for us right here in Loisoida for five seventy-five a month. And don't you know they busted their asses to make that nut every month for me and Estella?"

She fell silent, and Casey put his arm around her shoulder. Aquila's sister Estella had become a crack ho, and was knifed to death several years ago. Even now, Carla couldn't mention her without tearing up.

Wiping a thumb under one eye, she continued. "As late as 2007, something like a hundred billion in property in New York was sold over a three-year period. But the slick bastards on Wall Street got way too drunk on greed and their own supposed goddamn infallibility. It wasn't enough they were making twenty, thirty, a hundred times what a conductor on the subway makes or, Jesus, let's not even think about what some broken arches, middle-aged maid pushing their supply cart for ten hours a day makes in one of the hotels. Hell, what they make in my hotel," she snapped. "When the pigs got through hogging it all up and the meltdown happened, this goddamn city went topsy-turvy. Empty stores on Fifth Avenue, furloughs for city workers, homeless shelters closing . . . I mean shit, we're one step away from airlifting homeless families out of the city. It's cheaper than actually making the effort to improve their situation. Plus lately we've got rolling blackouts 'cause, surprise surprise, there's no money to fix the goddamn turbines."

She put her hands on her hips, the kimono drifting open to reveal tantalizing flashes of her taut body as she stood, arms akimbo, declaring class war. "What we ought to do is first waterboard these muthafuckahs to find out where they've hidden our money, then string them and their asshole-licking enablers spewing their bile on right-wing T.V and radio up in the middle of Central Park to the cheers of the people they shat on." Her voice remained perfectly even while her eyes blazed with rage.

Casey stared at her as Carla walked to the kitchen. "Damn, Che Guevara," he muttered. "Remind me to never cat off at you."

She turned to him, her eyes slitted. "Who said you haven't already?" She whirled and continued toward the kitchen. "I'm going to make a frittata with fresh cantaloupe, chicken maple sausage, and fresh-squeezed orange juice. That sound good to you?"

"Yes'um."

"Good." She pointed her middle finger at him. "And your scheming ass better not assume I'm fixing you this kind of breakfast every morning. Or any kind of breakfast, for that matter."

"No, ma'am."

She almost gave him the finger again.

After eating, they went their respective ways. Casey'd gotten a call from Becker. "Got some cribs I want you to check out. One setup in particular is this sweet little apartment on West Seventy-third tricked out with secret doors, passageways, and whatnot."

"Secret doors?"

"It was custom fit for this financier who once owned a piece of the Yankees. This was gonna be where he brought his broads when down in the city."

"While the wife and kids were off in the 'burbs, right?" Casey observed.

"Exactly. He wanted to get his fly honeys in and out on the QT, hide some of his assets, that kind of skanless behavior. It's in a building that's underwater now. The developer's run off, and there's a fight between three finance companies over who owns the title. So right now these spaces are rentin' month-to-month."

"What you mean by 'underwater'?"

Becker explained the real estate term about owing more than what the property was worth.

"Sounds good, man, but how'd I explain I fell into a place like this to Lomax?"

"This is New York, deal city, baby. Sheeit, he knows from your past you got legitimate connects. We can create a story he'll buy. Make you something like the assistant super on paper or something like that."

"You got a rundown of former associates of Rono's who've fallen out with him? I'm talking about cats with their own operations now."

"What you got in mind?"

"A powwow."

Becker chuckled unpleasantly. "The ones I can think of offhand would slit both yours and his throats as soon as look at either one of you. 'Sides, ain't none of 'em gonna back your play against Rono anyhow."

"Probably right, but I got to chase it down to make sure."

"I'll ruminate on it."

They made arrangements for Casey to see the apartment and two other locations that might serve as his work space. He would pay cash through an intermediary to keep his name off any utility bills. He had other money stashed away, so covering the rent wasn't a problem. Besides, soon he was either going to be back on top or get killed trying, so not having a long-term lease was the least of his worries.

Casey called Kenny Saunders to see if Lomax had been around, but got his message machine. He tried the man's cell, but got no answer there either. He decided to head over to Harlem and do some shopping to make himself temporarily visible. That also meant some low-level VK slangers might spot him, but that might work out to his advantage, as they'd spend time looking for him there rather than in Midtown. Though he was careful to reconnoiter the Roosevelt's exterior each time he came back. He also decided to buy a permanent cell so he wouldn't give Lomax an excuse for not reaching him anytime the PO wanted to get in touch.

On the way uptown, he decided to change course and retrieve a stash of money he had in the Castle Hill section of the Bronx. He wasn't running low, but it bothered him that Rono's reception committee had been waiting for him at the Vidalgo yard in Queens. Did that traitor think so little of him that he only sent two, and then only to warn him to keep to his own concerns? Didn't that fool know the VKs *were* his concern?

Rono must have put eyeballs on several of Casey's businesses after he got sprung. Casey doubted his stashes were still being scoped now, as it would be a waste of manpower, given there was day-to-day VK business to conduct. But it'd been nearly a week since he was out, so how long would Rono lay in the cut? He certainly didn't believe Casey would simply fade into the background. So far the hounds weren't full-on hunting for him, though Casey had purposely avoided areas where he knew the VKs hung out.

This uneasy peace wouldn't last. If the roles were reversed, he would have been taking steps to sanction his enemy the day he got out. That it hadn't happened yet must mean Rono didn't want blood in the streets because he had some sort of deal in the works. For all he knew, coming at Casey would mean retribution from those who were still down with the former VK leader.

Where he was heading now wasn't—or at least shouldn't have been—a locale known to Rono. One of the first rules of being an effective gang leader was to never tell your captains about all your assets. Also, more than one of his safe money locations had people who knew he was out and who'd let him know if they were under watch. But better to check personally to make sure his stash was where it should be. He'd need the money soon enough anyway if he was going to rent one of the places Becker had in mind.

Reaching his destination, he was pleased to see the Hidalgo Quik Mart still existed. Twenty years ago it had a different name, but it had been a corner market then too. He walked into its air-conditioned interior and up to the twentysomething woman sitting behind the counter. Bored, she chewed gum as she leafed through a gossip magazine with fingers tipped with glossy black nail polish.

"My name is Marcus Casey," he announced.

She glanced up at him. "Good for you."

"Sometimes called Crush. You might want to call the owner about me."

"Yeah? Why's that?"

He put a twenty on the counter. "Humor me."

She glanced at him again, then snatched the bill and returned to looking through the magazine.

Casey leaned on the counter. "Today, while I'm still young and good-lookin,' huh?"

She made a put-upon face and produced an iPhone from beneath the counter. Hitting speed dial, she held the device to her ear while focusing on a cellulite-exposé pictorial of the beachwear of various actresses Casey had never heard of.

"It's me," she said to whoever answered her call. "Some dude is here." She assessed him again, mid-chew. "Looks, you know, like he's been around."

Loudly he reminded her of his nickname.

"Okay," she said, handing him the iPhone. "She wants to speak to you."

"Hello," Casey said. "This Hidalgo?"

"For your purposes, yes," an older woman's voice said.

"When you bought this establishment, you were given certain instructions regarding me."

"How do I know it's you?"

"I'm talking into one of these iPhones. You on one?"

"Yes. Tell Heather to send me your picture," she said.

"I probably don't look the same from all those years ago."

"Let me worry about that."

"You're supposed to send her my picture." He held the instrument out to the black-nailed girl.

She huffed at the command, but obeyed. She listened as the woman on the other end gave her instructions. She hung up, got off the stool, and walked to an opening leading to the back. "Well, come on," she said impatiently.

Casey followed her and they wound around behind the refrigeration compartment. She knelt to shove some cardboard boxes of beer out of the way. The short skirt she wore rode up, revealing a

.22 automatic in a holster on her upper thigh. She pointed at the raised wooden floor planks. "Here you go." She walked away, popping her gum.

He counted the planks from one end and stood behind a column of Red Stripe in the glass case. Revealing dirty, sectioned tiles, he again counted from the top of the exposed area to the correct square. Momentary panic assailed him when he tried to loosen the square and it didn't budge. Realizing it was sealed tight from two decades of built-up grime, he used one of his keys to scrape the gunk out of the edges. At last, he was able to get the tile up using the tip of his key, revealing a safe's dial.

Closing his eyes, Casey shut out the hum of the refrigeration equipment. He visualized several numbers, routes, addresses, and other important facts he'd committed to memory long ago. Dialing the combination, he heard a click. The door, designed to blend in with the tiles, was supposed to spring open. He dialed the combination again, and again got a click, but nothing happened.

"Shit," Casey swore. He stood over the tiles, hands on his hips, then stomped his heel on the door a few times. It soundlessly eased open on hydraulic hinges. Checking his six one last time— just in case the counter girl got it in her head to try a double-cross—he chuckled as he bent over and reached for three tightly wrapped, brick-sized packets. He also removed another packet. It was a fifteen-shot 9mm Beretta. The sidearm was bound in wax paper tied around a double set of rags soaked in Cosmoline. He briefly debated whether to take the piece or not, then decided to keep it with him.

After putting his trove in a plastic shopping bag, he resecured the empty floor safe. As he walked out of the store, the girl behind the counter was filling out a relationship survey in a women's magazine. He caught a glimpse of a kid down one aisle, out of her sight before a shelf of snack treats. He red-eyed Casey.

"Don't even think about boosting them Ho-Hos, Pablo," the girl said loudly. Pablo cussed and Casey departed with a grin.

On his way back to the Roosevelt, he got a message from Saunders to call Lomax.

"Mr. Casey, how goes it today?"

"Just fine, sir, just fine."

"You out job hunting?"

Casey replied cautiously, aware the PO could and probably would check up on what he'd say. "I might have a line on a dishwashing gig." A condition of his parole was to seek gainful employment, not necessarily secure such. Still, if pressed, he better have several plausible addresses for Lomax to check out.

"Why don't you come in for a visit tomorrow, okay? Say around ten A.M.? Not ten thirty. That fit into your schedule?"

"Anything you say, Mr. Lomax."

"Okay, then." He ended the call.

Casey bought a sports bag to hold his money and gun, then put the whole thing in the Roosevelt's safe. Carla would ensure he could keep it there, under the assumed name of Willard Motley, after he checked out. After arranging that, he got another call.

"Crush," Hank Graves said on the other end, "found out something might be of use to you."

"What's that?"

"A few of Rono's boys been hangin' at this strip club out near La Guardia called P. J. Woodside's. A high roller I know from San Antone was taken out there recently and given his pick of slanted pussy."

"Why you being so charitable, Hank?"

"Just tryin' to back a winner, brother." He hung up.

Casey glared at his cell. Graves volunteering information was most likely shiesty, but a lead was a lead—even if it did mean willingly popping up on Rono's radar. He hadn't asked Carla about the two Asians he'd run into in the Village. He wasn't about to draw her deeper into his game. But then why keep messing around with her? Somebody was bound to get serious, and where had that gotten him before? Used to be he burned through shorties like a square would his shirts. But after two decades doing his bid, the shit he'd survived inside the joint and inside his head, he was a far cry from the cocky boss baller who'd been sent away. Added to that was the death of his son, whom he'd barely known except to see occasionally during visitor's day. Everything he'd lost flashed before his eyes: Dani, Antonio, the VKs—his entire life. . . .

Suddenly overwhelmed, like being gut shot, Casey sat at the desk in his suite, looking out but not seeing the city beyond the window. A hand to his face, he felt as if his body were in free fall, being sucked into a swamp of despair. He remained immobile for several minutes, vividly reliving his betrayal. . . .

"This sit-down is fuckin' historic, Gul," Casey said, exuberantly grasping his second-in-command by the upper arms. "Blood in the streets, homies we grew up with dead and buried, but we've made it this far."

"We gonna take it all the way to the top, Crush," Gulliver Rono said, a big smile on his face.

Casey remembered the questioning faces of the various gang leaders he'd assembled that day. It had taken cajoling, promises, and chilling more than one obstreperous knucklehead, but the sit-down went forward. A student of underworld history, he'd modeled his meet on the infamous Apalachin Summit that brought gang leaders from different countries together, hosted by Joe the Barber in the late 1950s. Casey had put his summit together after months of one-on-ones and smaller meets with allies and rivals.

"It's time we put a squash on this tit-for-tat shit." Casey's words offered endless irony filtered through the decades. "Knocking off each other over bullshit is bad for our business and only gives the cops, the DEA, FBI, IRS, all these cocksuckers an excuse to get more money for their special task forces. While we all up in each other's bumpers, they just waitin' on us to fuck up so they can take us down."

Marcus Casey remembered bringing the side of his fist down forcefully on the table to drive home his point. Then the shouting started and the black helicopters swooped low. Doors were battered in, windows burst into shards as stun grenades flew inside. Heavily armored tac squads of cops and feds invaded the chateau.

One of the gang lords snarled, "Benedict!" at Casey, who looked around in shock, trying to comprehend how this had happened.

Then, for all to see, it became crystal-clear as the knife stabbed him in the side, the power of greed behind it so strong it cracked two of his ribs. Collapsing in pain and rage, breathing hard, one of his lungs deflating like a popped balloon, sweat coating him like a shroud, Casey rolled over on his back. The first thing he saw was Gulliver Rono standing over him, a triumphant grin on his face as he casually tossed the bloody blade aside. Funny, despite everything happening around him—other gang members being taken down or trying to fight their way out, his own captains running everywhere—at that moment, Marcus Casey, about to black out, the rough hands of the law on him, his life ebbing out of his body, didn't see the big light or the vast darkness.

Instead, all he saw was Bob Ford. Or rather, the actors who'd played Ford in the several movies he'd seen about Jesse James. How Robert Ford, one of his gang, one of his trusted saddle pards, had shot James in the back like the yellow coward he was.

The cops had grabbed him up, handcuffed him, and slammed him "accidental-like" into doorways and walls. Casey would have laughed at the absurdity of it all, if he'd had the strength.

. . .

Standing in his hotel room, Casey absently touched the scar beneath his shirt, shallowly breathing the manufactured air. The cops had driven him around for a long time, yelling insults and racial slurs while they roughed him up. It was obvious the law was hoping he'd die before they got him medical attention. But he hung on because he had to hang on—he had to live to kill Rono. But Mack D had taught him, through many examples, including those damn Shakespeare plays he'd made Casey read, that revenge was best tempered with a grander vision.

"*Oftentimes, to win us to our harm, the instruments of darkness tell us truths, win us with honest trifles, to betray us in deepest consequence,'*" Mack D would recite. Also in *Macbeth* had been this passage, seared into Casey. "*False face must hide what the false heart doth know.'*"

But present matters still needed to be addressed. Looking at his watch, Casey decided to go to a couple of businesses, pretending to look for work to cover his ass and satisfy Lomax.

Walking around outside, he ventured into Times Square, passed by one of the tourist shops offering models of the Empire State Building with a rubber King Kong hanging off of it, or Rudy Giuliani fright masks. There was a giant outdoor monitor at a Best Buy, and when he heard the phrase "City Hall psychic," he paused. On the large set played a news report about a rumor that the mayor consulted a so-called medium for advice. They cut to hizzoner's press secretary vehemently denying this as a scurrilous whisper campaign by the mayor's opponents.

Casey recalled what Becker had said about Nozinga's clientele, and imagining who those persons unknown might be. He rode the bus and randomly entered several shops, from a Starbucks on the changing Lower East Side to a froufrou sandwich emporium in Tribeca.

As he'd hoped, no one was hiring. One frank owner-operator even confided, "Man, half the time I don't trust myself near the register. And you fresh like baby's breath out of the pen? Sheeit."

He was surprised at the response of a fiftysomething Chinese-American woman at a chop suey café in Chinatown. She wore a form-fitting black skirt ending below the knees and a stained white shirt. Her gray-streaked black hair was pinned back and her knowing face spoke of a wanting life.

"You did time for murder?"

"No. Running a criminal enterprise." They'd tried to make him for several corpses that had turned up over the years, but couldn't get any of the charges to stick.

They stood in the busy and cramped kitchen area, which must have been 110 degrees at least. She looked him up and down. "You know how to handle yourself, huh?"

"Sure," he said.

"You okay washing dishes from dinnertime till midnight, one in the morning?"

"Not a problem."

"You could go all night if you had to, huh?"

Casey raised an eyebrow. "Well, I—," he began.

"Gimme your number, handsome. I might call you." She leaned on the metal counter, watching him write.

10

That night Casey went out to P. J. Woodside's. The club was far enough off the flight path that the planes didn't rattle its stucco as they came and went, but the hum of them taking off and landing could be heard in the distance.

Woodside's was the kind of strip club given to faux classiness, if that could be bestowed on an establishment where nearly naked women shook their butts and crotches in horny customers' faces. The low-slung cinder-block building was set back on a swath of gravel with a blacktopped parking lot off to one side. The tricolored neon sign out front was relatively sedate and a satellite dish was hitched to part of the roof.

Forking over the cover charge, he ambled inside. Led Zeppelin's "Black Country Woman" gurgled over the speakers as a small-waisted, large-breasted black woman in a fluorescent orange wig did her number on the stage. Several men of various ethnicities and ages ringed the stage, occasionally throwing bills at her. She grabbed the back of a long-haired guy's head and crouched down, opened her legs, duck-walked forward, and grinded on his face. Whoops of delight could be heard over Jimmy Page's guitar.

Casey went to the bar, and when the topless bartender came over, he asked, "Brix around tonight?"

"I don't think he's gonna be in tonight." She was about thirty, pretty and lean-muscled. Her hair was long and frizzed out in various directions.

Casey shrugged. "That's too bad. I'm in from Philly to do a little business. I was told Rono's crew would treat me right. Young. Asian delight, if I'm not being too explicit." He grinned.

"Philly where?"

"O-Trays," he answered, using the name of a gang there that would have an OG like him in its ranks. "They call me Ced."

She smiled back. "You shoulda said so. Go on back. I'll see to it." She pointed to a far corner, and he headed that way. A large man stood before a velvet rope and an old-fashioned steel door with rivet heads outlining it like something out of a Depression-era speakeasy. The guard had been given the okay sign from the bartender, and he opened the door, saying, "Down on the left."

Casey went through into a corridor with a row of cinder-block-walled cubicles on both sides. Each open doorway had a red velvet curtain that reached to the concrete floor. Subdued lighting was provided by low-wattage sconces along the walls. The sounds and smells of sex assailed his senses. On his left, a cubicle halfway down had its curtain drawn back. He walked in to find a padded chair and a low concrete ledge built into the wall that held a futon mattress covered in a sheet and light blanket, with a towel on top. Next to it was a sink and wastebasket.

Casey sat in the chair.

Soon a young woman appeared at the opening. He guessed she was Filipina, with flawless, tawny skin, shoulder-length black hair with brown highlights, heavy hips, and thick mascara. She wore a black thong and high heels. The areolas on her large breasts swayed slightly with hypnotic power. She closed the curtain.

"Hi," she said. "I'm Baybay. What you like, stud?" Her English was accented but clear.

Casey held up a thousand in hundreds folded over, the wad of bills hidden by his hand, figuring they had cameras everywhere. "I want you to blow my fuckin' mind, baby."

She frowned. "What's your game? You undercover po-po, tryin' to make a bust? You can't entrap me. You have to say what you want."

Casey smiled and shook his head. "I'm the furthest thing from a cop you'll ever see."

She sized him up for a second, then like a cat moved closer and straddled his lap, reaching down to squeeze the bulge in his crotch. "You feel real enough. So what you want, baby? Want to fuck me deep in the ass, then come in my mouth? Watch me dribble your man juice down my chin?" She smelled of whiskey, cigarette smoke, and perfume. There was as little emotion behind her words as a waitress reciting the lunch special.

Casey put a hand on her warm back and brought her closer. He assumed the cubicle was bugged. She started kissing his neck. He whispered in her ear. "This money and another grand is yours if you tell me what you know about Grace Phan."

"Why?" She reached down and began rubbing his protruding crotch.

"I got a score to settle with Jai and Kelta." He hoped he said that low enough.

The girl, who Casey guessed wasn't more than twenty, didn't react, didn't give anything away. She leaned back, grinding on him. She got off him and, bending over, slowly undid his zipper. She gently pulled his member free and began stroking him. "Take your pants down," she said, fixing her gaze on him.

Casey did so, his boxers and black trousers down around his

ankles. She sucked him first, then got on, taking his erect penis in her red-nailed hand and inserting it herself. She rode him slowly and said softly as she made kissy face, "I can't stand that bitch. You gonna cut her head off?"

He grabbed her waist tightly. "I'll let you do it."

The woman smiled, showing even, discolored teeth. She put more energy into her lovemaking.

"Yeah, daddy," she gasped, "fuck me good. Give me that sweet, sweet black dick."

He licked and bit those taunting nipples as she pounded against him. They both worked up sheens of sweat as they kept at it. Bucking on him rapidly, about to consummate their act, Baybay tongued Casey's ear. "Corner of Halsey and Throop, Bed-Stuy, two o'clock tomorrow." Given how long it had been, he was surprised that he'd managed to last for some time. When he climaxed, she immediately stopped her motions, got off him, and sauntered away.

"Fuck," he exclaimed, slouching in the chair. "Sure beats spankin' it by a damn sight. Shit, Baybay."

He got himself together, cleaned up, and exited the cubicle. There was no other way out except back through the metal door. Along the way, another client exited a cubicle next to him. He was an older white man in a three-piece suit, open collar, combing his silver-white hair back in place. Casey stopped as the other man gave him a sheepish look.

"Great place, isn't it?"

"It sure is, Your Honor." Smirking, Casey moved past the other man, who frowned at him, his face coloring. The white-haired man was the judge who'd sentenced him. Casey knocked on the door and it opened. He went back to the bar as the older man scurried to the door.

"You didn't like the girl?" the topless bartender asked, registering his dour expression.

"She was slammin'." He watched the older man leave, tempted

to follow and beat the hypocritical shit out of him. How would he explain that to Lomax? "Give me a Johnnie Walker Black, double."

"Your wish."

Casey centered himself. The bartender returned with his order. "Here you go, Crush."

That brought him out of his funk. "What?"

"You wouldn't remember me." She looked down at her ample chest. "I was skinny and buck-toothed then."

Heat flushed through Casey, and he had to force the words through his suddenly dry mouth. "That right?"

She leaned closer. "Don't freak, Crush. I ain't gonna give you up. Not after what you did for my mama, Faith."

The pressure dissipated, and he stared at her through a twenty-plus-year-old lens, imagining her when she was ten. "Charlotte? Charlotte Hart?"

She giggled. "Hell of a stud to come rollin' into this den of whackness. What the hell was that 'O-Tray' bullshit?"

Casey ignored the question and took a swallow of whiskey. "What the hell you doing slingin' here?"

She looked past him, then back. "Long story that we can go into elsewhere." A new customer came to the bar. "Gimme your digits when I swing back."

Casey sat there, one of those setups containing cut lemons, limes, olives, and cherries near him on the inner ledge of the bar. He sipped steadily, considering the writings of the English philosopher Thomas Hobbes, whom he'd read and reread so many times in isolation. His central tenet was Determinism, that all human action is caused entirely by what you did before, and not by the exercise of will. But, of course, you had to exercise your will to make anything happen in the first place. He and Mack D went around and around discussing this conundrum—a conundrum that had brought him here to this strip club and reconnecting to a person out of his past who might have a role in his present.

Charlotte Hart came back, working a shaker in her hands. Her breasts bounced mesmerizingly up and down. Casey told her the number of one of his disposable cells and finished his drink. She hadn't charged him, but he put money on the bar.

"That big one in the corner's been eyeing you," she said, picking up the two twenties.

"I know." He'd noticed him after his session with Baybay. "One of Rono's?"

"Yeah, an enforcer. Calls himself Thick."

"Okay, baby girl, I gotta bounce, thanks for the heads-up." He walked out of P. J. Woodside's into the humid night.

Also coming out into that night was Thick, an imposing individual who specialized in beatdowns that left his victims permanently damaged. He'd had brass knuckles specially made that spelled out PAIN in heavy letters on one set. The other spelled out HURT. He'd slipped them on in barely contained anticipation of taking care of Marcus Casey.

Thick had come by his nickname for two reasons: his massive body—which was the reason he thought people called him "Thick"—and his not-quite-altogether-there mind. Although he'd been warned Gulliver Rono didn't want Casey touched by any of the Kings, when he saw the man himself chatting to the bartender, that warning was forgotten in the rush of Thick's excitement at taking care of a problem for the boss.

Outside, he squinted into the darkness, the harsh, overhead arc-sodium lights casting deep shadows off the parked cars. He scanned the lot before tromping down an aisle, his broad head swiveling back and forth as he searched for his prey.

"Hey, Haystacks," a voice called from between two rows of cars.

He turned, swinging a huge arm as Casey ducked. His large left shattered the window of a parked BMW. Its alarm whooped as Casey came up inside the reach of those massive arms and stabbed the paring knife he'd palmed off the bar into the pulsing veins on Thick's tree trunk of a neck, plunging the small, triangular blade in and out several times.

Spouting blood, Thick was still upright, and leveled a blow at Casey. This caught him flush in the chest and he wheeled back, his sternum cracked. Thick advanced and Casey got in position with a spin move learned from a martial artist he'd met in the joint.

"Got you now, bitch," Thick said in a surprisingly high voice. He closed his big arms on Casey, crimson staining the upper part of the man's leather jacket.

Casey brought the knife up and into the soft part of the muscle behind Thick's jaw and then faster than the larger man had time to react, he shoved the knife deep into his ear, twisting the handle.

"Oh, you muthafuckah." Thick groaned, a tear tracking from his watering eyes.

Casey got free as Thick had to divert a hand to staunch the new flow of blood from the side of his face. Casey drove an elbow into his solar plexus and followed with a kick of his heel into the imposing man's knee. The combination of strikes staggered him. Head down, breathing hard, he stared at Casey as the several punctures in his neck area streamed red.

"You gonna start getting light-headed from blood loss," Casey advised. He'd nicked his carotid artery. "You might want to get those wounds looked at soon."

Thick tried to charge forward, blinking and wincing. But Casey had punctured his eardrum, causing an onset of vertigo. With his double door–wide torso, Thick was like a child's wind-up toy lacking necessary gearing. He weaved and moved his big hands around, but halted like he'd run his spring down. He simply stood there and bled.

Casey walked backward, keeping eyes on him. There were a few individuals in the parking lot, but no one dared get too close. He turned and left. Thick didn't pursue him.

Casey returned to his suite at the Roosevelt. Lying in bed, he thought about Charlotte's mother, Faith Hart. She'd been a projects girl, slang product, and a single mother at sixteen. She was on her way to being yet another ghetto statistic, but Faith had larger aspirations than being a gold digger or stick-up kid. Working up from corner dealer, she had branched out and organized other young women like herself into "coke clubs."

Through a boojie public defender, Hart made discreet but lucrative sales to the lawyer's career women friends at their book club gatherings and sorority meetings. She even did some negligee-and-coke parties. It was a sweet hustle, and Hart ran it with a velvet fist, ensuring that she and her tight crew did well. So well that word leaked out, and she started to get pushed up on by rivals, including a chump calling himself Kor, the name of a Klingon on the original *Star Trek*.

Hart knew she couldn't hold out against Kor for long, and aligned with Casey's Vicetown Kings. But Kor had seen the profit rolling off her operation and licked his chops, intent on controlling Hart's crew. Casey sent word to back off, but one evening a sniper shot Hart in the back, severing her spine. Though the hitman was brought in from out of town, Casey put money and intimidation on the streets and uncovered the shooter's name. It didn't take long to put the deed at Kor's doorstep.

Four of his lieutenants were sent to the Promised Land and Kor was found decapitated, his body roped to a chair on a muddy bank of the Hudson. His head was in his lap, and a note pinned to his chest read: *Where No Man Has Gone Before*. Casey paid for Faith Hart's treatments and put something aside for Charlotte.

On his back with one arm under his head, Casey heard traffic sounds from below as New Yorkers went about their business or pleasure, some legitimate and others illicit. He lay there, imagining what each person was doing. With a smile at being just another face in the crowd, Casey drifted off to sleep.

11

Casey sat in Lomax's outer office the following morning, having arrived a few minutes before his scheduled appointment. The parole officer wasn't there yet, so he observed the personnel go about their day. There was a bearded PO in his shirtsleeves, gun in a belt holster, joking with a tall, white-haired woman in a flower-print dress holding several file folders. A butch female PO, tight shirt, broad shoulders, cuff links clinking on her belt, stalked through wearing tan Dockers and heavy biker boots. Others typed at computer terminals as a smallish man with a slight limp carried a near empty coffeepot to a kitchen area behind a cubicle screen.

"I appreciate your promptness, Mr. Casey," Lomax said, stepping through the open doorway.

"I try not to keep CP time."

"I would have assumed that, but it's good to see you in action as well. Come on in."

Casey followed him into his inner office and sat as Lomax

hung his sport coat on the old-fashioned wooden coatrack. The tie he wore today was a mélange of scratchy lines of different widths and subdued colors. *The man sure likes his ties*, Casey thought.

Lomax threw his empty coffee cup in the trash and told Casey he was going to get some more coffee and would be back in a bit. After a minute, Casey got up to stretch his legs. Casually looking around the office, he got the shock of his life. On Lomax's desk were surveillance photos of his run-in with Jai.

FUCK!!! His first instinct was to run, then he thought he could just steal the photos, but before he could move he heard Lomax's voice down the hall. *Keep cool nigga, nail it down, keep cool,* Casey silently repeated to himself as he sat back down.

Lomax walked in, sat behind his industrial metal desk, and took a sip of his coffee. He picked up the photos, glanced at them, then tossed them in the trash. Casey's head spun as he watched all this go down. Before he could think or even breathe, Lomax pulled an electronic monitoring device from a drawer.

"As you've no doubt surmised," he began, "this is tied to this," he pointed at his circuit board and map on the wall next to his desk. "Some of the gentlemen and ladies under my charge are easily—misled, shall we say." He looked up then back at his device while he tapped its keyboard. Two of the glowing dots beeped on the grid and went out.

"Those two were violated and sent back to the hoosegow."

Shit, here it comes.

Lomax leaned back and looked at Casey. "You know Derek Webb or Francis Hardy, better known as Low Rise?"

He'd seen both names in Saunders's file. "Nope."

"Webb manages the dope sellers in the part of the Bronx the VKs control. Low Rise is his enforcer."

"Yeah, well, I don't associate with criminals anymore, remember, Mr. Lomax?"

Lomax rose and stepped over to the grid, placing a finger on one of his red dots. "Low Rise's main squeeze is a stripper who rooms with a girl called Arpage Anson. You know of her, don't you?"

"Can't say that I do." Casey knew the case well, however—it had been the talk of the yard while the trial had been going on. "A veterinarian sent up for offing her old man and his girlfriend. She put knockout drops in their drinks one night. They awoke tied hand and foot in a locked room with some possums shot up on meth. Them goddamn, bug-eyed, tail hangers bit and scratched them to death." He wasn't a fan of possums to begin with, even less so after hearing about this.

"Given her old man was wanted on a murder beef, her mouth-piece argued extenuating circumstances, and she got relatively light time. But I like to keep track of her," Lomax said. "These two dangerous broads got a crib in East Harlem." He rattled off an address on 116th Street.

"Like I said, Mr. Lomax, I don't know these people, so . . ."

Picking up where Casey left off, Lomax said, "So if you do bump into them, you will know they're trouble. 'Hopefully they will be off the streets, by any means necessary.' That's a Malcolm X quote, right?"

Jesus H. Christ, what in the fuck is up with this dude? Casey stared at the man, his gaze betraying nothing as he tried to figure out the rules of the strange game they were playing—which Lomax apparently either already knew or was making up as he went along. "Uh, yeah."

"All right then. What's up on the job front?"

Casey gave him the names and general locations of the businesses he'd visited.

Lomax nodded absently, absorbed again in a readout on his tracking device. "Keep up the good work, Mr. Casey."

"You want me in next week?"

Lomax raised his head just enough to look at him over the top of his glasses. "I'll let you know."

Casey got up, still watching the PO as if he were about to spring another surprise on him before he left. When he hit the street he called Saunders. "Dude, I just went through the weirdest shit, are you at the crib?"

After Casey left, Lomax pulled the photos and the police report detailing the incident from the trash can. Lomax doubted Casey could be convicted in a court of law over these photos, as his face was not particularly clear. But being a parole officer, he had a lot more leeway. A lot more. He put the report back in his drawer and made some notes on a pad of paper.

"Soon enough, Mr. Casey—you won't be able to wait much longer."

Casey walked into Kenny's crib and ran down his review with Lomax. Kenny sat there with his face screwed up and said, "Damn, nigga, what's this dude's game? You think he's giving you the green light to cap Low Rise?"

Casey ran his hands over his head. "I don't know, man, I ran down a bunch of shit in my head on the way over here. What if Low Rise is under surveillance by some other law enforcement agency? It could be a special task force of the NYPD, the goddamn state cops, or even the feds."

Kenny nodded. "Oh right, so they stake out the girlfriend to get to Low Rise to get to Rono's captain?"

Casey shook his head. "But why in hell go to such elaborate measures when he has photos of me jolly stompin' Jai?"

He sat down and looked at the ceiling, then finally said, "Or maybe he just has a particular beef with Rono, and wants me to settle it. Okay, do me a favor, call Shinzo and have him get me a layout of that apartment. Also, see if he can plant a bug in the girl-friend's place."

"Done deal. Anything else?" Kenny asked.

"How you feel about digging up facts on a law authority type?" Casey asked.

Kenny laughed and said, "I knew that was coming. Let me see what turns up."

"Solid, I'll hit you up later."

Casey headed over to Bed-Stuy, where he saw both signs of re-vitalization and stalled efforts at revamping the area. Some store-fronts sported clean and bright awnings and freshly washed windows and swept steps, while around the corner sat forlorn, empty shells, many covered in gang signs, including the VKs' tag. Kids ducked and dodged traffic on their scooters and street sales-men hawked watch knockoffs and bootleg DVDs. He took it all in as he closed in on the location where he was to meet Baybay. He flashed back to their encounter at the club. *Damn, that broad had skills.*

Casey searched the facades of the apartment buildings, won-dering which one housed her and her fellow captives though they must not have been under twenty-four-hour watch. The way he understood how this trafficking bullshit worked was the girls, smug-gled or enticed over here illegally, couldn't run far since the money they made—and some had quotas of a grand or more a day—was taken from them by force. No money, no ID, and if you didn't know English or the lay of the land, then where the hell could you go? But it didn't surprise him that Baybay had been so matter-of-fact about meeting him once he told her the score. She struck him as a dame who was down for whatever it took for her to get out from under.

Up ahead, a figure detached itself from atop a stoop and came toward him. Baybay was in jeans and a tight cotton top, her hair pulled back in a bun. Without her heavy eye makeup she looked even younger, but still sexy as fuck.

She didn't say a word, but held out her hand.

Casey produced a sheaf of folded hundred-dollar bills in his palm. "As promised."

She tried to hide her excitement, but Casey knew what was up. They entered a neighborhood deli.

"You want some coffee?"

"No thanks."

She went over and plunked down at a small table with two rickety chairs next to the cold case of juices and sodas.

Casey got a cup of coffee and sat down. "I want everything you know."

"I was fifteen, poor like a muthafuckah back in Baguio City on Luzon. Five brothers, two sisters, none of us had much going. Mom dead, daddy working long and hard for little money in an electronics factory putting together plasma TVs and shit for all you rich Americans."

Casey didn't say a word, sensing she had to say what she was saying—*needed* to say what she was about to tell him—and was content to just listen for the time being.

She took a sip of his coffee, then continued. "There was this ad for nannies on a flyer going around, you know. Me and my older sister said, hell yeah, why not? Despite our family saying it was dangerous." Sadness flitted across her face for a second before she stuffed it back down inside.

"First we were brought to Chicago by snakeheads. Didn't know shit, green as fuck, but I did what I had to do so we could survive and get away. Shit got bad real quick, tried to escape, didn't make it."

She fell silent. Casey broke it, knowing reliving the past was as dangerous for her as it was for him. "And your sister?"

"Dead," she said flatly. "Killed in front of me to teach me a lesson."

"That's messed up."

"It's fucked up any way you look at it."

"That why you don't give a shit?"

She hunched her shoulders. "Do or die, right? After that I got sold to Grace Phan and brought to New York. That was, oh, 'bout two years ago."

"You deal with Rono at all?"

"I seen him a few times; I see his guy Brix all the time."

"Bancroft got a thing for you?"

"Most men do, sweetheart. I know you liked what I put on you the other night—didn't you, daddy?" She could switch her voice from ice to honey and back again like other chicks flipped a light switch.

"Come on, kill that shit. This ain't no game."

She straightened up and said, "Brix likes to think he some helluva player. Bang us, take us shopping, like he's some pimp." She sneered. "He's just another trick in a nice suit."

"Ever been to his place?"

"Oh yeah, it's a pretty boss crib; a couple of months ago he took me and a few of the others there to entertain these older dudes he wanted to impress."

"Who were they?"

"No idea."

"You sure don't seem too nervous 'bout bein' seen in public. How'd you get out today?"

She gave him that loopy grin like he'd seen in Woodside's. "Rono used to send his men over to watch us while we watched TV." She laughed hollowly. "But that was a waste of manpower. I heard him argue with Jai, so that stopped. So now some of the older women keep order, see? They get better clothes, maybe get to go to a movie, treats like that."

"Like trustees in a prison. They've been beat down psychologically and want favors from master. You telling me you're supposed to be one of the guards?"

She laughed loudly. "Nigga, please. Marci's on the day shift over here, but that ho's got a habit." She tapped her nose. "Us girls get candy from our regulars and feed 'em to her. As long as we get back in a certain time, she don't say nothing."

"What's to stop you from just walkin'?"

Baybay patted her cleavage, where she'd tucked the bills away. "Till you came along, I didn't have the paper. Now, I'm in it to win it, just like you are." She leaned forward. "I want that bitch Grace's head on a spike, and I'm willing to do whatever to make it happen."

"How many apartments do Phan and Rono have?"

"Don't know for sure. But at least two here in Brooklyn and another in Manhattan. I did overhear Bancroft talking to Kelta about some Uptown pad in the club last week." She jabbed a finger at him. "You know that bitch is bi, right? She likes to get freaky with the girls. I think her and Phan got a thing for each other. Anyway, they were talking about this shipment coming in. But it didn't sound like the normal shit. Something big's about to go down, and the VKs are trippin' over each other to make sure everything goes down smooth."

"They said all this in front of you?"

"No, in front of Char."

"You and Charlotte are tight like that?"

"Yeah, that's my homegirl. Why you think she sent me in to you?"

"Wait—are you two planning a move on Phan yourselves?"

She folded her arms. "Now that you're here, shit yeah."

Casey chuckled. Baybay smiled thinly in reply, then said she'd better get back.

From a distance, she pointed out the apartment building she

and the others lived in. She also told him the apartment number, and then walked away, hands in her pockets, her apple ass cheeks twitching in her tight jeans as she went.

"One damn tough piece of cake," Casey muttered, watching her go for a moment before turning and heading in the opposite direction.

Back at the Roosevelt there was another message for him. Not on the house phone, but in an envelope left at the front desk. It was simple and direct:

Eight tonight. Lion's Mane Props. CMZ.

Champa Munoz had hit town.

12

Casey met Champa that night at the prop house on the edge of Koreatown in Flushing. As he went in, he passed a prostitute who seemed a bit out of her element, but she staggered away before he could say anything.

"Damn, homes, don't you age?" Champa said, his smile revealing a mouth full of gold teeth.

"My nigga, what it do?"

"You know, makin' that paper here and there."

"Grey Goose." Casey raised an eyebrow. "You makin' out a'right."

"Indeed."

There was a bottle of the premium vodka and two filled glasses before him. He slid one of the squat tumblers to Casey. The two sat in a set of faux Louis XV chairs and desk, clinked their glasses, and drank. Champa had been thick-bodied the last time Casey had seen him. Now—and he was near Casey's age—he looked slimmer in the legs and buffed out in the upper body.

"So what happened to you—you get on Atkins or something?"

"Turned semi-vegetarian 'bout six, seven years ago."

"No shit?"

Champa touched his stomach with his glass, cubes clinking. "Gut shot after an armored car job, half my damn stomach gone after my operation. Intestines infected, twice." He blew air through his mouth. "After that, hamburgers, chorizo, most any kind of heavy meat fucks me up, like I'm getting stabbed or some shit. Trust me, you don't wanna hear about how I'm up on the roof of this sports stadium in the middle of Tulsa, pulling a snatch on one of them self-help seminars. We're torching our way through and I gotta take a dump in a corner to keep from embarrassing myself."

"You're right—didn't want to hear that. Yet I have."

Munoz laughed, pouring more vodka for himself and Casey. "It wasn't as hard as you might think. Though I still have to have my *carne asada* burro, no matter how bad I suffer for days afterwards."

"Enough," Casey said, holding up a hand as he took another taste.

Champa laughed at the expression on Casey's face. "But how 'bout you, dawg? You ain't been on the outside for what, a week, and suddenly you movin' and shakin' like you never left? Rumor mill's been crankin' overtime since you back in the game."

Casey leaned back in his chair. "Anything I need to know 'bout?"

Champa studied his drink for a bit. "Anyone comin' out of Attica or the other max pokes in the area, all they talkin' 'bout is how you somehow worked an understanding between pretty much every gang on the streets of New York. That true?"

"Pretty much, except for a couple stragglers. Once I get the VKs back, I got it arranged that New York streets will be run like a corporation. All the big bosses are down, I just need to connect with their captains to make it friendly."

Casey got to enjoy a rare moment—seeing Champa Munoz utterly speechless. He drained his drink in one gulp and poured another. "Nigga, I'd think you was frontin' if you didn't look so goddamned serious. How the fuck did you manage to herd all them ballers into goin' along on this ride?"

Casey sipped his vodka before answering. "It didn't happen overnight—nothing does in the can. Once I got my head on straight and figured out what I wanted—Rono tits up and the VKs back—a friend of mine turned me out about how the VKs and all the gangs could be more than the sum of their parts. And you'll never believe where the idea came from."

"I'm listenin'."

"Henry muthafuckin' Ford."

Champa's eyebrows raised. "What?"

"A hundred years ago, Ford paid his workers five dollars a day— much higher than any other factory at the time. His turnover— which plagues our own businesses, let's face it—dropped to virtually nothing overnight. He was into vertical integration, controlling not only the manufacture of a product, but also either the raw materials used to produce it, its retailing, or all three if possible. At the height of the Ford Motor Company, them cats was processing their own steel, turning it into cars, and selling them at their own franchises coast-to-coast. For a long time, people hardly knew there were any other cars besides Fords."

Champa frowned. "Okay, the cracker sold a shitload of cars back in the day. How's that figure into your game?"

"Simple—everyone treats all these various operations more like businesses than loose enterprises. Divide the city into set districts and assign a crew, and only that crew, to handle one aspect of the empire. Tighten up how we act, both toward the customers and our own people. Set and enforce some goddamn rules, like no perkin' while on the clock. Pay our own a share better than what they can get anywhere else, and institute a system of bonuses— you sell more, you make more—simple as that. Pay everyone decent, and they won't be lookin' to promote themselves by cappin' the next man up. No skimmin' off the top either; if this works like it should, there'll be more than enough paper to go around."

"They musta laughed your ass outta the yard when they first heard your ghetto finance shit."

Casey smiled, remembering those early days when hardly anyone listened to a word he had to say. "True dat, so I didn't just tell people about it—I showed them."

"How so?"

Casey's smile grew broader. "The crew I left inside basically took over all the illegal shit happenin' in Attica. The other crews have a slice, each handles one aspect—drugs, toilet hootch, legal counsel, specialty items from outside—but it all flows under VK eyes. If my boys don't like somethin', one word is all it takes to put an end to it. And you know what? Inmate-on-inmate crimes actually dropped for the first time in a decade."

"Da-yamn."

"Damn straight. Muthafuckin' warden even got a commendation from the mayor on how he'd 'cleaned up' Attica. 'Course the sorry peckerwood couldn't tell anyone the real reason the cons weren't busy beatin' the shit out of each other—the VKs. If you should ever find your sorry ass there, just drop my name, and you'll be taken care of, G."

Champa clinked his glass against Casey's. "Ain't never planning on goin' in, but shit do happen. So what came next?"

"Word got 'round on the prison wire that I was makin' shit happen. It still took a lotta years—four just to get the favors traded to get meetings with the bosses themselves—but I had nothin' but time on my hands, and a lotta plannin' to do for when I got out."

"You spent all your time in the joint settin' this up on the outside? What if you didn't get here?"

Casey shook his head. "Mack D taught me to not worry about the shadow of impending death, like the *samurai*. When those sword-swinging muthas were in battle, they had conditioned themselves to expect to die at any moment. Once a man conquers his fear of death, he can concentrate on accomplishing whatever he desires in his life."

He sipped again. "Once I had their ear, I explained the situation, and found many who were more than willing to listen to reason. Then, it was only a matter of figuring out what each crew coveted the most, and then brokering arrangements to let them have it."

"That all sounds a bit too convenient to me."

"Shecit, nigga, it only took me twenty years to pull this together."

"And you and the VKs gonna be the overall enforcers? What about those who don't wanna get on board?"

Now it was Casey's turn to smile thinly. "They get one chance, and if they turn it down, they are removed from the equation— permanently. No room for renegades in this deal."

Champa chuckled. "Sounds charming, but I hope you don't mind if I stay on the outside on this one. I prefer my life free and easy, not answering to anyone."

"I got no problem with that, easy rider. As long as you're still available if I need your talents, that is."

Champa held up his glass. "You pull off this crazy plan, homes, I'll be the first to congratulate you. And shit yeah, you know I'm always 'bout getting that paper." He drained his drink, then put the glass down on the desk with a thud. "In fact, it's funny that you called when you did, Crush. I was just thinkin' how I could use a guy like you to hit a lick I got word of, right here in the city."

Casey set his glass down. "I'm listenin', but I gotta tell you straight, I don't know how this figures into my plans."

Champa showed his teeth in a predator's grin. "You will after you hear what I got to say, I guarantee it. I want you to be part of a four-man crew takedown of a money wagon. And not just some random ruffian's shekels either. Oh no, this chedda comes straight from the deep, dirty pockets of your former homeboy, Mr. Rono."

Casey leaned forward. "You have my attention."

"Your boy's been saving his nickels and dimes for a rainy day, and it's coming soon. The Colombian cartels wanna make it snow all over the Big Apple, and they think Rono's the weatherman. After all, the U.S. still remains a growth market for the candy the VKs trade in."

Casey wondered if this was the group Baybay had entertained. "Including the sex trafficking?"

"Yeah, but they're looking to step up their game in a major way. Seems he and that Grace Phan're putting an 'I Spy' operation in place. Ingratiatin' their girls with politicians and big business types. Get the goods and sell that shit to whoever wants to pay the price. Rono wants the blow to loosen lips and the girls to shake their tits to get all the dirt he can dig up." Munoz poured more vodka for both of them.

"How much?"

"Ten point five mil, give or take a hundred grand. Comes through this Friday."

They clinked glasses again on that. "How the hell you know all this, Champa?"

"Inside track, baby. Brix Bancroft set this up."

"The silver-haired brother?"

"I'm comforted to know you ain't been sleeping while on the outside."

"He's looking to take Rono out."

"Yup, sound familiar?"

"No shit. What's your connection to him?"

Munoz smiled. "He asked around among our various thieving friends, lookin' for someone who hadn't been on the scene for a while, and word got to me."

"Nice to be recommended," Casey grunted.

"Ain't it though?"

"You concerned about Bancroft pullin' some okey-doke? I've had bad experience with turncoats," he said without sarcasm.

Munoz rolled the glass between his large, calloused hands. "That's why Jupiter Jenkins is the fourth one in on this. She's got balls bigger than all of us, plus she's worked with me before. And you and her pops were down back in the day." Junko Jenkins had gone up against Rono after he'd overthrown Casey. He'd died hard, taking a roomful of Rono's boys with him in a grenade explosion.

"Huh—thought she went straight." Casey raised an eyebrow, recalling their conversation at the repair yard.

Champa shrugged and sipped. "With that much chedda on the table, people tend to rethink their priorities."

"Looks like I'm gonna have a chance to hurt Rono and line my wallet at the same goddamn time."

"Ain't that some shit?"

They laughed and drank some more before Casey asked, "Who's the other man on this? I assume Bancroft is supposed to cap Rono while we rob the shipment." The thought of someone else capping Rono twinged Casey's stomach, but he dismissed it. If Rono got gone and his hands were clean, wasn't that all for the better than risking his freedom just to end that mother personally?

"I figure on using Walker for our wheelman. He's not shy around a gat either."

"Sounds right. He's steady as hell, won't panic if things go south."

"I don't intend for that." Champa Munoz went on to explain the cash was coming from the Caymans after a rinse. It would be flown inside plasma TVs via a factory in Jamaica into Kennedy. There airline personnel, also on Rono's payroll, would remove the hidden cash, which would be transported in a hearse for a funeral.

"A real funeral?"

"One of the Vicetown Kings slanger's big mama kicked the

other week, and they kept her on ice as they knew they'd be moving the money now. The switchout from the airport is supposed to happen at the funeral home—that's where we do our thang."

"Slick," Casey admitted. "Do you know who handled the rinse, the banker?"

Munoz said, "No. Bancroft knows, but he wasn't sharing." He went on to inform him where the four would meet the following day to rehearse, and they said their good-byes outside the prop house.

Casey hadn't mentioned his feelings for Carla, but he knew he'd have to tell Champa eventually. It wouldn't do for him to find out otherwise. Goddamn broad had put him in a trick bag, yet it wasn't like he was trying to extricate himself now, was it? He sighed and walked on.

The evening had turned cold, and Casey zipped up his cotton workingman's Windbreaker that he zipped up as he walked. He tried to sort out his feelings about this job, which was both opportunity and hindrance. Not only would he be denied his right to kill Rono himself, he'd then have to deal with Bancroft. Would the captains and lieutenants be loyal to the cat they already knew? Close ranks around the new leader? Over the years in prison he'd gotten enough word to know Rono's inner circle was with him for the money, but he'd earned little respect.

It meant something to Casey that while he was certainly nobody's idea of a choirboy, he had the respect of his men and women—because he respected them right back. Without that, all you had was a pack of wild dogs, ready to pounce on the leader at the first sign of weakness—just like Bancroft was about to do.

Casey came out of his reverie at the sound of gruff voices. He looked up at a trio of struggling figures in the distance.

"The fuck you gonna do, ya fuckin' jig?" one in a backward baseball cap said harshly, shoving a gaunt figure trapped between him and another white boy.

"Yeah, bitch," the other one said. He held a baseball bat and hit the man they were tormenting in the back of his legs, making him sink to his knees.

Casey stalked toward the three, who stood on a barren patch of overgrowth and detritus among the buildings in this industrial area. He could see them clearly in the security lighting from a nearby truck lot. There was something familiar about the man the two were pushing around.

"Fuckin' homeless moulie," Backward Cap announced, kicking him as he tried to rise.

"Goddamn alley bats're bringing down the neighborhood. Take your nigger ass back to Brooklyn or wherever and beg there." The bat man raised his weapon to bring it across the shoulders of the downed man, who struggled to get up again.

"Put it down, muthafuckah," Casey warned.

"Get to steppin,' asshole. This is none of your concern." When his partner hissed something in his ear, Backward Cap advanced on him.

"You wanna bank on someone, cracker? Here I am." Casey feinted with his raised arms, then lashed out with a kick, his heel catching the drunk bully flush in the solar plexus. The blow bent him forward, and he vomited. Casey followed with a right to the jaw that sent him to the ground. He was already turning to face the second man, but the bat wielder was right there and whacked him on the back and shoulder blade, sending a bolt of pain shooting down his arm. Casey grunted and ducked the next swing, the bat whistling over his head, then charged, wrapping his arms around the other man, his legs churning to keep the thug off balance.

"Let go, nigger!" the bat man yelled. He stamped downward with the grip end of the bat into the middle of Casey's back, but Casey didn't release him. They both went over, tripping on a large piece of junk.

"You gonna get schooled, you fuckin' jig," the bat swinger gasped as they grappled.

"Your mama's a jig." Casey got in a punch to the man's nose, making him howl, then disengaged himself and got to his feet. The other one shambled toward him, but the gaunt man jumped on him before he reached Casey. They both fell to the ground, snarling and scrapping.

Casey turned to see the man with the bat, his nose bloody, also upright. His weapon raised and cocked, he rushed Casey again. Forearms up, Casey grimaced as he took the blow across his arms. Even through the pain, he reached out and hugged the bat as his attacker tried to pull it back.

"Gimme that," he wheezed.

"You got it." Casey swung his foot up into the other man's crotch and simultaneously twisted his body, wrenching the bat free.

"Fucker—," the drunk bat swinger blared as he folded like a cheap card table, clutching his privates.

Casey swung the bat like he was hitting one out of Yankee Stadium. He connected with the man's jaw and there was a *pop* as he went down like a felled tree. Casey stalked to where the other two were wrestling and he tapped the bat on the cap wearer.

"Wha—?" He looked up with startled eyes that immediately closed after Casey hit him across the face, crushing his nose. He went over in a fetal position, hands to his face, mewling in agony.

Casey wiped his prints off the bat with his shirt tail and threw it over the fence into the truck lot. "You all right?" he said to Ten Spot. The panhandler was sitting on the ground, legs drawn up, and his arms around his knobby knees.

"I'm okay."

"We gotta bounce—come on."

"Don't forget my face, nigga. I'm going to cap your monkey ass," the one with the broken nose said, rocking among the weeds.

"Not tonight you ain't." Casey kicked him in the stomach and he vomited on himself.

He got Ten Spot on his feet. "Wait." The tall panhandler looked around in the half-gloom and spotted his backpack. He picked it up and the two hurried away.

"What the fuck you doin' out here?" Casey asked. For a second, he imagined that Ten Spot had been following him, then dismissed the idea. He might be out of practice, but not that much. He damn sure would have seen him.

"Can't jus' hustle in the usual places. Lot of them limousine liberals out here feel sorry for us have-nots."

"And a lot of them crackers like your two dance partners like to gang up on a brother and chunk your ass for kicks."

"Life ain't nothing but a chance," the other man said.

Casey handed him two twenties. "Get yoself somethin' to eat, man." He made to part ways.

"Back in the day I was a good soljah, Crush."

"I know."

"I can be again. I can be useful to ya."

"Okay, Ten Spot."

"No drama, man, on the real." He stepped closer. "You gonna get back on top, ain'tcha?"

"I'm on parole, homes."

Ten Spot showed those surprisingly healthy teeth of his. "I know, I know, why the fuck should you tell me anything? But I can prove my worth. I can do a job."

Bemused, Casey asked, "Yeah, and what job is that?"

"I know some of Rono's houses where the mixin' goes on. I know delivery times and shit."

Casey poked a heavy finger into the street bum's chest. "You stay the fuck away from Rono. You don't wanta get involved in anything he's doin'. You just get yourself together, ya hear?" He started to walk away again.

"Don't you worry, Casey, I'm on this. I can soljah up."

"Leave it alone, Ten Spot," Casey called back. He took a cab back to Manhattan, had the driver drop him off a few blocks away, and walked the rest of the way to his hotel. He took a long soak to lessen the soreness his body would be feeling from the bat blows. After a tumbler of Hendawg, Casey fell into bed and slept like the dead.

Rono had been waiting for the call ever since that Asian hooch had called one of his slangers and said she'd seen Marcus Casey going into a theater shop in Flushing. He'd immediately had Derek Webb contact the two crackers who'd owed the VKs a favor and told them to get their asses down there and take Casey out. He gave them the number of a burner, instructing them to call when the job was done.

Once the plan had been put in motion, Rono paced the floor of his penthouse, too keyed up to relax. He wanted that goddamn phone to ring so those cracker assholes could tell him that they'd put Casey out of his misery. Finally the cell phone vibrated in his pocket, and Rono held up one hand to quiet the rest of the room as he flipped it open with the other. "Go for Rono."

For a moment, he didn't hear anything, then heavy, labored breathing wheezed out over the small speaker. "Ow—goddamn it, that fuckin' hurts. Yeah, look, we found your guy, but we ah—we couldn't take him down."

Rono's lips compressed into a thin line as he comprehended what he was hearing. "Say that again, muthafuckah."

The man on the other end sounded like he was speaking through a mouthful of cotton balls. "Look man, we set up right where your guy told us t'be. Even had some old nigger bum we was usin' as bait by beatin' on him, figuring all those porch monk—all you guys stick together, right?"

Rono didn't answer. The guy continued, his words coming faster and faster. "So he comes out, sees what's goin' on, and moves in. We tried to take him, but Ralphie got all fucked up—I hadda take him to the hospital, I think his jaw got broke bad."

"I don't give a rat's fuck about your homeboy, what I give a fuck about is Casey still walking the streets, goddamn it! Why didn't you just draw down on his ass and shoot him!"

"All right, all right, I know we fucked up. We didn't expect that a forty-five-year-old nigga fresh from the joint was going to be a problem."

Rono took a deep breath, squeezing the cell's plastic case until it creaked under the pressure. "This don't even come close to squaring accounts, you hear me? You two ain't off my shit list, not by a damn sight!"

He slammed the phone closed, then hurled it across the room, watching it explode against the wall in a spray of plastic and circuit boards. "Is there no one who can handle this guy once and for all?" he shouted at the assembled group, all of whom had gone stone-silent, staring at him with drinks in their hands and cigarettes or joints forgotten between their fingers. Just then one of Rono's drunken soldiers tried to conceal his laughter at a text message he got. Rono spun around, drew his SIG, and put one straight in his dome. The whole room freaked, half of them hitting the ground screaming, the other half frozen stock-still.

"Do you people think this is fucking funny! This muthafucka is threatening my lifestyle and alla yours! Do I have to threaten your life to get someone to handle my muthafuckin' lightweight!" Rono eyeballed everyone and they all averted their eyes, not wanting to give him a excuse to make another example of one of them.

Rono flapped an arm at them. "Party's over—everybody get the hell out." People started to move gingerly toward the door. Rono leapt onto the coffee table, scattering drugs and drinks everywhere, and roared, "I SAID GET THE FUCK OUT!" They couldn't leave fast enough, scrambling over each other in their rush to the exit.

ICE-T and MAL RADCLIFF

Once the room was empty, Derek Webb closed and locked the door. He walked back into the living room while Rono stepped off the table and slumped down on the couch, head in his hands. Rono looked at the table, his hands scrabbling for something to calm his mind. Finding a fat philly, he applied flame and inhaled, letting the potent Purple Kush do its thang. Exhaling, he shook his head. "This muthafuckah's like a ghost, Derek, always coming back when I think I got him put away."

Derek plopped down in an overstuffed chair on the other side of the room and regarded his half-baked boss. "Rono, you know I roll how you roll, but in this case, I think we got to rethink our strategy 'bout Casey."

Rono raised his head and reached for a rocks glass and a bottle of Crown Royal XR, the phat blunt still in his other hand. "I'm listenin', dawg."

13

Still moving a bit stiffly after the corn squabble, Casey checked out the apartment in the Midtown West building Shinzo had recommended. Standing at a window, he could see nearby Central Park between two other buildings. There was a split-level main room, a sectioned-off kitchen, and a full bathroom between two bedrooms, one more spacious than the other. Furniture and appliances had been left behind, testifying to the speed with which the previous tenant had left his tilt.

Becker couldn't be there, but he'd provided a crude blueprint showing the location of disguised switches to the hidden compartments. There was even a passageway to a back stairwell that could be accessed via the master bedroom through a hinged bookcase. The place was perfect.

Learning where to find and how to activate the switches took some time, but afterward Casey left a message for Becker to make the arrangements so he could move into the place. He'd discussed it with Carla, who said she could probably find a real estate agent who would front that she'd obtained the rental for him. Casey would have to kick her back a fee, but the story should satisfy Lomax. Though Casey was beginning to doubt whether Lomax would care what the cover story was as long as it was the least bit plausible. His PO had an agenda, and Casey needed to figure out what it was before he got ensnared any deeper in the man's machinations.

He went out and grabbed lunch at a diner. Afterward, he got a call from Becker.

"You want to drop by and get the keys?" he asked after telling Casey he could move in that day.

"Yeah, but I need to get my stuff over at the Roosevelt first."

"I'll have Li pick you up."

"Cool. Make it about one thirty," he said, glancing at his watch as he walked back to his hotel room. He called downstairs for Carla, but she was out. He left a message on her cell and gathered his belongings. Five minutes before the appointed time, the front desk called to tell him Li had arrived. He went down and got in the restored Jaguar sedan.

"Thanks," Casey said as she pulled away.

"Always a pleasure," she said. "Shinzo's at Madam Nozinga's, so we'll need to swing by there first."

"He see her pretty regularly?"

She turned in profile and smiled sweetly, but said nothing. Casey didn't press the issue—he respected a soljah who didn't jaw jap. They arrived at the woman's building, but Becker wasn't downstairs yet. He came out several minutes later and got in the back with Casey. He was effusive. "Have a good session?" Casey joked.

"The best," Becker answered. He produced three cheroots, and they all smoked on their way to the office.

Casey wondered if the medium kept a handwritten log of her clients or maintained a computer database. A computer might be difficult to hack, but he was sure he could find someone to get into it. Though if he were the madam, he'd keep that shit in a ledger in a really good safe. Walker was good with safes. He asked blandly, "Are we celebrating an auspicious occasion?"

The pretty chauffeur exchanged a look with Becker, both laughing lightly. "This is a hell of a town, Crush," his friend said. "A hell of a town."

Becker maintained an office in a warehouse along the Hudson River, near a new development. There was a fenced-in parking lot, but Li brought the car to rest in a narrow area beside a side door. The markings on the warehouse announced it as a refrigeration parts distributor. The three entered and walked through the facility, which was filled with what looked like real merchandise, covering all makes and models.

Casey looked around at the various motors and assorted machinery. "So this is legit? You're selling parts?"

"On this floor," Becker answered. They entered an elevator and he punched in a code. They descended for a bit, and the doors opened on several long worktables where women and men were assembling purses. Other packed shoes in fancy boxes. There were several men in trendy suits on stools at intervals in the long room including three manning monitors.

"Those guys," Becker said, beaming, "have rotating views of the roof and perimeter." He enjoyed being able to impress Casey.

Casey picked up a shoe with a buckle. "Quality knockoffs—leather, not plastic. Nice work."

"We can essentially make the exact same product, charge half their markup, and still rake in plenty. Louis V, Prada, Gucci, Juicy Coutoure, and so on. We do different designers in various cycles—keeps the feds guessing as to who's distributing what. Right now we're on purses and shoes."

"You assemble everything here?" Casey asked as they walked through.

"Got a pipeline to Guangzhou," Shinzo admitted. "That's the

goddamn counterfeiting factory center in China. We get what we call incompletes, than retool them here into particular brands."

"That's tight." Casey nodded appreciatively. "You handle the electronic brand name knockoffs out of China too?"

"Yeah," he said, suddenly distracted. "Now and then, but the profit and ease is better on this shit." He said something in a low voice to one of the men on the stools, then turned back to Casey. "Look here, our parts trucks help move our goods throughout the city." They made the circuit and headed back toward the elevator.

"See these?" Becker pointed at various small nozzles interspersed along the ceiling among the sensor-activated water sprinklers. "If we get raided these release a cloud of soot and gunk. That way the items get doused. That also means those forensic fucks would have to clean the purses up to present them as evidence and my mouth-piece would argue contamination and get it thrown out."

"That's some impressive shit, Shin," Casey said. With the proper infusion of paper, Becker could take his operation way beyond the five boroughs. No doubt that notion had also crossed the other man's mind. "You get a lot of competition in the knockoff market? Say, from the Black Lotus?"

Becker's expression turned cagey. "Why you wanna know?"

Casey held up his hands. "You mentioned a pipeline to Guang-zhou. Word on the street is the BLs are flooding the market with their own high-end brands." Kenny's report had been thorough. "The last thing you want is a price war, I suppose."

Becker and Li exchanged glances. "You been out what, a week, maybe? Where you gettin' this intel from?"

Casey smiled. "Sheeit, nigga, you ain't the only one with a psy-chic!"

Shin laughed and shook his head. "Aw, nigga, please."

"But let's get back to my original point—is the Black Lotus a problem?"

Becker stared at him before his face broke into a broad smile.

"Nozinga told me this morning that you'd be the key to solving one of my issues in the near future. Now ain't that some shit."

Casey shrugged and held up his hands. "What can I say?"

"We just got word from our factory overseas—the hometown Lotus is comin' down on 'em hard to supply them exclusively. We could find other suppliers, but not at the same quality or anywhere near the price."

"That's a situation, all right," Casey mused.

"Damn straight. You got a plan to eliminate this growing thorn in my side?"

"Oh yeah, brother—I got lotsa plans. But what I need to know is if you'll back me when I go into action."

Becker grinned. "Nigga, you know I got tips. Put a gat in my hand or let my dawgs loose, I'll back your play 'til we either on top or in the ground."

Casey grinned back. "My nigga."

They rode back up in the elevator and Casey and Becker worked out the financials and he got the keys to his new apartment. Li drove him to his new place, and he unloaded what little he had. As he was finishing up, he got a call from Carla.

"What up, big boy?" she teased.

"Your boy's gone legit. I'm standin' in my new crib." He told her the address.

"Oh, are you mine now?" He could hear the smile in her voice.

"As much as anyone's, I s'pose."

"Want me to come over later? Bring some takeout?"

"That sounds great, but I got to do some homework, so some other time."

Her voice cooled. "Am I always going to be at arm's length, Casey?"

"For now, I got to keep my head in this game, but you know I'll work something out." Casey said good-bye, then hung up.

All night Casey studied the file Kenny Saunders had assembled, rereading the parts on Gulliver Rono, the VKs, and the other two gangs. He made additional notes on all of them, including what he'd learned since being released. Champa's takedown was going to accelerate his timetable or derail it, but that couldn't be helped. The robbery was going to happen with or without him. Better to be a part of the action, particularly since he'd earn his cut, which would finance the rest of his operation. But would Champa go up against Bancroft if he did overthrow Rono? And what about Jupiter Jenkins? Seems she'd take her cut and bounce; that would be the smart move. Too bad, as he could use her skills.

Still, if Rono went down, there would be days of disarray and infighting as Bancroft solidified his base. That was exactly what had happened when Rono had betrayed him, Casey recalled. Sitting in jail, awaiting indictment and trial, word from the streets came easily. A good number of captains and lieutenants down, enforcers and soldiers down to slangers had broken or outright initiated hostilities against Rono. A lot of good men had died in the following weeks, and a lot of suckas rose to the top.

Attacks and retributions had rocked the city, the bloodletting spilling out among affiliates in Chicago, Atlanta, and Los Angeles. In the end, Rono had survived, but the Vicetown Kings Casey had erected from damn near nothing were not the same. He took some satisfaction in knowing that Rono had bitten off more than he could chew. But his own hunger wouldn't abate until he had the chance to retake and remake the Vicetown Kings again.

Keyed up, he couldn't concentrate on his notes anymore, so he did his prison cell routine of exercises, including two hundred diamond push-ups, two hundred sit-ups, and, using the edge of the couch's frame with his arms behind him, an equal number of dips. He finished and sat on the floor, breathing hard. Tomorrow he'd get some free weights and one of those pull-up bars. Shit was ratcheting up and he had to keep his mind civilized but his body savage.

Toweling off, Casey tried to remember whose quote he'd just mangled. Well, whoever had first said the words, it was a truism he believed. Mack D believed it too, and he was locked down for life and then some. Casey would have to find out if it would be a violation to visit him in prison. Mack D was the reason he'd survived all that shit, and he couldn't let the older man simply fade away. Despite what he'd said during the last week of Casey's incarceration.

"You know Satchel Paige was right, don't you?" Mack D asked. They stood side by side, assembling alternators for several models of Celicas. Toyota, like many car manufacturers, subcontracted a portion of its low-end work to prisons. Where else could you get willing workers for twenty-one cents an hour? Wages so low they undercut hourly rates, even in Southern right-to-work states with little or no organized labor. Let alone what was left of a unionized work force in other states. Particularly post-Meltdown, with the domestic auto industry still recovering.

Casey had just reread Paige's autobiography, *Maybe I'll Pitch Forever*, chronicling his playing in the Negro Leagues, and his role in opening the Major Leagues to black players. Screwing together an alternator housing, he asked, "'Bout what? Personally, I like Rule Five: 'Avoid running at all times.' But I'm also really down with Number Six: 'And don't look back—something might be gaining on you.'"

Mack D just nodded and smiled, his fingers flying as he attached wires inside the alternator. "But you're forgetting Number Three: 'Go very light on the vices, such as carrying on in society—the social ramble ain't restful.' You remember that when you're on the outside, now, ya heard? I know you got lots of plans and such, but they won't do you a bit of good if you don't stay out of here or out of the ground long enough to make 'em happen."

"Indeed."

. . .

149

Mack D's message was clear. Casey took a shower, alternating cold and hot water. Afterward he felt centered, and rather than study his notes, he started reading the opening chapters of a dog-eared copy of *God's Bits of Wood* by Senegalese writer and filmmaker Ousmane Sembène. The story involved many issues, from a railroad strike to the African armed struggle against colonialism. Casey appreciated the novel's various components, but was always struck by the lessons its protagonists learned from organizing and being prepared.

By 1:00 A.M. he was feeling tired, and thought about Carla. If she was here right now, they'd be in bed and the last thing they'd be doing was sleeping.

All in due time, baby girl, all in due time.

Condensed breath floating from his mouth, Casey stood in a marshy area not far from Newark Airport the following morning. The sun was rising and both humans and inanimate objects were awash in grays. Jupiter Jenkins was dressed in jeans and a hoodie, her head covered against the chill. Champa and Casey were in black chinos, heavy boots, and cotton Windbreakers. Walker wore tinted glasses, and was dressed in jeans and an open flannel shirt over a thermal tee.

"Bancroft's man swerves the lead car, crashing it. Walker and me let loose with these bad rascals from the opposite roofs." Munoz hefted a chunky Milkor MGL Mk. 1 handheld, six-shot grenade launcher that looked like the biggest revolver ever made. It was the twin to another one still in its case atop the hood of the hooptie he'd driven here. There were two other cars too, representing their targets. "We're gonna be unleashing canisters that are a combo of tear gas and halothane. It'll make 'em cry and be disoriented simultaneously. By the time we're thirty seconds in, they won't know if they're dead or alive."

Casey and Jenkins exchanged wary glances, both knowing all too well how Champa loved this shit.

Champa pointed at them. "You two swoop in on the Escalade in front of the hearse and neutralize the guards while me and Walker rappel off the roofs. You two will then snatch the casket and take up the panels underneath while Walker gets the car and I take care of the ones inside the funeral parlor. Bancroft says there won't be but a few, all unarmed civilians. The main action will happen outside, making sure all of Rono's niggas are down and out."

"A million is roughly twenty pounds of one-hundred-dollar bills. Those fill one of those big metal attaché cases, so there'll be ten of them," Casey observed. "It would be unwise to take off in the Escalade, so that means we're transferring them to the car Walker's driving."

"Correct," Munoz affirmed.

"So that means three of us are grabbing two cases each at any given moment, assuming one of us covers them."

"What you thinkin', Crush?"

Casey was imagining himself warm in the arms of the man's ex-wife, Carla Aquila. But instead he said, "I'm thinking a lot of this job depends on your boy Bancroft. His man doing his move at the right moment is key to this."

Champa replied, "If he doesn't do the block with the lead car then, yeah, the score is screwed. But we're unlikely to be exposed if the shit goes down hard."

Casey nodded. "You gave him the cover story too, right? Just in case."

"It's cool, Bancroft will set the stage for us just right. It shouldn't matter, since Rono'll be tits up a few minutes after he hears who supposedly hit his money train."

"Yeah, well, better safe than sorry." Casey knew far too many cocky muthafuckahs who'd thought they had everything nailed down, then ended up in the ground 'cause they didn't allow for the crazy shit. He had no intention of following their example.

Jenkins asked, "What about this dude in the lead car? He's gonna be goofed up by the gas too."

"He knows, Jupiter," Champa answered. "He also knows he's a dead man if Bancroft doesn't kill Rono at the same time we're doing this."

"I just meant he's not gonna be any help on site, is all," she said. "We all have to be on our ones and twos. No missteps."

"That's why we're here. Let's get to work." Champa clapped his hands and the quartet went through their paces. Munoz and Walker had previously erected plywood platforms representing the two-story buildings they would be atop of as the convoy went past. The small procession would leave the cargo area of JFK and return to the city and the funeral home. It was there that the money was scheduled to be taken out and the body would go on to the church.

Casey and the others practiced again and again, getting grimy as they ran the plan over and over, each one in the right place at the right second. They were ingraining their moves in their heads and reflex muscle.

Casey was elated to be involved in righteous criminal activity at last. It was the difference between being a spectator and a participant. He had to be on the grind. This was his freedom.

14

Brixton Bancroft clipped the nail too short on his little finger and winced. Examining the reddening under the head of the nicked nail and skin, he touched his tongue to the minor injury, then did the nails on his other hand. Putting the clippers back in his dresser drawer, he removed his hairbrush, glancing over at the bed and the shapely Vera Hammond, still sleeping in it.

After a pass with the brush, Bancroft gave a last look at his reflection. In the next forty-eight hours, he'd either be top dog or a corpse. This must have been how Rono felt all those years ago. And where was Crush Casey in all this? If his play was successful, Casey would certainly be a factor. He'd been ID'd at Woodside's as the one who'd attacked Thick. Not just attacked him, but nearly killed the gigantic banger, which was impressive in and of itself. Clearly he'd been there scouting, but seemed to have gone to ground afterward. Rono was already nervous and distracted about Casey, given his focus on the impending deal with the Colombians.

Bancroft had formulated his plan a few months ago, but he knew the odds weren't ever going to be better than at this moment. Striking now would eliminate Rono, then he'd get rid of the deadwood that punk-ass had gathered around him, and finally he'd renegotiate the deal that sucka had made with the cartel— he'd been the one who reached out to them in the first place, after all.

He would make them understand that the ten million was an initial payment for exclusive purchasing rights for their top product. The group wouldn't like it, but they'd swallow the bitter tea. They knew the VKs had the most extensive drug network on the East Coast, so they'd have to back his play if he was the new contender.

Bancroft brushed lint from his tailored silk sport coat. The lush life hadn't spoiled him any, and he'd kept his ear to the ground. When he'd heard through the grapevine about a smooth takedown of a money drop Champa Munoz had engineered in Arizona, he knew Champa was the man to heist the money train. He'd gotten in touch via Walker, and the rest was smooth sailing. It was a shame that he'd have to double-cross Champa and his team afterward but he still needed the money to pay the Colombians. And he also needed Rono as distracted and jittery as possible before he took care of the man once and for all. After Bancroft consolidated his rule, he'd move on those Black Lotus fuckers, who'd been cutting into profits on the south side. Champa had given him the cover story, and he'd gleefully gone along with it, fitting the last piece into his plan to install himself as the kingpin of the VKs. Smiling, he checked his shave once more, turning his head to the left and to the right, then laughing out loud.

"What's so funny?"

"You are," he answered in his rolling baritone, crossing to the bed where Vera Hammond yawned and stretched her lithe body. Bancroft sat next to his lover and took her in his arms.

"That right?" The blanket had fallen just enough to reveal part of her left breast and nipple, which hardened as Bancroft softly rubbed it. She reached up for him and they embraced passionately. He never got over it, but a remarkable aspect of the woman was her lack of morning breath. *How is that possible?* he'd wondered more than once.

"I still can't help being nervous about this," she said, her hand pressed to his chest, resting over his heart.

"Me too. But everything's in place. Munoz and his crew are set."

"Who's on it?"

"The crew?"

"Yeah, the crew."

"Champa has this vet buddy in on the job, and he said he'd fill out the other slots with local talent. He vouches they'll take care of business, and that's all that counts."

She stared. "You better know what the fuck you're doing. Dixon isn't exactly a bruiser."

He pinched her thigh. "He'll come through—the choice spot I promised him, he goddamn well better. You just make sure you got the shit covered on your end, woman."

Bancroft kissed her one last time, then headed out to meet his destiny.

Ike Lomax sat in the back of O'Farrell's Tavern and eagerly began devouring his piled-high pastrami sandwich slathered with coleslaw between thick slices of fresh-baked rye. He chased each delicious bite down with swallows of Samuel Adams Imperial Stout.

A slender, dark-skinned black man in a dark suit and rectangular glasses approached his table and sat opposite him, unbuttoning his coat.

"How's it hangin', Mr. Fulson?" Lomax said after swallowing a mouthful. "What'll you have?"

"Something stiffer than that," the other man said, pointing at the beer.

"Comin' up." The parole officer waved at the waitress, who took Fulson's order for a vodka tonic.

"Grey Goose," the slender man specified. The waitress nodded and went away. "Are you aware Champa Munoz is back in town?" He reached for one of Lomax's fries. Meticulously he scooped ketchup on his prize and chewed it.

"The fellow that likes to make things go boom," Lomax declared. "This info is from the joint task force supposed to be on him?"

"Sort of, yes. Actually, he's an all-around armaments expert. But the task force has been reassigned, absorbed into a larger concern that doesn't affect our operations here."

"Hmm—so, if Champa doesn't have them breathing down his neck anymore, he's ready to do some business," Lomax remarked. "He must be up to something. What about your Mr. Casey?"

"What about him?" Lomax had more of his beer. "You think he's met with Munoz?"

"As a known former criminal associate, I don't have any reason not to." His drink arrived.

Lomax responded, "Hell, you could blame Casey for MLK's assassination with that kind of pretzel logic."

Fulson managed a weak smile. "Him being a child at the time only barely takes him off the list of possibles." He drank some of his cocktail. "Munoz did freelance work for Casey when he was consolidating his leadership of the Vicetown Kings."

Lomax looked off into the gloom of the bar, then back at his guest. "Oh yeah, I remember a few cats having their rides getting blown to the Promised Land with them still in 'em."

Fulson smiled. "I heard about one individual—Deadeye, they

called him because of a false eye—who put his hand on the door-knob to his apartment after opening the security screen, and was electrocuted on the spot."

Lomax chuckled evilly. "Damn, Fulson—that's some diabolical shit." He ate some more of his sandwich, watching the slender man. "Best Reuben on this side of town—sure you won't join me?"

Fulson held up his glass. "I'm on a liquid diet thanks to the heat coming down on me from upstairs over all this. I'll be chasing this with Pepto if we don't break something on the Colombians soon." He sipped again, regarding Lomax over the rim of his glass. "So, why you like this cat Casey so much anyway?"

"Relax, I'm not suffering from Stockholm syndrome or some shit. I simply appreciate ingenuity."

"Law enforcement personnel, after repeated interaction with lawbreakers, often take on their attributes." The slender man drank again.

"Sometimes ruthlessness calls for ruthlessness, Mr. Fulson. Is that not what engages us in the service of the greater good?"

Fulson displayed another weak smile. "If that's what helps you sleep at night. Nonetheless, it might behoove you to keep closer tabs on your man, particularly now that he's moved out of the Harlem walk-up."

Lomax swallowed, wiping his mouth with a paper napkin. "Oh, I won't let him flit away. Besides, if your suspicions are correct, I imagine we'll be hearing from Casey soon—or at least of his exploits."

Fulson stared into his drink. "Tiger by the tail and all that. Isn't there some kind of parable about the master swordsmen you beg to come to your village to run off the brigands? Only once that's done, the swordsmen realize they've got a sweet setup and stick around, becoming the new overlords."

"More like we're about to let the tiger loose, hoping we've aimed it in the general direction we intended. 'Cause you know damn well you keep holdin' that tiger's tail too long, he's gonna turn around and they'll be calling you Lefty."

"Blowback on you or me?"

Lomax worked a piece of gristle from between his teeth with his thumbnail. "Too damn late in the day to be frettin' about that, ain't it?"

"I like to fret. I need to fret." Fulson drained his glass. "Hell, in my job, it's practically a requirement for promotion."

Lomax signaled for the waitress again. "Then, brother, you better make this one a double. Could be that shitstorm's about to hit."

Fulson rotated his head, an audible crack accompanying his grateful order for another drink.

15

At 7:24 A.M. on an overcast Friday morning, Tommy Dixon sharply turned the black Escalade's steering wheel as the small convoy arrived at the funeral home. The SUV screeched sideways in the narrow passageway, the front bumper crunching against the cinder-block wall at the rear of the building.

"The fuck, Tommy?" Buster Goldwyn swore beside him as the white Caddy behind them smashed into their rear panel, the driver of that vehicle stomping on his brakes. The hearse was behind the white SUV and behind it was another black Escalade.

Dixon was jumpy and grabbed at the door handle, trying to get out. "Where the hell are they?" he muttered.

"S'up with you, man?" Reflexively, Goldwyn reached for Dixon, who'd worked himself into near terror the last few nights with bad dreams about being caught and tortured. He'd slipped his gun in the side door pocket earlier, and now came up with it in his hand. Turning, he fired point-blank into Goldwyn's stunned face.

. . .

The Mount Zion Open Arms Funeral Home was a complex of buildings, cinder-block structures added on to the main converted 1920s-era mansion over time. One part, which stuck out in an L-shape, was the embalming section. The employees jokingly called it the packing and shipping department, as this was where the bodies were also placed in their caskets and wheeled back to the viewing room. The embalming room had a second story over it that held chemical supplies and spare casket parts.

It was on this roof that Walker popped up and fired four of the tear gas–halothane combo grenades. Champa was on another second-story warehouse rooftop at an angle opposite the funeral home. He let loose with another four canisters around the rear vehicles as VKs poured out, guns bristling, their lungs and eyes hindered by the disorienting cloud.

Casey, his chest covered in a level-four bulletproof vest and wearing a gas mask with full face visor, came around the back end of the last vehicle on two coughing gangstas trying to see into the gray.

"Yo, we're bein' hit!" one of the soldiers yelled as he fired at the moving form in the cloud.

Casey's semiauto Mossberg boomed, and double-aught buckshot tore into the man's stomach and groin, spraying crimson, fleshy pulp against the side of the Escalade. There was a choke on the end of the barrel to concentrate the spread pattern. The blast sent the dead man's body sprawling against the vehicle.

The second man had stumbled to the tail end of the SUV in an attempt to get clear. He was about to unload his silver-plated SIG SAUER on Casey's back when a throwing knife blurred through the haze and sank into his throat. He gurgled loudly as he drowned in his own blood.

Casey glanced at Jupiter Jenkins, who quickly moved past him to remove the weapon. Getting back on track, Casey resumed his hunt for the rest of the convoy crew.

Inside the embalming room were three employees, two maintenance men, and the home's lead embalmer, whose job was to aid Rono's crew as ordered. All of them had their hands in the air as ordered by Champa, clad in all black and also wearing a gas mask and vest. On the tables and counters were the various devices and cosmetics used to prepare bodies, including aspirators with gauges, needle guns, glues, and the highly flammable embalming fluid of ethanol, formaldehyde, and methanol. On a wall were two large anatomy charts, male and female.

"Everyone just relax and this will soon be over," Champa assured them. He tossed the head embalmer duct tape and plastic restraints. "Tie up those two."

"Oh yes, oh yes," she said, moving quickly and deftly completing her task.

When she was done, Champa snatched the tape and tore off a large piece. "Now hold very still."

Outside Casey approached a coughing, teary-eyed VK with a homely face in a snap brim hat and clubbed him to the ground with the butt of the shotgun. He hit him twice more, hard, making sure he stayed down. Jenkins, an adherent of *muay thai* kickboxing, shot an elbow into another VK's chest while putting a heel into his knee, dislocating it. He buckled as she brought her knee up rapidly into his face.

As the man Jenkins beat on crumpled to the ground, Casey ran after a soldier who'd run out of the gas, which was now dissipating. The VK soldier flapped his arms and turned wildly around in a circle, laughing and muttering, "I'm a junior bird man, look at me fly." The halothane, a narcotic gas that produced euphoria, had done its work. Casey lowered his shotgun, socked the man instead, and he dropped to the ground like a marionette with its strings cut. Casey hurried back to the vehicles, Jenkins right beside him.

Jenkins kicked Tommy Dixon hard in the face to make it look convincing. The gas had taken out the remaining VKs, all of whom were in a torpid state and easily bound with duct tape on their mouths and zip-ties around their wrists and ankles. No one had either the presence of mind or the time to dial out on their cell phones. Even if they did, Munoz had set up a signal jammer on his rooftop to thwart reception.

The absconders got busy on their main goal. Casey jumped in the driver's seat of the last Escalade and backed it up, clearing a path to the hearse itself. Opening the Cadillac's rear swing door, they grabbed the casket and let it clatter to the ground on its rollers with Casey shoving it out of the way. Walker drove in at the same time, having rappelled down the wall and jogged to an '86 Crown Victoria LTD station wagon a block away. Expertly he backed the Crown Vic behind the funeral home, stopping the car exactly ten inches away from the rear of the hearse. Having rigged a switch at Casey's suggestion, Walker popped open the tailgate by pressing a button on the dash. Casey and Jenkins tossed in the metal cases of money two at a time. Walker remained behind the wheel of the idling car and Munoz, who had come out of the embalming building, covered them. When they were done loading up Champa yelled, "Count." Jenkins answered, "Ten," and Casey said, "Ten." Then they dived into the rear of the station wagon, Casey pulling up the tailgate as Munoz got in beside Walker, who peeled away the moment everyone was inside. Their watches read 7:31 A.M.

Munoz took out his burner cell phone and speed-dialed a number. He let it ring twice, then smashed it against the window frame and threw the broken instrument onto the roadway.

. . .

Brixton Bancroft received Champa's call. He pretended to listen to a message and excitedly said to Gulliver Rono, "Gul, some mutha-fuckahs just hit our shipment."

The two were in the back office space of Magic Sword, a video games distributor owned by the Vicetown Kings in Kew Gardens. Framed posters of lurid art advertising killing zombie hordes and slaughtering monstrous aliens decorated the walls. The plan had been for the money to come from the funeral home to here.

Rono, who'd been talking to one of his bankers, jumped up from behind his desk. "WHAAAAAAAAAT!"

"Lemmy's chasing 'em, let's go." Lemmy was the one Jenkins had killed with her throwing knife.

"GODDAMNIT I KNOW WHO DID THIS SHIT! What did Lemmy say?" Rono asked, flipping right the fuck out.

"They were masked. But he said he thinks he knows where they're heading."

"How the fuck's he know that?"

"Heard one of them shout when they were driving away some-thing about the grease plant. Then heard a language he knew was Asian."

Rono had a shocked look on his face. "It wasn't Casey, it was those motherfuckin' Changs."

This idiot's losing his fucking mind, Bancroft thought. "Yeah," he said. The Black Lotus in the area was run by a tight-knit group of cousins who collectively went by Chang. Originally from Hong Kong, they ran part of the grease retrieval business in the five bor-oughs, particularly among Asian cuisine restaurants. The Changs had carved out this niche due to the vacuum created when the FBI had arrested a number of the traditional Italian American mob-sters involved in this endeavor. But the Changs had their hands in other rackets, and had clashed with the VKs before.

Morning traffic clogged the roads and bridges into Manhattan, but the direction they were heading took them into a section of Queens called College Point. Bancroft took as many residential streets as he could. The fiction he'd created for Rono had to be plausible. He was taking the VK leader to an area that had been going to be converted into shops and housing overlooking Flushing Bay—until the private and public monies ran out. Now finished buildings sat next to partially completed husks.

The Changs' bayside facility was a fairly new fixture that turned culinary grease into biodiesel and bioburner fuel. They'd even gotten a green award from the local chamber of commerce. Bancroft parked some buildings down from the conversion plant among a stand of framed but hollow buildings.

"We'll sneak up on them," he said, getting out of his car.

Rono had his gun out, a heavy Colt Delta Elite 10mm. "These muthafuckahs gonna be sorry they fucked with me," he vowed.

Close up, creeping forward at his side, Bancroft let his leader pull ahead. Then suddenly he turned and buried his drawn knife in Rono's side. How poetic, to deal with the gang lord in the exact same manner as Rono'd dealt with Marcus Casey. He wanted to see the pain and fear on his face as the life left him. Only the feel was wrong, Bancroft immediately knew. The tip of the blade had connected solidly, but failed to penetrate as deeply as he'd expected.

"What the fuck!" Rono pulled away, his eyes wide as he glared at Bancroft. Blood, but not enough, blossomed on his shirt.

"You're fuckin' goosed?" Bancroft was so surprised that he forgot about the pistol in his other hand.

"Madam Nozinga told me true . . . like always," Rono gasped. He'd made sure to pull on his Kevlar woven undershirt that morning. Not as heavy and thick as a bulletproof vest, the material had nonetheless slowed the blade enough that it hadn't penetrated fatally.

Bancroft raised his gat, but Rono's big gun boomed first, echoing in the open rafters of the building's shell. The 10mm round tore into Bancroft's chest, dropping him where he stood. His pistol clattered to the dusty floor, crimson leaking down his sleeve.

"She couldn't see why," Rono said, stalking toward his downed second-in-command. "But she said it was some kind of double cross. Figured—" He coughed, red spray dotting his mouth. He was still upright, but would have to get attention for his wound. "Figured it would be one of the crew. You know, I kinda bet it'd be Dixon, he's greedy like that. And what with his gambling, he ain't never seen that kind of money together all at once. Get the big eyes and big ideas."

"Eat shit," Bancroft wheezed, bloody foam bubbling from his mouth. "I don't give—two fucks 'bout you—and your mutha-fuckin' fortune-teller. Casey's gonna get your jive ass anyway." He seemed to run out of any reserve he had, and his head fell back against a partially stuccoed brick wall.

Rono stood over him. "What the fuck does that mean—you working with Casey, HUH?" He ground his pistol's muzzle in Bancroft's gaping wound. "Answer me, you fuck!"

Bancroft groaned in agony, then his lips split in a bloody smile. "Tell 'em—to bury me—in my charcoal gray suit. Think you can—remember that—you punk-ass bitch?"

Rono thought his head was going to explode. He drove his gun deeper into Bancroft and screamed, "WHERE'S MY FUCKING MONEY!!"

Bancroft twisted and convulsed on the floor like a fish out of wa-ter, his face a study in pain. His shirt was drenched in red and his labored breathing was heavy and wet. Rono jumped up and shot him in the knee as Bancroft screamed. Rono walked over and crunched his heel onto the ruptured knee, cartilage and bone cracking and splintering. Bancroft cried out again, on the verge of passing out.

Rono, cupfuls of sweat pouring off him, bent over the dying man, again wincing from the knife wound.

"My money, you half-breed mongrel cocksucker. Who's got my cash?"

"You gonna have—a lot of explainin' to do. Hate to be—in your shoes right now. . . ." Bancroft started laughing and coughing.

"The fuck's so fuckin' funny?" The boss of the VKs shot him in the face, splattering his clothes. Rono straightened unsteadily and shot Bancroft three more times, demolishing his facial features. "No open casket for your punk ass." He shambled to the car and cursed. The keys were still in Bancroft's pocket.

He got back out of the car and returned to the body. He bent down, a hand slick with blood pressed to his side. Wrestling the keys free, he rose unsteadily to his feet and shot the dead man in the face one more time. Driving away, he used Bancroft's hands-free cell phone to call Low Rise.

"Get yo ass over to College Point." He gave him the location.

"What's up, Gul?"

"Pick up Brix's body. Bleach up the area. Take Spud with you."

"What?! Shit, what happened?"

"Shut the fuck up, nigga, and do as I tell you. Get the body," he repeated, "and sanitize the scene. And tell that crazy Arpage to get her nose out of the coke and meet me at my place. Tell her she's got some sewing to do."

"Yeah, I—"

Gulliver Rono clicked off and concentrated on driving and not passing out. He knew he'd have little time to recuperate. He had to get his shit back in a hurry or lose the whole goddamn deal with the Colombians. There was only going to be a limited amount of time to find that money. He'd toss Bancroft's apartment, but doubted there'd be anything there. For damned sure he was gonna make the ones who stole his money pay. But before he got patched up, there was another matter to take care of. He called Big Sally and told him to get over to Vera Hammond's apartment. "Slap that bitch around a little till I get there," he said.

"On it," the quiet, big man said.

"Wait," Rono said, phlegm in his voice. "She could be at Brix's place. Send a couple of soldiers there and you go to her place."

"Okay."

Big Sally didn't ask why Rono didn't sound like his usual self over the phone. He was not bothered by such nuances, and besides, his boss had a hair trigger these days. He liked assignments where he was told to do a specific thing, and that's what he was going to do now. The idea of terrorizing Vera Hammond excited the shit out of him. He liked how she looked, and he loved to see the fear in pretty women's faces when he got rough with them.

In the cab, however, it occurred to him he was gonna have to tell her something for her to let him up. He'd been to her apartment building once or twice to pick up Brix, but why would she buzz him up if Bancroft wasn't there? Rono hadn't told him what to say, and he wasn't about to call back and get cussed out for being stupid. He wanted to move up, and you didn't get to do that without showing what they called initiative. The cab stopped at her building, and Big Sally paid and got out. He walked up, worrying his bottom lip.

Given this time of the morning, people were exiting for work, and he was in luck and didn't have to come up with a convincing lie to tell her over the buzzer. A pudgy woman with a pudgy face was leaving and she smiled briefly at Big Sally as he nodded to her and caught the door before it clicked closed as she left. Because of his wound, he'd been wearing cargo shorts recently, but had put on regular pants over his bandages, a dress shirt, and his only blazer, figuring it would help with his camouflage. He was pleased with himself as he rode the elevator up to Vera's floor.

He knocked at her door and said, "Hey, Vera, it's Big Sally, Brix sent me to get you. It's urgent." He was proud he sounded so professional. The ho wouldn't know what was coming.

On the other side of the door, Vera Hammond's breath caught in her throat when she heard Big Sally's words. She knew he was lying, knew his being here meant Brix was either dead or being worked over.

"Hold on, be right there," she called back. She'd been pacing back and forth in the living room nervously for the past hour when she didn't hear from Brix by half past. She was in her red mini and the patent leather high heels that always turned her lover on. She'd planned to do him atop Rono's desk later to celebrate. But now she had to be resourceful to escape. Hers was a modern building, so there was no fire escape, and the only way in or out was the front door. But if she let Big Sally in, she would be trapped for sure.

Striding to a kitchen cabinet, she pulled out a small container of French roast coffee and opened it. Rooting around in the grounds, she pulled out a flash drive sealed in a plastic Baggie. Grabbing her purse, she stuffed the drive inside, then steeled herself, yanked open the front door, and stepped into the hallway, banging the door shut behind her.

This took Big Sally by surprise. He glared at her, open-mouthed.

"Let's go," she said boldly, striding for the elevator.

"Yeah, but—," he began, coming after her. She pushed the button for the car.

"No time to waste, right?" The elevator was busy at this hour and the door opened on several tenants on their way to the ground floor. Hammond stepped partway in, Big Sally right behind her. She smiled at one of her neighbors, a smallish man she'd seen before. He smiled back, and she put a hand on his crotch.

"Hi," she enthused huskily.

The man looked shocked and extremely happy at the same time. "Uh, hey—," he managed.

Hammond grabbed his shoulders, spun him around, and shoved him into the larger man. The other occupants reacted as the doors began to close on Big Sally's frame. He stumbled backward and threw the smaller man out of his way. Hammond put a spike heel into the enforcer's thigh, which she knew was tender because Bancroft had told her about the wound.

"Bitch!" he screamed, lunging for her. But the people in the elevator were panicking now, and a heavy, blue-jowled man with glasses and an expensive suit got between Big Sally and his target. They tangled as Hammond pounded for the fire stairs at the other end of the hallway.

Big Sally had his ivory-handled Colt out and clubbed the blue-jowled man to the floor. "Get back here, bitch!" He let off a shot that punctured a fire extinguisher on the wall next to the exit door. Foam and white mist hissed out as the door banged open and Hammond went through. Big Sally was in motion. Though he could walk pretty evenly with his healing wound, the stress of trying to run, particularly given the kick to his thigh, had him moving in more of a loping gait.

In the stairwell, Hammond paused long enough to slip off her heels and stuff them in her purse as she continued her descent. She could make better time barefoot, and as she went she heard the big man lumbering after her. He kept yelling, but from the echo she knew she was getting closer to the ground floor than he to her. Another shot rang out, but the bullet went wild, ricocheting off the metal stairs before embedding itself in the wall. She pushed the crash bar on the door that let her out in the lobby and hurried through, scared but determined.

She slipped on the waxed floor, sliding on her butt toward the front door. Her soles hit the glass and she was up and out on the street, running full bore for the first cab she saw.

By the time Big Sally huffed into the lobby area, Vera Hammond was gone. He swore and wiped sweat from his face with his large hand as he lurched around, unsure of what to do and dreading the reprimand that was sure to come from Rono.

Sirens wailed in the distance and Big Sally walked swiftly as he could away from the building. He vowed to get Bancroft's bitch for clowning him and getting away. Oh, he'd make her eyes go really wide when he got ahold of her. Really wide and white, like goddamn china saucers.

16

In a sparse apartment atop an empty storefront among a row of foreclosed properties in East Harlem, Casey and Champa monitored the early afternoon news on radio and a small HD TV with rabbit ears. After their score, they'd dumped the station wagon several miles from the funeral home. The four had changed into street clothes, then burned their overalls and gloves in an empty metal barrel Munoz had secured for that purpose. They transferred the cash equally to four duffel bags, minus Munoz's expenses and Bancroft's end. The four then walked several blocks over from different directions and took another car Walker had parked in a residential neighborhood.

In the car, Casey had said, "I wish you and your kids the best, Jupiter."

"You know you ought to take your share and get out too, Marcus. Why put yourself through all this?" Unsaid, Casey knew she foresaw him sharing Rono's fate.

"I can't see my way to doing anything else, Jupiter. It's not like

I'm gonna open a juice bar or whatnot." He wasn't sure he was gonna live too much longer anyway, but the course of his life had been set way before today.

"It's your world, homie. Don't let the treachery get to you," Jenkins said.

Walker had pulled up to Jenkins's car. She gave Casey a hug, and gave a farewell salute to the other two. She tossed her duffel bag, containing more than one and a half million dollars, into the trunk, then drove off. She'd already taken her children out of school, and would pick them up at a friend's place. Casey had known better than to ask where she was heading.

Walker then drove the car out to the Green Acres Mall in Valley Stream, near the border of Queens. The three wiped down the sedan and left the keys in the ignition. From the mall they walked to the nearby Long Island railroad station.

"Okay, you two, nice working with professionals." Walker stuck out his fist and Champa gave him a pound, as did Casey.

"You're not going on vacation, are you?" Casey asked.

What might have been a smile flitted across Walker's face. "Not yet." He nodded at Casey and, shouldering his duffel bag, took the stairs up to his train.

Casey and Munoz came back into the city to the empty apartment Shinzo had prepared for them. There was nothing about the robbery on TV. Nor was there any news about Gulliver Rono's body being found yet. Casey didn't necessarily give that any meaning, though each knew that if Brixton was going to make a bold move, he'd want Rono to be on display to send the signal to any doubters. However, the idea of someone else coming in and taking care of Casey's business—what had kept him going in the joint for two decades—was starting to fuck with his head.

"What you think?" Munoz asked Casey as he unwrapped a cold cut sandwich purchased from an Asian deli.

"I think it ain't a good idea to start asking every sonofabitch we know if that bastard's dead." Casey had called Shinzo already, but hadn't heard back from him. He stood and paced the small room. The more he thought about it, the more he hoped that Bancroft had failed. He still relished the idea that Rono would die at his hands.

Munoz bit into his sandwich, chewed a huge mouthful, then swallowed. "Let me ask you this: if Bancroft was successful, then what? Would you still sit back and let him run the VKs?"

Casey just looked at him while opening a bottle of juice, but didn't take a drink.

Munoz continued. "Oh, I'm sure if Rono is dead, you'd want to be satisfied, I guess is the word. Like letting Bancroft take out fools loyal to Rono. But then"—he pointed his sandwich at Casey—"the problem would come up that ol' silver head couldn't have you running around going all Frank Castle on him, icing the deserving and whatnot. What kind of example would that set for the troops that he was the new top dog? Plus, you might take out somebody he would find useful, even if he'd been riding Rono's jock."

Casey had walked to the window while Champa was talking, and now looked out at the street below. "Very considerate of you to be contemplating my welfare, Champa."

He shrugged and said, "Always try to see the big picture." He ate more of his sandwich and drank his iced coffee.

Casey glanced at his bag of Fritos and chicken salad sandwich, but he couldn't eat. He was too worked up, even though he'd tried to be cool about this moment. If Bancroft had killed Rono, that destroyed the goal that had sustained him for twenty years. Now what would he do? Take out Bancroft? He couldn't work up any enthusiasm for the idea. But hadn't Mack D warned him to prepare for the unexpected? He drank some of his juice, his stomach churning. *You'd think after twenty years of planning, I'd have already worked out this shit,* he thought. Not knowing what else to do until he got word about Rono, Casey walked over to the bags of money, staring at them.

"You know," Champa said, drawing his pistol and laying it on the card table, "if I was a temperamental nigga 'bout you havin' eyes for Carla, my mitts on this piece might make you real nervous right about now."

Casey turned and regarded Champa, annoyed and also aware that he'd left his own gat on the table, now several feet away. "Yeah, and?"

Champa patted the barrel of his gun, which was pointing away from Casey—at the moment. "In fact, one could suppose that I brought you in on this job, and then planned to cap yo' ass after the deal was done, doubling my share and taking care of the competition in one stroke."

Casey mulled this over—he couldn't really see Champa doing this, but put a woman between two men, and all kinds of crazy shit could go down. He didn't say anything—if it was cool, it was cool. If it wasn't, well, he'd only dig his hole deeper. He just stared at Champa until the other man's face broke out in a broad smile.

"Relax, nigga, I'm just fuckin' with ya. What you and Carla do is you and Carla's business, ain't none of mine." His expression turned serious. "In fact, the two of you have my blessing. Lord knows I put her through enough hell while we was together—you just make sure you treat her right, you hear?" He tapped the butt of his 9mm. "Otherwise you an' me'll be having an altogether different conversation."

Casey stared at him for a few more seconds, then shook his head. "You a funny nigga, Champa—like I don't have enough shit comin' down on me right now, I gotta put up with you playin' Dr. Jekyll and Mr. Hyde too?"

Champa shrugged. "You gonna eat that?" He pointed at Casey's unopened chicken salad sandwich. An irritated Casey whipped it at him hard.

. . .

Vera Hammond finally relaxed and stopped looking out the curtained window every few minutes. Confident that she was safe for now, she reviewed her situation. Whether what she and Brix Bancroft had was love was not a debate she was going to have at the moment. On her own since fourteen, she'd had her share of relationships go bad. Every time she'd started over, and would do so now.

The apartment she'd fled to was one Hammond kept under another name, across the river in Union City, New Jersey. After getting away from Big Sally, she'd hid here to lay low and plot out her next steps. Again, she imagined Bancroft might still be alive and being worked over by Rono right now. But more likely he was dead and gone. Since she hadn't told her lover about this place, she assumed she had a few days, maybe even a week or so to get her shit together. Rono would put soldiers and money on the street to ascertain her whereabouts. She could run, go to Chicago, or return to the West Coast.

Rono had connects in Chi-Town, but not much of anything in Southern California. Still, he was a vindictive cocksucker, and would expend the effort to chill her just to close matters out with Brix. Or worse, he'd try and force her to be his woman, and she would not abide such a disgusting situation. He'd wind up killing her anyway or she him, and she'd have to be on the run once more. But maybe, she reasoned, sipping a glass of vodka to help her focus, she should only look like she was running, but really start working to bring Rono down.

Notions of revenge didn't motivate Hammond. She felt bad that Bancroft was probably dead, but this was about her future now. Rono was a limited sort. Marcus Casey, at least from what she'd heard about him, might be something different. He'd been under Rono's radar since getting out of prison, but neither Rono nor Brix felt that was going to last very long.

Legs crossed in her stylish print skirt, sitting and sipping her joy juice as if she were about to head out for a shopping trip on Fifth Avenue, Hammond decided to reach out to Crush Casey. Not only did she have knowledge of Gulliver Rono's operations, but she had an ace to play as well. Brix Bancroft had kept a video diary of the misdeeds he'd done in the service of the Vicetown Kings. He'd made the running account in the event he was arrested and could work a deal if he provided this explosive eyewitness testimony. With her help he'd compiled these snippets onto a single flash drive and destroyed any other versions of the data. That same flash drive was now securely nestled in Hammond's purse, and wouldn't be leaving her person any time soon, unless it was to broker a deal for her safety.

What Brix did in terms of his confessions certainly spoke to how he'd come to trust her, but she quickly shook off such sentimentality. After all, wouldn't Brix be about business if she was the one lying cold and alone somewhere? And right now, the only ass she had to worry about was her own. It would be better to come at Casey straight, lay out what she had in mind and how it would benefit both of them. Then get back at the motherfucker who'd put him away and killed her lover. But that meant, she concluded as she finished her vodka, she'd have to confirm what had happened to Brix. It would mean exposing herself, but not so much that she'd get her head chopped off. At least she hoped not.

Hammond had two disposable cell phones, and texted Arpage Anson on one of them. The former veterinarian now worked as a sales and public relations rep for a consortium of discount dentists who went under the banner of Diamond Brite, a cuddly anthropomorphic polar bear in a bowler holding a big toothbrush for their logo. She roomed with Monica Kyle, the girlfriend of VK enforcer Low Rise. Anson and Hammond had known each other from their club days, and she'd indicated she was throwing her luck behind

Brix. After sending the text, the handsome woman decided she'd wait until she heard from Anson rather than ask around too much.

Arpage Anson was busy sewing up Gulliver Rono's knife wound in his penthouse overlooking the Hudson. He was lying on his leather couch, a doubled bedsheet underneath him to soak up blood and other body fluids. Anson sat on the coffee table, tending to him. She'd had him inhale a diluted solution of isoflurane, a horse tranquilizer, in a handkerchief to stop him from squirming around. But he was consumed with anger and seemingly oblivious to physical discomfort.

"I shoulda bled that sonofabitch traitor," Rono admonished himself. "Take the knife he meant for me and done up his pretty face. He'da talked then." He took a deep inhale on the handkerchief. "This is some good shit, Arpage."

"Just lay still, Gul. I'm almost done."

Rono's face clouded with deviousness. "You got them scalpels and saws and all that?"

"They took my license, Gul, you know that," she said, cinching her stitching.

"But you can get 'em again, can'tcha?"

"What you getting at?" She recleansed the wound in preparation to apply gauze and tape.

"Just figuring two and two, that Brix wasn't in on this attempt at usurping by himself." Rono wasn't much of a reader, but did enjoy those paperbacks of sword and sorcery tales like Conan the Barbarian and Thongor, where such terms as "usurper" and "berserker" were used with regularity.

With the anesthesia calming him a bit, he observed, "I need to be more centered. Can't get carried away like I did this morning."

He took another sniff. "Already got eyes out for that highbrow twist Vera. She got away from that dumb ape Big Sally." He smiled lopsided at her. "You two are friends, right?"

"We used to run together now and then back in the day. But that don't mean shit." Her hands steady, she applied the tape.

"But you could call around and see if you can get in touch with her. Ask her over, friendly like. Maybe go out for a drink." He put his hand around her wrist, loose, but she knew he could apply pressure at any moment. "How would that be?"

"The fuck I care happens to that bitch." She began packing up her supplies. She kept them in a Diamond Brite sales case replete with the sunny polar bear logo. "But she's not stupid, Gul. I get all girly-girl with her at a time when she knows you got people out scoping for her, she's gonna be suspicious."

Rono sat up, considering this. "I know that, bitch. Tell her you're concerned for her. Tell her you heard some street chatter that she mighta been in on this, but she's gotta, you know, convince me she didn't have anything to do with it."

"You want me to lure her to someplace where you can go all Hannibal Lecter on her?"

Rono raised his hands. "If she's innocent, I can find out quick. Like her corpse of a boyfriend, I'm sure she can't stand to let anything happen to that model's mug of hers. A couple of swipes of the scalpel across the face, and she'll blubber like a baby. 'Cause somebody sure as fuck got my money, and I'ma get it back on the rilla."

Anson doubted Hammond would fold so easily. And if she was in on the snatch, wouldn't she be long in the wind right now? "I'll see what I can do."

"That's what I'm talking about." He crossed to a desk and peeled off some bills from a wad he'd plucked out of a drawer, put four one-hundred-dollar bills on the coffee table. "Thanks, huh?" He walked off to his bedroom, the handkerchief to his nose. Turning on his plasma-screen TV, he flopped onto the bed, sitting against the headboard. Fascinated, he watched a program about a model airplane flying competition.

Anson stepped out of the penthouse and checked her cell phone in her purse. She'd turned it off, and when it lit, she saw she had a text from Vera in her message box. She instantly felt sick and wondered if she was going to get caught in some cross fire. She started to text Vera back on her way to the elevator. As she did so, she looked up as the doors opened on Low Rise and Big Sally getting out. The big man was still limping from his excursion chasing Vera Hammond.

She blinked hard because she still had her phone in her hand, the screen tilted down as the two men approached.

"How's Rono?" Low Rise asked.

"The patient will survive," she said, trying to be as natural as possible while letting the hand holding her phone fall to her side.

"You crack me up, Arpage." He and Big Sally moved past and through the double doors of the penthouse. Big Sally, looking contrite, grunted.

In the elevator, Anson put her phone away. She could feel sweat breaking out under her clothes. Back on the street, she texted Hammond about what happened and reluctantly set a meet for later that day. When Anson returned home, she wrote down the numbers she needed for business and then methodically disassembled her cell. She was glad her roommate had apparently worked one of her so-called "extra shows" after grinding it out at Woodside's last night. When she first came back, she had peeped into her room, and saw the girl was out cold, her fluorescent orange wig atop one of the bedposts.

Anson flushed smaller pieces of her cell phone down the toilet, then went out to buy a prepaid one. The former veterinarian was crystal clear on her motivations. Sure, she and Hammond were friends, but this was about her getting ahead. Now maybe

Hammond had the balls and desire to break off a piece of the VKs for herself, but that wasn't what Anson wanted. Vera's old man, who was now probably chopped up and scattered over parts of the city, had failed to take out Rono. How much money was stolen Anson didn't know, but she had the good sense not to press Rono about it when she'd come over to his place. He was wound up tight then, seething about Bancroft's betrayal and the shipment getting ripped off.

Anson was willing to take a chance and get in good with Hammond if she could, since her girlfriend might just know who took the money, and that'd be a start. That didn't mean it was going to be easy getting any part of the score, but it was a damn sight better than fronting for a bunch of second-rate tooth doctors more whacked out on their anesthetics than their patients. And if things got sticky, if she let slip a hint to her roommate and got Rono on her own ass, she'd give up Hammond and anybody else double quick to save herself.

Arpage Anson had no delusions about what she'd do to make sure she survived. Only, with another birthday having come and gone not more than three weeks ago, she'd like to do some of that surviving in style.

17

This broad can be trusted?" Casey asked.

Champa's eyebrows rose. "Your guess is as good as mine. She hasn't given us up to Rono yet, otherwise there'd be a huge muthafuckin' bounty on our heads."

"Whaddya mean 'us,' round eyes?" Casey joked.

"True dat," he admitted. A day had gone by since their heist, and earlier that morning Vera Hammond had gotten in touch with Shinzo, who'd confirmed that her boyfriend Brix Bancroft had failed in his attempt to unseat Rono, and paid with his life. She'd laid out some of her proposed deal to Champa, and had said she would get back in touch after she conducted more of her due diligence. "She certainly wasn't all teary and sniveling about how she had to pay Rono back for what he'd done."

"Nothing wrong with wanting revenge," Casey said.

"For sure. I'm saying she comes across as a cold-eyed chick who's about getting even, but also 'bout getting right too. This doesn't smell like a setup to me. Plus Shinzo's checking on her."

"Depending on what he says, no sense in me being shy. When she gets back in touch, we both meet with her."

"Bet," the other man said. The two knocked fists and parted company. Champa headed downtown, and Casey reviewed where matters stood. He was juggling several balls, grenades really. One slip, and it would all blow up under him. There was no choice but to pull this off, or be destroyed in the attempt.

Rono was going to be on alert, but he'd be hella anxious to get the money back. Not simply a matter of pride, Rono also had to show his future snowflake partners that he was a competent leader. Casey wanted to know more about the Colombians, hence another reason to talk with Vera Hammond. What he didn't want was to finally eliminate Rono, then have this bunch breathing down his neck and inherit his predecessor's obligations. The Colombians might be gearing up to remove Rono for mismanagement anyway, and wouldn't discriminate between one nigga in the top seat and another.

Being a goddamn gang boss in this here twenty-first century ain't nobody's idea of fun, so why do I want it so bad? Casey had enough money now so that he and Carla could go away and live, not exactly like a king and queen, but well enough. Neither of them had extravagant tastes. Still, he had certain weaknesses. What it all came down to was that the Vicetown Kings were the only thing that Casey could call his own. He'd built them up from a loose collection of dope slangers and hustlers to an organization spread across the U.S.—a true force to be reckoned with in the underworld. *And I'll be goddamned if I'm just gonna stand by and watch some no-account nigga like Rono take apart everything I put together.*

Checking his watch, he calculated the time to take care of an errand before keeping his appointment with Mal Yurik. It was definitely time to order up some distinctive attire. He did have a thing for quality threads—not a department store full of 'em, but a few choice pieces hanging in his closet. In a way, the threads symbolized the old days, but he hoped they also foretold what was to come.

If nothing else, I'll have a good-looking suit to be buried in, he noted sagely as he descended into the subway.

Rono's brows furrowed, the scar on his head pulsing in time with his ill-concealed anger. He resisted the impulse to snort more of the shit that crazy twist Anson had introduced him to. Refocusing, he asked, "Tell me again, Bark?"

The VK soldier had gotten his nickname because of his bulldog-like face. Right now that face was puffed out and purple on one side where he'd been butted by a semiauto shotgun held by one of the thieves. The injury had given him a reccurring dull headache, and being sweated by his gang leader wasn't helping his recovery either. He shifted on his battered leather couch and squinted in the afternoon sunlight.

The two sat across from each other in Bark's apartment on 153rd Street, not far from Rucker Park at 155th and Eighth Avenue where various basketball tournaments were held. Rather than call in his soldiers who had been on the money convoy, Rono had decided to drop in on a few out of the blue see if he could catch them slipping. A good general was always in the field, he'd determined. That, and he had a huge mad-on to find out anything about who'd lifted his fuckin' chedda.

"Like I said, Gul, the first thing I know is the lead car went sideways blocking us and we crashed into the back end. There was a boom from a gun up front, we jumped out with our heaters blazin' when them steppers released that funny gas, makin' us all loopy as hell."

This was consistent with what the other soljahs had told him or what had been reported by the ones he had out hunting down his benjamins. The Colombians weren't sweating him directly about the theft—yet. But he knew he better show he could handle his shit. If he didn't get those funds back, they might not be so eager to continue doing business with the VKs.

He continued interrogating Bark. "So at no time do these hitters give up a name, calling out to the other or something like that?"

"Not a fucking thing, Gul. Leastways not while I was conscious, you know. They had their thing down, man. Not a wasted step among them. Shit was military."

"Why'd the front car swerve when it did? You said the shot happened afterward, then the gas grenades were launched."

Bark shrugged his shoulder. That made his face hurt. "Fuck if I know. Ask Tommy. He musta seen something."

"Nigga, don't you worry about what I intend to do," Rono growled.

"I ain't about trying to tell you how to run shit, Gul," Bark said, hunching his shoulders protectively.

Rono stood and gently patted Bark's face, making him wince. "Get yourself some rest. I want you back in rotation quick, ya feel me? You got your duties, and you gotta be keeping your ears open for my loot."

"Of course, Gul. I understand."

"I know you fuckin' do," the gang lord said gravely. As he left the apartment, it flashed on him he better see what Marcus Casey was up to as well. This would spread his forces thin, but he had no choice. Casey had been off the goddamn map since getting out and that was unnatural.

He stopped for a moment, thinking things through. *Is it possible that muthafuckin' Casey hit me?* Shaking his head, he chuckled at the notion. *That broken-down punk might be good at beatin' on a coupla crackers in the 'hood, but even he couldn't put together somethin' like that a week after getting sprung. Naw, someone else lifted my paper, and I'm gonna put a world of hurt on 'em when I find who done it.*

Double-parked outside was the Hummer, driven by one of his enforcers called Jojoe. Rono had picked him today because he was crafty. Of course, after the Bancroft incident, he'd have to keep an eye on this ambitious bastard too. *It's getting hard out here for a gang lord,* Rono lamented.

Jojoe was a muscular six-three, had a couple of years of college under his belt, and liked to do the *New York Times* crossword puzzle almost as much as he liked three-ways with a mother and grown-daughter combo he dated. He put aside the folded newspaper at seeing Rono exit the building. He'd been leaning against the vehicle's fender and straightened up.

"Where to now?"

Rono had a foot up on the Hummer's running board. "You know Shinzo Becker?"

"I know who he is, yeah."

Both got inside the vehicle. "He's got a club on Flatbush in Brooklyn. You go over there tonight and scope it out. Don't do nothing but observe, understand?"

"What'm I looking for?"

"Right now, anything. Hell, Crush Casey might show his punk face there. I know they stayed in touch while he was locked up."

Jojoe pulled out into traffic. "You want me to take out Casey, why don't I just go find him directly?"

Rono shook a few drops of isoflurane from a canister into his handkerchief and inhaled. "'Cause you start asking around 'bout him, he'll go invisible on me for sure." Now he regretted not having him killed the minute he set foot outside. Of course, he'd tried to have his cap peeled back several times while he was inside, but that tenacious nigga hadn't had the decency to lay down and die. On one level, Rono still regarded Casey as washed up, not a threat. But there was also the nagging possibility that if he wasn't killed, eventually he'd come after Rono.

Jojoe shrugged. "I know how to make what you call discreet inquiries." He was eager to move up, get his stripes. He took out Casey, Rono would have to recognize his initiative.

Rono gestured with the handkerchief in his hand like some long-ago earl of the highlands. "Okay. Discreet like a muthafuckah for sure, but yeah, you go on the hunt for Crush." He paused and added, "Take Jai on this with you. He's looking to move up too. Let's see if he hasn't gone soft from man-handling them bitches all the time. 'Cause frankly," he snickered, "I think that ball buster Kelta is tougher than him."

Jojoe chuckled as well, but turned serious soon enough. "But I'm in charge," he said.

"Yeah, nigga, you in charge, so don't disappoint me." Rono sat back, enveloped in the relaxing cloud moving across the top of his brain. He knew he had to be careful with this drug, which he found out was used on animals. But he liked the symbolism of that, having imagined himself as the king lion for years. This shit would put him out if he used too much, but he liked the drowsy, numbing effect the anesthetic had on him and that it didn't last too long, just enough to dull the pain in his side and take the edge off, but not leave him foggy or dull. He seemed to emerge from his restful state with renewed clarity as to his next moves.

Rono said, "Speaking of our Asian pardners, take me to Phan's playpen, Jojoe. Call her and tell her to have a couple of those slant-eyed curlies ready. I gotta relax. Fact, when you drop me off there, you take Jai and go on the prowl for Casey straightaway."

"No problem," the other man answered, dialing Grace Phan on the hands-free.

A shiver went though Gulliver Rono. Whether it was a side effect of the isoflurane or an impulse of what was to come, he couldn't say. Thereafter he rode along in bliss.

A few miles away, Low Rise and Big Sally intercepted Tommy Dixon as he exited an all-night card game in Brooklyn. Dixon was a hard-core poker player, and could often be found making the rounds of underground games. He'd had a good night, and was smiling as he came up into the light from the unmarked set of rooms below the sidewalk, his pockets heavier by six Gs. The bruise Jupiter Jenkins had left on the side of his face had turned black and blue, darker than his skin.

"Yo, man, we been lookin' for your funky ass half the damn night. Why didn't you answer your cell, nigga?" Low Rise complained as Dixon saw them coming.

"I keep my celly off so I'm not distracted," he said. Big Sally loomed close on one side of the man. "Them cards was talkin' to me."

"The only distraction you should be worried about is Rono and his money," Low Rise said.

"'Course I'm worried," Dixon answered. "What's good for the boss is good for all of us, right?"

There was a hum in the pocket of Big Sally's jacket and he removed an iPhone. He looked at a text message on it and showed it to his partner.

Low Rise told Dixon, "Rono wants to know what made you stop the lead car you were driving when y'all were coming in from the airport."

Dixon felt his skin tingle with heat at the question, but remained calm, imagining he was back at the tables, running a bluff on another player. "Saw one of those punks on the roof with a bazooka or some shit." He'd practiced his answer over and over, until even he almost believed it.

"Yeah?" Big Sally said quizzically.

"On the reezie," Dixon responded. "One of them peeped up and I knew right away something was goin' down. I hit the brakes, the 'Lade went cockeyed, and I got out ready to blast. Only they shot those damn canisters with the goofy gas. At the same time, Goldie was gettin' out and took one in the grille." The three were standing next to the steps going down to where the game had been. The remaining players had exited as well. One glanced at Dixon momentarily, then kept walking.

"How come Goldie didn't have his piece out?" Low Rise asked. "Rono's snitch inside the department says the boy was dead on scene with his gat still in its rig on his belt."

"Fuck I know, man—mad shit was going down. Goldie wasn't always the coolest head. Maybe he panicked."

"That right?" Low Rise said.

When he'd shot Bobby Goldwyn in the face, Dixon had had the good sense to open the passenger door so he'd fall out of the SUV. His blood was splattered on the vehicle's interior, but he doubted Rono would be going back to his inside man to get the forensics report. At least he hoped not. Still, he had to give them somewhere else to sniff.

"What about Brix's old lady? She might have something to say. They were tight."

"She's in the weeds right now. But we'll get her. No ho's gonna outfox us."

Casey was on the phone with Omar Atkins as he exited the subway. He'd already told Atkins about Bancroft's demise, and how he was going for broke himself. "Time to get on the grind, man," Casey said. "You need to get your peeps together and take care of that little job I laid out for you."

"'Bout goddamn time," Atkins replied. "I'm tired of chasing after pennies like some rookie. I'm muthafuckin' due too. By the way, there's a sideshow goin' on in town tonight out in Queens. You wanna roll?"

"Nigga, let me be the one that's creative," Casey jibed.

"My man, this is about strengthening our hand for the surge," Omar said seriously. "Trust me on this and bring your checkbook."

"Okay, we'll see," Casey said, still dubious. They set a time.

Casey saw he'd received a text from Kenny Saunders. He'd done his research on Lomax and wanted to talk, teasing Casey with a line about Lomax having once been a cop. Casey nodded at this as he arrived at the tailor's shop. It fit Lomax's style—to a point.

The Old World–style wooden sign still hanging over the front door announced YURIK'S QUALITY MEN'S TAILORING. In the window were fashionable suits and sport coats, alongside a display of shirts and ties. He stepped inside, the small metal bell attached to the door tinkling.

"Very good, Colonel," a handsome older woman with immaculately coiffed white hair and squared shoulders told a large-bodied man holding a felt hat and standing at the front counter. She made a final notation in a carbon-copy receipt book and handed the customer his copy. "Your suits will be ready in three weeks or possibly a little less."

"Thank you," the man said in an accent Casey knew was African, but wasn't sure which country. "Do let me know." The colonel turned, a stern-faced dark man with dual parallel tracks of scars on one cheek. Nodding slightly to the newcomer, he put on his hat, and exited.

"Mr. Casey, welcome back." She held out a hand bedecked with heavy rings. A row of bracelets tinkled softly on her sinewy arm.

"Mrs. Stockpool. Looking proper as always." He shook her hand.

"Thank you, kind sir. Please, take a seat. Mal will be right with you. He had to take a call in the back. Can I get you anything? Fresh guava juice, perhaps?"

"Yes, ma'am, thank you."

As Casey sat in a comfortable chair near a table covered with bolts of various fabrics, Fulson and McCormick focused on a particular monitor among several others in a small, spare office several blocks from the tailor's shop. They watched the scarred man in the felt hat step to the curb to hail a taxi.

"You think Colonel Achebe knows Casey?" McCormick asked his colleague. He was in rolled-up shirtsleeves, his tie loosened around his neck. The high-rise office they were in was well lit and pleasantly cool from efficient air-conditioning.

Fulson shook his head. "Doubtful. They certainly didn't spend any time together just now in Yurik's place."

"Could just mean they're being cautious, not wanting to say anything in front of the suit maker."

Fulson pointed out, "Nah, Yurik's known for being a man of discretion. His clientele ranges from CEOs to musicians to the likes of these two gents. Many paths have crossed in that shop over the decades, and all sorts of conversations have taken place among individuals you'd think wouldn't have anything to do with one another."

"How come you're so damn versed in the doings of Mal Yurik?"

"Because, old stick," Fulson answered, "not only did I thoroughly read my predecessor's files, but I also did a personal exit interview with the man. And don't forget our Mr. Lomax was in plainclothes, safes and lofts squad first, then homicide detail, before he went over to the parole department. He tried for years to get a bug inside the shop, but Yurik has his business swept regularly." Which was why these men were restricted to external surveillance, tapping into closed-circuit traffic cameras.

Since both had read the material their researchers had compiled on the Colombian cartel, Fulson didn't have to add the reason they were watching the tailor's shop. They knew that several members of the drug empire liked to dress well, and a reference for Yurik had come up in some of the digging.

McCormick indicated the monitor displaying Yurik's shop. "What do you think?"

"Let's at least see if anyone else of interest shows up while

Casey gets his fitting," Fulson said. "After all, fashion is tempo-rary, but style is forever. Or something like that."

"I like it how you're always dropping your little bon mots."

"Lord knows I try," Fulson said dryly.

"You figure Munoz and Casey for the takedown the other day?"

"I like 'em for it just fine."

"If it was VK funds, was it a shot at the Colombian deal or Rono himself?"

Fulson stared at the screen. From the downward angle of their spycam, he watched Casey through the shop window as he talked with the stoop-shouldered Yurik, pointing at a swath of cloth the old man held. Finally he answered, "I believe Crush Casey has had twenty years to hone his plans, and is hell-bent on making 'em hap-pen. And too bad for any sorry motherfucker who gets in his way." He paused. "And he intends to look good as he does so."

Both men laughed heartily, then returned to their surveillance.

Inside the tailor's shop, Casey ordered a dark gray pinstripe, a blue serge, and a three-piece suit in a color called Cary Grant black. The vest on this one and the jackets of the other two suits included hidden pockets for a few pieces of equipment Casey had obtained from Kenny. He also procured a blazer and several shirts and ties by Hugo Boss, Dolce & Gabbana, and, for old times' sake, Yves Saint Laurent.

"Lovely choices, Mr. Casey. So glad you retained your sense of understatement," Yurik said as he handed several of the shirt-and-tie combos to an assistant.

"You're the best, Mal." He counted out stacks of hundreds on a glass countertop. Mrs. Stockpool hovered nearby, busy rearrang-ing a row of handkerchiefs at the end of the counter. Casey smiled inwardly. The old calculator would know if he was short a quarter, and wouldn't be shy about calling him on it.

Yurik held his bony fingers on the cloth tape measure draped around his neck. "Time hasn't seemed to mark you, young man, but my hands hurt more every day, and the knees ache whether it's rainy or sunny." He sighed. "Enough prattling. Shall I have your goods delivered?"

"Yes, sir." He gave instructions for the suits to be delivered to the Roosevelt. He knew Gulliver Rono didn't frequent Yurik's shop nor did any of his captains or lieutenants. From what he'd heard, this establishment was on Rono's banned list, given Casey's association with Yurik. The only reason he hadn't burned it down was because of the master tailor's other clients, who walked both sides of the line. Rono didn't need to bring down that kind of grief on himself.

"I do hope you'll be around for future business, Crush," Yurik said as Casey's disposable cell chimed. He didn't answer it.

"I intend to be, Mr. Yurik."

"Good to hear. Wouldn't want my competition to be getting your trade."

"No chance. Nobody can beat you, Mal."

"Be well, sir." He shook Casey's hand.

Outside he didn't recognize the number on his disposable cell, but hit redial. The other end clicked on.

"Crush," a female voice said.

"Who this?"

"Charlotte," the P. J. Woodside's bartender answered.

"What up, girl?"

"Baybay found out something you might want to know."

"That right?"

"Rono showed up the other night to let everyone know he wasn't feelin' no pain, no strain. I wasn't workin', but she was. Shame what happened to Brix, huh?"

"Goddamn shame. Everybody knows he's dead?"

"Word got around the club that he would no longer be making

appearances. That's how it was phrased. Jai's already angling for his job, ya know?"

"Baybay tell you this?"

"Naturally," the bartender went on. "Jai made sure he was on-site. Laughing at Rono's jokes and generally burying his nose deep in that punk's ass."

Casey said, "Good for both of them."

"Knew you'd be pleased. Talk soon." She severed the call.

Casey pondered the implications of what Charlotte had told him. Certainly Rono making such a public appearance meant he was playin' the loss of his bankroll cool, keepin' up appearances. But every hour that went by without a lead on where his paper had vanished would doubtless make him more anxious and more impatient to find it. Casey intended to exploit that weakness to the very end of Rono's life.

Yeah, all the way to the end, he reminded himself as he got Kenny Saunders on the phone and told him he'd drop by later to go over what he'd dug up on Lomax. He then tossed the burner down the gutter. This was no time to be getting sloppy.

18

Omar Atkins sat in a silver Escalade across the street from a bustling restaurant in Chinatown. With him were two other freelancers, a con man known on the streets as Blue, and a huge mountain of muscle named Quick. Both were known and trusted by Omar, and both were more than ready to put in some work. The restaurant they were casing was a confirmed hangout for members of the Black Lotus.

Omar drained his soda and belched. "'Kay, let's go over it one more time. With masks on and guns out, we go in. Quick, you cover the customers and make sure no one tries to be a goddamn hero. Blue, you watch the door—anyone comes in, you make sure they're stopped. I take the register and deliver the message. We should be in and out in ninety seconds. And remember—we ain't out for blood, but if any of these slant-eyes tries anything, you put 'em down, double-quick. Any questions?"

The two other men shook their heads.

"Both of you goosed?"

Two silent nods answered his question. Their identical baggy, black hoodies and sweatpants hid both their bulletproof vests and their guns.

"Then let's do it to it." Omar checked the action on his SIG SAUER .40 caliber, making sure a round was under the hammer, and waited for the others to check their pieces and give him the high sign. When everyone was ready, they got out of the car, leaving it running with the doors locked. Omar had the remote door lock in his pocket, so they could get back in and bounce quickly when everything was said and done.

Crossing the street, they paused at the restaurant's entryway, set in a small alcove, to pull the ski masks down over their faces, then stormed into the building.

Typical Chinese restaurant excess greeted them, with calligraphied paper lanterns hanging over about a dozen tables and a half-dozen booths, all occupied. The place was a riot of color, with red predominating, and just about everything else, from the window frames to the placemats, edged in gold.

"Nobody muthafuckin' move!" Omar shouted as he rushed the maître d's station. The slim man on the other side was already going for something under the podium until Omar smashed his nose in with the butt of his pistol. The headwaiter collapsed to the ground with a startled grunt. Omar swept the room, looking for any trouble. Quick had the place covered with his compact HK MP5K submachine gun, while Blue divided his attention between the door and the startled customers.

"Don't nobody try anything stupid, and you'll be back to eatin' your fried rice and eggrolls before ya know it." Omar hauled the dazed maître d' to his feet and shoved him toward the cash register.

"Do you—have any idea of the mistake you are making?" the man mumbled as he was hauled along.

"It's you muthafuckahs done made the mistake crossin' the VKs, bitch." Omar threw him forward so his chest smacked into the counter. He waved his pistol at the girl behind the station and set an unzipped sports bag on the glass. "Tell her to open it and put all the money inside. Any funny shit, and you die first, then she dies. Tell her!"

"Thirty seconds," Blue called out.

The man rattled off a string of Chinese, and the girl moved to do as he said. Omar kept an eye on her hands as she shoved fat stacks of cash into the bag. It was already gonna be a profitable hit—besides what Casey was paying them, he'd also said they could keep whatever they got from the till.

The girl had emptied the compartments, but Omar wasn't through. "Take it out." When she hesitated, he pressed the muzzle of his pistol into the back of the man's neck. "Tell her I ain't frontin' and she better take out that muthafuckin' tray."

The maitre d' spoke again, and she slowly removed the tray, revealing slim stacks of hundred-dollar bills lining the bottom of the register. "Keep that paper comin', girl."

"Sixty seconds!" Blue said from the door, having just gotten the drop on a pair of flashy-looking men who'd entered. He frisked them expertly, relieving them of their weapons, then motioned them to a nearby table. One of them looked like he was thinking about making a move, but Quick growled deep in his chest, and the seething man stayed put.

The moment the cashier finished emptying the register, Omar grabbed the bag, zipped it shut, and slung it across his shoulder. He stepped close to the maitre d'. "This your only warning. The Black Lotus has twenty-four hours to return the VKs' money, or we'll hit every restaurant, every dry cleaner, every grocery store you muthafuckahs own till we get it back."

"What are you talking about—"

Omar rapped the man's head with the barrel of his pistol hard enough to shut him up. "Pass the warning up the chain, ya feel me? Twenty-four hours."

He stepped back, keeping an eye on the nearest customers as he walked backward toward the door. A commotion at the rear of the room made him turn his head just in time to see a busboy pop out from behind a screen, aiming a sawed-off shotgun at the trio.

"Down!" Omar shouted, grabbing the floor as the scattergun boomed, its pellets destroying a painting of fog-shrouded mountains above his head.

Most of the patrons shouted or screamed and ducked under their tables, but a suited trio sitting nearby decided to make their move. Hurling bowls of hot-and-sour soup and dishes of pressed duck and lo mein noodles as a distraction, they went for their pistols and tried to get the drop on the robbers.

Quick more than lived up to his name, stitching one with a three-round burst that sent him toppling backward over his chair. Omar nailed another with two shots to the groin, sending him to the floor, screaming in agony. Blue double-tapped the third man just as he was about to draw a bead on Quick.

Omar gave it a beat, then popped up, tracking movement near the screen down the sights of his SIG. He put three rounds through it and was rewarded by seeing the shotgunner stagger out, blood adding one more stain to his dirty T-shirt before he collapsed to the ground, the shotgun dropping from his lifeless fingers.

"Ninety seconds!" Blue said, covering the rest of the patrons with his pistol while holding the door with his free hand. Omar stepped toward the exit, also covering the terrified men and women alongside Quick. Omar left last, calling back to the maître d'. "Remember—twenty-four hours, or the VKs come back for what's ours!"

He stepped outside, inserting a small rubber wedge between the door and the frame, ensuring that no one inside would be able to leave for a few minutes. Turning, he stripped off his mask and left the alcove, crossing the street to the Escalade and getting into the driver's seat. He pulled out, cutting off a compact car, which honked angrily as the driver shook his fist. Omar grinned and gunned the engine, sending the SUV zooming off into the late afternoon traffic.

In the Bronx, Big Sally hit a man called Prawn—a corruption of "pawn"—in the stomach, bending him over in pain. "Aw, shit, why the fuck you do that?" he gasped.

"You wuz running buddies with Brix," Low Rise pointed out, leaning against a stack of boxed Blu-ray players. "You and him been knowin' each other before you came into our thing. He set you up in this operation." Low Rise waved a hand lazily about the warehouse space, filled with various stacks of electronic equipment.

"I ain't got nothin' to do with no missin' money," Prawn said, grimacing and holding a hand to his midsection.

"How you know about that?" Low Rise asked sharply.

"Come on, Rise, everybody fuckin' knows."

Big Sally swatted the man with one of the Blu-ray cartons, knocking him into a stack of Xboxes and scattering the video games.

"Hey, you oversized fuck," Prawn yelled, "this is precious merch you wreckin'!"

Low Rise gestured to Big Sally, who limped over, grabbed the man by his shirt, and forced him over to Low Rise.

"Rono got us out beating the muthafuckin' bushes, understand? Any and all connections to Brix, he's got soljahs chasing 'em down."

Big Sally began throwing around boxes of expensive equipment.

"Tell him to stop that."

"Gimme something," Low Rise demanded. "You got eyes and ears on the street. You musta heard somthin'."

Big Sally had an Xbox in each hand and hurled one, then the other at a brick wall, smashing both. He laughed hoarsely at his destruction.

"What the fuck you want me to do, Low Rise?" Prawn seethed. "You and the big nigga can tear up everything in here, but it won't change my story. I didn't have nothin' to do with that robbery."

Big Sally gleefully jumped up and down on a boxed plasma-screen TV like a kid in a playground. He didn't seem to mind his wounded leg anymore.

"You better give me something," Low Rise repeated. "I've been gettin' the empty hand since yesterday, and you better believe Rono's all up in my ass over this."

The harried Prawn shook a finger at the enforcer. "Let me shake the trees and see if I can't turn up somethin' for ya." He glanced over at Big Sally continuing his reign of terror. "And you better remember Rono gets his cut of this, and Frankenstein there is fuckin' up the profits."

Low Rise glared at him then yelled, "Cut that shit out!"

Big Sally held a carton containing a laser printer over his head, ready to bring it crashing down.

"Put it down," Low Rise told him.

Big Sally looked as if his favorite pet had just died, but carefully placed the box atop others like it.

Low Rise poked the lanky man in the chest. "Get busy and get results. If I gotta come back here, you know we'll be breaking up a lot more than just these fancy record players."

Prawn swore a raft of profanities as he watched the two leave and straightened up his inventory. Then he started making calls, looking for any scrap of info that would get those two hardasses off his case and onto someone else's.

"So he was on the NYPD for thirteen years?" Casey said.

"Made detective, shiny gold shield, a few medals," Kenny Saunders confirmed. They sat in his apartment drinking bottles of Heineken. The air was on, effectively combating the humidity that had risen outside. "He worked safes and loft squad and homicide."

"Why'd he quit?"

Saunders smiled, tapping the notepad between them on the kitchen table. On it was his neat, precise block printing. "There was this one case. Good-looking grad school chick found in her parked car strangled with one of those S&M dog collars on, her own panties stuffed in her mouth."

Casey took a casual sip and waited.

Saunders went on. "Suspicion falls on this professor she was seeing. Older dude, married, the whole bit. Seems they got their kink on regularly, only his story was for the last month or so she hadn't been giving him the time of day, nada. He finally jams her up, and she tells him what he's already figured. She's got a new mule kicking in her stall—this egghead she says, is not worthy to wipe the sweat off this dude's balls."

"Reason enough for a man to nut up and kill her," Casey observed.

"That's what the cops figure, only Lomax, who isn't assigned the case, but hears about it the way cops do, sees it differently. This broad was in shape, strong, so how did the prof get her in the dog collar to strangle her? Like she was gonna give him one last pity fuck for old time's sake? Plus, he goes down to the morgue to view the body and knows he's seen her before."

Saunders paused to drink. "The dead girl had been one of the students he'd interviewed about a year and a half before in this other case, one he worked involving a murder in a dorm room. That one did turn out to be the boyfriend."

"Where you going with this, Kenny?"

His friend chuckled. "Lomax keeps on this, and finds out his captain also remembered this honey from the other incident. At some kind of community better-relations-with-law-enforcement function, sponsored by this neighborhood group she belonged to, they meet up again and soon are getting it on freestyle."

"He killed her?"

"Yep. Shit got out of hand in one of their sessions. At least that's what the captain maintains. There's fallout from this, naturally, and Lomax ain't down with catching the flack. The captain was well connected in the department, one of those rising-star types and whatnot."

"But Lomax presses," Casey said.

"Yeah," Saunders confirmed. "It winds up with a hung jury in court, so the captain walks free, but your boy ends up on a number of shit lists."

"He's forced out."

Saunders was holding his beer and tipped it toward Casey. "That all went down in ninety-nine."

"Since then he's worked for the parole department?"

"Actually, he dropped off the map for a few years. He shows up again in oh-four, when he's a PO."

"What he do in between?"

Saunders held an open palm up. "Don't know. Couldn't find anything on him for that time."

"He got family?"

Saunders shook his head briefly. "Don't seem Lomax has ever been married, had any kids, or been hooked up with, what you call 'em, life partners hanging around either."

Casey asked, "Anything else?"

Saunders picked up his notepad and flipped pages. "He was on a couple of task forces back when he was in the department."

"That's not unusual."

"No, but one of my sources for this info is from this clerk in the parole department. She tells me Lomax has some fed friends who drop by for lunch now and then. Has to be dudes he knows from them days." Saunders added, "And if you had buddies in the government, wouldn't you try and get on with them? Why be just a dude wet nursin' a bunch of knuckleheads?"

"Maybe he did try, only what happened when he was a cop scuttled all that."

"Maybe," Saunders answered, a skeptical look blossoming on his face. "But why did he lay the four-one-one about those two in the VKs on you? That's the kinda shit would get him fired. But it's like he figured you could use the info."

"Maybe to set me up," Casey opined.

"Or use you to get bigger fish, Crush. No offense, brotha, but until you're a shot caller again, you don't have the same stature as Rono."

Kenny's cell phone buzzed, and he checked the text message he'd just received. "My, oh my. Seems one of Rono's hustlers is burnin' up the streets tryin' to get a line on his boss's missin' money." His face split into a huge grin. "Now, you wouldn't know anything 'bout that, wouldja, Crush?"

Crush held up his hand like he was swearing to be a Boy Scout. "I cannot tell a lie. I had absol-fuckin'-lutely nothing to do with Gulliver Rono's missing ten million dollars that was supposed to pay off the Colombian drug cartel."

Both men laughed, then Casey got serious. "You put that word on the street like I toldja?"

Kenny waved his phone. "Sheeit, nigga, by the end of today, Rono gonna be screamin' to take the Black Lotus down for hittin' his money wagon. Prawn won't be able to pass this hot potato up the chain fast enough, believe me."

"Now that's what I'm muthafuckin' talkin' 'bout, dawg," Casey said, holding out his fist for Kenny to pound. "'Bout time to put the second part of my plan into motion. Say, you remember Ten Spot?"

Saunders's face clouded with thought, then cleared. "Sure. Cat used to be an A-number-one slanger, fuckin' fearless. But he broke the rule about a man and his product. Dope messed him up good."

"Know where I might find him?"

"Why?"

Casey smiled a Cheshire grin.

"Big-time Crush Casey," the man called Jawjack drawled laconically. "Heard your aged ass was back among the living. You all fag now from your time in the joint? Come here lookin' for some young boys who like to play the violin?"

"I'm looking for Ten Spot. Understand he runs errands for you now and then."

The two were at his desk in an open area toward the rear of a musical instrument sales and rental store Jawjack managed. His real hustle was selling weed and other feel-good drugs, a candy man to session musicians. Jawjack was low on the food chain, but was supplied through Rono.

The heavyset man leaned back in his swivel chair, putting his feet on his desk with the soles facing Casey. There was a half-eaten order of fried catfish in a Styrofoam container on the desk. His feet were small, considering his girth. Several trumpets hung on the wall over him.

"You know, Casey, I wasn't a big fan of yours when you was around, an' I like you even less these days. Now get the hell out of my establishment 'fore I have to make a call." He picked his teeth with the end of a matchbook cover. A salesperson and several customers were in the store, including a nine-year-old girl with afro puffs earnestly playing a piano in another part of the store. The presence of the people emboldened Jawjack. What could the chump do?

Casey stood, and without a word locked a hand on the man's ankles.

"Hey—," Jawjack protested.

Casey yanked the man's feet off the desk and sent him over backward. Jawjack yelped as he landed on his ass. Casey took a drawer out of the desk and busted it over the man's head. Jawjack sagged backward, and Casey crouched, got in closer, a heavy stapler in his hand.

"Ten Spot," he repeated. The customers hurriedly exited the store and the salesperson blinked and watched with his mouth hanging open.

"You don't know what you're—"

Casey banged the side of the stapler against Jawjack's head, eliciting a dull thud. Jawjack's head hit the wall and some of the trumpets fell on him. "I don't like repeating myself," Casey said.

Jawjack swallowed and said, "There's a couple of regular places where he begs." He told him the locations and added, trying to save face, "Don't think I'm not marking this down, Casey."

"You do that." Casey hit him again with the stapler and he wilted to the floor. Rising, Casey took a slice of white bread from the takeout container and put a piece of catfish in it, then peppered on drops of hot sauce. He folded the bread over and walked out of the store munching on his sandwich.

The girl, absorbed in her efforts at Duke Ellington's version of "Money Jungle," hadn't stopped playing as the salesperson bent to see about Jawjack.

19

That evening, after a light dinner, Casey and Carla strolled along the water on the Brooklyn Heights Promenade. Rain threatened in the distance. Both wore trench coats, hers a stylish deep blue edition by Land's End, his butter-soft black leather.

"You've been rather circumspect tonight," she remarked as they walked.

"I don't even know what that word means."

"Keep being funny."

He put an arm around her waist and gave a squeeze. They passed by a bar and grill overlooking the walkway and the Manhattan skyline beyond. Voices bolstered by alcohol erupted from within. The couple went on.

"Champa called me today," she finally said.

"What he have to say for hisself?"

"Wanted me to know he'd seen our daughter. Said they had a good time catching up."

Casey absorbed that and nodded his approval.

She stopped. "It's coming down, isn't it, Marcus?"

"Yes." Tenderly he put a hand to the side of her face. "You want details?"

"Am I supposed to be flattered you're suddenly not trying to keep anything from me?"

Before he could answer, he was interrupted by a new voice.

"Yo, you Crush Casey, right?"

The couple looked back and saw three black men approaching them. The trio were dressed hip-hop casual, one in a hoodie, the other two in baggy sports jerseys and watch caps with sports logos on them. They'd come out of the bar Casey and Aquila had just gone past.

"If I am?"

"We want to be down for your shit, man," the oldest one said. He didn't look more than twenty-two. The three sauntered closer; the cloud of weed and alcohol wafting off them nearly made Casey's eyes water. "Word on the street is you 'bout to make a major move. You back to stir it up, ain't you?"

"We can slang like no muthafuckahs can," the second one said, holding his arms out wide. "Like muthafuckin' Walmart, son."

Carla snickered.

"I'm not recruiting, gentlemen." He touched Carla's elbow as a signal to leave, but he knew better than to think there would be an end to this prattle. There wasn't.

"You don't think we know what we doing?" the third one, in the hoodie, blared, incensed. His over-large jeans sagged so low he had to continually grab at them to prevent them from falling off his skinny legs.

"Think you better than us, nigga?" the second one scoffed, moving his head from side to side. "Running around on your tired-ass rep." He looked at his friends for confirmation of his assessment.

"We been holding it down on the real." The older one came up, invading Casey's space. "Maybe you and your bitch here should go find a porch where you can sit and watch the fireworks from your rocking chairs." The trio chuckled.

Casey was about to go into motion, but Carla was faster. Her hand came out of her purse, and she put a Smith & Wesson M&P9c compact semiauto in the older one's face. "Your mama's a bitch. Now go away and play gangsta somewhere else, baby lokes."

The trio was shocked—the last thing they expected was a fine sistah to draw down on them.

"Whoa, hold up, bitch, ain't no need for that."

"Get to stepping, youngstas."

The trio slowly backed up, trying to preserve their ego after having just been served by a woman that could have been their mother.

Casey grinned. "What the hell you doing walkin' around with a gat?"

She glared at him incredulously. "It's the company I keep."

A light drizzle began as they resumed walking.

Later, in her apartment, Casey leaned back in his chair, taking another sip of his Johnnie Walker Black, neat. "What did you wanna be when you were a kid, Carla?"

"An architect." She was lying on her stomach on the bed, in pajamas, reading a book about politics. "Wanted to build buildings for the people. The real people, I mean."

"No shit." His gaze traveled up her legs. "Did you pursue that?"

"Sort of, but other stuff got in the way."

"I heard that." He sipped again.

The silence lengthened, but not uncomfortably so, then she asked, "You always wanted to be a kingpin?"

He chuckled. "When I was, I don't know, nine or ten, the only thing I wanted to be or do was play baseball. I couldn't think of anything better than being in the sun and hitting a fastball or leaping up at the left-field fence and bringing one down."

"Yeah, that's right, I remember you used to have those different baseballs in a long glass in your office."

"Yeah," he said, his voice taking on a grayer shade. "Had Willie Mays's autograph on one, Hank Aaron's on another. A lot of those cats, Reggie Jackson." He stared wistfully beyond the walls.

"Rono have 'em now?"

Casey didn't answer and she turned to see him leaning forward on the edge of the chair, staring into his whiskey as if it could take him back in time.

"What is it, baby?"

His voice was hoarse and soft. "Rono made sure I found out that when Antonio was nine, he gave him those baseballs as a birthday present. Like it was from him."

Carla stared at him.

"I never got to take my boy to a baseball game, Carla." He looked away from her, inhaled, and let out his breath in a long *whoosh.*

She sat on his lap and held on to him. Casey rested his head on her chest and thought about the last time he'd seen his son alive. . . .

"You gonna do what?" he said into the handset, aware the bulls could be listening in.

"I gotta line on a little somethin'. It's an easy run, five minutes in and out, low risk."

Angry, for a moment Casey could hardly focus on him. He'd always seen Antonio from behind the thick, shockproof glass, the barrier distorting his features slightly. Sporadically over the years, he'd seen his son grow up behind that glass. He wore baggy designer jeans, a Yankees baseball jersey, and brand-new unlaced Nike high-tops. His attitude wavered between sullen and hopeful, and Casey realized Antonio was asking for his approval in a roundabout way. Crazy, too, how he favored his mother so much.

Danielle had been killed when Antonio was six years old. The police claimed it was a hit-and-run. In the joint, Casey had put the word out that he'd pay dearly to anyone who could tell him otherwise, but he'd never uncovered anyone to prove his suspicions that Rono had been behind the incident. Granted, Rono's low opinion of women meant he didn't consider females as potential enemies. But the agent of her death remained unknown.

With no other legal guardian available, Casey's only child had entered the foster care system, as cruel and unusual a punishment as had ever been created, as far as he was concerned. Ten years later, a man-boy slouched in front of Casey, affecting an attitude he'd done nothing to earn, and looking to make his name any way he could.

"Look, little nigga—" Antonio tensed, and Casey dialed it down. "Who the hell's puttin' you up to this? Is Rono tossing you a bone?"

"Yo, Pops, ease up, will ya? Ain't no one twistin' my arm. Couple of homies I know need a lil' help, that's all. I gotta be making moves, y'know—"

"What about what we'd talked about? I'm hoping to be up for parole in a couple of years. Been keepin' my head down and my nose clean, and you're a big reason why. Once I'm out, then you and me can make some real plans. I don't need you in here with me, that's not a reunion that'll make me happy, you feel me?"

"Pops, you trippin', I can't wait till you get sprung. I gotta get a place of my own, the foster folks are really crampin' my style, you feel me? Shit, this is a powder-puff job, ain't nothin' to worry 'bout."

Casey leaned close to the glass, his mouth pressed into the handset. "You goddamn idiot. Take a good look at who you talking to and where we havin' this conversation. You wanna end up in here right beside me? Or even worse? The gangstas and slangers out there'd just as soon cut your throat as look at you, if not for kicks, then to get at me. Understand?"

Antonio shrugged, reminding Casey of himself at that age— figuring he had all the answers. "All the more reason I got to show that I can handle myself out there. Don't want nobody comin' at me just 'cuz I'm your seed."

Casey's mind and heart were both racing, his blood pounding in his ears. "Antonio, they gonna come down on you for no reason at all, just 'cause they don't like the way you look, or what you're wearing, or just 'cause they want to. Look, if you need some scratch to get by on, I can handle that, but I'm tellin' ya, boy, don't do this, just wait until I get—"

Now his son leaned closer to the glass, anger and frustration on his face. The bored guard in the corner gave a cursory glance over, then sank back into his practiced lethargy.

"Look here, Pops, I been waiting a lot of long miserable god-damn years for somethin' to happen. I ain't waitin' no more. I'm doin' my own thing now. It's my time." With that he pushed back from the booth and stood. "See ya when I see ya."

"Antonio, listen, at least let me know when you're done. Will you do that for me?" Casey heard the pleading in his voice, and hated it. He smacked the glass, trying to get his boy's attention as he cradled the handset down on the other side of the glass and walked out, and got a lazy half-wave from his son, who didn't turn around as he left the room.

Five days later, he got word Antonio was dead.

"You're taking a big risk, having me drive our beauty into this neighborhood." Li's eyes met Shinzo's in the rearview mirror as she maneuvered the Jaguar down a cracked, potholed street. "Don't even see any alley rats to covet it down here."

Shinzo Becker reclined against the plush backseat and puffed on his cheroot, then blew a smoke ring out. "If anything happens to it, I'll just take it out of your salary, gorgeous."

Her brown eyes flicked to him again. "You sure you want to do this? All the years we been rollin', I've never known you to agree to a meeting in another gang's 'hood."

"Maybe not, but my boy Casey needs a favor, and he needs it done like lightnin'. Only way I could get a meeting this quick was to agree to come to them. Gonna hurt my negotiatin' advantage, too."

"And I *really* cannot believe you agreed to come alone. For all we know, these *gwai los* could be planning to cap your ass the moment you step inside."

"Life's a gamble, my dear, but Nozinga assured me that my time ain't at hand just yet." Shinzo grinned as he kept an eye on the squalid Bronx neighborhood they were driving deeper into. Only the luxury sedan's headlights pierced the gloom, as every streetlight had been broken long ago. "'Sides, I gotta ace in the hole they'll never see comin'."

"And what's that?"

"Why, you, beautiful, of course."

She smiled thinly as the Jag rounded another corner, then drove up a street lined with nondescript warehouses on either side, with corrugated metal walls and roofs, and many blacked-out windows. Halfway up the block, a large garage door rattled open, throwing a large square of yellow light into the blackness of the street.

"That's our stop. Pull in slowly and—"

"I know, be ready for anything."

"That's my girl."

If the outside street was deserted, the inside of the warehouse was jumpin'. At least three dozen Mexicans were scattered about the cavernous interior, some playing dice, others grouped around a huge projection television playing a video game, and another group standing in a circle cheering and waving fistfuls of cash. Blunt smoke hung in a thick, blue haze over everyone and everything.

Shinzo could hear fast *mariachi* music, heavy on the accordion, over a pulsing bass beat that shook his car windows.

The Jaguar attracted immediate attention from a half-dozen bangers, who drifted over to admire the low-slung, sleek car. All of them had one thing in common—a stylized tattoo of a grinning devil on their arms, hands, or in some cases even their faces. A couple of them reached out to touch the Jag's glossy finish. The garage door closed behind the car, sealing them inside.

"Goddamn it, now I'll have to get her detailed again." Li glanced back at Shinzo one last time. "You ready?"

"You know it."

Li got her game face on and opened the door. A loud chorus of hoots, wolf whistles, and catcalls erupted from the Latinos clustered around the car. Shinzo smiled—Li was his secret weapon in more ways than one.

She went to the back door and opened it, then just as quickly whirled around, her right arm pistoning out in a stiff jab to a gangsta who had gotten a little too close—like his hand squeezing her ass close. The *cholo* staggered back, surprise on his face as he tripped and planted his butt on the stained concrete, surrounded by the laughter of his homies.

Shinzo unfolded himself from inside the car and shook his head as he gazed down at the Blood Devil picking himself up from the floor. Even though the warehouse was large, the hot, still air stank of sweat, blood, and weed. "I wouldn't advise takin' any more liberties with my chauffeur, son."

His words had no effect. Insulted in front of his crew, the gangsta spat on the ground and pulled his hand from his pocket to reveal a switchblade that he flicked open. "Gonna carve me up some slant *puta*!" Shrugging off his friend's hands, he stalked toward Li, who awaited him with her hands at her sides, seemingly relaxed.

The knife man lunged forward, the blade slashing toward Li's face. Her hands blurred into motion, the left one striking the wrist of her attacker's knife hand, deflecting it as her right shot out, fingers stiffened in a hard jab to the homie's throat.

He stopped as if he'd just run into a wall, the knife flying from his fingers as both hands went to his neck as he started to make choking noises. Li kicked the switchblade back under the car and watched the Blood Devil gasp for air, his face turning red as he fell to his knees. Then, slowly, he returned to his normal color as he was finally able to suck air into his paralyzed throat. The rest of the bangers all took a small step back, but still surrounded the two guests.

Shinzo sighed. "I warned him not to pull that kind of shit, but some folks just gotta learn the hard way."

"*Basta!* Enough!" A thick-shouldered bald man shoved his way through the crowd and stared down at his fallen soldier. He was dressed in the standard *cholo* outfit—chinos, wife-beater T-shirt, sneakers, and a flannel shirt with the top button closed. His face, however, was another story—tattooed across the entire left side was a bright red devil's head, complete with horns and a wicked grin curving up his cheek. "Get this *chivala* out of here—I got business to discuss, and I don't need his dumb ass fuckin' it up any more than he already done!"

Two others grabbed the spluttering ganger by the armpits and hauled him off. The rest of the mob broke up and drifted away, save for two hard-eyed bangers who hadn't said a word or moved a muscle during the entire incident, but had just watched the whole thing unfold with their arms crossed. Shinzo had pegged them for the real muscle as soon as he'd gotten out of the car.

The newcomer nodded at Li. "Excuse my homes—he's more than a little *borracho*, and gets a l'il grabby around a fine *senorita* like yourself."

Li didn't say a word, but just red-eyed him, her stare as cold and hard as any gangbanger. The man shrugged and moved to Shinzo. One of the bodyguards shifted his attention to them, the other kept watching Li. "So, you got some *cojones* comin' down here all by your lonesome, Becker."

Shinzo glanced at Li. "I felt I was suitably protected for the occasion—after all, we're just here to talk business, right, Jesus?"

"I figure that's the only thing'd bring your ass into our crib this time of night. So what's so important you couldn't discuss it with one of my slangers?"

"I gotta problem, and I'm hopin' you and your boys are the solution."

"I'm listenin'."

Shinzo shifted his position, looking at the ground. "Well, it's about Marcus Casey."

"No shit? Yeah, we heard he was back on the streets. Is he still pushin' that 'all gangs work together' shit?"

"Yeah, and he's pretty hard-core about it. Problem is, if he takes the VKs back, then you gonna have a big problem on your north side."

Jesus thumped his chest. "The gangsta hasn't been born yet that I fear. Let him try anything—me and my boys'll put him in the *microondas*."

Shinzo held out his hands, trying to avoid wincing. The punishment Jesus referred to, meaning "microwave," involved putting someone in a stack of gasoline-soaked tires and burning them to death. While Becker was stone-cold, he wouldn't wish that kind of death on anyone. "Hey, homes, I meant no disrespect. Still, I didn't think you'd want an all-out war when there are other ways to handle the situation and rake in some extra loot in the process."

"*Sí?*"

"Casey wants to offer you another chance to sign on with his operation. Wants to meet with you and the rest of the Blood captains, work out a deal."

Jesus spat on the floor. "Already gave him our answer the first time. The Blood Devils answer to no one!"

"And I understand that, man—don't be hatin' on the messenger. Thing is, I figure you and your boys could agree to meet him, then bring in a few of your heavy hitters and take him out once and for all. You do that, you know Gulliver Rono would give you a pass on your action down here. Hell, he'd probably even break off a little piece for takin' care of this problem for him."

Jesus regarded Shinzo in the dim lights, the wheels inside his head turning. As cool and composed as he looked, the club owner felt cold sweat bead on the back of his neck. If Jesus cottoned to the con he was runnin', there was no way Li or he was getting out of there alive. . . .

The Latino gangsta's brow furrowed. "Man, I thought you and Casey were tight. Why you droppin' this in our lap all of a sudden?"

"Things change, my man. When Casey was in the joint, I had my pick of action all over the city. But with him out and actually startin' to pull this all together, he's gonna want me to fall into line too, payin' tribute and all that shit, and that just don't set right, ya feel me?"

Jesus nodded slowly. "I can respect a man's desire for independence."

"See? We got more in common than most folks might think. So, whaddya say?"

Jesus stroked his chin, then nodded. "Tell him we're interested in setting up a meeting to hear what he has to say. You know how to get in touch with us to arrange the rest. Once everything's in place, we'll take care of this *mayate* once and for all."

"Solid. I'll pass the word along and make the arrangements."

Li walked to the back door and opened it again, letting Shinzo get inside before closing it and sliding behind the wheel. The garage door opened again, and they sped out into the night.

Only when they were several blocks away and heading for the nearest freeway did Shinzo exhale in relief. "Baby girl, I've done some muthafuckin' crazy shit in my time, but what just happened has to rank at the very tip top."

"True dat," the gorgeous Asian replied, making Shinzo chuckle as he flipped open his cell and speed-dialed Casey.

"Yo, homes?"

"What it is, playa?"

"Just planted the hook in the BDs. Looks like they're gonna take the bait, we just gotta reel 'em in. You seem to have a knack for makin' enemies out here, boy."

"Muthafuckin' Devils just too uppity to get into line, so they gotta be taken outta line—permanently. That is damn good news. Whatchu need for the next step?"

"Just a time and place for the meeting—these *loco* bangers are ready to rock and roll at a moment's notice. We gotta find somewhere out of the way where all these crazy fucks you wanna bring together can shoot it up without any citizens gettin' capped."

"Well, you the black Donald Trump of real estate, I'm sure you can find a suitable locale for this to go down, right?"

"How'd I know you was gonna leave this to me?"

Casey's deep chuckle rumbled over the phone. "Sheeit, nigga, I can't be doin' all yo' work for ya, didn't Nozinga tell you that?"

Shinzo laughed. "Like you ever did, muthafuckah. Seriously, I'm on it. Look here, speaking of gettin' shit done, I also may have a sit-down set up with Two Stroke."

"No shit?" Ellis "Two Stroke" Bledsoe ran an outfit in the New England area out of Providence.

"Seems Rono seriously punked him on a cigarette-smuggling deal a few years ago and he ain't forgot. Ol' scarhead bragged about it too, and our boy's been waitin' for the chance to settle the score."

"Keep on that good work, playa."

"Don't I always, brother?"

. . .

Clicking off the cell phone, Marcus Casey sat quiet and immobile. Back on point, he mentally reviewed the specialists he'd lined up for his operation. Even realizing he was deficient in several areas of expertise, including those simply effective with a gun or an assault rifle, it was foolish to contemplate a full-on assault on Rono and the VKs. There was no way he could recruit enough soldiers or afford to do so. There was also Rono on the hunt for his money, and sooner or later that meant whether or not he found out Casey was involved, his former second-in-command would have to devote energy to taking him out too. But Casey intended to strike first and fatally.

20

Vera Hammond rubbed her gloved hands together and told herself to stay calm, even though her stomach was doing flip-flops. If she'd made a mistake and this was her last night of living, then so be it. This was the life she chose, and if necessary, the price she would pay.

"Hey," a voice said behind her. Starting, she turned to see Champa Munoz appear from around a building. A brisk wind blew in off the East River, and she heard splashing from somewhere out on the dark water. "It's good to be wanted, huh?" he joked.

"At least Rono doesn't know who you are," she responded. "But that only drives home why I need to get out from under the boulder hanging over me."

"You could leave town."

"You haven't, Munoz," she noted. "And my guess is you've stayed because you got other work. Does it involve Crush Casey?"

Munoz cupped his bare hands and blew into them. He hadn't worn gloves. "Bitch, don't get all up in my business."

Vera remained cool. "*Our* business. As you pointed out, we have a mutual interest in eliminating Gulliver Rono."

"Besides a nice pair of legs, what you bringin' to the dance?"

"Evidence to put the heat on Rono."

Munoz shifted on his feet. "No offense, but there are certain individuals who aren't too concerned with sending Rono to the joint. More like they plan to send him to eternity."

Hammond had already considered this. "Then they'd want this material never to see the light of day either, as it also implicates certain Vicetown Kings enterprises."

"Okay bitch, you on a tightrope right now."

"Just trying to tease you."

"So you have this evidence?"

"It's safe, and only I know where it's located. But if anything happens to me in the next twenty-four hours, an associate of mine has instructions to send it direct to the *Times*." This last part was pure bluff, but Hammond was pretty sure Champa wouldn't push the issue, since he had no way of knowing whether she was frontin' or not.

"What about Rono's banker? Now that would be useful to know," Casey said behind her. He walked over to Munoz. He was larger than she'd imagined, though he moved fluidly. Unlike Champa, whom she could play with a bit just to keep him off balance, she instantly saw that Casey was not a man to fuck with.

"I can get that too."

"Can you get me to him?" Casey asked.

"What's in it for me?"

Casey and Munoz exchanged a brief look. Casey pointed a finger at her. "That's why you haven't run. You want a piece—okay, let's hear it."

Hands in her jacket pockets, her shoulders rose and fell.

"You got ideas for slangin' to the soccer moms out in Suffolk?"

Casey said, only half jokingly. Faith Hart's suburban enterprise had been an earner he meant to duplicate.

"I'm thinking even more white-collar upscale."

"I could see that—you got a certain sophistication about you," Casey allowed.

"So, how do we do this?" Hammond said.

"I'm hurt. You don't trust us?" Munoz cracked.

She cocked her head at him. "I'm the one got crosshairs on my forehead at the moment. I don't have such a luxury, do I?"

Casey spread his hands wide. "Who does?"

She smiled. "So you say."

"All of us got the mark right now," Munoz commented. "The big parade is getting ready to come down Main Street."

"Meaning I shouldn't lollygag," Hammond observed laconically.

"One other thing," Casey said. "You know where Rono's apartment is, right?"

"I do. I know a few other locations of interest as well."

He said, "Then we got something to work with."

"Let me see what I can line up on the banker. Wouldn't want you to think I wasn't an earner."

"All right, then," Casey answered.

"I'll be back in touch."

"I look forward to it."

Casey and Munoz walked off in one direction and she in another.

Later that evening, Omar Atkins guided the Jeep Wrangler between a chopped and lowered Buick deuce and a quarter and last year's Porsche. He shut off the engine and Casey, Champa, and he exited the vehicle.

There were numerous cars parked around the semi-completed sports arena. The consortium of developers had run out of funds with only this shell to show for their efforts. Around the area were various clearings for planned restaurants, trendy bowling alleys, and the like. It was as if they'd come to the end of civilization on the installment plan.

Now the skeletal structure was home to other, less-organized urban entertainment. At least a dozen pimped-out whips rumbled and roared in a large area, surrounded by metal bleachers filled with spectators, from well-dressed men and women enjoying cigars and champagne to colors-wearing gangstas puffing on blunts and talking smack. Thick-bodied men in black slacks and T-shirts stationed every few yards made sure to keep the peace.

Casey kept scanning the crowd, looking for too-familiar faces. "Don't know if I really wanna be showin' my face 'round here, man. This seems a bit too high-profile, given what I'm puttin' into motion shortly."

Omar clapped him on the shoulder. "It's all good, dawg—everyone knows this is neutral ground. Ain't no one gonna mess with you here."

As the trio moved through the crowd, a patron recognized Casey and excused himself from his date, saying he had to go to the bathroom. But what he really wanted was a quiet place to drop a dime.

Gulliver Rono was an impatient man. He always preferred to make the move, not just be reactive. That's why he'd tried to take Casey out all those years ago; the fool had become complacent, wanting to broker a truce among the gangs. What the fuck was that all about? It was better to keep them scrapping among themselves, that way no one got any ideas about getting too big, and trying to take on the VKs. Long ago, Rono had rationalized that he'd done what he'd done for the survival of the Vicetown Kings. The fact that he'd moved into the top spot was only natural—he had the vision to lead and the will to succeed.

His cell phone's ringtone blared, "Mo Money, Mo Problems" by Notorious B.I.G. Rono picked up. "Yeah?"

"Is that bounty still open on Casey?" the patron asked on the other end.

"Bet your muthafuckin' ass it is. You dead sure it's him?"

"Hell yeah, I am. How do I get my money?"

"Where's he at first?" Rono got the location, and told the voice on the other end how to collect. He then called Derek Webb. "Yeah, Casey's been spotted." He gave the location. "Send two cars of our boys down there, and you tell them to bring me back his muthafuckin' head."

They found seats halfway up in the grandstands. The promoters of tonight's event had women in skimpy outfits delivering food and drinks from portable kitchens stationed nearby. Mounted above the lot filled with cars were several digital cameras that would stream the contest for those paying for the download on their computers.

"Interesting," Casey muttered.

"Just wait till the show starts," Atkins promised.

"What's your pleasure, gentlemen?" one of the servers with commanding cleavage asked. Discards rested on the tray she carried.

They ordered and presently she returned with their drinks. Spaced about the circular area were the kind of lights on crane arms used by highway personnel for work in the dark. "Not bad," Casey allowed.

"This crew been puttin' on this kinda show for the past few weeks. They got this shit down," Atkins noted, sampling his double scotch.

The three men sat back and watched the show. There were bounce contests and drag races, with each event broken up by a small group of performers who did everything from dance numbers to magic tricks.

As they watched, Casey asked Omar, "So what's your connection to these . . . people?"

"The big chick who was out earlier, the one who did the striptease with the python?"

"Yeah?"

Atkins showed yellow teeth and waggled his eyebrows.

"You bangin' her?"

Atkins nodded.

"Lucky muthafuckah. Does she bring that thing to bed with her?"

"Heh."

The evening's entertainment came to a finale with a four-car multi-race. Casey and his crew let the crowd disperse, then Atkins led them to a group of large tractor-trailers as the rest of the group began to disassemble the bleachers.

The master of ceremonies greeted Omar as they walked up. "Mr. Atkins, so good to see you again. And you've brought friends. Wonderful. My name is Mr. Gray. How can I assist you gentlemen this evening?"

"My associates need to see the full range of what you have to offer."

"Forgive the indelicacy of this next question, Mr. Atkins, however, I'm assuming that your associates have the ability to purchase on the spot?"

In answer, Casey unzipped the sports bag he was carrying. The arc lights fell on the stacks of hundred-dollar bills inside. "I believe Mr. Franklin can attest to the current state of my healthy bank balance."

"Excellent, sir, excellent. So sorry to have to ask, but there's been a spate of recent customers with, shall we say, less than stellar financial resources. Step right this way, gentlemen."

Mr. Gray escorted the three men to a guarded and padlocked trailer. He produced a key out of Omar's ear, then opened the door and unfolded a small set of metal steps. "Come right in, gentlemen, and take a look at what we have."

Casey walked in to find a veritable arsenal, with everything from pistols to sniper rifles hanging on the walls and arranged neatly on tables. On one table he saw a variety of other munitions, from smoke and tear gas grenades to even larger antipersonnel weapons. He whistled long and low.

"Omar, you done good, my man. I think Mr. Gray and I can definitely do some business."

"Now I think you'll find this little beauty of particular interest as you and Omar embark on your . . . activities, Mr. Casey." Mr. Gray showed the men several items, and Casey selected what he needed from them. Money was exchanged, and then the three men loaded the back of the Wrangler and drove away.

They'd just turned out of the sideshow's parking lot when Champa looked behind them. "Yo, homes, I think we got company." Casey and Omar both checked their six, and sure enough, a black Lincoln Navigator with tinted windows was on their tail and coming up fast. Casey barely had time to draw his pistol before the big SUV rammed them hard, and then the gunplay started.

Omar Atkins wrenched the steering wheel to the left, making the Wrangler skid sideways on the access road. Casey blew out the passenger side window and let off shots from his 9mm at the Navigator swooping in on them. A rattle of automatic fire ripped into the Jeep, sending shards of metal and glass into Casey's back as he ducked for cover.

"Backseat!" Atkins yelled as he punched out the Jeep's starred windshield. "Lift it up!" He powered the vehicle off the road toward some tall weeds. Another car, this one a customized Nissan Skyline GTR R34 pocket rocket, also roared at them from Interstate 78.

"Ain't no one gonna mess with us on hallowed ground, huh, muthafuckah?" Casey red-eyed his soljah as he yanked on the rear seat. "Ain't no one gonna bother me, here, huh?"

"Well, they did wait till we was out of the parking lot," Champa said with an evil grin as he crouched behind Omar's seat, a Desert Eagle .357 in his hand.

Casey glared at him, then lifted the rear seat up on its hinges, exposing an H&K MR7 and an Ingram MAC-10 chambered in .45 caliber underneath. He grabbed the Ingram just as Atkins swerved to avoid a collision with the Nissan, which had driven up near the rear fender. Unlike the Navigator with two in it, there was only the driver in the street racer. He tried to shoot at the Wrangler while he drove, but wasn't particularly effective as his rounds pinged about. But that didn't mean he couldn't get lucky.

Atkins cut right, heading for the road again as the Navigator roared after them. The shooter on the passenger side leaned out and unloaded his Uzi at them. The bullets took out the rear window and tore into the cargo area. Atkins was driving blind for a moment, hunched down as he was to avoid getting hit.

"Tree!" Casey yelled.

Atkins rose up and spun the wheel just in time to avoid the collision. The side of the Wrangler scraped the oak with a shriek of crumpling metal.

"Aw, damn, that was a custom paint job!" Omar moaned from behind the wheel.

"What the hell's wrong with you, nigga! I'd be a damn sight more concerned about those hitters behind us than the goddamn paint on this bucket!" Casey had managed to get into the rear, shoving the backseat down again. He popped up in a break between bursts from their opponents and swept the Ingram's muzzle at the Navigator, the room broom emptying its magazine in under a second. He missed the driver, who turned the big vehicle in time, his rounds buried in a cluster in the SUV's side.

"Where's that fuckin' rice burner?" Atkins called as automatic fire echoed all around them.

The customized Nissan raced into view on their right, the Navigator gaining on them from behind. The Nissan's driver had his passenger-side window down and cranked off more shots. A round barely missed Atkins and shattered his rearview mirror. He wrenched the wheel hard right again, trying to broadside the Nissan, but the agile sports car avoided his Jeep with ease, then swung back for another try at them.

"Goddamn, you boys gonna do something 'bout these guys doggin' us, or just keep playin' with yoselves back there!" Omar shouted.

"Casey, take the SUV, I got this mufu." Champa had armed himself with the HK, yanking back the cocking lever and grinning like the crazy nigga he was. He popped up in the backseat and unloaded all thirty rounds of the 9mm into the Nissan.

The other car's windshield disintegrated, the burst of bullets punching through and into the driver behind it. Half his face was blown off, and his lifeless hands slipped off the steering wheel. The GTR went out of control as if it was a radio-operated toy and someone had just stepped on the remote control. The low-slung sports car turned in a wide circle, but the dead man's foot jammed on the accelerator pedal made it go faster and faster. The car went up on two wheels, then flipped, rolling several times across the roadway and back into the bordering field. The Navigator had to maneuver around the upended Nissan as Atkins put several car lengths between them. The smashed-up GTR's momentum brought it to rest on its top in the tall weeds, a lost object of car culture art.

Atkins took a marked exit off the road again, this time right into the acreage of a parking lot belonging to a closed outlet mall. He drove at an angle toward the front under the ghostly phosphorescent glow of the security lights atop their poles, the Navigator gaining ground. A round of fire issued from their pursuers. The left rear tire of the Jeep was clipped and everyone inside heard the pop. Within seconds the tire began to shred and soon they'd be rolling on the rim.

"One chance," Atkins said, looking nervously at Casey.

"Do it!" Casey and Champa had both reloaded their weapons and braced themselves.

Atkins stomped on the brakes. The Jeep's tires squealed and smoke clouded behind them as the Navigator's shocked driver reacted by applying his brake and trying to veer off. But the big SUV plowed into the Jeep's right rear section, which crumpled upon impact. Casey had scrambled into the front passenger seat just in time, otherwise he'd have been trapped in the twisted metal that had been the side of the Wrangler a second ago.

The crash affected the Navigator too, snapping the bushings and tie rod of the front left tire so that the SUV wouldn't move anymore.

The driver had bashed his head against the windshield, dazed. The shooter was pushing him out of the way to get a shot off when both Casey and Champa fired into the Escalade, the flurry of rounds killing both men inside the vehicle instantly.

"Oh shit, can't a brotha catch a break?" Atkins complained. In the near distance, a strobe light of a police helicopter swung about in the darkness as it got closer.

"We done wore out our welcome here," Casey said as all three clambered out of the heap that had been the Jeep. He grabbed whatever he could salvage from the back and distributed it between the other two, then grabbed a final armload for himself. Pausing long enough to rip part of his shirtsleeve off, he lit it with Champa's Zippo, and stuffed it in the gas tank opening after Atkins twirled the cap off. The three fled into the darkness beside the mall as the Wrangler exploded, followed by the Navigator a few seconds later. Not only did this draw the attention of the police helicopter, but it also destroyed the evidence. Omar had already made sure to register the Jeep in a fake name, should forensics manage to raise the vehicle ID number off the charred engine block.

The three sweated in the warm night as they ran through thickets and underbrush until they could no longer hear the commotion they'd caused.

21

Two Stroke Bledsoe turned his stern, lined face from the view off the observation deck of the Empire State Building. With panoramic vistas of New York City surrounding him on three sides, he snugged the collar of his camel-hair coat tighter around his neck. "Guess I'm getting sentimental in my old age."

Casey chuckled. "Uh-huh."

"My mom brought me here when I was a kid." He pointed at the floor. "I remember her showing me the Statue of Liberty, the Chrysler Building, all that, laying the histories of these buildings and such on me. The struggle it took to make each thing happen, and that they all took vision and drive. And how I could also have my place in history if I applied myself."

"You did apply yourself." Casey glanced at the face of a sweet little girl as she gave him a gap-toothed smile, then scampered off to catch up with her family.

"But not exactly like Mama intended," Bledsoe said. "Still, like any other chump-ass tourist, whenever I come to Manhattan, I usually come back here." He shook his head from side to side. "Just like a sucker. How's the view from up here now that you're a free man?"

Casey looked out at the horizon, savoring the feeling of freedom. "Much of it looks the same. 'Course, there's been some big changes since I went in, too." He waved at the gaping hole in the skyline where the World Trade Center towers used to be, now swarming with construction equipment and crews working on the new 1 World Trade Center building.

Bledsoe snorted. "You're assuming they're ever gonna finish that thing."

Casey nodded. "Yeah, ain't that some bullshit. They finally got something righteous to do and they still manage to blow it."

Bledsoe looked out at the skyline again. Gray had creeped into the hair on the side of his head. "It's still a great city, no matter what anyone else says."

"True dat." Casey paused, wanting to choose his next words carefully. "It sounds like a load of bull when I say it out loud, but that's part of why I'm doin' what I'm doin'. This city needs help, and there's only one way I know of to do that."

The corner of Bledsoe's mouth crooked up in a wry grin. "Fortunately your plan involves regaining control of the largest gang here, otherwise you wouldn't have a hope in hell of pullin' anything off." He shook his head. "You don't need my or anybody else's blessing in this, Crush. But if it makes you feel better, I won't shed no tears should Rono go to the Happy Hunting Ground."

"I didn't want to see you about that so much as what happens if I'm successful."

Bledsoe's eyebrow arched. "You still talkin' 'bout an eastern seaboard hookup? An affiliation of crews like you tried back in the day?"

A wind had come up. "Even larger. Nationwide. But even more than that—an empire that would make your mama proud. Taking

care of shit our way. Earn you that place in history—if unofficially—
that she told you about all those years ago." This was the first time
he'd articulated what he'd been conceiving to someone outside his
own circle, and it sounded right, natural.

Squinting, Bledsoe regarded him. "You not talkin' just about
quelling internal beefs. You're saying Batman-vigilante type shit."
They'd walked off to one side of the deck.

"It isn't like we haven't had to regulate our communities before.
Keeping the peace is good for us. And I'm damn sure not saying
we'd be a buncha psalm singers and apple polishers either. That
ain't us. We'd still have to do our thing. Only not so goddamn
chaotic, Two Stroke. Working in a disciplined network rather than
at cross purposes."

"Why you reachin' for this now, Crush?"

"Now you gonna get me soundin' sentimental."

Bledsoe said, "I ain't much on being Robin Hood, man. I'm
more a Reverend Ike kind of nigga—the best way to help the poor
is not be one of them."

"Amen," Casey said as they both snickered. Casey sobered first.
"I'm serious 'bout this, Two Stroke. You agreed to meet because I
know you've been thinking it too. I know about those rec centers
you've financed."

"What—I like basketball."

"Sure you do," Casey said.

Bledsoe snorted. "Plus, I want those young niggas where I can
see 'em, seein' as how they can't shoot straight nohow."

"Maybe we're two old softies these knuckleheads don't have no
room for." The wind kicked up again, making Casey slip his hands
into his pockets.

"I'm old, not dead, nigga. I bet the wolves still got some bite
left."

When they were the only two riding down from the observation deck in the elevator, Bledsoe spoke, his voice flat. "Like I

said, Crush, I'll back your play. I've even got a few hitters I can loan you. Right now, you and I agree on one thing—we both want to see Rono gone."

The doors opened, and the two men exited into the three-story lobby, the ceiling rising above them. "Now on this other thing, I ain't jumpin' in with both feet, but if you do what you tell me you're gonna do, let's say I'll keep an open mind when we meet again."

It was better than Casey could have hoped for. Bledsoe wouldn't commit personnel to Casey just because of their friendship. He was gambling, he'd calculated the odds, but wasn't ready to go all in until he had an idea how Casey's hand was gonna play out. That was all right with Casey—this whole operation had been a gamble from the start, so what was one more risk on top of it all?

"'Preciate it, Two Stroke. In a minute."

"One."

Bledsoe would have his men in town by tomorrow, which worked out perfectly for Casey. They pounded fists and parted company downstairs.

"Goddamn. Muthafuckahs. Goddamn muthafuckahs!" Rono had been saying various combinations of these two words for the past ten minutes as he paced back and forth across the living room floor. Almost all of his captains were there, everyone silent and sitting at nervous attention. This must have been what Hitler's generals felt like in the end. Too scared to take him out, yet too scared to leave. Near the entryway to the kitchen, Derek Webb stood with his hands clasped behind his back.

"Nothin' but a buncha GODDAMN MUTHAFUCKAHS!" Rono whirled and roared at his assembled top crew. "HE'S JUST ONE FUCKIN' MAN!

"I mean, what are we?" Rono paused, waiting for an answer.

"The Vicetown Kings—the VKs," Webb said, knowing no one else would have the balls to reply, and not wanting Rono to get any more pissed off than he already was.

"Goddamn right we are—the Vicetown Kings—the VKs. The biggest, baddest gang in the entire muthafuckin' city. Ain't nothin' goes down here that we don't have a piece of, that we don't know about, that we don't allow. And now, in the space of twenty-four muthafuckin' hours, somebody rips off my MUTHAFUCKIN' *TENMILLIONDOLLARS,* and MARCUS-MUTHAFUCKIN'-CASEY KILLS THREE OF OUR SOLJAHS and both of 'em get away clean!"

"We'll get that money back, Gul," Low Rise said from the couch.

Rono slowly turned on him, the scar on his head seeming to pulse with righteous indignation. "Really? You gonna do that for me? On the rilla? When's that gonna happen, Low Rise?" While he was talking, Rono had slowly stalked toward the other man, and now loomed over him, making Low Rise sink back into the couch, his wide eyes darting back and forth, begging for help from anyone else in the room. The rest of the crew stayed stone silent, waiting for Rono to unload again.

"'Cuz you know what I see when I look around here, Low Rise? I don't see a bunch of the most bad-assed shot callers, the captains of the Vicetown Kings. I see a bunch of LIMP-DICK PUSSIES SITTING ON MY FURNITURE, LICKIN' MY MUTHA-FUCKIN' SHOES, AND MAKING GODDAMN EXCUSES FOR WHY THEY HAVEN'T FOUND MY MONEY OR KILLED MARCUS-MUTHAFUCKIN'-CASEY!"

He paused to take a deep breath, then looked around and shook his head. "This ain't the Vicetown Kings I know—none of you cocksuckers are fit to wear our colors." He stalked among them, every captain he came near shrinking away. "When I called this meeting, you all slunk in here like whipped dogs with yo goddamn tails between your legs. Didn't none of you have the brains or balls to say, 'Can't make it, Gul, I'm still beatin' the streets and the bushes for your money and Marcus Casey, and I ain't comin' in till I get 'em both.' Goddamn punk bitches, the fuckin' lot of ya.'"

While Rono continued ranting at his captains, a knock on the penthouse door caught Webb's attention. Slipping his HK P7 out of his waistband, he held it at his side while walking over to answer it—a nigga couldn't be too careful, even up here.

He cracked the door just enough to peek out, seeing the VK soljah named Bark on the other side. He caught a glimpse of at least two other figures in the hallway, but knew if Bark had brought them up, they were on the level. "Whatchu want? Rono's tearin' new assholes all up in here, so I suggest you bounce if you know what's good for you."

"Then lemme in, 'cause I'ma 'bout to make his muthafuckin' day. Got a slanger here says he got a line on Casey."

That got Webb's attention. "Really? Bring him in here."

Bark stepped back and waved the first, smaller figure forward. "C'mon, git yo ass up here."

The kid, no more than fifteen, stepped forward, dressed in baggy designer jeans and a red-and-white LeBron James basketball jersey, his ball cap cocked to one side. He just stared at Webb, his eyes flat.

"You carryin'?"

The kid shook his head.

"What you hear 'bout Casey?"

The teenage slanger shook his head, his stare turning insolent. "What I got I tell only to Rono."

Webb red-eyed him while admiring the punk's nuts at the same time. "'Kay, baby loke, it's your show, but if he don't like what he hears or thinks you're frontin' to get in good with him— well, you brought it down on yoself, ya feel me?"

The kid didn't react to the implied threat. "Let's do it."

"You all hang here a moment—gotta talk to my man."

Webb strolled back into the living room, where Rono was build-ing himself a good head of steam again. "—Sheeit, the only ones who might have a line on what Casey's doing right now are Jojoe and that fuckin' slope Jai Kitsuwon. And if that muthafuckah brings Casey down, well, all I'm gonna say is that I'll be lookin' at a buncha sorry niggas that let a pimp—a real muthafuckin' *pimp*—show all y'all up."

Webb stood to one side until his leader noticed him. "What, nigga?"

"Got someone here you'll wanna talk to, Gul. Says he got a line on Casey."

"Is that a muthafuckin' fact?" Rono vanished into his bedroom while Webb brought the three men into the living room: Bark, the kid, and the third man, a bum with a brand-new backpack, dirty clothes and falling-apart shoes, and strangely clean, white teeth.

Rono reappeared, strutting up to the three. "What you got for me, Bark?"

The VK gangsta nodded at the kid. "L'il G here said he over-heard him"—he pointed at the bum—"jaw jappin' 'bout Casey. He tol' me, we both went and got him to bring him to you."

Just like that, Rono went from boiling over to cool as ice. He slung his arm around Bark, the other man tensing a bit, but trying not to show it. "That's my dawg." He turned to the others in the room. "You see this? This is what I'm muthafuckin' talkin' 'bout! While you fools are sittin' on yo dumb asses watchin' me pop a muthafuckin' blood vessel, my nigga Bark is out takin' care a my business. Here, man, lemme break off a piece for ya."

Rono's free hand went into his pocket and pulled out a thick bankroll. He counted out ten benjamins and handed them to the man. "For a job muthafuckin' well done. Why don't you hang for a bit, kick it up in here?" He turned to glower at the rest of his captains. "There might just be a spot or two openin' up in management soon—could be the ticket you need to step up your game, dawg."

"Solid, Gul." Bark had already tucked the money into his pocket, and eased back away from Rono to a clear spot against one wall. If he felt the dark stares from several of the other captains, he wasn't showing it.

Rono noticed, however. "Hey—no red-eyein' Bark here. I find out anyone messed with him because he fuckin' *did his job,* they gonna answer to me! Now, where's the baller at who found this broke-down nigga?" Rono looked around, his eyes falling on the kid. "You the man who brought this to me?"

The kid had been tough with Webb, but in Rono's presence he seemed to shrink into himself, and only nodded silently.

Rono smiled, looking almost friendly for a moment. "You got a handle, l'il G? Can't just keep sayin' 'hey you' all the time."

"They call me Tone-D."

"Tone-D, huh? A'ight, I'm down with that. You a DJ?"

The kid puffed up a bit at actually conversating with the gang kingpin. "Hell no, I rap."

Rono's grin grew wider. "No shit, playa? Maybe you oughta throw some rhymes down for me later—if you got any skillz, I can hook you up with producers, record labels, whatever you need, dawg."

The kid's eyes widened. "That, uh—that'd be great."

"A'ight. In the meantime, take this"—Rono peeled off ten more benjamins and handed them to the kid—"and you come see me in a few days, and we'll see if you got any flow. Now bounce on outta here, youngsta, I got business to conduct."

The kid grabbed the money and took off for the door in a flash of red. Rono turned to the last man standing alone in the room. A puzzled look crossed his face. "You look real familiar, nigga. Now why the hell is that?"

"That's Ten Spot, Gul, he runs errands for Jawjack out of his music store," Big Sally rumbled. "Man used to ball all outta control—he could move more rock than anyone, ever. Too bad he started using his own product—now you all lookin' at is what's lefta him."

Rono glanced at the other man. "That the truth, old man? You used to be some legendary baller, used to slang with the best of 'em back in—sheeit, musta been back during muthafuckin' Prohibition, old as you look."

Several of the captains chuckled at the dig, then everybody fell silent, waiting for the old man's reply.

Ten Spot cleared his throat. "Nope."

The answer took Rono by surprise. "No? Whatchu mean 'no'?"

Ten Spot turned his head to stare Rono right in the eye. "I didn't slang with the best. I *was* the best."

No one moved or spoke for several heartbeats. Rono just stared at the old bum, and Webb was sure he was gonna have to clean up another dead nigga off the floor in a second. Then Rono chuckled, the low sound growing into a loud laugh that was shared by the rest of the captains in the room. It continued for a long while, everyone laughing at the old man, who stood stiffly, having returned to staring straight ahead.

"Goddamn, grampa, I didn't know we had a muthafuckin' pimp in the house!" Rono feigned wiping a tear of laughter from his eye. "You a piece of work, old man, you got heart." His expression turned serious. "Jawjack's place, huh? The same place that Casey was at a couple days ago? Now ain't that a muthafuckin' coincidence." Rono was holding something black in his hand, tapping it gently against his thigh as he walked around Ten Spot, who stood perfectly still and looked straight ahead. "So, my boy Tone-D says you were barkin' off 'bout Marcus Casey. What you know 'bout him?"

"I know he came into a lotta money recently."

The words hung in the air, making Rono freeze as he was walking around Ten Spot's back. "That so? How'd you get the four-one-one on that?"

"I panhandle all sorts of places—clubs, bars, restaurants. Them rich people, come out after eatin' their fancy meals and drinkin' their wine, they see me after gettin' all fat and happy, makes 'em feel guilty, you know. I make good bank outside a four-star restaurant—"

Rono gritted his teeth, making the muscles in his neck stick out as he controlled his temper. "I didn't ask for your muthafuckin' life story, gramps, I asked how you knew Marcus Casey got his mitts on a lot of paper."

"Right, right, sorry. So I'm doin' my thing at this real swanky restaurant in Brooklyn, Dominique's on the Pier—I can usually get a few bills before they run me off. Anyway, who do I see but Casey and some fine piece of tail come out, looking like they's livin' large, all happy and shit. The valet brings their car 'round, and Casey peels off a hundred and says, 'Keep the change, Gulliver Rono's payin' for this anyway.' They all laughed like he was Chris Rock, then they got in a car and drove away."

"Really? And you been spreadin' that story around on the streets, old man?"

Ten Spot looked at him again, a strange gleam in the old man's eye. "Well, you gotta admit it's a damn funny story."

"Really? Well, you look me in the muthafuckin' eye and see if I'm laughin'." Rono stared at him for a moment, daring the old man to say anything. Ten Spot remained silent. Rono began walking slowly around him again.

"That's a good story, old man, but there's one thing you didn't know. Ya see, I had a little talk with Jawjack yesterday, and he told me Casey had come to his store lookin' for you."

Rono breathed deep, then exhaled, shrugging out of his dark gray suit jacket and handing it to Derek Webb. "You know what

I think, gramps? I think Casey and you cooked up this little story to make me fly off the handle and come after him blind."

Rono stopped, just behind Ten Spot and a bit to his left. Silence fell over the room for a moment before the VK leader broke it. "So you know what we're gonna do—"

He flicked the wrist of the hand holding the black tube, making sixteen inches of rolled black steel spring out from the end. Raising his arm, Rono smashed the metal baton just under the back of Ten Spot's knee, making him drop his backpack, shout in pain, and collapse to the floor, clutching at his spasming leg. The old man rolled back and forth, tears springing from his squeezed-shut eyes.

Rono stood over him, tapping the end of the baton into his empty hand. "Nigga, you gonna tell me everythin' you fuckin' know 'bout Casey. And 'fore we're through, you gonna tell me things you didn't even know you knew."

He kicked the backpack across the room as the baton rose and fell, rose and fell, the meaty *thwacks* broken only by the howls of agony reverberating through the penthouse.

Casey had put the word out to Charlotte Hart, Hank Graves, and a couple of others to get ahold of Baybay to see if she had any more inside dope on what moves Rono was making. He heard back from Graves late that night she was in a Beaux Arts–style '30s era apartment building on Riverside Drive on the Upper West Side. If he got there at first light, she'd meet him in the underground garage.

Casey wore his jean jacket as he entered through a heavy metal door that had been left ajar for him. It was set in stonework next to the grilled gate the cars entered and exited through. He walked down a concrete ramp into the garage, the low wattage from overhead bulbs providing weak illumination.

Parked about were mostly late-model cars. He turned his head slightly at the sound of a car starting and looked at a 1958 Lincoln Continental Mark II. An older woman with bouffant hair, also from another time, was behind the wheel. She smiled at Casey as the electronic gate opened. Casey's eyes followed the car as it went up the ramp and he noticed that the cable to the closed-circuit camera in a corner of the ceiling had been cut.

Suddenly he sensed peripheral movement and shifted his body. To his right stood Jai Kitsuwon and to his left was a man he didn't know. Their intent was obvious. Kitsuwon grinned broadly as he raised a pistol with a suppressor on the end of it.

Casey backpedaled and dived to the dirty floor behind a Volvo as the other man unleashed rounds at him. The bullets ripped into the skin of the car and the assassins advanced, still firing. Casey twisted and threw one of the mini flash-bang grenades he'd gotten from the sideshow arms dealer, rolling it under the Volvo. It skittered across the floor, and went off in a heated flash at Kitsuwon's feet, the sharp crack echoing through the parking level.

The Thai was instantly blinded by the brightlight. "Cocksucker!" he shouted, feeling about. Casey drew his next surprise from the inside of his jacket and rose to a crouch, ready to spring it on the annoying little Thai man.

Jojoe had averted his eyes and was less affected, though he too blinked hard to dispel the white spots swirling in his vision. He was looking for the nearest cover just as he heard a sound he couldn't decipher. Kitsuwon pirouetted on his right foot, colliding with Jojoe.

"Fuckin' dude knifed me!" he screamed indignantly. He was feeling about his chest and touched the end of the blade without a handle protruding slightly from his jacket beneath his rib cage. "Can you believe this shit?" Kitsuwon wailed. "He got me with one of those goddamn trick knives." He started around, his vision still not clear.

Jojoe grabbed Kitsuwon, his eyes seeing normal again in the half gloom. They ducked behind a row of cars, listening and waiting. "Can you see yet?" he asked the other man.

"Yeah, yeah, almost," Jai said, going to one knee and breathing hard.

"Can you shoot?"

"Fuck, yeah!"

"Watch the elevator leading to the apartments," Jojoe ordered. From where they were, Kitsuwon could see the elevator doors as he looked over the cars' hoods.

"He doesn't seem to have a gun, but he sure as hell is armed with some nasty toys. I'm gonna flush him out. When I do, you pop him, ya hear me?"

"I got you, man." Sweating, Kitsuwon winced as he altered his position. Jojoe figured the blade was causing internal bleeding, but he had no choice except to trust Jai could bring their target down. He couldn't stand still and have Casey lob a frag grenade or some shit on them.

Jojoe crept off, planning to sneak behind the cars in a wide circle, then work his way back in. The garage was L-shaped, so there were cars facing one way, with a line of others perpendicular to them. He snuck forward, alert for any disturbance. Sneaking along the side of a Lexus, Jojoe heard a footfall and popped up to see Casey out in the open. In the milliseconds it took for him to get off his shots, his target had flung what looked like a handful of marbles to the floor. Only these were some type of smoke pellets that burst into a cloud, masking his form. Jojoe wasn't about to rush into that pall, and hunched down again, still looking for the right opportunity.

The smoke drifted across to where Kitsuwon was. He rose partially, firing into the white grayness, anticipating Casey's stealthy approach.

"Right here, asshole," Crush Casey said at his side. Jai swung his pistol around, trying to aim, but Casey simply grabbed his wrist and twisted, forcing him to drop the gun. He calmly kicked the shorter man in the stomach, dropping him to his knees. Casey scooped the pistol up and aimed it at Jai's face.

The elevator door binged open and an older couple exited, talking to each other. Casey's hand came up, the pistol tracking the couple just as Jojoe burst from cover and ran behind them, blocking Casey from taking a shot. Shoving the frightened couple forward roughly, Jojoe reached the elevator, slipping through as the doors binged shut.

The woman stumbled to her knees and her husband bent down to help her.

Casey stalked over to Kitsuwon, his back to the two, having turned up his collar.

"Oh my God, Harold. He's going to shoot that man!"

"Be quiet and get to the car, Mildred, this is none of our business."

"Oh, Harold!"

Kitsuwon's eyes fluttered as he lay on his back and briefly focused on Casey as he put a bullet through his heart. Casey ran up the ramp and out the door, making sure to wipe down the latch as he went. He'd made sure not to touch any of the cars. He took the suppressor off the pistol and put the handgun in one coat pocket, the silencer in the other. He walked on, willing himself to blend in with the early morning pedestrians.

22

"ook, the thing is you make these horny motherfuckers believe they have the biggest dick you ever saw," Baybay explained to one of the newly arrived sex slaves, a Vietnamese girl named Pho Doc Binh, who had been rechristened Sandi. She wore a short pleated plaid skirt, white blouse knotted below her high, round breasts to show off her lean stomach, and chunky shoes. At seventeen, she looked exactly like a naughty schoolgirl from the pages of manga porn, right down to her sullen expression.

"Maybe I bite his thing," she said.

"And maybe you get your throat cut, dumbass."

Binh looked evenly at Baybay. "Why you do this? You like me."

"I'm exactly like you, that's why I do this. I'm trapped. You're trapped."

"I want go home."

Baybay shook her head. "This is your home now. Deal with it."

Binh said something in Vietnamese, then, in English, "Bullshit."

"That's what I'm talkin' about. Use that anger," Baybay said. "See the people who have hurt you in the faces of the men you have to suck and fuck and see them in the fire. See them over and over again hurt and crying, until you can't feel anything anymore."

"Like you." Binh lit a cigarette, blew smoke into the air.

Baybay glanced at the door, not wanting to show how accurate the other girl's comment had been. "Yeah, like me."

Binh was about to say something else when Baybay heard heels clicking angrily on the stairs outside. "Shh, the Dragon Bitch is coming." Hearing their madam talking in the hallway, she crept to the door to listen.

"Are you serious? . . . When did this happen? . . . That stupid fuck! . . . Jai always was biting off more than he could chew—in every sense of the word. . . . Yes . . . who was he looking for? . . . Really? . . . And she was the one who serviced him at Woodside's as well. . . . Yes, I think it's high time you had a talk with Baybay personally. . . . I'll bring her right over. . . . Within the hour. . . . Of course she'll be yours to do with as you like, Mr. Rono . . . we cannot have girls acting out of control like this. . . . Of course . . . we'll see you soon."

Baybay's insides turned to water as she heard the conversation. *Fuck fuck fuck!* She didn't know how, but they knew she was working for Casey. Quickly she snuck back to the leather couch and sat down, pretending to be engrossed in the television show while her mind raced through and discarded possible plans of escape.

"What's the matter?" Binh asked, stubbing out her cigarette.

"Nothing—lemme have one of those." The Vietnamese girl slid one out and Baybay lit up. She hated the taste, but right now it might be the only weapon she'd have. She blew smoke out and looked over as the door slammed open, revealing Grace Phan standing there in a tailored crimson pantsuit.

Grabbing the remote, she angrily clicked off the cartoon movie the sex slaves had been watching. "Keep that shit off and get these girls ready," she snapped at Baybay. One of the girls, a doe-eyed beauty from Estonia who'd been enjoying the program, looked away and lowered her head.

"Get up, Baybay. We're going for a ride," Phan said.

Baybay rose slowly, dragging on her cigarette. "Come on, girls. Where we goin'?"

"The rest of you stay where you are," Phan snapped. "Just you, Baybay."

"Why?"

Phan stalked to the Filipino girl and grabbed her chin, squeezing hard. "Because I said so, you ignorant slant whore!"

That was all it took. "Fuck it," she said aloud, bringing up the cigarette and aiming it at the other woman's eye. Phan jerked her head out of the way just in time, and the burning ember sizzled into the skin on her cheek.

"You ungrateful bitch!" Phan released Baybay, but her other hand came up in a roundhouse slap that nearly knocked the Filipino over, sending her staggering back onto the couch. She got to her feet as Phan pulled out a small compact, examining the burn on her face. "Goddamn it! You worthless piece of street trash, you'll pay for that!"

The other woman stared at them, and Phan took her eyes off Baybay to bark, "What the fuck are you looking—"

That's when Baybay slugged her. Hard.

"Wha—?" Phan cried out, staggering across the room.

"Fuck you, fuck Jai, fuck all you goddamn pimps and smugglers!" Baybay screamed as she tackled Phan, sending her into the television, which rocked on its base before toppling to the floor. Two of the other girls screamed as the women grappled, pulling hair, scratching at each other's faces, and throwing wild punches.

"Ungrateful whore!" Phan said, throwing her knee into Baybay's stomach. The younger woman rolled off her, gasping, and the madam scrambled to her feet and kicked Baybay in the head. She went to her purse to get her cell phone, but was surprised when Baybay jumped on her back and sent her crashing to the floor again. Bleeding from broken skin on her forehead, Baybay smacked Phan in her nose, making it bleed. The older woman rocked Baybay with a stiff-armed shot to her temple, shook loose, and crawled away on all fours. Grabbing a straight-backed chair, the disheveled, bleeding madam pulled herself up just as Baybay lunged at her again. Phan grabbed the skittish Estonian girl and pushed her into Baybay, then snatched her purse from the coffee table and ran out of the apartment. By the time Baybay had disentangled herself, grabbed Phan's cell from the floor, and chased after the woman downstairs, she was nowhere to be seen.

Spitting blood from her mouth, Baybay slowed down and took a deep breath, but kept walking, waiting for a shout from the apartment building or a heavy hand to land on her shoulder. When she rounded the corner of the block, she took off again, and didn't stop for ten minutes, until the stitch in her side brought her up short. Ducking into a corner store, she got the key for the restroom and splashed cold water on her face, then stopped her nosebleed with a compress. When she'd caught her breath, she pulled out the phone and dialed a number, whispering, "Come on, come on, pick up, pick up."

"Who dis?" a familiar voice answered.

"Char? It's Baybay."

"Baybay, what's up? What's the matter, you in trouble?"

"Damn right—I'm on the street and in the wind. I need a place to lie low immediately."

"Okay, where you at?" Baybay gave her the address of the store. "Good—stay in there, don't come out for anyone until they tell you either Crush Casey or I sent them. Got it?"

"Okay, I'll wait here."

"I'll have someone there as soon as possible. Just hang tight, girl, you'll be all right."

"Thank you, Charlotte . . ." Baybay hung up the phone, not wanting to let the other girl hear her cry. She sank to the floor of the bathroom, tears streaming from her eyes as she realized just how close to being killed she had come.

Lomax had worked up a man-sized appetite after going through all of the data that had landed in his inbox overnight, and had ordered an Italian meatball parmigiana sub from the Manhattan Diner a few blocks away. He'd supersized it by adding fresh buffalo mozzarella and basil, and the aroma coming out of the white paper bag was making his mouth water. Licking his chops, he carefully slung his tie—a silk reproduction of Monet's *Water Lilies*—over his shoulder, tucked a napkin into his collar, and prepared to feast.

He was about to take his first bite into hoagie heaven when his phone rang. He looked from the sandwich to the phone, then back to the sandwich. The black Bakelite rang again, reverberating inside his skull with its insistent din.

"Ain't that always the way?" he muttered, setting the sub down carefully on his cleared desk. He licked a bit of sauce off his pinkie, and picked up the receiver. "Lomax."

"It's Fulson. Hey man, where's that storm you promised me? I'm lookin' out the window, and it's sunny skies and sixty-five degrees in the city. My bosses are starting to make noises that involve the words, 'waste of time and manpower,' and 'lateral transfer to Shit City, Nebraska.'"

Lomax leaned back in his chair, idly wondering if he could sneak a bite or two and talk to his federal contact at the same time. "You tell those DEA cats to just chill out and let things play. There's all sorts of shit goin' down in the big city, my man—you just gotta know where to look."

"That's all well and good, brother, but I need something to

whet their appetites, otherwise they're gonna come down on me like a ton of shit, and once the flow starts, it's all downhill from there."

"Damn, man, you keepin' me from my lunch with this paltry request. All right, I'll humor you. Keep in mind that I'm givin' you the raw data here, 'kay? It's up to you to spin it to the suits."

"Don't worry about that, I just need something to tell them. We're laying out thousands of dollars on these offices and surveillance, and so far it hasn't turned up jack-shit."

"All right, all right, keep your drawers buttoned. Let's see, let's see." Lomax grabbed a thick folder labeled VICETOWN KINGS from the floor next to him, and flipped through the top few pages. "Okay, item one: Approximately three days ago, the Vicetown Kings started shaking the streets up and downtown, eyeballin' really hard for around ten million dollars in nonsequential bills."

"Holy shit! Why you telling me this now?"

Lomax ignored the excited agent and continued. "Word 'round the campfire is that this money was earmarked to purchase a huge— with a capital H—load of cocaine from the cartels in South America. If Rono can't make the deal, the coke never arrives in the city."

"What? How does that help me? I work for the *Drug Enforcement Agency*, remember? We need to arrest people and confiscate the drugs they're trying to move *into the country*, not derail pending deals—all this gets me is a ticket to friggin' Nebraska."

"Fulson, Fulson, Fulson—anyone tell you you worry too much?"

"All the time—like I said, it's a job requirement. Please tell me you have something else."

"'Course I do, I wouldn't leave you hanging. Item two; The same day the money got pinched, Brix Bancroft, the VK's second-in-command, was found with his face shot off in an abandoned industrial complex at College Point in Queens, all by his lonesome."

"And?"

"With no other bodies in sight, I'm theorizing that he was either behind the heist and got capped when Rono found out, or he tried to take Rono out in the confusion, and got iced instead."

A low moan came from the receiver. "Lomax, you're making me sick. *Please* tell me all these bread crumbs you're laying down are leading somewhere."

"Elementary, my dear Fulson. Third: Last night, three gangbangers named Trey-Dog, Rolla, and Cherry Bomb were found in various states of death along a half mile of the BQE, one with his face shot off, the other two roasted in their Escalade. All three were known associates of Gulliver Rono, and all were card-carrying Vicetown King members."

"Antacids . . . where's my antacids . . . ?" Through the speaker, Lomax heard desk drawers opening and closing and frenzied searching. "Every word coming outta your mouth's making my ulcer flare up."

"Well, suck down your milk of magnesia or Rolaids or what have you, 'cause my sandwich is getting cold, and I'm about to wrap it up. Fourth on our list, and the final piece of the puzzle. Early this morning, Jai Kitsuwon, an Asian known for procuring female flesh for unsavory purposes, and also associated with Mr. Rono, was found shot to death in an underground parking garage on the Upper West Side. Vice has long suspected the VKs of running high-priced call girls out of that area, but haven't had much to go on—until now."

"What the hell does *any* of that have to do with the cocaine pipeline from South America Rono's trying to build?"

Lomax sensed Fulson was really trying to keep his temper, but couldn't resist one more jab. "I connect all the dots, and still you do not see the big picture. Here's the deal: With Rono missing his bankroll to buy his boatload of Colombian flake, he's going to do whatever he has to to get that money back and make the deal—rob, steal, kill, whatever. In short, he's going to get sloppy, cut corners, what-have-you. Since the DEA is *supposed* to be cracking down on organized crime as part of their war on drugs, this should make them happy, since sooner or later, Rono's going to do something that will put him on their radar. A bust of a major gang lord in my fair city should burnish your badge very well."

Fulson's voice was hesitant. "Well . . . maybe . . . okay, that a start."

Lomax frowned at his counterpart's reticence. "You're damn right it's a start, and a good one. Second, someone's been taking out VKs all over the place. While I'm not gonna place any blame or name any names, you and I both know who's behind that. I strongly suspect our avenging angel also had a hand in the armed robbery—it's exactly his style, filling his pockets while hurting his enemy at the same time. Point is, I expect a major dust-up brewing that involves the Vicetown Kings, maybe even in the next couple of days. When that happens, all sorts of skipskaps and scalawags are likely to be shaken loose."

"Yeah, about that? I already got enough heat coming down from above—the last thing I need is them to catch wind that our star player once walked on the dark side his own self. Are you sure you can trust him?"

"Sure, as much as I can trust an ex-gangbanger who once ran the largest street gang and criminal empire in the city." *I don't think now would be the time to let him know that Casey has aspirations of regaining that crown either,* Lomax thought. "But you don't have to worry about that—handling him's my problem, not yours."

"Not if he doesn't produce something I can dump on my superiors' desks—if that doesn't happen, it's both our problems."

"If you say so. Anything else you need?"

"*Anything* else I need? Anything *else* I need? Are you telling me you expect me to take this load of suppositions, random gangland slayings, and evasions and half-truths and make a credible case out of it? Are you *insane?*"

Lomax rolled a shoulder. "Isn't that what you government suits do best—spin gold out of straw? Like I told you, man, I'm just giving you the raw data—what you do with it is your prerogative."

"Oh, my God . . . I might as well start packing my bags right now."

Lomax shook his head. "Tell you what—why don't you try to wrangle twenty-four hours out of your bosses, and let me see if I can turn up something more concrete?"

Fulson sounded like a man who was already packing his bags for a transfer to Bumbleshoot, Idaho, for the next two years. "Yeah . . . I'll see what I can do. . . . Just promise me you'll be in touch in twenty-four hours."

"I promise, my man." Whether Lomax would have anything of import to relay might be another story, but he knew his boy Casey was getting ready to make his move, and when it went down, all sorts of interesting things were bound to shake loose. "Maybe you should take the afternoon off, get yourself a massage, take a steam, you know, relax a bit."

"Yeah . . . maybe I should, since this might be the last time I get to see the Big Apple for a long time."

"All right, I'll be in touch as soon as I have something. Now if you'll excuse me, I'm going back to my lunch."

Fulson's voice was growing fainter. "Yeah . . . okay, Lomax . . . I'll talk to you later."

Hanging up the phone, Lomax picked up his meatball hero and smiled. It was still warm. He raised it to his lips again, then paused as a thought struck him. Holding the sandwich in one hand, he picked up the phone and dialed a memorized number. It rang and rang, then went to voice mail, a computerized, feminine voice telling him that the customer wasn't available, and to please leave a message.

"Mr. Casey, I trust this message finds you beatin' the streets of our fine city for gainful employment. I think it's time for another meeting. Let's say my office, four P.M. today. I'm sure I'll see you later."

After all, he may be doin' some of my work for me on the sly, but that don't mean I can't put a little bit of the fear of God—or in this case, his parole officer—into him either.

Hanging the receiver up, Lomax finally bit into his meatball sub.

Hank Graves had the crack whore who called herself Trebly bent over a stack of mattresses in the storeroom. Her jeans were bunched down around her ankles. She didn't wear underwear when working, only when sleeping.

"Oh, yeah, baby, do me, big daddy, do me," she intoned huskily. Every once in a while she'd get on a friend's computer and check out the free porno sites to brush up on her role-playing. She'd even been interviewed on one of them, *Crack Ho Diaries.*

Graves grunted as he put himself into his work.

She was firing up her crack pipe in a practiced maneuver as Graves did her from behind. But suddenly he stopped, though he hadn't come yet. No matter. Trebly inhaled her narcotic lovingly and deeply, her tongue going numb from the smoke. Fumes drifted from her mouth, momentarily blotting out her vision and the despicableness of her bottom-feeder life. But the feeling didn't last long. It never did.

"Goddamn, Graves, you take 'doin' the nasty' to a whole new level." Crush Casey turned his cold eyes on the ho. "Get whatever cash he's got in his wallet."

"Whatever you say, boss man." Trebly shook loose her trick's rapidly softening cock and shimmied into her pants, still holding her crack pipe in one hand. Bending down, she sifted Graves's pants until she found his wallet, and swiftly emptied it, her eyes widening at the several hundred dollars in her hand.

"Now get the fuck out of here, and you never saw nuthin', got it?"

She nodded at the big black man and scurried for the back door without looking back.

"Crush," Graves began. "Look, man—"

Casey hit him twice across the bridge of the nose with a chair leg he'd broken off. Graves sagged against the mattresses, his pants and bikini-style underwear tangled around his legs.

"Crush, man—it wasn't like that—," Graves started again. Blood was splattered over his face, his nose bent to one side.

"Uh-huh," Casey said. He brought the chair leg down on Graves's head so hard it snapped in half. Bits of wood stuck out of Graves's scalp. He put a hand to the burgeoning lump, his eyes glassy and unfocused.

"Crush—you gotta listen to me, man—they had me jammed up."

"Stop whinin' and stop lyin'." Casey grabbed him and hoisted him to his feet, then pushed him onto the top mattress. Drawing the pistol he took from Jai, he pressed it into Graves's beer gut. "You set me up, you punk-ass muthafuckah. Now you better gimme somethin' I can use."

Graves scooted back to the wall, as if he could somehow get far enough away from the black muzzle of the pistol. "What do you want? What can I do?"

"Except die?" Casey glared at him like a man about to squash an irritating bug.

"What can I do, Marcus? What the fuck do you want from me?"

Casey described the shooter who got away. "Who is he?"

"Jojoe, they call him Jojoe," Graves said, gulping. "He's smart, wants to earn his button. He's, uh—he's been on the hunt for you."

"Woulda been nice to know that earlier." Casey gestured with the gun. "Known associates?"

"Shit, I—I don't know." He closed his eyes, waiting for the bullet.

"Get yo' drawers up. You got calls to make."

"Sure, Crush, sure, whatever you need, man." Prodded by Casey, he stumbled into the back office. Casey followed, screwing the silencer onto the end of the extended barrel.

At his desk, Graves made those calls and gathered a handful of names and hangouts for JoJoe. "See, man, see, I came through for you." Graves finished writing and turned an expectant, hopeful face up at Casey, only to see the suppressor leveled on his eye. His expression crumpled, but before he could open his mouth to beg for his life one more time, Casey shot him through the right eye. He slumped across his desk as Casey took the list in his gloved hand. Keys could be heard rattling at the front as one of the employees arrived to open the store. Casey exited through a side door.

Walking along, he regarded the list Graves had prepared. He made a mental map and plotted where the closest location was, planning to start there and work his way out, as one of the spots was in the Bronx and another in Queens. In fact, it was high time to start operating like a boss again and not a lone gunman.

He called Omar Atkins, and found the freelancer in a very good mood. "Hey dawg, good to hear ya. The 'VKs' delivered that message to the Lotus, and they are pissed off and lookin' for pay-back."

"Good, 'cause we 'bout to give 'em somthin' else to chew on. In the meantime, I gotta submarine assignment for you," he said.

"Hit me."

Casey filled him in on recent events and finished with, "Sit on this house in Queens and be on the ones and two for this Jojoe."

"Smoke 'im?"

"If you get him in your crosshairs, and you got an escape route, yeah. Otherwise, lay in the cut and observe."

"Cool. By the way, my boys said if you got any more work like that last job, they're in."

"You trust 'em, right?"

"Like my mama on the stand cosignin' for me."

"If they want in on what's about to go down, we can use all the hitters we can get. I'd need to know right away if they can play. I'll double the pay on this one, but let 'em know it's more dangerous."

"Sheeit, nigga, what day in NYC isn't? I'll make that call and get back at ya." Omar clicked off.

Casey then called Shinzo Becker. Li, the chauffeur, answered. "Have him call me," he said when she told him he was busy at the moment. "It's important. I need some eyes out for a sucka."

"Understood," she said. "Shinzo gave me a message to pass along if you called. The Blood Devils are ready to go."

"Excellent. We'll be settin' it all up in the next twenty-four hours. Tell Shin I also need that location we talked about as soon as possible. He'll know what I mean."

There was an advantage to being mobile—he wasn't tied to any one place, while Rono had to defend his physical assets. What did Che say? *War is always a struggle in which each contender tries to annihilate the other. Besides using force, they will have recourse to all possible tricks and stratagems to achieve the goal.* *Yeah, it's definitely time for some tricks,* Casey thought.

His phone buzzed, signaling he'd gotten a voice mail. He dialed up to hear Kenny's voice. "Crush, holla back the moment you get this. Ten Spot delivered the package, but got into a bit of a jam, and ended up in the hospital. I'm headin' over there right now."

Crush dialed Kenny and had him swing by and pick him up. Thirty-five minutes later, they were standing outside Ten Spot's room, talking to his doctor.

"You're this 'Crush' Casey?" The doctor, a tall, slim Indian, asked. "He won't stop asking for you. Are you relations?"

Casey resisted the urge to bulldog through the skinny doc and get in to see his boy. "Yeah, I'm his nephew. Can we see him?"

"Normally I wouldn't recommend it—he's still under the effects of the sedative we gave him so we could set his ribs. Four of them were broken, along with his right leg and left arm. He has a severe concussion, and both hands were injured pretty badly. He's lucky he didn't get a punctured lung on top of everything. But if letting you in might calm him down, be my guest."

Casey and Kenny walked into the room. Ten Spot lay like a faded ink stain on the clean white bed. The nurses had washed him, so Casey could see his face clearly for the first time, see what the ravages of drugs and street living had done to him. It wasn't pretty; his skin was wrinkled and pitted from years of abuse, both from his environment and what he'd done to himself.

When he saw them, Ten Spot's face lit up. He gasped and tried to sit, but winced in pain, and eased back down on the tilted bed.

Crush was at his side, helping him lay back down. "Easy, Ten Spot, easy, don't go hurtin' yourself any more. What the hell happened?"

The old man wheezed with every breath he took and motioned Casey to come closer, his lips working as he tried to form words. "I delivered the message—just like you tol' me to. But Rono didn't bite. Tried to beat—the four-one-one out of a nigga—but I didn't—tell 'em nothin'. Kept my mouth shut—just like you'd want me to."

Crush straightened, but Ten Spot grabbed his arm with his plastered hand, wincing as he did so. "Crush—didn't I tell ya—I kin be a good soljah for ya? Didn't I tell ya—I could make it happen?"

Casey bit his lip, knowing he'd put Ten Spot in harm's way in the first place. He figured Rono would push Ten Spot around a bit and kick him out on his ass, not beat the man to within an inch of his life. "Yeah, man, you did good—real good. Now just relax and let those pretty nurse honeys take care a you for a few days, okay?"

"Yeah, right on—knew I could do it—get my shit straight

and—get back in the game. Workin' for Crush Casey again—just like the old days. . . ." Ten Spot's head nodded as the sedative took hold, and his eyes drooped closed.

Casey ran a hand over his mouth as he stared down at the old panhandler who had risked his life to help him. "Wasn't supposed to go down this way, Kenny."

Kenny Saunders rubbed his hands together. "Ten Spot knew the score when he took the risk, Crush, you know that. We all knew what we were gettin' into when you hit the streets again. Hell, he's lucky—we could be standin' in the morgue right now, staring at his body under a sheet, you dig?"

"Yeah, I hear you. I want you to make sure the bill is covered, every last dollar—I'll repay you later."

"Ain't no thang, man. You lookin' at a nigga with a 710 credit score."

"Okay, let's bounce."

Seeing Ten Spot in the hospital had shaken Casey, as much as he was loath to admit it. Back in the day, he'd be the first mufu to send out a team of hardasses to cap some fool who'd deserved it and if his boys took their lumps or a bullet during, that was just the price of doing business. But his time inside, along with his many conversations with Mack D, had given him a new appreciation of the people who were working alongside him. They weren't just disposable pawns—they were living, breathing entities, with their own desires, goals, and frailties. Ten Spot had risked everything to deliver that news to Rono, and look where it had gotten him—all because he'd wanted to impress Crush again.

Shaking his head, Casey silently vowed to be a lot more careful, especially when the time came to take out Rono. He couldn't afford to make any bigger mistakes.

He caught Kenny Saunders's eye. "Hey, brother, one more thing? Can you get me a line to Rono direct? I gotta message I wanna deliver to him personally. It's time we put an end to all this, and I know just how to do it."

"Can do, dawg. Gimme an hour or two, I'll getcha those digits."

Later, having so far come up empty with sighting Jojoe, Casey was at the apartment above the empty store. He and Champa were going over an inventory of weapons and other equipment on hand.

"What I hear from the jungle," Champa began, "is Rono's shakin' the goddamn trees lookin' for you. Word is he's paying two grand for any info, and five and up for a direct sighting." He chuckled. "He goes any higher, even I'd consider turnin' yo' ass in."

Casey red-eyed him while slapping a magazine into an HK MP5 submachine gun. "That ain't funny, man. And now you the one without a gat nearby."

Champa held up his hands, a broad smile splitting his face. "All right, be cool, nigga, shit, I'm just playin' witcha, that all."

"Some kinds a playin' ain't worth the trouble, homes."

"Da-yamn, you a jumpy cat recently, you feel me? Anyway, the VKs ain't the only ones on the warpath. Seems someone done poked a stick into the Black Lotus down in Chinatown too. Somethin' about the VKs thinking the Lotus hit their money wagon a few days ago—and they been hittin' back on the outskirts of VK territory recently. Killed four slangers in the past day alone."

Casey shook his head as he set up a row of flash-bang grenades, checking each one for any problems. "Ain't that a shame? Gotta be careful out there nowadays—never know when the right word in the wrong ears could stir up a whole mess a trouble."

Champa nodded. "True dat. Then there's the Blood Devils— lotta people on the street sayin' they preppin' to make a move against a major player. But no one can find out who the target is, or what's goin' down."

"Really?" Casey's eyebrows arched in surprise—he hadn't

thought the Devils would have considered him that much of a threat. "Well, them small gangs who get too big for their britches either get one over on whoever they wanna chunk, or die tryin'."

"All this goin' on, and you just sittin' here countin' yo' bullets." Champa whistled in admiration. "You been the spider pulling the strands of all these webs, ain'tcha? I gotta give ya credit—the old Casey woulda charged in guns blazin' and takin' out anybody and everybody who wasn't down. But you gone all Machievellian and shit on me now."

Casey stared at him. "Mack D schooled me that there are many ways to bring an enemy to you, and attack when it is most advantageous. He was particularly fond of this quote: *'If the enemy general is obstinate and prone to anger, insult and enrage him, so that he will be irritated and confused, and without a plan will recklessly advance against you.'*"

"Works for me. Is that more of that Sun Tzu shit?"

"No, another nigga called Chang Yü, who kicked a lot of game on how to defeat opponents when you're outnumbered or outmaneuvered." He checked the action on a FMG9 machine gun, then noisily refolded the weapon. "Make no mistake—the war is on, man. But how it's goin' down is what's different this time." They continued with their inventory of mayhem.

Champa's sat phone trilled, and he answered, listening. He said, "Okay, got it, Vera." He wrote on a pad. "This is cool. Yeah, yeah, more good shit. Thanks." He closed off the call and held up the piece of paper. "Now we know the banker's identity."

Casey waited.

"Vera been scopin' that data file she got from Bancroft." He tore the sheet off the pad and handed it over to Casey, who also read it. "Our girl's also gettin' that list together on Rono's locales. 'Parently there's a lotta stuff in that file."

Casey held up the sheet of paper. "But we got this right now."

"We do indeed," Champa agreed.

When they were finished with the inventory, Casey's cell rang. "Yeah, Kenny? Just a sec . . ." He scribbled a number down on the paper with the banker's name. "Okay, cool, that's good lookin' out, my man."

He hung up, then pulled out a burner. "Watch and see how I make a nigga irritated and confused." He dialed the number, then held the phone out so Champa could hear both sides of the conversation.

"Go for Rono," the ragged voice on the other end said.

"Guess who, nigga?"

There was a pregnant moment of silence before Rono spoke again through gritted teeth. "You dead, nigga, I'm talking to a dead man on this cell. Hello? You hear me, muthafuckah?!"

Casey gave it a beat, then continued. "I just thought I'd call and thank you for your generous contribution of ten mil to the 'Crush Casey livin' large' fund. You have yoself a nice day, ya hear?"

Casey snapped the phone shut, and broke it in his large hands. "That'll make Rono come to us at a place of our choosing, I guarantee it."

A slaughterhouse chuckle rasped from both men as they kept preparing for the upcoming bloodbath.

23

The next morning, Crush Casey, fitted to the nines in Mal Yurik's black suit, his eyes hidden behind a pair of Sean John sunglasses, entered the busy lobby of a building on Wall Street and strolled over to the security kiosk.

"Jefferson Humphries to see Mr. Cobb."

The security guard, his thick arms and torso swathed in a gray sport coat, gave Casey a cursory glance as he called up appointments on his monitor. "Last-minute addition this morning—you're a lucky man—Mr. Cobb almost never has free time in his schedule."

Crush regarded him indifferently over the rims of his shades. "Luck has nothing to do with it, son." And it didn't—Becker's guard pal Teddy also moonlighted at this building, and he was romancin' one of the secretaries. It had been easy to slip Casey into the appointment book for a ten-minute meeting—he wouldn't even disrupt the man's morning schedule.

Satisfied, the guard tapped a clipboard on the counter. "Sign in, please. You know where you're going?"

"I do, thanks." Casey wrote the false name with his left hand. He was naturally right-handed, but had practiced an awkward yet legible way of writing with his left for years when it came to situations like this. He nodded good day and went up the elevator to the forty-first floor of the skyscraper. He was let out into a sedate but tasteful lobby for a suite of offices and he told the receptionist whom he was there to see. After less than a minute, he was led back to the lush corner office of Garland Cobb, who acted as co-CEO of Pegasus Investments, along with his younger brother Harlan.

Some four decades ago, Garland Cobb had been a kid from the streets running numbers for a sports bookie when he lucked into meeting Vasili Machinko. The underworld banker took a liking to him, and Cobb learned his craft under the older man's tutelage while Machinko had served as Casey's laundryman. After Rono had Machinko taken out, Cobb inherited the apparatus Machinko had built over time. Although Cobb was displeased at the cause of his success, business was business.

A fit, energetic man in his early sixties, Cobb was in shorts and a T-shirt on his treadmill doing a power walk when Casey entered. He slowed the pace while extending his hand to Casey, who braced himself to see if the other man would recognize him. While they'd never met face-to-face, as Casey had done all his business with Machinko directly, there was no telling where Cobb might have seen his face—or if Rono had already warned the money launderer to be on the lookout for him.

His concern was unwarranted—Cobb pumped his hand twice and let it drop. "Mr. Humphries," he greeted Casey, breathing easily.

"Call me Jeff," Casey replied. He remained standing near Cobb as he continued his exercise.

"Forgive me, but this was the only way I could squeeze you in now. At my age, I can't be missing my scheduled workouts."

"I completely understand."

"So, the appointment reminder was a bit vague about the reason you're here."

"I'm here to deliver a message from my employer."

Cobb eyed him speculatively. "Which is?"

Casey stepped back from the treadmill, looking around the richly appointed room. "I don't mean to be insulting, but you do regularly sweep this office?"

"Of course I do, young man."

"Very well. I'm an associate of Marcus Casey."

Cobb's salt-and-pepper eyebrows rose, but his arms and legs never stopped their rhythmic stride. "Is that so?"

"It is. He wanted me to meet with you to apprise you of the change in leadership that will occur with the Vicetown Kings soon."

That got Cobb's attention. He dialed the speed of his treadmill down to a slow walk, but didn't stop. "Are you threatening me in my own office?"

"Not at all, sir. As you have said, this is a business meeting, and I am simply notifying you of the change in the Vicetown Kings' business affairs that will be happening shortly. Mr. Casey would like to retain your services on behalf of the organization. He has very ambitious plans for the future, and sees no reason to disrupt what has been a very equitable arrangement for both parties."

"I see." Cobb stared at Casey for a moment, then shook his head. "That goddamn *macher*'s back after twenty years, and he just expects everything to go back to the way it was?"

Casey smiled slightly. *Damn right I do.* "I'm afraid I'm not at liberty to disclose the reasons why Mr. Casey tasked me to give you this message—he simply asked that it be done, and that is exactly what I am doing. Should you wish to set up an appointment with him once the hostile takeover has occurred, I'm sure that can be arranged."

"'Hostile takeover'—heh, that's rich." Cobb eyed Casey speculatively. "What's to stop me from calling security and having you hauled off to jail for extortion and intimidation?"

Casey smiled. "I would guess the incriminating files, made by Brix Bancroft, detailing your intimate involvement in Rono's business. The papers, the police, the FBI, and the SEC—all of them would be very interested in taking a closer look at some of Pegasus Investments' off-the-book deals." Casey spread his arms out to encompass the plush office. "You and all of this would become just another sad casualty of the Wall Street collapse."

Cobb came to a stop on the treadmill. "And if I think you're bluffing?"

"Mr. Casey has already planned for that contingency." Casey withdrew a small digital recorder from his pocket and pressed the play button.

"—Garland Cobb, now there's a piece of work." Bancroft's disembodied voice filled the room. "He and his brother Harlan of Pegasus Investments do with money what we do with rocks, guns, and pussy—slang it around. Only they take it from coal-black to bright white, washin' that filthy lucre until a nun would swear on a stack of Bibles it came to her right from the U.S. Treasury. If you open the file labeled 'Pegasus,' you'll see the various investments the company has had a hand in on behalf of the Kings—"

Casey clicked the recorder off. *This Internet thing has a definite future,* he thought. Vera had e-mailed Kenny the voice snippet he had just played off the flash drive, which he'd downloaded into the recorder. It had all worked perfectly.

Cobb frowned. "Casey can't possibly implicate me without destroying the Kings as well—he'd be a fool to sacrifice everything that's already in place by throwing me to those SEC schmucks."

"Mr. Cobb, surely you of all people understand that the 'Vicetown Kings' is, at its heart, just a name. The organization itself can fade into the shadows while your no doubt messy and very public trial is splashed across all the front pages and the nightly news. Then, while you're serving three-to-ten in a cushy, minimum-security federal penitentiary, we will simply absorb the enterprise previously known as the Vicetown Kings and relaunch our business ventures under a new name. You and your brother, however, will still have lost everything—your entire fortune, your good name, your standing in the community."

Cobb's face had faded from its ruddy hue to a shade of pale white chalk. "How long do I have to decide?"

"Mr. Casey is willing to grant—" Casey's cell phone trilled. He pulled it out and checked the display. "Please excuse me, but I have to take this." He opened the phone and raised it to his cheek while turning away just enough to ensure that Cobb could over-hear his side of the conversation. "Yes, sir?"

"Hey, Crush, you still sittin' in that cabbage shuffler's office?" Shinzo Becker's cheerful voice sounded in his ear.

"Yes, sir, I'm with him right now."

"You tell that old Jew that Crush Casey is tellin' him to get with the program or he'll be floating tits up in the Hudson by mornin'!" Becker laughed long and loud.

Casey kept his expression impassive. "Yes, sir, I'll certainly pass on your regards to him. Was there anything else you needed at this time?"

"Yeah, you wanted that address where the shit's gonna go down tonight, right? Well, I found the perfect place for you, a foreclosed slum apartment on Taylor Avenue, in Parkenbush." He named a building number, which Casey repeated out loud, along with the street and neighborhood.

"Yes, sir, I'll be sure to have everything prepared for this evening."

"A'ight, then, I'm off to plant a bug in the ears of the BDs. They gonna bring the blood and thunder with 'em, I guarantee it."

"Excellent, sir, that is most satisfactory. Yes, I'll call you when my business here is concluded." Casey flipped his phone closed and turned back to Cobb. "Please forgive the intrusion, but some calls simply cannot go to voice mail."

"Of course . . ." Gone was the exercising master of the universe Cobb had been when Casey had first walked into his office. He had shrunken to a pale, stooped version of himself, and now stared out the window, seemingly lost in thought.

"Now, where were we?" Casey resumed his stroll about the room, passing by Cobb's austere glass-and-steel desk with his back to the other man for a moment. Pretending to admire a Lucien Freud original, he placed a surveillance device disguised as a writing pen with 360-degree fiber-optic view and microphone in the caddy atop the furniture. "Oh, yes, as I was about to say, Mr. Casey is willing to grant you twenty-four hours to give your answer. Now, did you have any other questions at this time?"

Cobb dabbed at his sweat-beaded face with a small towel. "I can reach you at the number you left?" He tossed the towel onto a straight-backed chair over his suit jacket draped on the back.

"Of course. I look forward to talking with you soon," Casey said.

"As—as do I." They shook hands again, Cobb's now clammy with sweat, and Casey left the building. Outside, in the flow of pedestrians, he whistled a tune and acknowledged the pretty girls with a broad smile.

He had barely gone a hundred yards when his cell phone rang again. It was Kenny. "Talk to me, playa."

"Man, you were barely out the door when Cobb called Rono, tellin' him everything that went down. You'll wanna hear Rono's reaction yoself—I thought that fool's head was gonna explode right then and there."

"Maybe I can play it as a lullaby to help me sleep at night. Did Cobb get the address right?"

"Oh, yeah, he told Rono three times. I'd say your company is definitely comin' to call this evening."

Casey nodded. "True dat, so we best have a suitable reception prepared for them. I'll jaw atcha later, brother. I gotta get all my dominoes in a row right now."

"'Kay, dawg, but you know where I am—you need anything, just holla at your boy, an' I'm there."

"Righteous." Casey disconnected the call and sent out a text message to a select group of people. It read simply:

It's on. Tonight.

Across the river, the morning was painted in foggy grays as Jojoe, in the company of a VK soldier named Lex, left a quiet house on a sleepy suburban street in Queens. The two walked across the lawn to the Porsche Cayenne idling in the driveway. Another VK soldier named Rudy Black sat behind the wheel of the vehicle, listening to a cut from a *Best of Run DMC* CD. Suddenly a figure dropped onto the hood of the SUV from a maple tree with bushy foliage overhanging the driveway. He was decked out head to toe in grays to match the sky.

"The fuck—?" Lex said, reaching for his piece.

The man, one of Slim Harwood's soldiers who favored knives, threw a heavy hunter's blade directly into Lex's forehead, right through the watch cap he wore. He blinked twice, his eyes showing white, and ceased breathing before he hit the ground.

Jojoe pulled his piece and shot at the figure, as did Rudy Black, blasting through the windshield. But the man had dropped some kind of smoke grenade on the SUV's hood, and when it had cleared, he'd vanished.

"Ain't this some shit!" Rudy Black had gotten out of the Cayenne and stood next to Jojoe, looking around, their guns ready. The door to the vehicle left open, "Walk This Way," played on the sound system.

Jojoe glanced at the dead Lex, at the same time fumbling for his phone to call Rono. He was turning back to Rudy just as the side of Rudy's head exploded in a spray of brains and bone.

Jojoe took off for the side of the house, but another bullet from the unseen sniper punched through the big muscle of his thigh and he stumbled to the ground, skidding to a stop in the dry, brown grass. Several pairs of hands hauled him up, and he was hit several times in the face by two soldiers supplied by Two Stroke Bledsoe. The dazed man was tossed into the rear of a Charger driven onto the lawn by Omar Atkins, who then took off down the street.

Across the street, on the rooftop of a two-story house with peeling paint, Walker quietly came down the ladder he'd put up at the rear. Inside the small bungalow lived twin sisters in their eighties. One of them was hard of hearing, but both had slept through the entire incident. Wearing gloves, he left the ladder where it was, broke down and repacked his Remington 700 rifle, silencer, and scope in a disguised tool case, and calmly walked to the pickup marked with a plumbing company logo, parked on a parallel street. He got in and drove off.

While a concerned neighbor had dialed 911, it was another six minutes before police arrived on the scene. When they did, "My Adidas" could be heard from inside the still-idling Cayenne.

24

Casey had just gotten the text message that Omar and his boys had snatched Jojoe when his phone beeped, indicating he had a voice mail. Playing it, he was surprised to hear Lomax's voice demanding a meeting at four that afternoon.

"Sheeit," he muttered, checking his watch to find it was a little after ten A.M. *Just enough time to get some shit done,* he thought. He texted Omar to take Jojoe where they'd discussed, and that he'd be there in an hour. Then he called Kenny and gave him the address of where the big party was gonna go down.

"Hey, playa, I need your electronic whiz kid to get over to the building and set those cameras up. He better take some muscle with him—the place might not be empty, if you know what I mean."

"I hear ya. If it's occupied, whaddya want 'em to do?"

"They best warn anyone there that a wreckin' crew's comin' through, and anybody who gets in their way is gonna get flattened. If anyone comes at them, tell 'em to do what they gotta do to defend themselves. The important thing is for him to get out there, get that footage, and get those cameras set up like yesterday. Also, you need to seed the street so the Black Lotus knows where and when this meet's goin' down."

"A'ight, when you want 'em to know? You pick the time, and I'll have someone whisperin' in the Lotus's ears in less than sixty minutes."

"Damn, dawg, whatchu doin', leanin' out the window and shoutin' to 'em?"

"Hey man, as soon as you told me who the other players were, I made sure to keep the lines of communication open twenty-four/seven. My weebles are ready to drop that dime the moment I tell 'em to."

"I hear that. Don't wanna give 'em too much time to call in an army or weapon up, so get the word on the street 'bout six this evening."

"Can do."

"Solid, my brother. And you got the list of things I needed taken care of?"

"It's all above the shop, son, ready and waitin' on ya. You movin' fast, anything I need to know 'bout?"

"Lomax called me in for this afternoon, so I gotta deal with his ass before I can get down to business. I'ma gonna get the players as ready as I can before heading over."

"Can't break it?"

Casey shook his head. "Naw, I've made every one so far, so if I bail, he might get suspicious. He's given me a pretty long leash—I don't want him tightening up on it now."

"I hear that." Kenny paused, and Casey got the idea he was working up the nerve to ask something. He simply listened silently while he walked. "Look, dawg, you need any more help tonight? You know I got what's needed, and I can kick a door down with the best of 'em."

"I 'preciate the offer, big stump, but this one you gotta sit out tonight. I need an airtight cover for this evening's activities, and guess who that is? As far as you're concerned, I was over just kickin' it all night at your crib, you hear?"

"I got yer back, go take care of business."

"I'll holla at ya once the deed is done, One."

"I'll be waitin'."

Hanging up, Casey caught a cab over to a fading industrial section of Bed-Stuy. Tipping the driver, he waited until the taxi was out of sight before walking down past several dilapidated warehouses to the fifth one, where a side door stood ajar. Walking inside, he trotted to the black panel van that was the only thing sitting inside. Knocking on one of the split doors in back, it opened and he climbed in.

Around him were Omar and the pair of Bledsoe's soldiers who'd participated in kidnapping Jojoe. The man himself was duct-taped to a chair and gagged, his eyes wide with terror. A sharp, pungent smell assailed Casey's nose, and he peered around Omar to see Jojoe sitting in a puddle.

"Damn it, man, I told you not to lay a hand on him."

Omar spread his hands. "Yo, homes, I swear, other than the hole Walker punched in his leg when we were takin' him down and a couple of smacks to keep him in line, we haven't harmed a hair of his nappy little head. I can't help it if this one"—he pointed at the knife man—"can spin stories of what he's gonna do to you with a blade that made punk-ass here wet his pants."

Casey ran a hand over his face. "Look, we still gotta use the van this evening, so get some Spic and Span, bleach, cat piss remover, I don't care, but clean that up, 'kay?"

"Ain't no thang—we'll have this smellin' like it came from the showroom."

Casey walked over to Jojoe and yanked the tape from his mouth, making the sitting man groan from the pain.

"Jesus Christ, Casey, I'll tell you whatever you want, just . . . just don't leave me alone with that guy."

"Where were you and the others headed this morning?"

"Rono had just called a general meeting—I didn't know where, I swear, Lex had the location, they were just picking me up."

Casey bent over and put his hands on his knees. "So, basically, you're no good to me anymore, are you, college boy?"

"Whoa whoa whoa, ain't nobody sayin' that. What you want me to do? I'm surprised Rono hasn't called me wonderin' where I am by now."

Casey grinned, a dark sight indeed. "Could be Rono ain't wastin' time on a sucka who doesn't answer his celly—probably thinks you're already dead."

"Hey, look, let me try to get ahold of him—maybe I can get some information out, get the inside dope on what he's plannin'."

Casey looked at the other three men, all of whom smiled back. "Sheeit, nigga, I already know what he's plannin'—he's getting every soljah he can find together and gonna come down and try to plant my ass in the ground." He paused, examining Jojoe from one side, then another. "Hmm, same cut, same general build—I'd say homes here and I share a bit of a passing resemblance, don'tcha think?"

The reactions varied, from nods to Omar fuckin' with him by sayin', "Hell, Crush, I can't tell—you know all you black boys look alike to me."

Everyone laughed; even Jojoe forced a smile to his lips. Casey grabbed his chin and stared at him one more time. "Yeah, Jojoe, I just thought of a way you gonna help me—but you ain't gonna like it."

He ripped off a new piece of tape and stuck it over the bound man's mouth, ignoring his frantic pleas. "Keep 'im on ice till later this afternoon. I got plans for this muthafuckah. You boys know where to meet up later, right?" The other three nodded.

Casey opened the door to the truck again. "A'ight, I'll catch you later." He wrinkled his nose. "And hose this fuckin' truck down before you go anywhere, goddammit!"

Realizing he'd better change before the meet with Lomax, Casey walked a half mile to an intersection nearer to civilization, then called a cab. On the way to his place, he called Carla, but got her voice mail. That caught him off guard.

"Hey, Carla, it's Crush. Look, I'm gonna be tied up tonight with that business we been talkin' 'bout, but I'll holla at you later once it's all done." He paused a moment, for once unsure of what to say to her. "Been thinkin' 'bout you, girl, and once I get things squared away, we'll get together." It was lame and he knew it, but what he really wanted to say, he wasn't gonna leave on no damn machine.

When he walked in the door of his apartment, he stopped upon seeing Carla sitting on the couch facing the door. Casey knew he'd locked the door when he'd left earlier that morning.

"How the hell'd you get in here?" He tried for a smile, but it didn't feel quite right, and he let it slip off his face. "I don't remember leavin' you a key."

Carla smiled a Cheshire cat grin. "Crush, Crush, sometimes you are far too trusting." She nodded toward the kitchen. "I happened to notice the diagram about the hidden passages and shit, and memorized how to access the back stairwell from the garage."

Casey shook his head, chuckling. "Always knew you were a smart cookie." Now that the opportunity was here to talk to Carla face-to-face, he found himself suddenly apprehensive. "You come over for a little afternoon delight?"

Carla held up her cell phone. "The thought had crossed my mind, you know, of greeting you at the door wearing nothing but perfume, or a sheet. 'Course, that was before I got your message sayin' you were headin' out to most likely get your ass shot off."

Casey had removed his suit jacket and was heading into the

bedroom. "Baby girl, now isn't the time for this conversation. I made my bones very clear from the start regardin' my plans and what was gonna go down."

"Goddamn it, Crush, don't you get it? You're a free man now." Carla followed him, the subtle scent of her perfume preceding her. Her smell made Casey pause, but he shook it off and kept changing. "I was hoping a few days or weeks on the outside might convince you there are other ways to live, different lives you could choose for yourself, instead of running back into the streets to ball hard until you get shot down like a dog." She turned away. "I had to live through that shit with Champa for years—I ain't gonna watch it consume you too."

Casey had pulled on jeans and a T-shirt, and now he closed the closet door and walked over to her. "Carla, it's you who don't understand."

She whirled on him, her hands beating at his chest until he caught them in his own. "What I don't understand is why you have to be so jackass-stubborn!" She stared defiantly up at him, tears brimming in her eyes.

"'Cause, sugar, it's the only way I know how to be." Carla started to say something, but Casey silenced her with a finger to her lips. "Hush now, and lemme speak my piece. Stubbornness been the only thing keepin' me alive since forever. As a boy, the streets tried to chew me up and spit me out, but I outlasted that and got into the VKs. I juked and jived and ended up takin' the whole gang over, and believe me, some a those cold-eyed muthafuckahs woulda seen me dead if they'd gotten the chance. I ruled the roost, then that punk-ass Rono cuts a deal with the feds and sticks a shank in my side, sends me to Attica, steals twenty years of my life. I wouldn't be here today if I hadn't vowed to get out and make him pay. That's what kept me going for the past two decades. And now, you think a couple of take-out meals and a plush crib gonna turn me away from achieving what I spent the last seven thousand, three hundred days workin' toward? Sweetheart, what I'm doin' is *all* I know. The Kings are my home—this gang shit is my life. Don't think I haven't enjoyed your charms, darlin', but there ain't nothin' you could say or do that would stop me from seein' Rono one last time face-to-face, and knowin' only one of us is walkin' away."

"Let go of my hands, please," Carla said. Casey did, and she threw her arms around him. "Goddammit, Crush, I just got you, and now you're about to go out into a shitstorm, and you might not come back. Don't you understand there's people in this world who care about your stubborn ass?"

Casey squeezed her tightly to him, drinking in every bit of her he could. "'Course I do, woman, but what kind of life would we have? That heist money wouldn't last forever, ya know."

"I got enough salted away that between yours and mine, we wouldn't have to worry 'bout it for a good long time."

"I don't do well being a kept man, girl." Casey shook his head. "There's only one place for me in this world, and that's back in charge of the only thing I've ever created—the Vicetown Kings. But don't you worry—they gonna be different once I'm back on top. I'm takin' your advice to heart and gonna make 'em a different kind of organization." The fact that he'd already been planning to do that didn't make any difference—he knew it was what she needed to hear. "And to do that, I'ma gonna have to survive to fight another day, you know that. Don't forget—it ain't just that you got me, girl—I just got you too, and I ain't planning on goin' anywhere any-time soon."

Carla kissed him hungrily, then took his face in her hands and stared into his eyes. "You look me in the eyes and promise me you're gonna come back."

"Yes, ma'am, I promise I'm coming back."

"Damn you, Marcus Casey—you'd think I'd learned enough by now to stop fallin' in with bad men." Her lips grazed his cheek, and moved to nibbling on his ear. "You got anywhere you have to be right now?"

Casey knew exactly where she was going, and although he still had shit to coordinate, he figured he had a little time. "Fireworks ain't gonna start for a few hours yet."

Carla disentangled herself and led Casey over to the bed. "Then the very goddamn least you can do is break me off something proper before you go runnin' out to play gangsta." She shrugged out of her tailored suit coat, revealing a sheer blouse, and underneath that her magnificent breasts, barely contained in a silky bra.

"I think that can be arranged," Casey said as he slowly pulled his T-shirt off. "Any requests?"

"Yeah—shut up, lie down, and get busy."

25

Gulliver Rono stalked around the rear area of the Magic Sword video games distribution offices like a caged panther. "So, other than this address where Cobb claims Casey's gonna be tonight, we got nothing on him or that freelance fuck Atkins?" he asked.

A sitting Derek Webb, with a stylish bucket hat on his head, spread his arms. "We come up dry. Since the dustup after they left the sideshow, Atkins has gone to ground too. He ain't at none of his usual spots."

Rono grimaced, his stomach acidic and churning for the last two days. The wound in his side burned something fierce, but he resisted the urge to claw at it or sniff a hit of tranq—he wanted his mind clear right now. "That means Casey's gonna make his play soon," he stated.

"We got money and all eyes out for him now, Gul, what else you want us to do?" a female lieutenant nicknamed Happy said.

"Get results, goddammit!" Rono barked at her and the others in the room. "Don't any of you get it? Casey ain't just an irritation to us—he means to bring us down! I mean, what the fuck? We gotta shore up the VK brand, understand? Can't have anybody thinking we slippin'."

"True dat," Webb agreed.

Rono ran a hand over his head. "What I can't figure is why Casey's man let slip the locate he's gonna be at right in front of Cobb? That don't make sense."

"Unless he felt he had the old man so scared he wouldn't call ya," Webb offered.

"Naw—I been underestimatin' that fuck since the day his ass hit the street—now I gotta try to think like his has-been punk-ass. He wants me to come to this fuckin' building so he can cap me—all right, I'll play that game. If that old broke-down nigga thinks he's gonna bushwhack me, he's got another think comin'."

He whirled on Derek Webb. "Get word to everyone you know is loyal to drop whatever the fuck they're doin' and get their asses here by six P.M. tonight. I mean fuckin' *everybody*. Then we all gonna go over to Taylor Street and kill every muthafuckin' nigga we see there. There's only one rule—no one but me takes out Casey. He's mine."

As he trotted up the steps of the parole department's building, Casey resisted the urge to check his watch yet again. He was early, but he knew every minute he spent away from the shop was one less minute he didn't have to ensure that tonight's job was gonna go down smooth. They were already improvising as it was, but the time was right, it was now or never—it wouldn't get any better than this. The fact that he wasn't dealing with one enemy, but three at once, was a complication that threw any normal plan right out the window.

The thought made Casey recall the key writings of the nineteenth-century German *Generalfeldmarschall* Helmuth Karl Bernhard Graf von Moltke, including one maxim Mack D had drilled into him: *"No plan of operations extends with certainty beyond the first encounter with the enemy's main strength."* Simply put, "No battle plan survives first contact with the enemy."

Casey had been impressed enough with that simple truth to track down and read a translated history of the Franco-Prussian War, the preparation for which had been overseen by von Moltke himself. The man's strategy was to plan as well as possible, and also prepare for as many potential outcomes as could be thought of, since the original plan would not be able to be carried out once the battle was joined.

And that was the problem—other than hunting down Rono and killing the bastard, Casey didn't really have a plan beyond getting the three gangs in the same place at the same time and letting them all scrap it out amongst each other. Only afterward would his own team come on the scene and clean up whatever remained. He'd tried to keep it simple, but with three enemies to try and anticipate, the variables were numerous and troublesome.

Bet that ol' Kraut bastard never tried pullin' off somethin' this tricky, he thought. He had no idea if or how any of the other players would react to his bait. If any of them cut and ran early, one or both of the other forces might still be too large for Casey and his crew to take down. And if one didn't show up, then he'd have to work out a contingency to eliminate them later. The permutations and possibilities were enough to make his head spin.

Worry 'bout right now right now, nigga—time enough to handle later when it comes, he thought. He had to keep this meeting with Lomax short enough so he could get back to business ASAP.

After checking in at the front desk, he made his way through the corridors to Lomax's office. He heard a familiar voice talking as he approached the closed wooden door with the pebbled glass window, and realized Lomax was on the phone. Casey slowed up, trying to listen to the parole officer's side of the conversation without appearing too obvious about it.

". . . I told you, about two hours ago the streets went real quiet-like, like everyone suddenly had something better to do than be out there. . . . Yeah, it's gonna go down tonight, I'm sure of it. . . . No, I don't have any more information—call it my finely honed instincts talking. . . . No, I don't know if he'll be overseein' it personally—whaddaya think, I'm the man's personal secretary? . . . Will you just calm down and trust me? . . . Yeah, I'll call you the moment I got anything. . . . All right . . . All *right* . . . Good-bye."

Casey stepped loudly to the door and knocked three times.

"Come in."

He opened the door and stood there, looking at Lomax for a second, really observing the man who had the power of freedom or imprisonment over him—a fact that was really starting to chafe at Casey. Lomax looked sharp as always, dressed in a slate-gray button-down shirt with a blue and green tie depicting painted water lilies on it. The ceiling fan lazily stirred the air, which smelled faintly of spicy tomato sauce, around the small office.

"Mr. Casey, punctual as always. Do step inside."

Casey strolled in and took his usual seat, eyeballing the PO as hard as he dared. *Wish this guy'd stop dancin' around and come at me straight for once.*

Lomax leaned back and interlaced his hands behind his head. "So, what have you been up to recently?"

And here it goes again, the same bullshit, Casey thought. *Are you staying out of trouble? Have you found a job yet? Do you have a place of your own?* For a second, he wished he could tell Lomax what he'd *really* been up to recently. That would impress the parole officer, no doubt—and earn Casey a one-way ticket back to the pen. His slow-burn anger flared again, and he spoke before he could stop himself. "I got a line on a real nice job."

Lomax's right eyebrow lifted, but he stayed silent.

Oh fuck, I'm in it now. Casey's mind raced as he tried to figure out what to tell his PO. "It's not a typical dishwasher or truck driver gig—this one—this one involves helping improve the city."

Lomax's left eyebrow rose to join its partner. "Go on."

"Yeah—it's a nonprofit dedicated to cleaning up neighborhoods, revitalizing them, and helping the community through outreach programs in schools"—Casey had read about such programs in *Time* magazine, and recently Shinzo had mentioned a friend of his that had gotten involved. He figured there was no better time to throw it at Lomax—"and making sure empty storefronts don't attract vandalism or vagrants, that kind of thing."

Lomax's eyebrows lowered in a frown. "I'm familiar with almost all of the urban programs in the city. What's the name of this— organization?" he asked, the pause between the words so slight Casey almost didn't catch it.

"It's just getting started, so they haven't gotten much press out yet. They're still tossing around ideas, but one of them is to call the program—Urban Victory." Casey tried not to wince—that sounded lame, even to him, but Lomax didn't seem to notice.

"And what exactly would your duties entail?"

"They've been looking for someone to perform outreach to the various communities—you know, talk to kids about the consequences of doing crime."

"And they think you may be the man for the job?" Lomax's tone wasn't condescending or incredulous; rather, he seemed to be taking Casey's bullshit story at face value. For his part, Casey was just trying to stay one answer ahead.

Casey looked at Lomax dead on and kept lying through his teeth. He knew he'd have to set up this operation quick, or potentially be thrown back in the joint. "Well, I do know the realities of doing crime *and* doing time, so yeah."

Lomax stared at Casey and grunted his skepticism. "I see. And do you have a contact number for this organization?"

"Well, as I said it's more of a nonprofit than an organization." Casey said as he warmed to his story. *This guy likes playin' it coy all the time—let's see how he likes it comin' at him.* "Many representatives from diverse areas and backgrounds coming together in a common cause."

"Sounds fascinating. As I asked earlier, do you have a contact number where they can be reached? You know I'll have to look into them and make sure it's a viable 'operation' and not a bunch of knuckleheads trying to shake down the city under the guise of a neighborhood watch program or some such."

Casey let the jibe pass without reacting. "Well, Mr. Lomax, I was wonderin' if I could ask a bit of a favor? I got the final interview tonight—so I was wonderin' if you could hold off until tomorrow before contacting them? I don't want them to think hiring me comes with problems. I hope you understand—this could be the break I been looking for to keep my life outside on track."

"Well, I'm all for that. The interview's tonight, you said?"

"Yeah—tonight sometime I gotta call them to confirm it."

"All right, Mr. Casey. You go to that interview, but the first thing tomorrow morning, I want an address and phone number of this 'Urban Victory' program."

"No problem, Mr. Lomax. Anything else?"

Lomax regarded him with a gimlet gaze for several long moments, and Casey was sure he was about to bust his ass back to Attica. He met the PO's hard stare with his own calm one, knowing that the first person to speak in a standoff like this was the loser. Just when he was about to clear his throat, the parole officer leaned forward. "Get out of here, and go take care of your business, Mr. Casey."

"I intend to, Mr. Lomax. I'll be in touch with that information first thing tomorrow." Casey stood to leave. *And if I don't call to-morrow morning, I'm most likely dead,* he thought.

He walked casually out of the office, resisting the urge to glance back over his shoulder to see if Lomax was watching him. Once out of the building, he made himself stroll along for a few blocks before whipping out his cell and calling Shinzo. "Hey playa, we on for tonight, right?"

"You know it, brotha. The BDs are straining at their leash to take you down. I thought we'd be seeing you at the shop?"

"Yeah, I'm heading over right now, but I need you to put something else into play for me. It has to do with that friend of yours running that nonprofit. He's about to change the name and get a big cash 'donation'." Casey outlined his conversation with Lomax, and the story he'd spun.

Shinzo whistled. "Wait just a goddamn minute, lemme get this straight—are you fuckin' tellin' me you told your own parole officer that you're gonna 'take a bite out of crime' by joining an urban renewal program?"

"Yeah, it just came out, and once I started rollin' it seemed to work better and better. But I need an office address and phone number I can give Lomax to satisfy him. Better have a remote answering service that can forward calls as well."

"Goddamn, nigga, I thought you was just gonna head over there and tell him some bullshit to keep him off your back for a day or so, not set yoself up as a concerned member of the community."

"Yeah, well, the conversation went in a different direction. Can you set it up?"

"Does the Pope still wear that pointy hat in public? 'Course I can set it up. I'll talk to my man today, he needs the money. You'll have everythin' you need by tomorrow morning—assuming we both live through the night, that is."

"There is that. Thanks, brotha."

"Ain't no thang, dawg. Now get your ass over here so we can figure out how we're gonna come out on top of this fuckin' suicide mission you runnin'."

"On my way."

After Casey had left, Lomax picked up his phone and dialed Fulson's number. When the DEA agent answered, he said, "It's definitely going down tonight—I just got confirmation from the man himself. . . . Hell no, man—I'm just gonna sit back and let it happen. . . . Don't worry . . . in one night Casey's gonna do what it would take a hundred cops ten years to handle. . . . I'll be in touch tomorrow with the details. . . . Later."

26

Casey wasted no time getting back to the apartment above the empty storefront. The rest of his crew was already there, going through various final preparations. Shinzo and Li were huddled around a flat-screen monitor, watching the footage Kenny's AV connection had gotten from the building earlier that afternoon. Champa and his two hired guns were laying out sets of gear for themselves. Omar and Bledsoe's two soljahs—introduced as Blade and Snap-Fire—were already dressed, the looks on their faces a mix of befuddlement and amusement at what they were wearing. At a card table in another corner, Walker sat methodically field-stripping and cleaning a variety of weapons. He glanced up to acknowledge Casey's arrival with a nod before returning to his work.

"Hey, look who's the last to arrive to his own muthafuckin' party," Champa cracked from the other side of the room. "Crush, you sure we should be wearin' this shit? I mean, da-yamn, I feel a little bit like we're consortin' with the enemy, ya know?"

Casey grinned, and rapped the helmet the other man was holding. "When we fall on whoever's left in that building, I want them to be struck with complete and abject fear. I don't know anybody else who will set them boys running as when they see us bust through those doors dressed like this. There's a few other reasons we doin' it. First, ain't no one gonna pick us out as the hitters behind this job—they'll just think the city sent out its big guns responding to a nine-one-one call. Also, it's good fuckin' shit—the clothes are made for the vests to go around without impeding movement, and the harnesses allow you to carry everything you need up top, without havin' to scrabble through your pockets for it. And that pot you're holdin' will deflect anything up to a 5.56mm bullet at ten yards—worth sacrificing your fashion sense for one evening, ya hear?"

"I guess. Just not used to going in in this particular disguise, know what I'm sayin'?"

Casey was about to check and see how Shinzo and Li were faring when his attention was caught by Bledsoe's two men talking quietly between themselves, each one casting an occasional glance over at Walker.

He strolled over to the pair. "Gentlemen, I just wanted to say thanks for y'all agreein' to gun up and help out on this little job. Do either of you have any questions?"

The two soljahs glanced at each other, then Blade spoke up. "Jus' one, and we don't mean any disrespect, but why's whitey along on this? We were given to understand this was gonna be complete black-on-black and various other colors, if you get my meanin'."

Casey smiled and clapped both men on the shoulder. "Dawgs, that skinny white boy over there is probably the single best reason any of us are gonna get out of this alive. Don't you worry—his shit is tight, and when everything's said and done, you'll be sky-high he's with us tonight, I guarantee it. Now make sure you're fitted and ready to roll in a few minutes, I gotta check with my other homies, and then we gonna bounce."

The two men nodded, and Casey moved to Omar. "Any problems delivering that package to the address?"

The other man shook his head. "It's ready and waitin' for Rono to pick it up. Cleared out everyone we could find as well, though it took some persuadin'. You sure picked a shithole for this all to go down at, dawg."

"Gotta keep my enemies off balance and confused, and what better way to do so than to put them on unfamiliar ground?"

Omar nodded. "I'm down with that, just as long as it doesn't trip us up either."

"You got a leg up on us, since you already been there, so I'm sure you won't let that happen, right, homes?"

Omar smiled and puffed out his chest. "You know it."

Satisfied, Casey crossed to Shinzo and Li. "How's the video reconnaissance goin'?"

Becker leaned back in his chair and rubbed his eyes. "Well, it sure ain't the muthafuckin' Four Seasons. The place is a goddamn deathtrap—rotten walls, nonworking appliances, no electric or heat. Man, I wouldn't let my dog live in a place like this, much less people. Gotta give props to your boy, however; he laid out everything nice and clean, along with the original plans to the place so we can see what's been jury-rigged and fucked with."

Casey nodded, knowing Kenny had used a contact at City Hall to get the building plans copied, scanned, and sent over before they went in. "Big dawg like yoself ain't scared, are ya?"

"Sheeit, man, if I'd known I was headin' into a rattrap like this, I'da had my shots updated, otherwise, Li and me are ready to hit it whenever."

"That's what I like to hear. I'm gonna get everyone together in a few to run through the plan one last time, so you two best get fitted.

Li, we made sure to have a selection of outfits that should work for you as well."

She nodded curtly, and she and Becker went back to reviewing the footage. Casey ambled over to Walker. "Where you at, man?"

The wiry man slapped the action closed on the lethal-looking semiautomatic rifle he'd been cleaning. "Potting Rono's boys from a hundred yards out. I gotta hand it to ya, Casey, you do know how to keep your hired guns satisfied—I don't even wanna know how you got your hands on an M-110 semiauto."

"People who know people, brother." When he'd seen the sniper rifle at the sideshow, Casey had known it was the weapon he wanted Walker behind tonight. "How'd that other long tom work for you?"

Walker smiled, one of the rare times Casey had seen the man's teeth. "You mean the heavy artillery—" He whistled long and low. "—I didn't bring it in 'cause I didn't want to alarm any of your homies, but it's ready to rock. Just make sure everyone secures those handwarmers on their helmets and doesn't take 'em off until the mission is over, you got me?"

"I'll check each one myself. Listen, you sure you don't want any backup at your position? If anyone cottons to where you are, they might try and take you out, which would put a serious crimp in our operation."

"Don't you worry about me—the missus and I worked out a system I've been wanting to test under field conditions, and it looks like tonight's the night. If anyone has the brains to figure out where the long rounds are coming from and tries to bushwack me, I'll have a nasty surprise waiting for 'em. I just need thirty minutes to set up, and I'll be good to go."

"Fair enough. I'ma run through the plan one more time in a few minutes, so be ready."

"You know I will be."

Casey looked around the room at all the activity going on, and the people willing to risk their lives to help him reclaim what was his. His grin didn't fade as he walked to his own set of clothes and equipment and started suiting up.

When he was finished, he made one last adjustment to his helmet and checked the fit of his gas mask before removing both and setting them on the table, then clapping his hands together to get everyone's attention.

"Everyone gather 'round for a minute." Once the rest of the crew was clustered at the table, Casey looked at each face for a moment before speaking again. "I ain't one for speeches anymore—as most of you know, the last time I tried to give one, I got a shank in my ribs for my trouble."

There was a chorus of chuckles from around the table, and Casey let them die down before he continued. "The point is that I wanted to thank each one of you for throwin' in on this, especially when you think about the odds against us. Everyone knows what we're up against, so if anyone's havin' second thoughts, or don't think they can handle their weight, now's the time to speak up. Won't be no disrespect—it takes a big man—or woman—to stare down what we're headin' into, but an even bigger one to admit if they ain't up to the load."

Everybody looked at everybody around the table, but no one said a word. Casey gave it a slow five-count, then smiled. "All right then. Everyone's wearin' the gear you've been given for this job, and you've all been briefed on taping those handwarmers on your helmets before we go in—I cannot stress how important that is. Basically, if you don't want to get a bullet through your chest by our sniper, make sure your warmer is activated, on your dome, and giving off heat before we put boots to the door.

"Once inside, use the flash-bangs to work over anyone in the rooms before you charge in and start shootin'. Remember—keep your eyes averted and your mouth open to minimize the shock wave, otherwise you'll pop eardrums, and I don't need anyone comin' out of this deaf."

He tapped the paper that covered the table. "We're restricting our movement to the first floor of the building only—no one's gonna chase after bangers who flee upstairs. Our long gun will be handling them, so just be sure to report where you see them go, and he'll take care of the rest. Everyone also has the team they've been assigned to, main groups of five and four, and each of those broken into teams of two or three. Just remember to stay together, back up each other up, and don't get too far ahead of anyone else. We're not looking for heroes, just take out as many of them as you can when you go in."

He spread a variety of mug shots around on the table. "And be on the lookout for any of these gangstas—they're the leaders of the Blood Devils, the Black Lotus, and the Vicetown Kings. All of them are to be shot on sight."

Champa asked the question Casey knew everyone was thinking. "What about Rono?"

Casey barely hesitated before answering, although he'd been wrestling with it all day. "Assuming he has the nuts to even show his face, if anybody gets a clear shot at Rono, you cap his ass, and I'll be the first to shake your hand." Casey held up his hands at the looks he was getting around the table. "I know, I know—if I had my way, I'd be offin' that fool personally, but this ain't no gangsta movie, where I got the luxury of challenging him *mano a mano*. If Rono shows up tonight, he's gotta die, and at this point I'm beyond caring who does it, only that it gets done. Am I clear?"

Heads nodded all around him. "All right, folks, let's get ready to roll out. Before we go, I got one more quote to lay on y'all from my cat Sun Tzu: 'Let your plans be dark and impenetrable as night, and when you move, fall like a thunderbolt.'"

He looked around at the faces staring back at him. "I don't know what the Kings, the Devils, or the Lotus are expecting, but I'm damn sure it's not each other. The very last thing they'll be lookin' for is us bustin' in on 'em as well, so we already got the dark and impenetrable plan all set up."

He picked up an HK MPA3 submachine gun, slapped a magazine into its receiver, and yanked the cocking lever back. "Now let's fall on 'em all like a muthafuckin' thunderbolt."

Immaculate in a Hugo Boss suit and tailored London Fog trench coat, Paul Chang sat in the backseat of his Mercedes Benz limousine, his brother Peter beside him. Their armored luxury car was bookended in front and behind by two identical Lincoln Navigators, both filled with the very best soldiers of the Black Lotus. All of the sixteen men had been on alert ever since the robbery of the Golden Duck Restaurant and the message delivered that the Vicetown Kings wanted their money back.

Neither Paul nor Peter knew what the other gang was talking about, but they were not going to let this insult to their *tong*'s honor go unavenged. They had already killed several of the VKs' street runners in retribution, but strangely, this had not brought the Kings to the negotiating table. Indeed, they had not heard anything at all from the other gang, leading the Changs to believe that the Kings were about to declare all-out war, perhaps over their previous disagreements with the Black Lotus. Though the brothers had heard the Kings were in a state of disarray, with their second-in-command having come to an untimely end, they didn't want to risk open combat with such a large gang.

When Paul had received word that several high-ranking members of the VKs would be at a particular address in Parkenbush, the Changs had immediately mobilized their soldiers.

Peter threaded a silencer onto the barrel of his Steyr TMP machine pistol and inserted a thirty-round magazine into the butt of the compact weapon. Next to him, his brother loaded an identical

gun. Their men were armed with a variety of black-market submachine guns and pistols, and all knew what this evening's mission
entailed.

Go to the building in Parkenbush.

Find the members of the Vicetown Kings.

Make sure none of them left the place alive.

It didn't matter whether they arrived first, and could set up an
ambush, or if they or came after Rono and his men—the Changs'
orders had been explicit.

Kill the VKs and restore the Black Lotus's honor—even if every
man had to die in the attempt.

Barefoot, Jesus climbed onto the hood of his custom-modified '59
El Camino and held up both hands for silence. The muttering and
macho comments from the group of fifteen Blood Devil *veteranos*
arrayed in a loose semicircle around him tapered off to silence.

Before he spoke, Jesus glanced down at the paint job on his
Pequeño Diablo—his little devil. The El Camino's hood was covered with a huge devil's face, complete with blood-red horns and
skin, a wicked smile, and red-irised eyes that gave anyone looking
at it the creeps. Many of his gangstas said they felt like the eyes
followed them as they crossed in front of the car.

Jesus loved whipping up his homies while standing on it—the
feeling of power as he stood on the biggest symbol of the Blood
Devils' power was intoxicating, and he felt it always gave his
speeches that little extra something to make his *compadres* fall in
line and do whatever they needed to get done.

*Like smoke some uppity ex-con who thinks he's gonna make the Devils
fall into line*, he thought, his dark-brown eyes scanning the hard-core
chucos he'd assembled for this mission. "Homes, we gotta problem."

The muttering began immediately, which Jesus knew was a
good sign. His boys were restless, ready to mix it up. Things had

been too quiet lately, and a job like this was exactly what they needed to stay sharp and spread the fear of the Devils on the street.

"That *puto* Marcus Casey thinks he can make us fall in with his vision of an empire controlled by him and those *maricón* Vicetown Kings."

The muttering of his men grew louder.

"Now, I know *ese* just got sprung from cold storage, and it seems he needs a lesson in how things run out in the real world. That lesson is that the Blood Devils answer to no one!"

His crew was getting more worked up, nodding and punching each other on the arms, their fists clenching as they thought about the insult that Casey had delivered in his offer to talk to them about joining his syndicate.

"It's a lesson I'm gonna enjoy teachin' tonight. And one that motherfucker won't ever forget—for the rest of his very short life!"

The bangers around him whooped and shouted, holding up their pistols, shotguns, and the occasional assault rifle.

Jesus unslung his SPAS-12 automatic shotgun and rested it casually on one shoulder. "After tonight, people gonna know not to try and keep the Blood Devils down! After tonight, all the gangs will learn what it means to fuck with us!"

The shouts and noise from the assembled gang members was almost deafening, even in the cavernous warehouse. Jesus held his shotgun above his head and began chanting, *"Rifa, rifamos! Rifa, rifamos!"*

The chant, loosely translated as "We rule" or "We're the best," was quickly picked up by the rest of the *vatos,* until the air echoed with sixteen men shouting at the top of their lungs.

Jesus stepped off the hood of his El Camino and slipped on a pair of combat boots, then got into his vehicle, accompanied by his brother Elbanco, who was toting a pair of Ingram Mac-10s chambered in .45 caliber—dangerous little submachine guns that could kill everyone in a room in under two seconds. The rest of his men were piling into two nondescript vans.

"*Vámonos,* Devils!" Putting the *Pequeño Diablo* into gear, Jesus laid rubber on the warehouse floor as he rocketed into the dark street outside, the two vans following as they headed for an abandoned apartment building in Parkenbush.

Gulliver Rono looked around at the motley crew of VKs Derek Webb had assembled. A dozen of his best men—*Those that are left,* he chided himself—all armed to the teeth and ready to smoke anyone who got in their way.

"Bunch of goddamn lifetakers and heartbreakers I got here." He grinned, lighting up a cigar. Rono was also strapped to the nines, his main weapons being a pair of massive, chromed Colt Delta Elite 10mms in twin holsters at his waist. His black spring-loaded baton was secure at the small of his back, and he had a couple other surprises for any muthafuckahs who got too close.

"A'ight, listen up, I'ma only gonna say this once. We're goin' in to smoke anybody we fuckin' see at that address, ya all feel me? No one gets out alive. Anyone sees Casey, you *do not* take him out—you get on the horn and call me, got it? Casey is mine. But I'll sweeten the deal by offerin' a cool ten large to the cat who spots him first."

Rono tossed on a silk longcoat that hid his pistols, then turned and stalked toward the door. "Now let's get going and chill that muthafuckah—I want his goddamn head on my mantelpiece afore the sun comes up."

27

Casey stood with his arms folded over his chest, stoic and silent on the outside. But inside his mind and gut were both churning, anxious for the action to start.

He wasn't the only one to feel that way. The entire van fairly thrummed with tension. Most of his people managed to hide it, but Casey felt it coming off the rest of them. Most of them, like Bledsoe's men, affected a too-casual air of nonchalance, leaning against the van wall, idly holding the butts or barrels of their guns. Champa channeled his preaction adrenaline into his fingers, tapping them against each other rapidly, index finger to thumb, middle finger to thumb, and so on. He swore it loosened up his hands for shooting, and also didn't make any noise when they needed to be quiet.

Omar, Shinzo, and Li all emulated Casey, each standing or sitting stock-still, waiting for the bullets to fly and the blood to spill. Of the three of them, Casey thought Li seemed the most relaxed, sitting on the metal wheel well, back against the wall, eyes closed.

That's one stone-cold honey, to hang with a buncha hardcore hitters and look like she'd give any of 'em a run for their money.

He leaned over Kenny's tech genius and scanned the flat-screen monitors. "Anythin' yet?"

The kid, a lanky, bespectacled nineteen-year-old who went by the handle of Tebber, shook his head as he adjusted the picture on one of the screens showing the entire street, as well as the front, back, and sides of the building. "Street's dead, man. Ain't nothin' goin' on out there at the mo."

Casey straightened up and keyed his throat mic. "Rooftop, you see anything?"

Walker's laconic voice drawled in his ear. "Nothing moving out here yet—just like the last five times you called."

"Just makin' sure, man."

"Since I'd like to live through the evening too, believe me, I'll let you know the moment when I see anyone who looks like our targets."

"All right, all right, ya don't have to bite my fuckin' head off, nigga." Casey checked his weapons one last time, then refolded his arms, wanting to pace the length of the van, but aware he couldn't take a step without bumping into one of the others.

"We got company." Tebber waved Casey over just as his ear-piece crackled to life.

"Three vehicles approaching slowly from the north," Walker whispered. "Musta turned off Morris Park. I see a pair of Esca-lades flankin' an Acura—probably Rono and his boys."

Casey's pulse quickened as he heard the name of his enemy. "Hold your position, rooftop."

"You sure? One bullet, and I could take care of that problem for you permanently."

"Not just yet—we need to cut off the head snake and his cap-tains all at once. Let the diversion do its work. Only strike when I give the word." Casey tapped Tebber's shoulder.

The hacker hit a button on his console. On the monitor showing the front of the building, a yellow light flickered on, the only
one in the entire structure.

"That oughta get his attention," Casey breathed. "Come on, you
sidestabbin' muthafuckah, go after that bait."

Rono had dulled the throbbing pain in his side with anesthetic
salve, and cleared his mind with a small pop of cocaine he'd sniffed
off his hand. He was cocked, locked, and ready to rock.

Along with Derek Webb, Low Rise, and Big Sally, he scanned
both sides of the street as they drove slowly down Taylor Avenue.
"What a shithole—figures Casey'd come here to do his business—
man's got no class."

Nods and smiles all around met Rono's comment, just as his
driver raised a hand. "Yo, Gul. This the locate. I think we here."

Rono looked out at the dilapidated four-story building rising into
the darkness. "Sheeit, I'ma get my Bruno Maglis dirty just walkin'
inside." He scanned the front of the building, spotting the dim yellow light in one window. "Think that chump's stupid enough to
leave the welcome light on for us?"

Webb put a pair of night-vision goggles to his eyes and peered
up and down the street. "I ain't got anyone or anything moving,
G. Time we wrapped this up and got gone."

Rono, who had just drawn his pistols, rapped the barrel of one
upside Webb's head, not hard enough to injure, but strong enough
to get his captain's attention. "I say when we muthafuckin' move,
nigga, you feel me?"

"Yeah, Gul, yeah—no disrespect."

"A'ight, get the boys together—we're going in. Pull up right in front
of this hole—I wanna show that fuck we ain't afraid of nobody."

. . .

"Movement 'round the back as well," Tebber announced quietly.

Casey stared at the monitor to see clusters of black-swathed men disembarking from a pair of gleaming Lincoln Navigators flanking a Mercedes-Benz limousine. All of them had night-vision goggles on and what looked like bulletproof vests as well. Each one toted some kind of automatic weapon, with various machine pistols and submachine guns in their hands. "Damn, these muthafuckahs came with the hard-core shit."

"Yeah, and their timing couldn't be better." Omar had come over to watch the show, staring at the silent wraiths flowing across the small courtyard in the back and up to the doors. "Think they'll be suspicious there's no guard?"

"Well, I couldn't steal five more VKs and plant them everywhere we needed a warm body, now could I?" Casey's sardonic comment made the others chuckle.

"Wonder where the Blood Devils are?" Shinzo mused. "Ain't like them to be late for a fight."

Just then Walker's voice hissed in Casey's ear. "Holy shi— Casey, you getting this? Check the roof of the building left of where the VKs are going in."

"Tebber, get me a visual."

The hacker tapped keys, then held up his hands. "Sorry, man, all my shit's street level. You didn't ask for eyes on the sky."

"Fuck." Casey tapped his mic. "What you got, rooftop?"

"Six, eight, ten—I got fuckin' movement all over the place. If the back-door men are the Lotus, then it looks like the Blood Devils are aimin' to get the drop on everyone by coming down from the high ground. Musta come in at the end of the block and're hoofin' it rooftop to rooftop. They're swarmin' the fourth floor and moving down. ETA to ground floor about sixty seconds."

"Death from above? Them Mexis're smarter than I gave 'em credit for." Casey twirled a finger in the air. "Everyone get ready— the shit's about to go down."

"Plan still the same?"

"Hell, yeah, once all these gangstas finish chopping each other into red meat. Make sure your handwarmers are activated and securely attached to the back of your helmets. Four go round back and cut off the Lotus, the rest of us take the front. Rooftop'll handle the upper floors once we flush them, you hear that up there?"

"Affirmative, unlimbering the big gun now."

Rono's men clustered tightly around him, everyone scanning the alleys, windows, and rooftops for anyone lying in the cut to whack them.

"Let's go bag me a jive-ass sucka," Rono muttered, taking the front steps of the building two at a time and stopping in front of the door. "Low Rise—getcher ass up here and open this door." Rono was pissed, but not stupid—if anyone was waiting to open up on the first one through, he'd be goddamned if he was gonna get perforated with bullets—that's what his peeps were for.

"Put a nigga behind the trigger." Low Rise took a deep breath and approached the door, his Walther MPK submachine gun snugged up to his shoulder as he came close. Pressing his ear to it, he listened intently, then stepped back, and reached for the knob, turning it slowly, then pushing it open.

The door swung wide easily, and Low Rise almost fell into the black doorway as he tried to steady himself and bring his subgun up to cover anyone waiting for them at the same time. Only silence greeted him.

On the other side of the doorway, his Colts at the ready, Rono peeked in just long enough to spot the glimmer of light coming from underneath the first doorway on the left. "Whatchu waitin' for?" he hissed, nodding for Low Rise to move forward.

Trying to look everywhere at once, Low Rise crept through the doorway, the muzzle of his MPK tracking anything that moved. The hallway smelled of bleach, stale fried food, urine, and vomit. Faded linoleum tiles cracked and shifted under his heels. About fifteen feet wide, the hallway continued to the back of the building, with a broad staircase taking up the middle of the corridor.

Knowing what his boss would want, Low Rise took a position on the far side of the door and nodded for Rono to come inside. Rono sent Big Sally in first, the huge hitter toting an AK-47 with two banana magazines attached to the one already in the gun, for easy reloading. The whole rig still looked tiny in his large hands as he stepped into the corner, where he could cover both the doorway Rono was about to kick in and the stairway. Two more VK soljahs, Bark and Fred Red, took up positions on either side of the stairs, one covering the darkness leading up to the second floor, the other keeping an eye on the rest of the corridor in the back.

Rono checked all his boys, then raised his two Deltas and walked in front of the door. He took one step forward and planted his boot into the pressed wood near the lock. The door splintered apart and flew open with such force that one of the hinges broke as it slammed into the wall.

Rono didn't care, he was already inside and yelling as he pumped round after round of 10mm bullets into the figure seated on the far side of the room. The man jerked back and forth under the impact of each shot, his white shirt and gray suit jacket sprouting holes and spurting blood as his chest was destroyed by the barrage. Rono stopped after a few seconds, as the man's head lolled on his shoulders.

Low Rise was right behind him, covering the corpse as Rono, breathing hard, waved him forward. "Check 'im."

Alarms ringing in his head at the lack of anyone else in the room, the banger walked forward, subgun at the ready, until he was close enough to reach over and lift the dead man's head up.

Jojoe's wide, dead eyes stared back at them, his mouth covered with a strip of duct tape.

Low Rise turned to Rono, terror in his eyes. "Shit, Gul, it's a goddamn trap!"

28

Even from where they were, Casey and his crew heard the thunderclaps of Rono's big pistols as he capped Jojoe. Everyone was clustered around the monitors now, waiting to see how the scenario Casey had arranged would play out.

Casey checked his weapon, then tapped Champa on the shoulder and nodded him toward the driver's seat of the van. "Here we go. Rooftop, make sure Rono stays in the building."

The words had just left his mouth when all hell broke loose.

A shotgun blast shattered the night and lit the darkened staircase for a second. Fred Red staggered back across the tile floor, crimson blooming on his chest from the double-ought buckshot that had pulped his rib cage. Gasping and wheezing, he died a few feet away from Big Sally. The big man, who had strapped together two bulletproof vests to cover his massive frame, sank to one knee and unleashed a full burst of 7.62mm bullets, letting the muzzle of the automatic rifle climb naturally up the stairs. He was rewarded with a scream of pain, then a body came tumbling down the stairs, the blood leaking from the *vato*'s legs darker than the large red devil's head tattooed on his bare chest.

"Kings, get the fuck in here and cover Rono!" Sally shouted to the rest outside as he yanked his empty magazine out, flipped it, and slammed the second one home. "Gul, you okay in there?"

His words were cut off by Bark's 9mm Uzi firing from the other side of the staircase. "Got bangers coming in from the back—Jesus Christ, they're everyw—!"

Big Sally heard a sound like ripping cloth, then saw Bark stagger backward under multiple bullets, his Uzi dropping from his hand as he fell to the floor.

"Kings, get the fuck in here!" Spotting shadowy forms approaching from behind the stairway, Sally let off another burst at knee height, hearing muffled cries as his rounds found flesh and bone. His ears rang from the AK's loud report, and clouds of burned cordite fouled the air. Another submachine gun opened up next to him, and he looked over to see Low Rise firing from the doorway at the silent horde coming from the back way. Two more Kings were shooting from the main doors, and one of them let go short bursts as he scuttled to Big Sally. "Where's Rono?"

Between short bursts, Sally shouted, "In the room to your right. Get 'im outta here!"

"Keep us covered, man!" The gangsta stepped back in front of the main doors when his head suddenly exploded, showering Sally with blood and brains. Sally stared at the twitching corpse in shock, seeing the back of the man's head pulped as if it had been hit with a sledgehammer. He checked the second King shooting in the doorway, only to see him go down too, the bullet entering the top rear of his skull and blowing out his entire face.

"Muthafuck! Shooter in the building 'cross the street. Two a you fucks go get 'im!" Sally screamed at the bangers still outside.

He alternated shooting at the group trying to come down the stairs and the ones that were splitting up and coming at him on both sides of the staircase. "Rono—move yo ass!"

Inside the bare room, Rono had whirled and was heading for the door when gunfire had erupted outside, making him hit the floor. A few feet away, Low Rise lit up the hallway with bursts from his submachine gun, shouting to his leader. "Rono, you gotta vacate, dawg!"

"No shit, muthafuckah!" Crawling to the door, he peeked outside just in time to see one of his boys get capped with a round to the dome. "Where the fuck you suggest I go?"

Low Rise ducked back inside, tore the magazine out of his Walther, and reloaded, yanking the cocking lever back. "We'll lay down fire for ya, you get to the door and out to one of the Escalades, 'kay? On three—one . . . two . . . three!"

He popped back out and held the trigger down on his subgun, spraying bullets as he screamed into the hallway. His angry shout was cut off suddenly as he whirled around and fell to the floor, clutching his throat as blood fountained from his mouth. Rono crawled to him, but saw his neck had been savaged by bullets, and there was nothing more to be done. He shrugged away the man's grasping fingers. "Sorry, dawg, but yo done for." He peered through the doorway just in time to see Big Sally get shredded by a hail of gunfire from several different weapons down the hall, still blasting his AK as he went to the floor with a crash that shook the entire hallway.

"Fuck this shit!" Rono stuck one of his Colts out the door and fired down the hallway, sprayin' and prayin'. At the same time, he pointed his other Delta Elite at the front window and shot it out, then holstered his guns and bolted for the window. Breaking glass from the bottom sill out with his elbow, he climbed out, dropping to the street with a grunt.

"Rono has left the building, repeat, Rono has left the building." Walker's voice confirmed what Casey was seeing between shots from his sniper rifle.

"Step on it, Champa!" Casey braced himself as the van took off out of the garage and turned left to head down Taylor. "All right, change in plans, people, listen up! Everyone's goin' in the front way—catch the Kings between us and the Devils and the Lotus! No one comes out alive, ya feel me!" He flipped the Plexiglas visor down over his face. "Everyone better have those hot spots on your helmets, otherwise you likely get a bullet in the back of yo skull! Champa, where my lights at?"

His wide grin visible in the rearview mirror, Champa flicked a switch, and the red-and-blue lights atop the van sprang into bright life, illuminating the letters emblazoned in foot-high white paint along the sides and back of the vehicle: SWAT.

Casey walked to the back door, ready to hit the ground. "The moment we stop, everyone's out and taking down bangers!"

"Comin' up on the block in ten seconds!"

On the roof across from the carnage playing out in the apartment building, Walker inhaled, then exhaled, and at the moment when his body was completely still, squeezed the trigger of his silenced M110, sending another 5.56 full metal jacket slug into a gangsta's head. As soon as the shot was out, he ducked down beneath the low parapet of the building and rolled to his secondary position, waited for return fire, then carefully popped up again and began searching for another target. Finding one, he centered the crosshairs, inhaled, exhaled, aimed, and fired again, knowing the man on the second floor was deader than Dillinger. Walker dropped out of sight again and rolled farther down the roof of the building, planning to scope the street and see which Kings were still alive before targeting those still inside the building.

As he moved back and forth, the metal fire door to the roof swung silently open, and two Kings crept out onto the gravel, Ingram M-11 "room brooms" ready to smoke the sniper Big Sally had said was up here somewhere. They moved out cautiously, one to the left, one to the right, staying in the shadow cast by the small dormer the rooftop door was set in.

As one of the gangstas peeked around the corner, searching for the shooter, his leading foot broke an invisible sensor beam that was set to trigger a sawed-off double-barreled shotgun mounted in a corner of the roof. Both barrels went off with a deafening roar, turning the thug's chest into bloody mush and dropping him where he stood.

The second banger ducked low and charged out, thinking anyone on the roof would be reloading. His first step triggered the second beam, connected to a second shotgun. As he was bent over, the pellets caught him in the face and groin, sending him down to the rooftop trying to clutch both his pulverized nuts and shattered jaw at the same time.

Hearing the scatterguns go off, Walker rolled around until he could see the roof and both downed soljahs. He zeroed in on the one still moving and took him out with one shot to the head. Just as efficiently, he put a second round into the unmoving one—just to make sure—then returned to his trap shooting around the apartment building.

Seeing a familiar figure fall out of a window in the front, Walker spoke into his voice-activated mic while keeping his crosshairs on the fleeing man. "C, don't know if you can see this, but Rono's buggin' out. He's making for the Escalade nearest to where you're gonna hit the street."

. . .

Rono had just picked himself off the ground when he heard squealing tires in the distance. Looking down the street, he saw a familiar windowless black panel van with a white roof and cherries-and-blueberries flashing on top.

"Muthafuck! The goddamn po-pos!" He took off for the nearest Escalade, yanking the driver out and climbing into his seat and slamming the door closed. "Stop that van, no matter what!" Twisting the key, he shoved the gearshift into reverse and floored the accelerator. The big SUV lurched backward, Rono cranking on the wheel as fast as he could to point the vehicle away from the bloodbath.

His driver, left standing on the street with an HK MP5 clutched in his fist, was illuminated in the bright lights of the SWAT van as it roared toward him. Frozen in the high beams for a second, he dove out of the way just before the van's grille would have turned him into roadkill.

Rono glanced over in time to see the front of the van grow large in the passenger side window. "Sheeeit!" he screamed as he jammed the Escalade into gear and tromped on the gas pedal. The SUV had just started to move when the bigger van slammed into its rear quarter panel, crushing the taillight and frame into the back passenger space and sending the entire vehicle spinning around in a complete 360-degree turn, jumping the curb and smashing into the front of the building, where it stalled.

In the back of the van, everything was chaos. When Walker had let Casey know Rono was splitting, he'd told Champa, "Ram that fuckin' Escalade!"

"He ain't goin' nowhere. Hang on!" Champa had just finished shouting his warning when the van had slammed into the back of the SUV with a teeth-jarring crash. Everyone was flung forward, and even Casey, who'd braced himself before the impact, was nearly knocked off his feet.

He was up just as quickly, however, and hit the door with one big fist, coming out with his HK subgun in his other hand. "A Squad, move out! B Squad, cover them! Go go go!"

Even as Shinzo, Li, Omar, and the others spilled out of the van and headed toward the front of the building, Casey was going around the far side, where Champa was meeting up with him. Tebber had taken his place in the driver's seat and leaned out. "Cell jammer's in place—figure we got four minutes to get the fuck out of here 'fore the real po-pos show!"

Casey just nodded and slapped Champa on the shoulder. "Let's finish that muthafuckah."

The two men moved on the silent Escalade, guns up, ready to smoke anything that moved. They reached the passenger side without any trouble, and Champa hooked the door handle while Casey covered him. On his nod, Champa opened the door and Casey moved in for the kill.

The interior of the SUV was empty, the driver's side door wide open. Above the scattered gunfire, Casey heard an engine roar to life and climbed up on the hood to see the other one start moving, pulling back to take off down the street.

"Hell, no!" Casey brought his subgun up to his shoulder and rattled off a long burst at the SUV, his bullets shattering the rear window and stitching a line of holes into the back door and bumper. Champa had rounded the corner and added his own gun to the mix, shattering a taillight and blowing one tire out, but the Escalade didn't stop, it just kept accelerating down the street.

"Muthafuck!" Casey looked around for another vehicle, knowing their van would never keep up with the SUV. His gaze fell upon the silver Acura, and he glanced at Champa, who already had a big shit-eatin' grin plastered on his face.

Without a word, both men sprinted for the car, Champa sliding into the driver's seat. Once he was down and strapped into the passenger side, Casey hit his radio to broadcast to the rest of the crew as Champa popped the clutch and burned rubber out of there.

"Everybody listen up—you got two minutes in there, then clear out like your ass is on fire and your hair's catching, got it?" Not waiting for a reply, he hit the button that lowered his window and stuck his head outside, MP5A3 at the ready, waiting for the crippled Escalade to come into his sights.

As they sped away, the boom of a very big gun echoed through the street and across the neighborhood. Casey glanced at Champa and grinned. "Walker musta finally uncapped the heavy artillery."

Back at the entrance to the apartment building, the rest of the team had put down any VKs who hadn't had the sense to get out while the gettin' was good. Shinzo had led his team in from the left, while Omar had taken the right and swept through anyone still standing outside like a freight train.

But once that was done, they'd been stopped cold by the combined buzzsaw that was the Lotus and the Devils. The two gangs seemed to have reached some sort of truce-under-fire, and were now both laying down a withering stream of bullets at the main doorway. Shinzo and Li had taken cover in the corner of the building by the stairs, and couldn't even peek over the landing to get a look at who was still inside.

"O, you got a way in?" Shinzo asked over the radio.

"Fuck no, not if I wanna keep my head on my muthafuckin' shoulders! That goddamn door's a death trap!"

"Okay, flash-bangs on three." Shinzo pulled one of the small grenades from his belt and yanked the pin free. Next to him, Li did the same. "One . . . two . . . three, now!"

He stuck his arm out just enough to toss the stunner through the shattered doorway, followed by Li. From the other side, Omar and his boys did the same, bringing the total of munitions in the foyer to five. Shinzo crouched down, closing his eyes, covering his ears, and opening his mouth to equalize the blast pressure that was coming.

Even through his closed lids he sensed the 100,000+ candle-power flashes going off, followed by the ear-splitting *bang*s from the grenades. Once it all died away, Shinzo opened his eyes and looked up to see gray smoke billowing out of the hallway.

"Go go go!" he said, scrambling to his feet and vaulting the concrete side of the stairs to gain the upper landing. Li was right next to him, with Omar, Blue, and Quick backing them up on the right. Seeing forms staggering about in the smoke, he took a deep breath, poked his submachine gun around the corner, and opened fire, chopping three men down.

"O, you take the right side, we got the left."

"Ready and able."

"Ready . . . set . . . go!" Shinzo ducked into the hallway, making for an apartment door a few yards inside on his left. The first thing he passed was a giant of a man, his face and upper chest turned into bloody hamburger, slouched on the floor in the corner near the door, a smoking AK with its slide locked back still clutched in his huge fists.

"God-*damn*!" Shinzo kept moving and had just taken his second step toward the door when he heard the unmistakable sound of a shotgun slide being racked.

"Fuck—Li, cover!" Leading with his shoulder, Shinzo hit the door of the apartment in front of him, breaking it completely off its hinges and sending it to the floor with him on top. Behind him, Li calmly fired short bursts as she ducked inside the room just as the shotgun somewhere down the hall roared, a slug punching a fist sized-hole in the wall above Shinzo's head.

"Sonuvabitch!" Rolling off the door and over to the wall, Shinzo heard a chorus of guns open up outside, the clamor nearly deafening.

"O, O, where you at?" he shouted into his radio.

"Pinned down on the other side, in the room we set the trap in. Can't go forward, and we ain't leavin' you here, either."

"Shit!" Shinzo was thinking as fast as he could when he was nudged by Li, who was frowning behind her visor as she pointed at the roof behind them. "Fuck, yeah, girl—we get out of this alive, I'm givin' you a fat raise! Rooftop, rooftop, come in!"

"Been waitin' for your call, S. What ya need?"

"Damnit, man, can't you see the front door lit up like a god-damn Christmas tree, only those ain't lights twinklin' inside! Think you can clear us a path down the hall?"

"Bet your ass I can. Better cover your ears—this one's gonna be loud."

"I hear ya—do it to it!" Shinzo ducked down and covered his ears, reaching up only to grab Li, who was still trying to peek through the door, and who nearly got a faceful of 9mm bullets for her trouble. "Damn, woman, what you tryin' to do, get that pretty face messed up? Just hang back and let our boy do his thang."

Jesus was riding the ultimate adrenaline high. With the advantage of the high ground, his team of *vatos* had pinned the two forces down, keeping the heads of both the black-suits in back and the SWAT team out front down with a withering hail of bullets. Flanked by two of his best men, both armed with AKs, he stood in the middle of the stairway, a bulletproof vest over his bare chest, the SPAS-12 shotgun chewing up the rotting walls and doors of the apartment complex. He didn't care what he had to shoot through to kill these fucks—he had enough shells in the double bandoliers crossing his chest to send everyone he got in his sights straight to hell.

"Come on, *putos,* stand and fight, why don't you?" He took an-other step down and sent rifled slugs through each door again, and was rewarded by a shout from his left. Turning, he put two more into that side of the hallway, but heard nothing else. Scanning the area for movement, his eye caught something on the roof across the street, the moonlight illuminating a figure hunched over a long, black piece of metal. He turned toward it, aiming the SPAS from the hip as he slid the fire selector from pump-action to full auto and bore down on the trigger.

Sixty-five yards away, Walker grinned as he sighted in on the ganger's torso using the thermal scope attached to the six-foot-long weapon he was lying behind. The man pointing the shotgun at him showed up as a brilliant blaze of red, yellow, and orange, the scope reading his body temperature against the blues and blacks of the cooler surroundings.

At this range, it almost wasn't fair.

"Hello, sunshine," he said as he squeezed the trigger, the massive *boom* of the Barrett .50 caliber M107 semiautomatic sniper rifle echoing up and down the street and through the entire neighborhood.

Jesus fell back against the stairway like he'd been hit with a sledgehammer moving at more than a thousand feet per second. The huge bullet had plowed straight through his vest and body and exited out his lower back, taking a grapefruit-sized chunk of muscle and spine with it as it burrowed through the stairs beneath him, still having enough energy to shatter the shoulder of a Black Lotus soldier crouched beneath the far side of the staircase.

His two henchmen stared at the body of their leader in shocked silence—a fatal mistake, as Walker's next round exploded the head of one clean off his shoulders. The last man standing made a break for the second floor, but Walker tracked his fleeing form through the wall with the thermal scope and squeezed off one more shot that punched through the running man's spine and exploded his heart, dropping him in his tracks.

The ear-splitting *boom*s continued, and under the heavy fire that punched through anything—walls, doors, floors—to reach its target, the scattered, shattered elements of both gangs began to fall back.

"Rooftop to O and S, what's left of the Devils are retreating upstairs, and I see a half-dozen Lotus making a break for the back door. I got the second floor and above, you clean up the ground."

"Roger Dodger." Shinzo came out into the hallway, which now looked like a small, vicious war had been fought in it, to see Omar and his team appear across from them. In the doorway stood Bledsoe's two men as well. With nods to each other, the seven commenced hunting while .50 caliber rifle shots steadily boomed out above their heads.

29

Champa kept the pedal to the metal as the Acura zoomed through the deserted neighborhood, not stopping for anything, even intersections. After reloading his HK, Casey had removed his helmet and kept quiet, knowing not to distract the man when he was in the groove.

Traffic was light at this time of night, and they only had one harrowing moment, when both men spotted a snack truck starting into the intersection they were about to fly through at seventy miles an hour. Casey couldn't help himself. "Champa—"

"Ain't no thang, nigga." Champa flicked the wheel to the right just enough for them to veer past, coming so close to the truck Casey glimpsed the driver's eyes popping out of his head in shock. Then they were across and gaining on the damaged and wildly swerving Escalade, red-orange sparks trailing from its busted right tire.

"Pull up on the driver's side," Casey said, undoing his seat belt and kneeling on the seat so his head and upper body were outside. He yanked the cocking lever back and sent a short burst into the rear left tire, blowing it out. The rear of the SUV settled lower, but Rono just kept going.

"Da-yamn, this is like World's Wildest Police Chases, man!" Champa shouted.

"Yeah, and if we don't stop that fool, we gonna have the real ones on our ass too!" Casey stole an occasional glance at the night sky, expecting a police chopper to light them up at any moment.

Rono stuck one of his pistols out the driver's side window and shot wildly at them, the bullets spraying and ricocheting everywhere but into the Acura.

Casey winced, hoping no innocents would be hit by a stray shot. "Damn it! Pull alongside, I'll cap this mad fuck right now!"

The two vehicles streaked through another intersection, which was mercifully empty. Champa came up alongside the Escalade, but as soon as Rono caught sight of them, he wrenched the wheel hard left, forcing Casey to duck back into the car just as the SUV slammed into the Acura's side. The heavier vehicle forced the luxury sedan to slew left toward the row of buildings lining the street.

"Watch it!" Casey shouted, seeing they were heading toward another apartment complex.

"I see it, nigga." Champa twisted the wheel hard like he was wrestling an alligator. The Acura shot into a side street like it was on rails. "Damn—gotta get me one of these, if we still alive tomorrow."

"Turn this fuckin' whip around, he's gettin' away!"

"He won't get far on those two busted rims." Champa found a narrow alley and nosed the car in, then reversed while cranking the wheel, sending them shooting back the way they had come.

"Hold up, hold up—he could come at us from the cut when we pop out."

Champa slowed down at the intersection, then pulled out and immediately came to a stop in the middle of the street. "You gotta be shittin' me."

Two blocks down, the battered Escalade sat facing them, its

engine racing. Champa licked his lips and glanced at Casey. "You two crazy fucks gonna do what I think you gonna do?"

Casey didn't turn his head, didn't even flick his gaze in Champa's direction. "You want out, you know where the door is, playa."

"Sheeit, no—this the most fun I've had in a long muthafuckin' time!" Champa revved the Acura's engine, answering Rono's challenge. "Just say when, dawg."

"Cover your face." Casey grabbed a Mossberg pump shotgun from the backseat and looked away before blasting two shots into the front window, punching two baseball-sized holes in it and starring the rest of the safety glass. Twisting his body, Casey got a leg up and kicked the windshield free.

"Punch it!"

Champa popped the clutch and hit the gas, making the tires scream as the Acura rocketed full speed toward the Escalade. Casey could see Rono's face twisted with fury as his crippled Escalade tried to gain momentum. His HK empty, Casey drew his Glock with an extended magazine and started leveling 9mm hollowpoints at the grille and windshield of Rono's now pathetic ride.

Somehow, Rono managed to keep the SUV rolling at them while returning fire with one of his pistols. The two vehicles drew closer together, the Escalade looming large in Casey's vision. Seconds before impact, the Acura's right front tire exploded. The car swerved hard right while the Escalade hit its tail, sending it spinning like a top. Guns and bullet casings ping-ponged all over the interior. Champa grunted as he grappled with the wheel, trying to maintain control of the whirling dervish. When the Acura finally came to a stop, he turned the car around to see the Escalade slowly limping away. It nudged the curb and stalled out, steam pouring from its shattered radiator.

"Christ, where'd you learn to drive—Champa?" Casey frantically searched the car for a weapon, but the first two guns he grabbed were empty. "Can you help a muthafuckah look for a goddamn piece?" he yelled before looking over to see his wheelman leaning back in his seat breathing hard, sweating his ass off, and holding his bloody neck.

"Goddamn . . . muthafuckah got lucky and tagged me. Feels like my collarbone's broke—again."

"Shit, lemme see." Casey leaned over to take a look, but was distracted by the sound of creaking metal. Glancing up, he saw the driver's door of the SUV open, and a bloody, beaten Rono crawl out, still clutching one of his pistols. Ignoring the silent Acura fifty yards away, he staggered down a nearby alley.

"Goddamn, this muthafuckah don't know when to lay down and die," Casey said as he tended to his friend.

"I'm cool, nigga, handle yo business and don't take all day." Champa reached down and pulled up a chrome-plated Smith & Wesson 500 Magnum revolver. He winced as he handed the five-pound monster to Casey and said, "For special occasions."

Casey took the gun with his free hand as he pulled out his cell and speed-dialed Shinzo, who picked up on the first ring. "C? We're just leavin'—everything's over and done with."

"Great, now I need you to get over to the corner of Taylor and Eighth, CH's hurt and needs a doctor."

"We're just stashin' the van now. Be there in five."

"Hustle up, nigga, otherwise the po-po's gonna get here first."

"Don't worry, we'll get him gone sure enough."

"Thanks, dawg." Casey hung up and turned back to Champa. "You sure you a'ight?"

"Go, damn it. I'm cool and the muthafuckin' gang."

Casey looked hard at his friend one last time to make sure he wasn't being heroic, then kicked the door open and headed after a walking dead man.

. . .

When he'd come to in the wrecked Escalade, Gulliver Rono's first thought was pure amazement that he was still alive. Blood streamed down his face from several cuts made by flying glass, and his suit and long coat were a complete mess, soaked in sweat and blood. Slapping his pockets, he found his cell, but when he pulled it out, the screen was dark. He tossed it away with a curse—no help from his soljahs now.

He stood with a groan, feeling pain flare in his side and his shoulder where he'd landed on it when the SUV had gone over. But he was able to climb up on the seat, shove open the passenger side door, and crawl out.

He glanced at the smoking Acura on the other side of the street, but didn't even think about going over and checking to see if Casey was still alive. All he wanted to do was get the hell out of there and regroup. If the old fuck was still alive, he'd deal with him later.

Climbing down from the SUV, Rono landed and nearly fell over on impact, but righted himself quickly and headed toward the nearest alley. He heard faint sirens in the distance, and needed to put as much space between himself and the accident—not to mention the slaughterhouse he'd fled from—as possible.

Breathing hard, he walked down the alley, one of his Colt Delta Elites gripped tight in his fist. From behind him, he heard footsteps, and turned to see a familiar form appear in the mouth of the alley.

"Goddamn it!" Rono raised his pistol and shot three times at Casey, making him duck for cover. Rono grinned, but his smile vanished when the other man popped back up with a huge, shiny pistol in his hands and fired.

Rono flattened himself into a recessed alcove as bullets blurred past. Feeling for the doorknob, he tried it, only to find it locked. "Fuck this." He put the muzzle of his pistol against it and squeezed the trigger twice, blowing off the knob. Shoving the door open, he was met with a blast of cold air, and realized he was entering a refrigerated warehouse. Peeking inside, he saw stacks of pallets filled with large crates of various products, from prebagged frozen fruits and vegetables all the way up to boxed steaks and sides of beef.

"Yeah—yeah, this'll play." Rono crept inside and started looking for a place to hide. *Find me a place to hole up and smoke that fuckah when he comes in.*

After his last burst, Casey sighted in and waited for Rono to make a break for it, ready to cut him down the moment the no-account punk showed his face. Several seconds ticked by without return fire or anyone breaking from cover. Casey gave it another ten count, then began stepping noiselessly up the alley, the muzzle of his pistol trained on where he'd seen Rono disappear.

When he got there, he saw a sliver of light coming from the recessed door, which hung ajar. Reaching out, Casey pulled the door open while moving to one side at the same time. No bullets blazed out from the other side. Casey risked a quick peek inside, catching a waft of cold air on his face and seeing stacks of loaded pallets.

Shit, he thought. The sirens were getting louder, and he didn't really have time to play cat-and-mouse with Rono. However, it appeared he had no choice. Taking a deep breath, Casey rushed in, heading for the nearest cover, a three-pallet-high stack of boxes filled with frozen asparagus.

Again, no fusillade of fire came from deeper in the warehouse. His breath fogging out in a white cloud, Casey tried to look everywhere at once. *Muthafuckah's had plenty of time to get set up and wait for me to walk right into his sights.* For a moment, he wondered if Rono had simply bugged out, but shook his head, dismissing the thought. If Rono ever wanted a better time to chill Casey once and for all, this was it. He looked around again, especially up at the pallets that reached halfway to the ceiling high above him. *Gotta get to higher ground, get the lay of the land.* Shoving the Smith & Wesson into his belt, Casey grabbed the cold wooden pallet above his head and hoisted himself up.

The climb was tiring, particularly because every surface he touched was freezing cold, numbing his fingers even through his shooting gloves. At last, however, he heaved and scrabbled one last time and hoisted himself over onto the top of the stack of frozen food.

Getting to one knee, he was drawing the pistol when he heard an ominous click from nearby. *Shit, muthafuckah had the same idea—!* Twisting his body, Casey tried to fall to one side while bringing the Magnum around so he could get a shot off, but Rono was already firing, and Casey felt impacts on his upper chest and a flare of pain in his shoulder. Too late, he realized he'd fallen too far back, and was now on the edge of the pallet. Before he could steady himself or get a grip, he slid over the side and fell to the hard concrete far below.

Casey'd had more practice than most in falling from high places. One attempt on his life in prison from a few members of the Aryan Brotherhood had been to bum-rush him and try to throw him from the second-floor corridor into the yard below. They'd managed to surprise him, but Casey had taken one with him, using the thug to cushion his landing. He'd walked away with a broken finger and dislocated shoulder. The skinhead had died of a broken neck—that, and Casey's two hundred seventy-five pounds crushing his chest when the two men had hit the deck.

So when he fell off the side of the stacks, he twisted his body in midair, managing to get his legs underneath him in time to take most of the impact. Most, but not all—he still hit the floor with enough force to jar the breath from his lungs and ring his dome against the concrete hard enough to make everything go black for a few moments.

When his vision returned, Casey blinked several times to see the nightmarish, blood-streaked face of Gulliver Rono looming above him. His hands empty, the pistol nowhere in reach, Casey instinctively reached up to throttle the grinning bastard, but Rono leaned back and brought his arm down, the slim black baton he held smacking into Casey's left forearm. Casey grunted in pain and rolled over, clutching the hurt limb to his chest. Before he could turn back or say anything, blinding pain shot through the back of his left leg as the baton *thwacked* into him again.

"Bastard . . ." Casey clutched his leg and rolled over to stare at Rono, who was coming in again, that damn metal baton cocked and ready to beat him to a pulp. He knew his vest had stopped most of the shots, only his right shoulder didn't seem to want to work right. If he could only get a few moments to catch his breath—

"Crush, Crush, Crush—good to see you again, dawg!" Rono's last word was punctuated by the baton coming down hard on Casey's injured shoulder, making the prone man shout in pain. "I missed you—'specially in the last few days, muthafuckah—since you stole MY MUTHAFUCKIN' MONEY!"

He flailed at Casey with the baton, smacking him on the legs, the arms, the head. Unable to get a bead on Rono, Casey just threw his arms up to protect his dome and tried to stay conscious until the other man was done.

"Oh, I got plans for you, muthafuckah. First, I'ma break your arms and legs so you can't go nowhere. Then, I'ma work on you my own self till you fuckin' *beg* to give me back every muthafuckin' dollar you stole. Then, well, I might just keep you as my personal muthafuckin' plaything—torture you for a while, then when I'm tired, give you a chance to heal up, and start all over again. You gonna pray for a cap in your muthafuckin' dome 'fore I'm through, but you ain't gonna get it—not for a very, very long time."

Casey shook his head. "Won't matter, Rono—I'll come back from the goddamn grave to put you down."

"Oh, oh—careful now, or I just might give you your wish." Rono was still strutting around Casey, who was flat on the ground. "'Course, mebbe that's what you want now—ya know, be reunited with that dead ho and your bastard kid."

"Antonio . . . his name was Antonio . . . and you fuckin' killed him, you sonofabitch!"

Rono threw back his head and howled with laughter. "'Course I did, muthafuckah! Don't get me wrong, I had plans to turn that little nigga totally against you—you know, mold him in my own image of a *successful* gangsta. Then, when you got out, I was gonna cap him right in front of you, make you watch as I wiped your seed from the earth, bitch! But that boy had ambition, you know what I'm sayin'—so he had to go. Set up a job for him—next thing I know, he's tits up in a warehouse in Jersey. Man, I woulda given anything to have seen your face when you got the news—oh shit!"

Roaring with rage and sorrow, Casey managed to rise to his knees and lunge at Rono. The other man danced out of the way, clubbing Casey across the face and sending him to the ground again. Rono clucked his tongue. "Sad, just sad. You nuthin' but a broken-down old fool, Casey. You ain't fit to wipe my ass, much less take over the Kings."

Casey had pushed himself up onto his knees again, and now leaned back on his haunches, his arms and legs screaming with pain. In his left hand he held the knife he'd drawn from the small of his back out in front of him.

Rono, standing a few yards away—straightened and regarded Casey with a smirk. "Whatchu gonna do now, playa? Crawl over here and cut my hamstrings?"

Now Casey was the one who smiled, his teeth white in the dim light, as he pointed the blade at Rono. "No, I'll gut yo ass from right here."

"What the fuck—" was all Rono said before Casey hit the small button on the hilt, sending the blade flying out to bury itself in the gang lord's stomach. Rono staggered back, one hand reaching up to touch the end of the blade sticking out of his abdomen, just below his rib cage. "Muthafuckah—"

Casey got to his feet and walked toward Rono, who was still staring at the metal sticking out of his stomach. He looked up at Casey, then his free hand went for the Colt on his hip while he raised the baton in his other hand.

Casey lunged forward, blocking the baton coming down with his forearm, pinning Rono's arm against the wall while grabbing his other wrist and squeezing—hard. Bones creaked under his grasp, and Rono whimpered with the pain. The heavy pistol slipped out of his fingers and clattered on the floor. "Casey—wait, man—"

"I been waitin' twenty years for this." Still holding the baton hand against the wall, he reached up and grabbed Rono's fleshy throat in his free hand, squeezing with all his strength despite the pain in his shoulder.

Rono bucked and flailed, trying to punch his enemy in the breadbasket, but the blows were absorbed by the vest, and didn't slow Casey down one bit. Rono's frantic fingers scrabbled at his attacker's crotch, but Casey turned his legs so that his thigh blocked them.

Wheezing and gasping, Rono vainly tried to suck in air through his closed windpipe. He raised his arm again and clawed at Casey's face, but Casey raised his eyes and nose out of harm's way. Rono then turned to his arm, trying feebly to break the immovable fingers crushing his throat, but they might as well have been a circle of iron. Casey only tightened his grip, feeling the windpipe flex and collapse under his hand.

Eyes bugging, blackening tongue protruding from his mouth, Gulliver Rono reached out one last, desperate time, his fingers scraping against Casey's throat. Casey shook him off and squeezed even tighter. Gulliver Rono choked, gasped, convulsed, and finally his head lolled to one side as the frantic light in his eyes dimmed and went out.

Casey kept up the choke hold until his fingers started to ache, making sure the punk wasn't faking. When he finally released his grip, Rono stayed up against the wall for several long moments before sliding to the floor, his sightless eyes already glazing over.

Casey stood over his vanquished foe for a long minute, almost unable to believe it was done. He and Mack D had often discussed the idea of revenge, whether it was a laudable or achievable goal. Looking at Gulliver Rono's dead body, Casey nodded.

"Goddamn satisfying."

30

The next morning, Grace Phan took the last of her money and jewels out of her wall safe and stuffed them in a messenger bag just as Kelta Cruzado stalked into the room.

"The car's here. Let's get the hell out of town."

They both hurried out to the Lincoln Town Car Cruzado had summoned to take them to Kennedy. Each pulled two large suitcases on rollers, along with the messenger bag Phan had around her torso by its strap. Wrestling the bags downstairs, they saw the car double-parked at the curb outside of Phan's building. The trunk was already open and the driver stood there at the ready. The sun shone brightly on the deserted street.

"Ladies," the driver said, "let me get those for you." He began loading the bags in the deep, plastic-lined trunk, the women glancing up and down the street impatiently.

. . .

Baybay had rehearsed what she was going to say to her tormentors, but what was the point? Coming out from where she had concealed herself, she walked up behind the two and put a bullet in the back of Phan's head. The older woman tumbled partially into the trunk, instantly dead.

"Oh shit," Kelta said, shaking her palms at Baybay. "Please don't do this—"

"Shut the fuck up." Baybay shot her twice in the face, the silenced gun coughing discreetly. Then she helped the driver, Omar Atkins, get the bodies and luggage in the trunk before they drove away.

Baybay didn't look back at the apartment building as it receded into the distance. *Thanks for the closure, Casey—my nightmare's finally over.*

At a graveyard in Queens, Casey, in his blue serge suit, rose from placing flowers in the buried tube fronting his son's grave. He figured it would be hypocritical to say a prayer, but he couldn't help but wonder if his son's restless soul, if there was such a thing, roamed about in search of an answer—

He stood staring at the simple marble tombstone for a long time, searching for words that were years too late. "I'm sorry, Antonio. I wasn't there when you needed me most. Even if I wasn't behind bars, I'm not so sure I wouldn't have fucked things up anyway. I lost sight of what was important, and we all paid the price. I suspect I'll burn in hell, but until then I won't forget what I've done, and I damn sure won't forget about you."

A tear dropped from his eye onto the fresh-cut grass. "I hope and pray you're at peace now."

He stood there for several minutes, looking at and beyond the grave, thinking about the ghosts of those long gone—and of those still breathing. Turning around, he headed for the gates, his hands absently patting the pockets of his suit jacket. He had the strangest feeling he was missing something, but he couldn't quite put his finger on it.

Nearing the graveyard entrance, Casey walked past two cemetery workers in their dirt-stained clothes. One handed a wire brush to the other as he cleaned off the battery posts on their electric cart.

This man joked, "Life's too fuckin' short, you dig what I'm sayin'? You gotta realize tomorrow today, baby."

"You ain't never lied," his coworker agreed with a laugh. They both gave respectful nods to Casey as he left. He nodded back as a light mist fell from the sky.

"Damn, man, what happened to you?" Mack D asked. They talked on handsets from opposite sides of the thick glass partition between visitors and inmates. Casey had come back to Attica using a fake ID and a few well-placed bribes.

Casey grinned ruefully. "Took a few lumps, but I did it, Mack. I took back what was mine."

The other man nodded. "Uh-huh. Grapevine's been burning up in here."

Casey didn't reply, suddenly at a loss for words now that he'd accomplished what he'd set out to do.

"So, you did what you said you were gonna do, how you feel about everything now?"

"I—I don't know." It had all hit home while standing over his son's grave. Once the initial rush of pleasure at seeing Rono dead had passed, Casey realized he was still standing on the burial site of his only child—and nothing would ever change that.

Mack D nodded again, as if he'd expected Casey's answer. "You got the Kings back, boss baller, but what was *really* resolved? You gonna tear up the streets again until you get taken down in a hail of bullets, or one of your flunkies tries to shoot you down, maybe even pulling it off this time? You know darkness only begets more darkness."

"You and I always talked about takin' the Kings in a whole 'nother direction, and I'm still down with it, but—"

"But nothing. Whatever a man can conceive, a man can achieve. You conceived your plan, you put it into motion, you achieved your goal. Time to make some new ones now."

"Who you quotin' now?"

"Me, nigga! You got decisions to make. You spent enough time in this goddamn place—now get outta here and handle your business."

Casey leaned forward, about to reply, but Mack D cut him off. "Ain't nothin' more to say. Go walk your path."

"I don't—I don't know about that."

"Yeah, but I do. I don't wanna see you around here visiting the walking dead anymore, nigga. Get out there and live your life, ya hear me?"

With that Mack D hung up the phone, nodded at Casey one last time, got up, and walked away.

As if on cue, his cell phone rang while Casey was leaving the prison. He flipped it open. "Yeah?"

It was Lomax. "Remember our follow-up meeting today? Drop by my office at one this afternoon—that is, if you're not too busy."

"I'll be there." He flipped the phone closed with a sour look, thinking about some way to get the PO off his back once and for all. He couldn't just cap the man—they'd replace him with another one anyway, one who might shorten his leash to where it would be impossible to handle his business. No, for now it was best just to go along and see what he wanted.

. . .

Later that afternoon, Casey strolled into Lomax's parole office. He saw the man himself in the hallway, talking to another officer. Seeing Casey, he nodded. "Just go on into my office, I'll be with you in a minute."

Casey nodded back and walked in, seeing the usual items—the large board with the flashing lights, the battered desk—and a radio tuned to an all-news station.

"*. . . And here's your news at the top of the hour. Police are still investigating what representatives are calling an 'apartment slum turned into a war zone,' that erupted last night in the Parkenbush neighborhood, leaving twenty-seven dead. Officers are looking for any witnesses to the battle that rocked the Bronx neighborhood yesterday, which they say may have involved at least three gangs clashing in some kind of winner-take-all battle. Although no bystanders were hurt in the incident, the NYPD has vowed to find the perpetrators and bring them to justice. . . .*"

Lomax hustled in, turned the radio off, and took his customary seat behind his desk. "Thanks for waiting, Mr. Casey, it's been a busier morning than usual around here. Have a seat, and we can get down to business."

Lomax shot Casey a look as he pulled a folder out of a drawer. "You all right? Looks like someone worked you over last night."

Casey touched the butterfly bandage over his eye—Rono had walloped him pretty good before he'd managed to ice the son of a bitch, and his face was still bruised and swollen. His voice was steady, however, as he'd practiced his story earlier that day until it rolled out smooth. "Well, Mr. Lomax, you know how some folks see anyone in a suit—white or black—as a target. I was coming back from my interview when two cats tried to bank on me— probably looking for some quick cash. I beat 'em off and got away, but they gave me a bruise or two to remember 'em by."

"I see. You weren't hurt too badly, I hope."

"Nothing but my pride."

Lomax nodded. "And that interview we talked about—how'd it go?"

Casey grinned, not minding the hurt in his cheeks and jaw. "I aced it. The other candidates didn't stand a chance. The job's mine as of this morning." He pushed a card that had URBAN VICTORY embossed on it, along with an address and phone number of an office building Shinzo had set up for him, across the desk. "I'll have my own cards in another week or so."

Lomax picked the card up and studied it. "Well, well. Good for you, Mr. Casey. I think this is the start of something very big for you."

"I agree completely."

Lomax flipped through his folder. "Terrible business in Parkenbush last night—I assume you heard about that?"

"Caught it on the news this morning—sounds like some bad people doing bad things to each other."

"You are absolutely correct. Someone sure went after a grocery list of bangers recently—really did our fair city a favor by cleaning up the streets. Even scared some of the bigger names into hiding—particularly your old friend Gulliver Rono—no one's seen hide nor hair of him lately. I don't suppose you know anything about his whereabouts, huh?"

"Not a clue."

"Well, that's okay, since it seems a small flash drive was found at the scene detailing the VKs' business with the Colombian cartel and some sort of cocaine deal."

"Imagine that." Casey could imagine it very easily. He'd had Vera select enough information on the VKs' deal with the Colombians—conveniently implicating Rono and all of the recently killed captains, of course—and drop it in the Escalade, ensuring it would be found by the right people.

"That's not all they found." Lomax was silent for several seconds, drawing it out. "They also recovered a gold medallion of St.

Jude—very similar to the one you wore during your first meeting here, actually."

Fuck! Casey resisted the almost overwhelming impulse to touch his neck even as he realized he didn't feel the light weight of the medal and chain on him. *That's* what was missing today! Rono must have snapped the chain when they were tussling, and Casey had been too amped to realize it. And with the inscription on the back, the NYPD could definitely tie him to the scene. That was it—the game was over.

I'll be goddamned if I give this jive-ass nigga the satisfaction of a confession. Casey locked eyes with Lomax for thirty seconds, neither of them moving a muscle.

Suddenly Lomax shrugged. "Unfortunately, when they inventoried everything in the evidence locker, the medal was missing. Seems someone swiped it—maybe for a souvenir. Ain't that somethin'?" He leaned back in his chair. "I'd think the owner of that St. Jude medallion would probably be pretty indebted to the person that took it."

Casey looked at Lomax, not breaking his stare or giving up anything; he'd played too many chess games in prison not to be able to decipher what was going on. He couldn't believe this, yet it was unfolding right before his eyes. "That sounds about right."

Lomax slowly nodded and took out another picture from his folder, regarding it for a moment before showing it to Casey. The man in the mug shot was thick and brutish-looking, with dead-black eyes under a heavy brow topped by an unkempt mop of long, thick, black hair. Casey had never seen him before. "Too bad they didn't get this one too—an Armenian mobster named Alek Petrosian. He's into all sort of bad shit: drugs, weapons, human trafficking, dog fighting—whatever turns a buck fast."

Casey simply replied, "Sounds like a menace to society to me."

The PO stood, the picture still in his hand. "Indeed." He tacked the picture of the man on his corkboard, then turned back to Casey. "You can go now."

Casey walked outside as if in a trance. Once the summer heat and noise of the city hit him, he blinked and shook his head. Mack D's voice echoed in his head once more, quoting Sun Tzu: *"Nothing is more difficult than the art of maneuvering for advantageous positions."* The only question was, who was maneuvering around whom? Every time he thought he had a line on Lomax, the man juked and jived and came out of nowhere—and everything he was doing seemed to be aimed at keeping Casey on the streets and operating. *But why?*

Shaking his head, Casey resolved to ponder this new wrinkle later. Right now, he had an empire to get back on track.

At the new Urban Victory offices in Queens, Casey and the crew he'd been talking to entered the middle-class suite of bland rooms.

Casey walked around a battered, secondhand metal desk and sat ready to conclude the next steps in cementing his organization. There was still drama to be quelled on the streets, but Two Stroke Bledsoe was already brokering a peace. The Blood Devils and the Black Lotus, their command structures shattered after the battle of the previous evening, were falling apart, with smaller gangs rushing in to claim the territories. Casey would bring them into line soon enough; right now he had other chickens to fry.

"Shinzo, is your brother still banging that Armenian broad?"

"Nope, he married her," he said with an explosive laugh.

Casey laughed too. "Poor bastard. Anyhow, we need to get invited to dinner next week. Can you set that up?"

"Sure, no problem." Shin knew not to ask questions.

"You got plans for me as well, stud?" Baybay asked.

Casey met her direct stare with his own hard gaze. "I sure do—you know how to get in touch with Phan's overseas contact?"

Baybay came off the wall at him, her hands balled into fists. "What? Nigga, are you for real?"

Casey raised his hand. "Whoa, chill out, girl, you jumpin' to conclusions without givin' me a chance to speak my piece. I said that to say this . . . we gonna take his ass down, as well as all his partners too."

She stopped at that, and Casey watched her mull over the possibilities. He gave her a beat or two, then leaned back in his chair. "Now can you handle this, or is it too close to home?"

Baybay's head came up again, and she stared at him for a hard second before nodding once. "Okay, Crush, I'll back your play— long as we get to put some muthafuckin' hurt on those slave dealers."

Casey nodded soberly. "You got it."

Just then Champa walked into the room with a sling around his arm, but dressed to the nines. Casey stood up and looked at him, admiring his threads. "Look at this pimp nigga, all silk-suited and eelskin-booted."

The room chuckled as Champa gave everybody a "who me?" look, then smiled at his old friend. "Well done, son. I gotta admit when you first told me what you was up to, I had my doubts. Shoulda known Crush Casey still has the biggest balls in the city."

Casey smiled. "Thanks, man, I owe you more than most."

"Shit, nigga, don't you know you can't owe family?"

Casey's eyebrows raised. "Is that so? So you wanna be down with all this?"

Champa nodded. "I'd forgotten what a muthafuckin' rush it was to pull jobs with you, nigga." He slapped the desk with his free hand. "So, yes, count Champa in—but first, I'ma do a little ressin' and dressin' in the Caribbean."

Everyone busted out laughing at that, Casey included. He got up, came around the desk, and hugged Champa, mindful of the man's injured wing. "Okay, my brotha. You get all rested and ready—there'll be plenty to do when you get back in town."

Champa and Casey knocked fists, and Champa walked out exactly as Carla walked in. He paused a moment to look her up and down. "Hey girl, you comin' to see me? I was just leavin'," he said with a chuckle.

Carla red-eyed him with mock disdain. "Oh, you real funny, Champa. By the way, your two girlfriends are downstairs wondering where their pimp is."

The whole room howled, as did Champa as he left.

Carla Aquila looked svelte and sexy in her tight-fitting designer business skirt and top. As she walked across the room, every eye was on that naturally swaying caboose.

Casey gave Shin the sign, and he in turn motioned to the others in the room. They all exited as Carla, hands on hips and shaking her head, came around the desk to a sitting Casey, who'd turned toward her. "Did daddy have a good day at work?"

Casey reached for her with a huge grin. "You know it, baby girl."

Atkins closed the door on the two.